Death to Touch

By Shaun Lewis

This man was handed to you by God's deliberate plan… But God would not allow the bitter pains of death to touch him… there was nothing by which death could hold such a man.

Acts 2 verse 23

1

OTHER BOOKS BY SHAUN LEWIS

They Have No Graves as Yet

and

The *For Those in Peril* WW1 series comprising:

The Custom of the Trade

Now the Darkness Gathers

The Wings of the Wind

Where the Baltic Ice is Thin

The Suicide Club

Chapter One
August 1941

Oberstleutnant Ernst Scholtz of the *Luftwaffe* returned from Berlin a bitter man. An expert in mine warfare and a former member of the German Navy, Ernst was now running the Air Force's mine development and trials unit at Travemünde near Lübeck on the Baltic coast. In 1939, he had developed a strategy that, had it succeeded, would have forced Britain to withdraw from the war by Christmas. It had very nearly worked, too. By deploying large numbers of Germany's new secret weapon, the magnetic mine, along the busy waterways off Britain's coastline and in the estuaries to her ports, the German Air Force and Navy had brought Britain's shipping to a standstill for several weeks. The Admiralty had been forced to inform Churchill that unless they could establish the nature of the new weapon that was crippling Britain's maritime trade and develop countermeasures, the war would be lost within six weeks. Fortunately, an incompetent *Luftwaffe* aircrew had dropped a pair of the new mines in too shallow water. They had been discovered high and dry at low tide on the mudflats off Shoeburyness. Two of the Royal Navy's experts in mine disposal along with their two assistants from HMS *Vernon*, the Navy's torpedo and mine warfare school, had displayed a suicidal disregard for their safety by not only rendering the two mines safe, but discovering the secrets of the new weapons. It had then been only a matter of time before the Admiralty's scientists had developed methods to provide some protection for both merchantmen and warships against the deadly menace.

Thanks to Ernst and his teams of scientists and experts from industry, the mines were still playing an important part in the German war effort, but it was a cat and mouse game to stay ahead of the Royal Navy's scientists and Rendering Mines Safe (RMS) teams. As the enemy devised new techniques to counter the latest versions of the German mines, Ernst and his team had to develop more sophisticated weapons and ensure that their new technologies were safe from prying eyes, including the use of booby traps. It had been the *Luftwaffe* who had taken the lead in deploying the latest mines both in the sea and on British cities as a terror weapon and, hence, Ernst had been recruited from the Naval Staff and promoted to lieutenant colonel.

Ernst's summons to Berlin to discuss the next phase should have caused him some joy. Although some of Ernst's colleagues in the *Luftwaffe* chided him for *their* failure to bring Britain to its knees, the High Command still had faith in mines to damage Britain's sea trade. Indeed, production of mines was at its peak and Ernst had just been given approval to develop and trial two new forms of influence mine. The first was almost operational. Although it required a mammoth undertaking by the Royal Navy's minesweepers, they were proving successful in sweeping the mines detonated by the influence of ships' magnetic signatures and their engine noise. In the short term, Ernst proposed deploying mines that would be detonated by a combination of magnetic and acoustic influences. However, he had been ordered to cooperate more with his former paymasters, the *Kriegsmarine*, since, following the invasion of Russia, the *Luftwaffe* expected to be more committed to the campaign on the Eastern Front in the near future. More importantly, Ernst had persuaded the High Command that a radically different firing mechanism would be needed and he had been given the funding to commence development of a mine influenced by the pressure generated in the water by a ship's movement. All in all, it had been a very successful visit to Berlin and a feather in Ernst's cap. It was his subsequent call on his brother's fiancée that had started his feelings of bitterness.

Ernst had brought up his younger brother, Max, following the deaths by starvation of their parents in the immediate aftermath of the 1914 – 1918 War. Thanks to Ernst's efforts, *Little Maxi* had trained as a pilot and now commanded a wing of Junkers 87 *Stukas* in the Balkans. Before leaving Germany, he had become engaged to Else, a young woman Ernst had found enchanting. However, Else's great-grandmother had been Jewish making her an eighth Jewish, too. Nevertheless, even under the 1935 Nuremburg Race Laws, Else had still been considered German-blooded and entitled to citizenship of the *Reich* – but that had been before the war. Now, it seemed that even the great-grandchildren of Jews could be considered as Jewish. Else had reported that local officials of the Nazi Party were now questioning her German citizenship and had suggested that she might be recategorized as *Mischlinge,* mixed breed. As a result, she might

4

not be permitted to marry Max, a non-Jew. Even worse, Else had heard that she, too, might be forced to wear a yellow, six-pointed star on her clothing from the first of September. Ernst had joined the Nazi Party several years earlier, but was, nonetheless, incensed by the news. His motive in joining the Party had been purely to gain professional advancement and he had not given much thought to the question of racial purity, but now the issue was close to home. Else bore none of the facial features common to the Jews and seemed as loyal to the Fatherland as he. How was he to tell Little Maxi that the Fatherland could treat its own citizens thus? For the first time in his adult life, Ernst was questioning a policy of the Nazi government.

To add to his bitterness, he had returned to Travemünde to find his cat, Gisella, extremely unwell. It was not for the first time and he had long harboured suspicions that a member of his staff was poisoning the poor cat as a way of hurting Ernst. This time it had been necessary to consult a veterinary surgeon, but without access to the necessary drugs, the vet had expressed pessimism about poor Gisella's chances of recovery. Ernst could not overcome his anger that somebody on his staff could harm a defenceless cat in order to satisfy a latent grudge against him.

*****

It was a mark of Ernst's status that he had now been given an assistant. *Leutnant* Franz Klein was a *Luftwaffe* reservist with no experience of mine warfare, but he was just what Ernst needed. Klein had been an actuary for an insurance company before the war and spoke good English. He was shorter than Ernst, a little overweight and almost completely bald. Unlike Ernst, he often wore spectacles. Ernst had taken an immediate liking to the man when they had met a few weeks earlier.

'I have done as you asked, *Herr Oberst*. Our colleagues in the *Abwehr* have supplied me with cuttings from the English newspapers that mention the British ships suspected of having been sunk by mines or torpedoes off the British coast. I have correlated them with our own reports of the laying of mines by the *Kriegsmarine* and the *Luftwaffe*. I regret that there is a huge margin of error in my tabulations.'

5

'That is of no great concern, Franz. We only need a broad outline.' Ernst smiled at Klein reassuringly.

'It was more difficult than you might imagine, sir. In many cases the names of the ships were not reported. I had to rely on casualty lists and these don't list the reasons for the ship's sinking.'

'Franz, stop worrying. I am only interested in broad conclusions. Have you been able to establish any patterns.'

'I have, *Herr Oberst*, but they are very… broad brush. Let me show you my annotated charts.' Klein unfurled the first of his charts, ironically produced by the Royal Navy's Hydrographic Office. 'The red crosses show my best estimation of where our aircraft, *U*-boats and *E*-boats have laid mines close into the shores of Britain. The black circles mark the approximate positions where enemy ships were reported as torpedoed. The blue squares merely show the approximate areas where the enemy has incurred casualties at sea. I cannot say exactly where the damage might have occurred… only the ports where the survivors were taken. Let me show you a few other examples, *Herr Oberst*.' Klein unfurled two more charts of the British coastline.

Ernst wasn't pleased by what he saw. It was obvious from the charts that the number of mines laid was out of proportion to the number of ships sunk or damaged. However, he still asked his question of Klein.

'And what do you conclude, Franz?'

Klein polished his spectacles before replying. 'I regret, sir, to conclude that the enemy has an efficient method for sweeping our mines, whether they are of the moored, magnetic or acoustic variety.'

'Indeed, Franz. It is as I suspected. Clearly, we must respond by some means or other. These little ships are proving a nuisance and must be dealt with. In anticipation of your analysis confirming my suspicions, I have already given the matter some thought. From now on, I can promise that the minesweepers will face a more difficult and hazardous task.' Ernst rolled up the three charts. 'Thank you for your work, Franz. It is excellent. I would like you to continue these correlations, but in future, I want to have information specific to the casualty rates of the British minesweepers.'

*****

Lieutenant Stephen Cunningham RNVR had never travelled north of Edinburgh until today and he was very much enjoying the scenery as the train steamed northwards along the Cromarty Firth. He was thankful for the recent thirty-minute refreshment stop at Inverness as he had missed breakfast in his Edinburgh hotel. Ever since his university days, Stephen had found difficulty in rising early and this morning was no different. Indeed, he had only caught the 06.33 from Edinburgh Waverley station by the skin of his teeth. Accordingly, he found himself standing in the corridor of the first-class carriage and had been forced to stand for the whole journey thus far. However, it had its compensations. The corridor was on the wrong side of the train to obtain the best views of the coast, but at least he could smoke and stretch his long legs. Once a keen athlete and, indeed, the winner of the *Victor Ludorum* trophy at Liverpool University for sprinting and the long jump, he had avoided cigarettes until the previous year, but these were changed times. After a few close encounters with death, he had started to drink spirits, but that was the road to ruin for an officer whose job was defuzing mines and bombs. Up close to a ton of high explosive ready to explode at any second, one needed not just steady nerves, but steady hands. No, smoking was a safer option to steady the nerves.

Leaning against the hand rail Stephen stretched his tall, skinny frame (half an inch under six feet), across the carriage corridor and arched his back. His hair was dark, but despite his relative youth of just twenty-five, it was starting to thin. He was short-sighted, wearing round cellulose spectacles, and he felt his nose was too long to make him attractive to women. Moreover, his shy nature and stutter put him at a further disadvantage with women. Even so, and to his eternal wonderment, he was in love with a woman who loved him, too. The previous day, he had bid a fond farewell to a beautiful, if slightly plump, redhead, Carol Templeton, at Kelso railway station. Carol was a nurse and had personally overseen his convalescence in her parents' home in the Borders after Stephen had been injured in a mine explosion the month before. He had lost one of his best friends in that accident along with his instructor from HMS *Vernon*. Was it usual in his trade to lose so many friends, he wondered ruefully, but thinking of his instructor, CPO Dawlish, he

7

remembered his words from their first days of instruction in the mysteries of rendering mines safe, '*Accept it now, sirs. As RMS officers, you're dead already. Now every day you live is a bonus.*' How truly Dawlish had spoken, Stephen thought. Despite being a pacifist, he was engaged in one of the Royal Navy's most deadly trades and yet he was extremely happy. Meeting Carol had shown him how every day of his life counted.

Chapter 2

It might have been the fag-end of summer, but that meant nothing to the Orcadians. The Orkney islands were one of the windiest spots in Great Britain and even in the summer the temperature didn't usually rise much above 60 odd degrees Fahrenheit. In Lieutenant Commander Bryan's experience of nearly twelve months based at Scapa Flow, four seasons could be experienced in a single summer's day. Like many of the soldiers, sailors and airmen based around the Royal Navy's huge anchorage of Scapa Flow, he hated the wild weather, the long winter nights and the tedium of the wartime routine. To make matters worse, HMS *Proserpine* (or *Proper Swine* as it was called by the sailors), the naval base at Lyness, was 500 miles from his hometown of Grange-over-Sands in Westmorland. Having grown up on the fells of the nearby Lake District, Bryan disliked the flat, treeless and seeming featureless landscape of Orkney's mainland, although he had to concede that the island of Hoy, where the naval base was sited, did offer some good hill walking even if only half the elevation of the Lake District peaks. But even had the Orkneys possessed a mountainous landscape to rival that of the Cuillins on Skye, it could not compensate him for being 800 miles from his wife in Havant, Hampshire. Until being appointed to this God-forsaken place, Bryan, as a torpedo and mine specialist, had been based at HMS *Vernon* in Portsmouth.

Bryan shivered as a cold gust of wind from the north-east pierced his Number 5's reefer jacket, despite the Coastal Forces sweater he was wearing underneath it. It was a bright day with only a few fluffy clouds scudding across the mostly-blue sky, but it was windy and the sea surface was marked with white horses. His petty officer came up to him. 'Smoke, sir?' The petty officer proffered a packet of the Royal Navy's *Blue Liners*.

'Thanks, PO. I don't mind if I do.' Bryan accepted the cigarette and light. He inhaled the thick tobacco deeply and gazed down to the beach on which his men were working. The sailors were securing with ropes and stakes three black, sinister-looking, metal globes fitted with spikes like overgrown hedgehogs, only these spikes, or horns, were far more deadly. Each horn was made of soft lead and contained a phial of glass which, when broken on contact with say the hull of a ship, released a chemical solution that set in chain an electrical pulse to explode the mine. But two of these weren't German mines. They had been laid by the Royal Navy to protect the eastern entrances to Scapa Flow until the new Churchill Barriers were completed by the Italian prisoners of war, only the north-easterly storm of the night before had washed them onto a northern beach of Burray, one of the islands to the south of the Orkney mainland. Normally, mines such as these exploded on beaching when the waves rolled them over and their horns struck a rock, but these had only met with the soft sand of this particular beach.

A sailor shouted to attract the attention of the petty officer and gave a thumbs-up sign. 'Looks like they've secured the bastards, sir, and they're all yours now,' the petty officer advised. The naval working party had secured the mines to ensure that they didn't float away with the tidal stream. Now it was Bryan's moment to start work on defuzing them. He was one of *Vernon*'s Rendering Mines Safe Officers (RMSOs) and the year before had been working flat out to make safe the many parachute mines the *Luftwaffe* had dropped on cities such as Birmingham, Coventry and Manchester, as well as London from time to time.

'No hurry, PO. May as well finish my fag first. The lads can shelter behind those rocks to the right whilst I'm on the job.'

'Fair enuf, sir,' the petty officer replied between drags on his cigarette. 'I 'ear you're due a spell of leave soon, sir. You heading for Pompey?'

'Yes to both, PO. I've a whole week off, plus three days travelling time. I can't wait. Apparently, there's a new RMSO due anytime to give me a break. Cunningham's the name. I'm told he's had a bit of a bad time recently and is coming up here for a rest... lecturing or something. Bit of a waste of his skills, but the admiral said he could stand in for me occasionally. You heard of him?'

The petty officer scratched his head a moment and then stubbed out his cigarette in the sand. 'Can't say I have, sir. He must be one

of these new RNVR types. You know, *Really Not Very Reliable.*'
The petty officer smirked at the quip.

Bryan, too, stubbed out his cigarette. 'A word to the wise, PO.
Don't let him hear you say that. This chap's got the George Cross
and the George Medal.'

Bryan was surprised to discover that the German mine was in a
very bad state and it looked as if it had been in the water since the
start of the war. Where had it come from, he wondered, and why
had it turned up along with two much more recently laid buggers? It
was badly corroded from its years at sea and several of the horns
were badly twisted. One was missing completely. Somebody had
had a lucky escape! The two British mines seemed in decent shape,
apart from being covered in oil, and he decided he would tackle
them first. He glanced across to his left at the work being done to
construct the second and third Churchill Barriers. Should he
evacuate the Italian POWs and the civilian workers from the nearest
barrier, he wondered, just in case? He decided against it. Were
work to be delayed on the construction, it would no doubt result in
an official complaint on the admiral's desk. In any case, he had
rendered safe dozens of these mines without a problem.

Bryan knew that technically, the mines shouldn't be armed and
should, thus, be safe. According to the Geneva Convention, when a
moored mine was cut adrift, it was supposed to disarm itself with a
strong spring that allowed the mooring spindle to return to its
original position, cutting any electrical circuit that might be involved
and neutralising the detonator. However, Bryan was experienced
enough to take nothing for granted. He knew that barnacles grew on
mooring spindles and, depending on how long the mine had been in
the water, there could be sufficient barnacles to prevent the spring
pulling back the spindle. He would assume all three mines were
armed.

He set to work on the first mine, but first swapped his wellington
boots for some waders as it still lay in about two feet of the surf.
With the benefit of considerable experience, he removed his watch,
too, and a small packet he always kept in his detonator box for the
purpose. Unrolling the white circle of rubber, he carefully placed his
seven-shillings-and-sixpence watch inside the tube, tied off the end
and placed the whole package in his jacket inside pocket. Now
should he become immersed in seawater, his watch would be

properly protected by the London Rubber Company's product known for its 'Durability, Reliability and Excellence', or *Durex* for short.

The mine was safe within thirty minutes. He had disconnected the electrical leads from the detonator to the primer along with the detonator and all he had to do now was to remove the explosive primer before burning out the TNT or main charge. The construction of most mines was similar and comprised three explosive components. The damage to ships was done by anything from half a ton to a ton of high explosive (HE) comprising TNT or amatol. However, the HE couldn't explode on its own or else it would be extremely unsafe to store or drop the mines from minelayers. Both the Royal Navy and Germans tended to use a two-stage method of initiation. A detonator was inserted into a primer. The detonator was often a thin copper tube containing a tiny amount of explosive, but sufficient to blow off a man's arm. It was triggered by an electrical impulse generated by contact with the mine's horns. In this type of mine the primer was a cylindrical tube containing picric acid. The RMS officer's job was to remove any detonators and the primer in order to make the mine safe. The main charge could be rendered safe by others, if necessary, by removal or burning.

With the help of his team, Bryan unscrewed the many nuts and bolts of two metal plates to expose the honey-coloured TNT within the mine. One of his team passed him a paraffin- soaked quantity of rags and a box of dry matches. 'Right lads,' he ordered, 'Time to withdraw.'

Bryan stuffed the rags inside the casing and at the third attempt due to the wind, set light to them. They soon blazed away and after three minutes or so, the explosive caught light to give off an intense heat and a thick, black and thoroughly obnoxious-smelling smoke. Bryan moved upwind to the second WW2 mine. This one was tethered a few feet up the beach and Bryan felt confident to remove his watch from its protective sheath and to replace it on his wrist. It was ten minutes past noon.

*****

At Invergordon the train discharged many of its passengers and Stephen was able to find a seat in a compartment containing only an elderly commander and a young army chaplain asleep in the opposite corner. From the commander's medal ribbons, it was clear that he had served in the last war. Stephen recognised the crimson and blue ribbon of the Distinguished Service Order amongst the campaign medals. From his grey hair, bald pate and Great War medal ribbons, Stephen judged the commander to be in his late fifties or even sixties. He in turn stared at Stephen keenly through bright-blue eyes and his eyes were drawn to Stephen's own medal ribbons. He seemed impressed.

'You don't see many of those about. The GC and the GM if I'm not mistaken. Don't think I've ever seen them in the flesh. Well done, young feller.' The commander leaned across towards Stephen and thrust out his right hand. 'Warburton's the name. Damn pleased to meet you.'

Cautiously, Stephen took Warburton's hand. 'C-C-Cunningham, sir.'

'Not related to ABC, are you?'

'N-no, sir. No relation.'

'Ah. So, what brings you up to this desolate land? Joining a ship at Scapa, I suppose.'

'N-n-no, sir. I'm to do some l-lecturing, b-but I don't know what on.'

'Lecturing? You can't be a ruddy schoolie with those medals. Come, come now, Cunningham. No need to be coy with me.'

'N-no really, sir. I'm an RMS officer and am being sent for a rest.' Stephen blushed with embarrassment.

'No need for shame, lad. I take my hat off to you chaps. You must have nerves of steel. No doubt you've been through a rough patch?'

Stephen paused before replying as he thought of all the friends and colleagues he had lost. 'I suppose I have, sir, but I think I'm f-fit for d-duty now.' He smiled as he thought of Carol. She had restored his confidence. Turning the conversation away from himself, he asked, 'And you, sir. Are you joining a ship?'

'No, worse luck. Wouldn't have me. Young man's game now, it seems. I commanded a cruiser in the last show you know, but I was pensioned off afterwards. Wouldn't even give me my old rank back, but I'd have jumped at the chance to come back as a snottie. No, boom defence is my line now.'

'I s-see, sir.' Stephen didn't really understand, but couldn't think what else to say, but Warburton picked up the conversation soon enough.

'Where are you from, lad?'

'L-Lancashire, sir. A t-tiny village near Lancaster. M-my father owns a g-garage there.'

'Bless my soul, Cunningham. I know that part of the world well. My late wife and I used to take a caravan that way… Near a place called Slaidburn. Damned fine fly fishing on the Hodder there. You know it?'

'Y-yes, sir. W-we're the other side of the F-Forest of Bowland. D-Dolphinholme, sir.'

Warburton thought for a moment and shook his head. 'No, can't say I've been there. Mind you, I've been to Lancaster. Fine castle.' Warburton was quiet for a while and seemed to be looking back into his past. Conscious of his stammer, Stephen resorted to habit and remained silent, too. He glanced at the view. The train was crossing a bridge over a firth of some sorts, but he was a physicist and not a geographer and, never having been this far north, he didn't know where they were. The padre began to snore gently in the seat beside him. Stephen stood to retrieve yesterday's newspaper from his case and this seemed to rouse Warburton from his reverie.

'You married, Cunningham?'

Stephen abandoned his quest for the newspaper and resumed his seat. 'N-no, sir.'

Warburton nodded. 'I understand. Too young and in your trade, probably not a good idea, hey? But don't rule it out for ever, lad. I had twenty-seven very happy years before cancer took my wife. When it comes, it'll be the making of you.' Stephen didn't reply, but smiled kindly at Warburton who was wiping away a tear from the corner of his left eye.

'You been on this train before, Cunningham?'

'No, sir. I've n-never been north of Edinburgh b-before, sir.'

'Almost a second home for me. I spent much of the last war at Scapa and frequently travelled this way. Used to be called the Jellicoe Express, you know, but Jack had his own name for it. The Misery Express they called it. No heads or catering onboard then,

you know. We used to have a 'bag mealy' and a good breakfast at
Inverness. Mind you, it wasn't so bad for some of the officers.
Used to have sleeping compartments then. It wasn't that bad a
service, mind, but ruddy long… Twenty-six hours from Euston, but
not much slower than now. I had to get from Hampshire, too.'

'D-did you t-travel up from Hampshire yesterday, sir?' Stephen
sensed that Warburton wanted conversation and the padre was still
fast asleep.

'The day before. I stayed at my club overnight. Can't believe how
bad things are in London these days, though…'

Stephen, of all people, was well aware of how bad things were in
London. He had been up close and personal with the *Luftwaffe*'s
magnetic mines dropped by parachute and seen first-hand the death
and destruction in the city. He listened with half an ear to
Warburton's complaints about rationing, the lack of whisky and a
myriad of other matters and thought about what Warburton had said
about marriage. Could it be, he wondered, that he and Carol might
marry? But what could a working-class, penurious, temporary naval
officer offer her? And as the commander had implied, in his line of
work it was highly probably he wouldn't survive the war anyway.
Such thoughts of how his relationship with Carol might develop
were broken when Warburton interrupted his monologue on…
Stephen couldn't remember quite what Warburton had been saying.

'Look over to starboard there, lad. That's Dunrobin Castle, the
seat of the Duke of Sutherland, but it was a naval hospital in my
day.'

Stephen cast his eyes to his right and saw a magnificent building
on a hill rising above the adjacent woodland. With its conical spires
in place of traditional towers it reminded him of a drawing of a
castle he had seen in a book of fairy tales as a child. He didn't think
he had ever seen a more beautiful castle. At that moment the padre
awoke and spoke for the first time in Stephen's presence.

'Ah, Dunrobin Castle. It's stunningly beautiful, don't you find?'
Stephen wasn't sure if he or Warburton were being addressed so he
didn't respond, but the chaplain continued nevertheless. 'It always
takes me back to my days at Cambridge. One vac, I and a bunch of
chums cycled down the Loire. You've never seen so many *châteaux*
in a single stretch.'

'That's down to Sir Charles Barry, isn't it, padre?' Warburton replied.

'Indeed. The architect of our Houses of Parliament. He had a hand in laying out the gardens, too. Modelled them on those at Versailles. Have either of you ever visited?'

Stephen merely shook his head, but Warburton replied. 'Damned great fire there when I planned to call. Can't recall exactly when. Before Jutland, that I do remember.'

'Quite right, commander. It was in 1915. I was still at Twyford then, of course, but…'

The padre seemed only too glad to act as Warburton's conversational partner, leaving Stephen to enjoy the views of the Sutherland countryside and coast in peace. Whilst he thought the coastline magnificent, he considered the inland landscape quite bleak and he remembered fondly the greenery of the fells and woodlands of his native Lancashire. Thinking of Lancashire, his thoughts turned to home and his parents and sister, Lucy, but inevitably, given his current euphoric state, his concentration drifted onto more recent memories of the beauty of the Borders countryside where he had enjoyed such an idyllic convalescence until only the day before.

*****

The second mine still had about twenty feet of mooring wire attached, trailing into the surf. It was badly dented and Bryan's specially-made 'C' spanner wouldn't fit the castellated slots in the security ring giving access to the detonator. Bryan was concerned that he couldn't tell the state of the insides of the mine, but short of having the mine taken out to sea and blown up, there was nothing he could do. This close to the new barrier under construction, he couldn't blow up the 800 pounds of TNT on the beach. In any case, it was a matter of principle amongst RMS officers that such measures were a last resort and a blow to professional pride. As he had so often done, he took a hammer and chisel and, after a few practiced strokes, released the holding ring. Very soon, the bung covering the detonator was exposed. Using a lever Bryan tried to prise the bung upwards, but it stubbornly refused to shift. He tried twice more, but it remained held in place by the sealing ring. Unhelpfully, the wind backed, too, to push the smoke of the first

16

mine's smouldering explosive in his direction. Bryan thought of withdrawing until the explosive had burnt itself out, but he still had to deal with the third mine and didn't want to waste time. He tied his handkerchief over his nose and mouth to resemble a cowboy and continued work.

This time he selected a larger lever and, after much grunting and sweat running down his sooty face, he managed to prise the bung upwards and it came away to the sound of a distinct, but muffled explosion. Bryan froze and the hairs on the nape of his neck stood on end. He knew that he should be dead. This close to the mine he should have been vapourised by the explosion. RMS officers didn't need graves. There wasn't enough left of the unfortunate to merit one. However, mercifully, he was still alive. He took his torch and felt inside the cavity for the detonator. It wasn't there, of course. As he had feared, the insides of the mine had been torn apart by the rough passage of the mine ashore. The battery supplying the detonator had been dislodged to expose its terminals and when he had released the rubber bung above the detonator the firing circuit had been made. He owed his life to the fact that the detonator had become dislodged from the electrical wires leading to the primer. Notwithstanding the chilly wind, Bryan broke out in a cold sweat, but there was nothing for it. He still had to render the German mine safe.

Bryan approached the German mine with much trepidation. It was a type with which he was familiar, but it was not just badly damaged, but badly corroded, too. He couldn't understand how the currents had brought it here or from where. However, that was something for the minesweeping flotilla leaders to resolve. He had his own problems, but to his relief, with a little persuasion from his trusty hammer and chisel, the keep ring came off easily and the bung came out easily. He placed his hand in the four-inch cavity to feel for the electrical wires connected to the detonator, but... he couldn't find anything. He should have been able to feel the wires and detonator. Again, he took his torch and peered inside. Suddenly, he was surrounded by a white flash that blinded him and threw him to the ground. He lay on the sand stiff as a board for several minutes. After a while, his hearing returned and he heard his petty officer calling him. However, he and his team remained sheltered behind

17

the rocks for the mandatory five minutes before the petty officer came over.

'Sir, sir! Are you all right?' the petty officer asked anxiously. Bryan remained too stunned to answer and just lay on the beach stupefied, wondering how he was still alive. Dazedly, he looked at his watch. The face was cracked and it had stopped at half past two. So much for Mister Durex and his earlier precautions.

The petty officer examined the mine and then knelt over Bryan. 'Jesus, sir! You're lucky to be alive.' Bryan thought the comment unnecessary, but felt able to raise his head. 'The det and primer have come adrift, sir and somehow you managed to make the circuit when you removed the bung. If the 'ole lot hadn't come adrift from the charge, sir, you'd be a dead man.'

Bryan was only too aware of the latter fact, but two similar close shaves in an afternoon were enough. It was a sign that it was time for him to seek new employment.

Chapter 3

Acting Lieutenant Commander The Honourable Thomas Montcalm RNVR was grateful that the head of the Admiralty's Directorate of Torpedoes and Mining (Investigations) or DTMI, Captain Arnold Maitland-Dougall, was late into the office. Montcalm, (pronounced Mon-com) and known by everyone as Monty, had been late for work after a late night returning from Oxford. There he had spent the weekend with Marcia Scott. He and Marcia, known as Marcy to her friends, had been undergraduates at Oxford together in the early 30s. Marcy had studied Mathematics at Lady Margaret Hall and Monty, Law at Christ Church. Marcy was working for the Foreign Office in a statistics department at a country house called Bletchley Park. Since Oxford, Monty had been called to the Bar and had followed a successful career as a barrister specialising in salvage until called up into the Royal Navy full time on the outbreak of war.

It had been a most pleasant weekend, Monty thought. He and Marcy were both keen sailors and they had managed to borrow a dinghy to spend a bracing day on an Oxfordshire lake. The night before, they had attended marvellous recital in Oxford. As students he and Marcy had just been good friends. She used to crew for him on his yacht *Firefly* on the south coast. However, since meeting up with her again by chance in May the year before, Monty had felt increasingly attracted to her. Last night, it had seemed that she was similarly attracted to him. A warm feeling came over him as he remembered her passionate embrace and kiss on the lips as they had said farewell at the railway station. Ordinarily, he had only ever received a peck on the cheek.

The warm feeling was rudely interrupted by the shrill of the ringing telephone. It was the Chief of Staff to Vice-Admiral Holt, the Flag Officer-in-charge of the Humber region.

'Is Captain Maitland-Dougall there?' asked Captain Palmer.

'I'm sorry, sir, but no. I'm not sure when he's due in. Can I help, sir? I'm his lead investigator.'

'Very well, Montcalm. We have a conundrum for you. Our minesweepers have been working flat out to clear the approaches to the Humber, but even after sweeping the waters thoroughly and declaring them safe for shipping, we're still experiencing underwater explosions, some of them dangerously close to the sweepers. It's very unnerving for the crews and we've had casualties, too. One broken leg and a couple of crewmen off sick with spinal damage.'

'Forgive the question, sir, but you are sure that no fresh mines have been laid since the previous sweeps?' Monty felt impertinent in asking the question of an experienced senior officer.

'Absolutely. First thing we thought of,' the captain replied curtly.

'Of course, sir, but I needed to check. It suggests that Jerry may have deployed a new mine variant and it needs investigation. I'll send one of our staff up there right away. To whom should he report, sir?'

'Send him to me, at Immingham. I'll then arrange for one of our best skippers to assist him with his investigations.'

'Thank you, sir. I'll attend to it immediately and send you Lieutenant Postlethwaite. He's one of our most experienced mining investigators.'

Monty replaced the telephone receiver and considered carefully the implications of Captain Palmer's news. In late 1939, Monty had been hauled out of a staff appointment in Portsmouth to help DTMI on account of his legal experience. It had been thought that his ability to assess and collate evidence forensically would solve the mystery of why so many ships were sinking in mysterious circumstances. Thanks to the discovery of the two mines on the mudflats of Shoeburyness, the Royal Navy had discovered that the Germans were deploying magnetic mines on the seabed in shallow waters. Armed with the knowledge, counter measures had been devised. Had they not, Britain would have lost the war by Christmas 1939. However, mine warfare was a cat and mouse game. Every time the Royal Navy RMS teams and the scientists came up with a solution to counter a mining problem, the Germans developed a new counter-counter measure and fitted booby traps to stop the RMS men learning the new secrets. One such development had been the invention of a magnetic 'clicker' mine. Such mines could be preset to ignore the magnetic influence of anything up to five ships before being triggered. It meant that only after the hard-pressed minesweeping flotillas have swept channels six times, could they be confident the waters were clear. Monty feared the Germans might have developed a new clicker mine with more than six settings. If so, it was very bad news for the country's minesweeping flotillas.

*****

Until Scrabster, Stephen's journey from Edinburgh to Thurso had gone rather well. The train had even arrived on time at exactly 14.30. Commander Warburton suggested Stephen join him and the chaplain for something to eat at the Railway Hotel before Stephen's crossing from Scrabster Harbour to Stromness, and then on to Lyness, but Stephen declined the kind invitation, despite Warburton's curious advice that he really ought to eat something prior to the crossing. Remembering the naval maxim, *never get separated from your kit*, Stephen had instead personally overseen the transfer of his tin trunk from the guard's van to the elderly bus ferrying the train passengers the short distance from Thurso to the harbour. Warburton and the chaplain were destined for different parts of the islands, so the trio bade each other a polite farewell at the station. Half an hour into the two-and-a-half-hour crossing of the Pentland Firth onboard a former mail steamer, Stephen was regretting the absence of a lining to his stomach.

Despite the sunshine and blue skies, the strong wind from the north-east had caused choppy waves. To make matters worse, the meeting of the strong current from the Atlantic and the North Sea, both funnelling through the narrow firth in opposite directions, often creates a lumpy crossing even in the calmest of weather. For Stephen, it was too much to bear. With no real experience of being at sea, it was not long before he felt very ill, indeed. The skin across his head felt extremely tight and his stomach craved to empty itself. He was not alone. Several men and women of all three armed forces were congregated on the upperdeck looking the worse for wear. It wasn't long before the vomiting started, to the immense amusement of a small group of seasoned sailors.

'Don't be a fucking idiot,' one of them called to a poor airman who had been the first to submit to Nature. 'If you're goin' to barf, then do it on the leeside, you nobber.' Sadly, for a young Wren also leaning over the guardrail to windward, the advice was too late. The airman's vomit was rapidly brought back inboard over her outstretched head. Stephen was desperate to avoid the humiliation of giving his stomach its wishes in front of Jack. The regular navy had a low enough opinion of the RNVR as it was. In his torment he recalled some advice he had been given to focus on the horizon. If only he could keep his stomach in check for another half hour or so, the ferry should be entering the lee of the island of Hoy, he reasoned.

To the glee of the watching old salts, dozens of passengers were now leaning over the leeside voiding their breakfasts and lunches. The smell was nauseating, causing Stephen even greater difficulty. Ten minutes later, a helpful Tar with a particularly cruel sense of humour passed around a bucket to those unable or too weak to find a gap to line up against the guardrails. As it passed him, Stephen noted it had been graduated so that the depth of its contents related to the wind strength and that it had then stood at Force 4. Stephen's stomach heaved at the sight and smell. Within seconds, he, too, was *yodelling the bucket.*

Thankfully, as Stephen had hoped, the sea was calmer on the western side of Hoy and he didn't have to lose his dignity again. He was impressed by the sheer-sided cliffs of the island and as the ferry passed Rora Head, somebody pointed out a huge sea stack of red sandstone rising from the seashore. He learned it was called The Old Man of Hoy. Notwithstanding the views, he was extremely grateful when the ferry turned into Hoy Sound and the entrance to Stromness. The sideways motion of the ferry seemed to stop immediately and it became obvious to Stephen that Scapa Flow made an ideal sheltered harbour for the Royal Navy. However, the majority of those who disembarked at Stromness were soldiers. Stephen was interested to see the soldiers comprised several regiments and corps ranging from the Royal Engineers and Royal Signals, to the Royal Army Service Corps and the Medical Corps, but to his surprise, no infantry nor gunners. Stephen asked if he might step ashore whilst the ferry unloaded its passengers and stores, but was told that the ship would be sailing again after thirty minutes. Instead, he remained on deck and enjoyed watching the activity onboard and ashore.

Sheltered from the wind, it was a pleasant day and Stephen soaked up the sun's warmth. Stromness looked to be a pretty little seaport and, prior to the war, must have been a quiet place to live, he thought. However, it now looked to have been taken over almost completely by the army. The houses along the seafront were interspersed with several wooden huts and in the fields behind the main town Stephen could see large camps of Nissen huts. To his surprise, several of the huts looked to be anchored down with steel hawsers about every ten feet down their length. He asked a sailor standing nearby having a smoke about them.

'Aye, well, sir. You've seen how it can fair blow here even in the summer, like. Well, jes imagine what it'd be like in the winter with thar winds blowin' a 'un'red miles an 'oor for days on end. It's the same in yon *Proper Swine*, sir,' he indicated with the butt of his cigarette. 'Thase hawsers hold the cabins doon and keep yer safe in yer bed at night.'

It was Stephen's first indication that he might have ended up in a place far wilder than his native Lancashire.

*****

Monty returned to his office after meeting a member of RAF Air Intelligence at Cockfosters. He had made a point of maintaining close liaison with the other services' intelligence directorates and it had paid off earlier in the year. Squadron Leader Alan Benson was a German-speaking interrogation officer at Trent Park, Sir Philip Sassoon's country home until his death. The house was now used as a special prisoner-of-war camp run by MI19. However, the 'Cockfosters Cage' was run more like a hotel than a conventional POW camp. The *guests* were given special privileges such as rations of whisky and regular walks in the grounds of the house, but were unaware that listening devices had been installed around the house. The previous year, the house had been home to many captured German aircrew and their conversations and skilful questioning by Air Intelligence officers had helped Monty discover details of a new mine, the BM1000, that could be dropped without a parachute like a bomb. However, whilst the house was now used as a POW camp for German generals and their staff officers, it was used, too, as a centre to interrogate other captured German personnel. When Benson had rung Monty, he had suggested Monty might wish to witness the questioning of a sergeant of the *Afrika Corps*, captured in the Western Desert. Monty had been intrigued as to the relevance to his department, but Benson couldn't explain his reasoning over the telephone and Monty had learned to trust Benson's judgement.

Excited by what he had learned at Trent Park, Monty was keen to brief Maitland-Dougall, but something in his captain's countenance curbed his enthusiasm.

'Is there something wrong, sir?'

'I'm afraid so, Monty.' Maitland-Dougall lit his pipe and sucked on it a few times before he was satisfied it was alight. He gestured to Monty to sit down. 'I've just been on the telephone to Captain Palmer at Immingham. Bad news, I'm afraid.' He drew in a few lungs full of tobacco smoke before continuing and Monty noticed the sadness in Maitland-Dougall's usually cold-grey eyes. Monty knew it was, indeed, bad news that was on the way.

'It's about Postlethwaite. He's in Grimsby hospital, severely injured! Captain Palmer arranged for him to join the *Rolls Royce*, a minesweeping trawler under the command of Skipper Romyn. According to Captain Palmer, Romyn is one of his best minesweeping skippers and has command of his own group.'

'I've met Leopold Romyn, sir. He's a legend in the fishing industry. You might recall, sir, that it was he last year who dived into the sea to lash two floating German mines so that they didn't explode on the shore of Yarmouth and damage the town. He wasn't even in the Patrol Service then.'

'Well, that's by the by. Postlethwaite never got a chance to find out. By the time he'd left Immingham and arrived at Grimsby, Romyn's unit was already at sea. Postlethwaite took a tender to meet the trawler at sea, but half a gale was blowing. The tender went alongside the trawler, but both boats were bucking wildly in heavy seas. Apparently, Postlethwaite either misjudged his jump onto the *Rolls Royce* or slipped, but he ended up hanging by his fingers over the side of the trawler. Before the crew could haul him inboard, he was washed into the sea just as the two boats came together. The steel plates of both boats crushed him like a grape.'

Monty was stunned by the news. To be injured whilst rendering safe a mine was a normal hazard of the trade for RMS officers, but to be caught up in such an accident was such a waste of talent.

'Look, Monty. I feel bad enough about Postlethwaite, but he had a job to do and that job still needs to be done. I've told Captain Palmer to expect you in Postlethwaite's place. A car will take you up to Grimsby as soon as you've packed an overnight bag.'

'Very well, sir,' Monty replied despondently. He knew from experience that Maitland-Dougall wasn't being callous. Monty had seen at close quarters how Maitland-Dougall cared deeply for his men, but he had been brought out of retirement for a reason. He was supremely professional and entirely focussed on the task. Monty stood to leave, but Maitland-Dougall beckoned for him to remain seated.

'How did you get on at Cockfosters?'

Monty's sombre mood brightened a little as he thought about the interrogation. 'As a matter of fact, it wasn't the wild goose chase we feared, sir. It was jolly useful.'

'So, what did this *Feldwebel* have to say that concerned this department let alone the Admiralty then, Monty?'

'It transpires, sir, that he comes from Eckenförde, the little Baltic port near Kiel.'

'I know it, Monty. It's where the Germans have their torpedo research factory.'

'Sorry, sir. I should have realised that you would know it,' Monty said contritely. 'Although the sergeant has no personal connection with the sea, his father is a foreman at the research establishment.'

'That is interesting. I don't suppose he's ever visited the factory, though?'

'Indeed, he has, sir. More than that, he has accompanied his father on a boat when testing torpedoes at night, sir.' Monty looked triumphant, but his boss was less impressed.

'Hang on a minute, Monty. Do you not think this chap was pulling your leg, perhaps for more favourable treatment? I know from long experience that one doesn't carry out torpedo trials at night. You need to see their run.'

'True, sir, but these had lights on the front of them.'

'Still sounds a bit rum. Did he seem to be speaking honestly?'

'I think so, sir. He seemed very friendly and straight-forward. He even seemed flattered to be questioned. Mason made all the questions seem so casual. But there's more, sir. The torpedoes didn't run straight. They weaved from side to side. Look here, sir. I had him draw me a picture of their run.' Monty pulled from his jacket a piece of paper showing a series of wavy lines. 'I just wanted to check there was not mistake in translation, sir.'

'Hmm. They must have had dodgy gyros. However, I can tell from your expression, Monty, that you think there's something significant here.'

'I do, sir. I asked Mason to establish how many of the torpedoes ran like this and the answer was *all* of them. The sergeant stuck to his story and said that according to his father, the trials had been a success!'

'I confess to being completely baffled, Monty, but you've convinced me that this is significant.' The captain shut his eyes and rested his chin on steepled fingers to think. Monty knew not to disturb him. After a few minutes of silence, Maitland-Dougall turned back to Monty.

'The Germans are cunning blighters and they don't do things without purpose. I think I know what they're doing, but I need to have a word with someone more expert on this when you get back from Grimsby. If my hunch is right, Jerry's perfecting an ingenious new weapon. Without countermeasures the implications could be enormous!'

Chapter 4

It was not only Monty's first ever visit to Grimsby, or Great
Grimsby as a local corrected him, but to Lincolnshire. His first
impressions weren't good. The whole town seemed to reek of fish,
but that was understandable given that something like ten percent of
the UK's fishing catch was landed there and a huge industry had
grown up in the town to process and distribute the fish. It didn't
help assuage Monty's olfactory glands that a stiff north-easterly
wind was directing the smell of fish from the docks across the town.
Moreover, despite it being the August bank holiday, the sky was
overcast and dark clouds out to sea threatened to bring in rain.
However, Monty couldn't help but be impressed by the number of
fishing vessels thronging the harbour. Many, of course, were no
longer employed on fishing expeditions. Monty noted the large
numbers whose winches and warps had been adapted to tow a
paravane rather than a trawl. Beneath the surface of the sea the
paravanes towed a cutting jaw. This was the sweep that cut the
tether of moored mines to bring them to the surface. The Royal
Dock in Great Grimsby was the base for Britain's largest
concentration of minesweepers. Forming part of the Royal Naval
Patrol Service, many of the vessels were manned by former
trawlermen as well as members of the RNR and former sailors of the
Royal Navy, many of whom had served during the Great War.

Notwithstanding the large number of RNPS vessels berthed
alongside in the dock, Stephen was disappointed to discover that the
Rolls Royce was already at sea on patrol. Like poor Postlethwaite,
he had no alternative but to catch a tender to take him out to the
minesweeper and, again, a heavy sea was running. The repetition of
history did not fill Monty with joy.

Fortunately, Monty was able to board the trawler without mishap –
and he didn't lose his luggage either. The *Rolls Royce* seemed an
inappropriate name for the converted trawler. She was hardly
luxurious, but she seemed sturdy enough to cope with Arctic winter
conditions and the crew looked a tough bunch, all of them fit-
looking with weather-beaten tans. As soon as Monty and his gear

were safely onboard, the skipper signalled his colleagues to begin minesweeping.

The trawlers worked as a team of three. Two trawlers swept the channel in line abreast whilst the third followed up and laid Dan buoys to mark the limits of the cleared channel. Like all the Humber minesweepers, *Rolls Royce*'s sweep comprised a long buoyant cable coupled with a short cable through which a heavy electric current was passed at six-second intervals. The gear was called the 'Double-L' or 'LL' sweep. The electric current created a magnetic field astern of the trawler pairs that was strong enough to detonate any magnetic mine lying on the seabed within the vicinity. The short cable, or tail, neutralised the magnetic field in the immediate vicinity of both trawlers of the pair and, thus, ensured no enemy mine could explode close to the minesweepers. The trouble was that the theory wasn't working and the Humber sweeper crews had been suffering casualties.

Sure enough, soon after the sweeping had started, it seemed as if the *Rolls Royce* had been lifted clean out of the water. To the accompaniment of a loud explosion, the stern was raised several yards and a giant wave crashed down onto the stricken trawler. Along with several others of the crew, Monty was thrown off his feet to the deck and he then understood the preponderance of broken legs and spinal damage amongst the minesweeper crews. Why did they volunteer, he wondered not for the first time. These brave men were the unsung heroes of the Royal Navy. Several times a day they risked injury or death, but none of the glory of the regular armed forces came their way. However, such thoughts were interrupted by the call of, 'Fire, fire, fire!' It seemed that the force of the explosion had set fire to the galley when the stove coals had been blown clear. Thankfully, the fire was quickly extinguished.

'How close was that, Skipper?' Monty asked of Romyn standing outside the wheelhouse.

'Oh, about twenty to thirty yards. Not too close, fortunately,' Romyn replied coolly and reached inside his coat pocket for his pipe and some tobacco. As he began filling his pipe, he added, 'What gets my goat is that we had already swept this channel this morning and reported it clear. But what can you do, hey, other than keep buggering on?' Romyn waved to the skipper of his sweeping partner to continue the sweep. Monty recognised that the problem the Chief of Staff had outlined was, indeed, a serious one.

To emphasise the severity of the problem, ten minutes later, another explosion shattered the peace. This time, it was 400 yards on the port beam where *Rolls Royce*'s partner had been just a few seconds earlier. All that could be seen of her now was smoke and flame amongst a colossal wave. Romyn immediately altered course towards the site of the explosion to offer assistance, but there was no trace of the trawler or her crew. There wasn't even any wreckage. The trawler had been swallowed whole by the sea.

'Must have gone right over it,' Romyn said calmly, but Monty could see the anguish on his face.

Monty assumed that the sweep would be abandoned and the trawlers would return to Grimsby to report the events and to mourn their dead colleagues, but to his surprise, Romyn merely ordered one of the trawler pair sweeping astern and to one side to break off and take over as his sweep partner. It was as if this was an everyday occurrence. Yet again, Monty was amazed by the quiet courage and dedication of the minesweeping flotillas. Clearly, these men reckoned that the work must go on regardless.

The stove had been relit and one of the crew had brewed a fanny of tea. Monty accepted a mug gratefully and, unusually for him, accepted, too, the offer of sugar. He hadn't taken sugar with his tea since the imposition of rationing, but today he felt in shock. However, he had barely finished his tea when a pair of Heinkels rudely interrupted the impromptu tea break. The two German bombers headed straight for the formation of minesweepers, but the Navy crews were ready for them. Gunners onboard immediately opened up with a mass of anti-aircraft fire. It was more than enough to dissuade the Heinkel pilots from pressing home their attack. They pulled out of their dive and climbed high into the clouds. Monty began to wonder whether he should have joined DTMI. He might now be in Portsmouth as the flag officer's legal advisor, convening courts martial and analysing punishment warrants.

A few minutes later, a sharp-eyed lookout hailed the sighting of two more aircraft, but this time they turned out to be RAF fighters. They waggled their wings in salute before they, too, disappeared into the clouds, Monty presumed seeking the Heinkel bombers as their prey. His attention was drawn to a tall, straight-backed member of the crew who had been one of those manning the anti-aircraft guns. Whilst most of the other members of the trawler were giving a cheery wave of departure to the retreating fighters, he was giving them a naval salute. Monty noted that on the breast of his junior rates' square-rig tunic he not only wore the medals of the previous war, but a crimson ribbon on which was pinned a bronze-looking cross. Monty turned to Romyn.

'I say. That chap over there. Is he wearing the ribbon of the VC?' Since April 1918 and the formation of the Royal Air Force, the dark-blue ribbon of Royal Navy Victoria Cross recipients had been replaced by the army's crimson ribbon so that now all three armed forces shared the colour.

Romyn checked who Monty meant before replying, as if more than one member of his crew might hold the VC. 'Aye, that's Desmond. He was a lieutenant commander in the RNVR during the last war. Apparently, he gained the medal during the Ostend raid, but I can't tell you more. He doesn't like to talk about it.' He pointed to a man in the bows. 'Old Middlemiss there, he won the DSM. We've a few old regulars sprinkled about my unit.' Monty was even more impressed by the calibre of RNPS men.

The afternoon gave way to dusk, but the day was still not yet clear of excitement. A third mine exploded abeam and close to *Rolls Royce*, dousing her once again with seawater and, on this occasion, a few fish. Clearly the trawler's fishing days weren't quite over yet. Fortunately, there was no damage to the sweeper or casualties amongst her crew. Monty plotted the position of the explosion in relation to the sweep and wondered if he had detected a pattern. He didn't have long to wait before being able to confirm his theory, as right on sunset, a fourth mine exploded directly ahead of Romyn's sweeping partner. For a moment the trawler disappeared in plumes of smoke, spray and green water, and Monty feared she may have gone the way of the earlier victim, but she soon appeared out of the spray and seemed intact.

The explosion gave Monty all the evidence he needed to complete his investigation and he went below to check the diagram he had brought showing the lines of force and strength of the magnetic field generated by the sweeps. It was obvious to him that the mines had been triggered in areas where the electrically induced magnetic field of the sweeps was at his weakest. Reacting to the Royal Navy's counter measures against magnetic mines, the Germans had retaliated by decreasing the sensitivity at which the mines were triggered. The ends of the sweeps generated the more powerful magnetic force of 0.6 of a gauss as this was the sensitivity of the mines recovered earlier in the war. Monty now calculated that abeam and ahead of the sweepers the force was down to 0.2 of a gauss and this was now enough to trigger the new versions of magnetic mine. Monty wondered about the motives of the German scientists. Had they learned through their intelligence services that ships were now routinely wrapped in electric cables to reduce their magnetic field, so called *degaussing*, or were they deliberately targeting the hardworking minesweepers? As far as he could tell, there didn't seem to be any changes to the mine clicker settings, but they had obviously been set to remain unarmed for the first two passes by the minesweepers. That at least was a relief.

However, despite having seen all he needed to be able to inform the Admiralty scientists to offer the minesweepers more protection, he could not return to Grimsby. With the descent of darkness there was insufficient light to continuing minesweeping so now the trawlers were tasked to escort convoys travelling up the busy east coast. With the density of merchant shipping plying the coast and the proximity of the German E-boat bases, the area the Humber-based trawlers were patrolling had become known as 'E-boat Alley'.

Soon after picking up their south-bound convoy, Monty and the other crew members heard the throbbing of heavy bombers approaching from the coast. Nobody was concerned as it was an established routine for the bombers of Lincolnshire to pass overhead on their way to a raid over Germany. One of the crew switched on the recognition lights and the other trawlers followed suit. The bombers continued their approach and above the heavy throbbing noise of their engines, Monty picked up the sound of bursts of machine gun fire. He knew enough about RAF operations to know that once the bombers crossed the coast, the gunners liked to test their guns. As an extraneous member of the crew, he volunteered to go below to make everyone a mug of cocoa. He had no sooner descended the steps than he heard shouting.

'The stupid idiots are shooting at us!'

Monty rushed back up the steps in time to see lines of tracer tracking across the sea towards the trawlers. Romyn personally switched off and then on the recognition lights, but the firing came closer and all too soon, the *Rolls Royce* and the trawler astern were hit. One of the crewmen just a few yards from Monty yelped with the pain of wooden splinter entering his arm. Monty hit the deck. He could hear some of the trawlermen not unnaturally uttering all sorts of oaths at the stupidity of RAF gunners, but Romyn decided more direct action was required. 'Open fire!' he ordered and muttered to Monty lying beside him, 'The bastards will only understand one thing. Retaliation!' Monty was horrified to hear it.

All the guns of the *Rolls Royce* opened fire as one against the aircraft overhead and within a minute, the bomber crews must have realised their mistake. The machine gun fire ceased and the signallers began flashing their own recognition signals. Fortunately, neither trawler had suffered serious damage and, once back on his feet, Monty couldn't see any signs that any of the bombers had been hit badly either. One of the crew members was applying a shell dressing to his shipmate's wound, but assured Monty that the wound wasn't serious. With the departure of the RAF bombers, all was quiet and the trawlers were able to get on with their business of escorting the merchantmen. Monty volunteered to relieve one of the lookouts in order to let him get an hour's sleep. At least it was something to do, he reckoned.

Nearly three hours later, Monty thought he might, too, take a short nap. The excitement of the day's investigations had now palled and he had had an early start from London the previous morning. He explained this to Romyn, standing in his usual spot in the wheelhouse puffing away on his pipe, but as he turned to exit the wheelhouse, he saw flashes of gunfire in the sky.

'Action Stations,' ordered Romyn and all the gun crews immediately closed up again.

The gun flashes were soon joined by slow and drunken lines of tracer renting the dark sky. Then there was a huge flash followed by a loud boom. One of the merchantmen was surrounded by a halo of white interspersed with yellow flames. *Rolls Royce* rushed to her assistance. Monty was grateful that after a short and furious attack, the E-boats had withdrawn after making their kill. However, it transpired that whilst the merchant ship had been torpedoed, she was still afloat and capable of making port with the assistance of a tow.

None too soon, but without further incident, at the break of dawn off the Norfolk coast, the Humber trawlers were finally able to hand over their charges to another escort. Romyn turned his force northwards for home.

*****

Stephen was extremely surprised and very nervous to be summoned to call on the Admiral Commanding Orkneys and Shetlands by the admiral's personal assistant. After all, he was a lowly lieutenant in the RNVR. With great trepidation, he disembarked from the tender to step onboard HMS *Iron Duke*, Vice-Admiral Sir Hugh Binney's flagship moored in Scapa Flow. Unlike some of the officers who preceded him in disembarking, he was not piped aboard, but received a friendly welcome, nonetheless, and was shown to the battleship's wardroom by a very neat Officer of the Watch. There he whiled away half an hour drinking tea and reading the previous day's newspaper. The news headlines were dispiriting. The Germans had broken through the Soviet Union's defences at Konotop and were now laying siege to Leningrad, the country's second largest city.

He was mightily relieved when the admiral's flag lieutenant entered the wardroom to say that Sir Hugh would see him shortly. The flag lieutenant escorted him to the admiral's great cabin beneath the quarterdeck of his flagship, but on the way, Stephen remembered that in his anxiety, he had left his cap behind. As he collected it, the flag lieutenant kindly reminded him not to wear it and nor should he salute the admiral 'tween decks.

Stephen had never met an officer so senior before and it seemed to him that the admiral's gold rings extended half way up Binney's arms. The left side of his chest was almost completely covered with different coloured medal ribbons. Stephen was completely tongue-tied and he felt his knees trembling. However, the admiral smiled benignly and stood to greet him.

'Good afternoon, Cunningham. I'm very pleased to meet you. Do take a pew.' The admiral gestured to a chintz-covered armchair by the fireplace.

'G-g-good afternoon, s-sir,' Stephen stammered in reply and sank gratefully into the armchair before his legs gave way.

'Tea?' Binney asked and without awaiting a reply, he nodded to the steward waiting at the open hatch to the pantry.

'You're probably wondering why I asked to see you, old chap,' the admiral continued.

'Y-y-yes, sir,' Stephen replied nodding.

'When I read of your appointment under my command, I was intrigued by your decorations. A GC and a GM! You must be an incredibly courageous man, Cunningham. I just had to meet you. You're not a relative of ABC, are you by any chance?'

'N-no, sir.' Stephen had become accustomed to the question about his possible kinship to his namesake, Admiral Andrew Browne Cunningham, the Commander-in-Chief of the Mediterranean Fleet. He was spared further conversation momentarily by the arrival of the steward with a tray of tea for two.

'Sugar, sir?' the steward asked. Stephen shook his head and allowed the steward to pour for him before serving the admiral. As Binney sipped his tea, it struck Stephen that the admiral must have had a succession of visitors, all of whom would probably have been invited to take tea. How did the admiral's bladder cope, he wondered.

'There's no need to be nervous, old chap. Somebody who's tackled as many mines and bombs as you, has nothing to fear from senior officers. After all, we all put just one leg in each of our trouser legs. How are you finding life up here?'

Stephen tried hard to follow the admiral's advice to relax, but it was impossible. However, the tea was beginning to steady his nerves and he could no longer feel himself shaking. 'It's v-very b-beautiful here, sir.'

'That's very true, Cunningham, and the people are charming. This is the second time they've had to put up with thousands of strangers fronting up here, but they seem extraordinarily relaxed about it and very friendly. But winter's a problem up here. It's boredom and not the enemy that's the killer up here… but every now and then we are troubled by Jerry,' Binney added quietly. In the early days of the war, a German *U*-boat had successfully penetrated the Flow's defences and sank HMS *Royal Oak*, sending over 800 sailors to their death. Nearer to home, HMS *Iron Duke* herself had been badly damaged by *Luftwaffe* bombing and run aground to prevent her sinking. She was no longer seagoing and only fit to act as a flagship and anti-aircraft platform.

'You need to get yourself a hobby, Cunningham. Do you walk?'

'No, sir, but I enjoy r-running when I have the t-time.'

'Excellent. You probably need to be fleet of foot in your line of work, hey? What about indoor activities? Do you enjoy the cinema? We have many excellent films showing ashore.'

'I prefer reading, sir. T-Trollope is a f-favourite of mine.'

'A good choice, old man, but a bit highbrow for me. I enjoyed his tales of Barsetshire, but couldn't get into his political novels. Wodehouse is more up my street.'

'Also, a f-fine writer, sir.' Stephen was pleased that his stutter was coming under control.

Binney looked at the brass clock on the bulkhead opposite and clearly decided that he needed to come to the main point of the meeting. 'How are you getting on with the lecturing? I understand you were a schoolmaster before the war.'

'I was, sir. T-teaching about unexploded bombs is fine, sir, but I'm not sure w-why I'm lecturing on w-what to do if taken p-prisoner, sir. I've never been a P-P-POW.'

'Oh, I shouldn't worry yourself about that. Just make sure you've read the handbook at least half an hour before you meet your class. It'll be a piece of cake.' The admiral finished his tea and laid his cup down on its saucer a little noisily. 'However, I could offer you something more challenging should you feel up to it, Cunningham.' He looked at Stephen expectantly.

'Anything, sir. I'm k-keen to help.'

'Good show. I knew that with your record you'd take that line. The thing is, Cunningham, we're in a bit of a bind trying to find a new Bomb Disposal Officer. The present incumbent had a bit of a nasty time a couple of weeks ago and has been sent to see the trick-cyclists. I've recently learned that he isn't fit to return to duty and is being sent south on indefinite leave. A pity as he was a good man. I know you're meant to be up here for a rest yourself, but I wondered if you wouldn't mind combining your duties of lecturing with working part-time as the BDO. It'd save taking another RMS officer off more pressing duties down south.'

Stephen was delighted with the offer and accepted it without hesitation. He would be glad to be back working with something familiar.

'Capital, Cunningham. I have every confidence in you, but I hope you'll not find the work too arduous.' The admiral rose to indicate Stephen's time was up. 'And remember... find yourself a couple of good hobbies to keep you occupied in your spare time. I enjoy sailing myself, but maybe not in the winter.'

Stephen left *Iron Duke* a happier man than when he had arrived.

Chapter 5

Two days after Monty's return to London, he and Maitland-Dougall met with a Captain Carslake to discuss the mysterious German torpedoes. Monty had never met Carslake before, but knew him to be regarded as one of the RN's experts on torpedoes and he had a reputation for being a genius, too. He and Maitland-Dougall explained what the captured *Feldwebel* had told them. Carslake wasted no time in giving his opinion.

'I can only draw one conclusion, gentlemen. The Germans have developed an acoustically-operated torpedo.'

'That's what I had feared,' Maitland-Dougall replied. 'We're going to have to develop some countermeasures PDQ.'

'I agree,' Carslake replied. 'The implications are quite horrifying.'

It suddenly struck Monty that he didn't understand the implications. He had been in too much of a rush to go to Grimsby beforehand, but now he felt he had no choice but to expose his ignorance.

'Why is this news so horrific, sir?' he asked politely.

Maitland-Dougall gestured to the other captain to explain.

'I would expect the torpedoes your tame *Feldwebel* saw were fitted with microphones in their heads. They would react to any sounds they received so, for example, were they to hear a noise to port, they would alter course in that direction. I suspect the wavy tracks your POW witnessed were as a result of noise transmissions from alternate quarters.

'As we all know, sound travels very well through water and that's how the dastardly *U*-boats detect our convoys – from the sound of the merchantman's engines. However, up to now, the limited speed of the *U*-boats underwater has meant that they have no choice but to attack the convoys from ahead and to allow the ships to pass over or close by them. Once the convoy has passed, the *U*-boats only options are to trail the convoy on the surface. They don't have the speed to follow astern whilst dived and, in any case, would drain their precious battery reserves. Obviously, shadowing the convoy on the surface when the *U*-boat has a superior speed puts the boat at risk of detection.'

'That I understand, sir,' Monty replied a little defensively. 'But how does such a new weapon change matters?'

Carslake glanced sideways at Maitland-Dougall with an expression that suggested he was lecturing a particularly dense schoolboy.

'I think that's a fair question,' Maitland-Dougall rose to Monty's defence causing Carslake to backtrack.

'Of course it is, Montcalm. I forgot that you are more of an expert on mines than torpedoes. The problem this weapon poses us is threefold. Firstly, the *U*-boats would be free to attack a convoy from abeam or astern. They could launch torpedoes almost at random. The torpedo would quickly pick up the noise of a ship's propeller and select the noisiest and, thus, likely aim for the biggest ship as its target. In any case, our convoys are shepherded in such a dense formation, an acoustically-guided torpedo could hardly fail to find a target. The second problem is that our escorts suddenly become more vulnerable. Up to now their greater speed has often tended to enable them to evade torpedoes, but no escort can outrun a torpedo locked onto its propeller noise. And finally, there is the question of our fast ocean liners. These ships have depended on their speed for safety and, thus, free to steam independently. Now all bets are off.'

'Thank you, sir. I now understand the problem clearly. So, what sort of countermeasure would you suggest?' Monty now fully understood the ramifications.

'I would suggest some form of noise-making decoy, much as we use to detonate acoustic mines… but clearly not housed in the bows.' Carslake laughed. 'That would completely defeat the object of the exercise. No, I had in mind something towed.'

Something registered in Monty's mind, but he couldn't quite recall what it was. Meanwhile, Carslake continued, 'The microphones in the heads of these torpedoes will be optimised for certain wavelengths. Your countermeasures would clearly need to match the same wavelengths. Clearly, it would help if you gained some intelligence on this or, dare I say it, recovered one intact.'

Monty suddenly remembered what he had been trying to recall. 'I think I might have an idea, sir. The Canadians have been developing a towed noisemaker for use as an acoustic sweep. I'll dig out the details. We might be able to get our scientists to adapt it.'

38

'Excellent, Montcalm. I think that might be just the ticket and I feel immensely relieved. Might I make a small suggestion, though?'

'Of course,' Maitland-Dougall replied. 'Be our guest.'

'It is just that you are clearly dreaming up something to *fox* the new enemy torpedo. Why not give your new countermeasure the codename *Foxer*?' Carslake chuckled at his idea.

*****

Three months passed by and there was no indication that the *U*-boats pattern of torpedo attacks had changed. There were no more reports of ships being attacked from astern than hitherto. In the meantime, Monty had worked with the Admiralty scientists to devise a noisemaker that merchant vessels could tow astern as torpedo decoys. In the absence of intelligence on the wavelengths at which the torpedo microphones would be set, Monty had asked the scientists to work on the wavelengths of an ordinary merchantmen travelling at ten knots. Thousands of the new *Foxers* had been manufactured ready for use, but the Naval Staff had ordered that they remain in storage until proof of the introduction of acoustic torpedoes was obtained. Monty felt pleased at his part in ensuring Britain was more prepared for the introduction of a new underwater weapon than it had ever been. Captain Maitland-Dougall had been pleased with his investigations in Grimsby, too. The subsequent adjustments to the settings on the sweeps seemed to have made a big difference and the casualties amongst the minesweeping flotillas had been reduced considerably. Monty had been informed, too, that his acting promotion had now been confirmed. However, this was not the time for him to rest on his laurels.

Monty was sitting at his desk one Saturday morning, wondering if the *Feldwebel* had seen something other than torpedoes in the water in the night, when the telephone rang. It was another DTMI officer, Lieutenant Martin Johnson RNR. Johnson was ringing from Barrow where he had been sent to investigate the torpedo load of a captured *U*-boat.

U-570 had been captured at the end of August. Whilst on patrol south of Iceland, she had been caught on the surface by an aircraft of Coastal Command. However, nobody in the boat had seen the aircraft before it dived again. The aircrew of the Lockheed Hudson dropped a marker where the submarine had dived and a couple of hours later when it returned to the surface, another Hudson was waiting for her. Before the German could dive again, the aircraft dropped two depth charges to damage the *U*-boat sufficiently to persuade her captain that he had to remain on the surface. His gunners tried to drive off the aircraft with their anti-aircraft guns, but were disabused of the notion by machine gunfire from the air. Faced with no option to escape by diving or to fight it out with the Hudson, the captain indicated his surrender. A series of aircraft then kept a continuous surveillance on the stricken submarine until a Royal Navy trawler, later backed up by a destroyer and other trawlers, arrived on the scene to take the submariners off their boat and to tow *U-570* to Iceland. In due course, the *U*-boat was transported to Barrow for its secrets to be trawled by several teams of experts from all branches of the Admiralty. Naturally DTMI hadn't wanted to be left out. *U-570* carried a full outfit of torpedoes. In any case, firstly, they needed to extract the torpedoes to make the submarine safe and Johnson had been given the task, but he had hit a complication.

'Sorry to be the bearer of bad news, Monty, but this job's not as straightforward as we first thought,' Johnson informed Monty over the telephone. 'We can't get at the torpedoes. The bow plates have been crushed by the depth charging and they're blocking the tubes.'

'Could you not retract them into the torpedo compartment, Johnno?'

'Sorry. No can do, Monty. The boat doesn't have any working machinery left. Even if we could withdraw the fish that way, I wouldn't recommend it. My fear is that the fish might be damaged, too, and in a dangerous condition. I wouldn't like to risk losing the boat should something untoward happen. She's too valuable for that.'

'It would ruin your day, too, Johnno.' Monty thought about what might be done, but couldn't offer any advice immediately. 'I'll tell you what, Johnno. I'll travel up straight away. We can't afford to take too long to make those torpedoes safe or else we'll be stopping the other specialists getting to work on the boat and her equipment. Expect me tonight. Can you fix me overnight lodgings?'

The journey to Barrow took longer than Monty had expected. There had been a heavy snowfall in the north and the snow was three inches deep as Monty's driver carefully steered him through the

Lake District. Knowing they would be in Barrow too late for dinner, Monty treated himself and his driver to a portion of fish and chips *en route* through Lancaster. The stop gave Monty an idea.

Once his task was complete, he would try to call on Lucy Cunningham, Stephen's sister, in Dolphinholme, very near to Lancaster. Monty had met Lucy when he and Stephen had stayed in Dolphinholme after defuzing magnetic mines in Liverpool the year before. Lucy was a primary school teacher. She was, also, a socialist and didn't approve of Monty's aristocratic and privileged background. Her forthright views had challenged Monty's political thinking. The younger son of an earl, he had not taken much interest in politics, but tended to vote Tory out of habit. However, investigating and defuzing mines in the working-class areas of London, Liverpool and the Midlands had opened his eyes to the poverty and harsh lifestyles of his fellow Man. He had not only not brushed off Lucy's mockery of his background, but enjoyed the experience. Lucy had a fresh and lively mind, as well as an attractive figure, and she seemed to welcome his attentions. They had been corresponding since their first meeting and met up twice more for tea when Monty had been in the north on business. Unfortunately, Stephen had learned of this relationship and, knowing that Monty was keen on Marcy, it had offended his Quaker sensibilities. He and Stephen remained friends, but were no longer as close.

The following morning, Monty accompanied Johnson to the shipyard. It was a bitterly cold day and snow lay all about the pavements of Barrow and within the shipyard. Monty could already feel his shoes absorbing moisture from the snow. With Johnson he climbed up the wooden staging from the dock bottom to the bows of the submarine. Monty had no choice but to agree Johnson's assessment of the difficulties in accessing the torpedoes. The only option seemed to be the use of an oxy-acetylene torch to cut away the crushed steel plates. Monty outlined his idea to Johnson.

'It's not a prospect that appeals, Monty, if you really want my opinion. Each of those torpedoes contains 500 pounds of TNT and there are four of them in the tubes. If we're not careful, the heat of the torch could be enough to cause the TNT to burn. That could then set off the pistols firing the warheads. It's not that I'm worried for myself, but there wouldn't be much of the *U*-boat either.'

Monty had to agree, but what else could he do? To make matters worse, it began to sleet. Monty had thought Barrow cheerless enough without the weather.

'Do you know how to use an oxy-acetylene torch, Monty?'

'No, I don't and I don't suppose you do either, Johnno?' Johnson merely shook his head. 'Then we'll find somebody who can.' Without awaiting Johnson's response, Monty descended the staging and approached a group of welders. It might have been a cold and wintry Sunday morning, but the war had to carry on and with it, shipbuilding.

One of the four welders acted as their spokesman. 'I reckon we could do job, but is there any danger in it?'

'I have to confess that there may be, but I can't see any other way,' Monty replied honestly and hoping to appeal to the welders' sense of honour.

'I see,' the welder replied. 'An' 'ow much explosive is there in them tubes?'

'500 pounds in each torpedo and there are four of them.'

'You must be jokin'.' The welder turned to his colleagues. 'Hear that, lads. 2,000 pounds of explosive... nigh on a ton. We'd all be blown to Kingdom Come. I don't know about you lads, but I've a wife and kid at home. I'll not risk it.' The other welders muttered in agreement.

'You'd 'ave to be daft to consider it,' one of them said.

Monty could see the men's points. It wasn't in their contracts to put themselves at risk of blowing up... and some of them might well be married, but all the same! The job had to be done and besides. With all the overtime these men were probably getting, they were all probably earning more than most RMSOs. He tried another approach.

'Of course, I'll be up there with whoever volunteers to do the job.' The men responded with ribald laughter to the offer of Monty's company. It was all rather trying. 'All right then,' he tried once more. 'If one of you would show me how to use the torch, I'll do the job myself.' This time, his offer was met with stony silence for a few moments before the youngest member of the group stepped forward.'

'I'll do the job for you,' he said.

'Wilf, you're mad. What're you thinkin' of?' several of the men asked almost in unison.

The welder turned to his mates and replied, 'I reckon that if this officer is so set on job, it must be important. An' none of us wants some amateur playin' with fire near explosives. He could take the whole yard down with him.' He turned back to Monty. 'No hard feelin's meant, sir, but I'm yer man.'

With huge relief, Monty joined Johnson and the welder on the wooden staging. However, it was still with much trepidation. Whilst he was now quite experienced in RMS work on mines and even bombs, he had never tackled a torpedo before. Nor had Johnson, a probation officer before the war, but he had at least been trained to do it. Monty used his finger to mark the area of steel metal plate that needed to be removed to give access to the first tube.

'If you're ready, start there,' he said to the welder.

The welder nodded and lowered his dirty goggles before bringing the flame of the torch to the metal. It cut through the plate like butter. It emphasised to Monty that the heat of the torch would be being conducted through the plating to the torpedo tube and then to the torpedo within. He tried to appear nonchalant.

Sparks flew in all directions, but the welder was nonplussed. He worked carefully and accurately followed the line Monty had indicated. He clearly knew his business as he was quickly done. Monty and Johnson went to lift the plate the welder had just cut, but Wilf held them back.

''Ang on a mo'. That metal'l be 'ot. Tak' these.' He handed Monty a spare pair of welding gloves and together they removed the cut plate and placed it on the staging. Monty marked the second area to be cut and Wilf recommenced cutting.

The weather turned worse and very soon, Monty's Burberry uniform coat was sodden and the melting snow was creeping down his neck. However, his and Johnson's nerves were too taut to notice. Wilf continue cutting regardless and soon he had cut away the second plate. They were half way through and, despite the heat of the oxy-acetylene torch warming up the torpedoes, nothing untoward had happened. Both Monty and Johnson began to relax.

Wilf set to on cutting away the plate blocking the third torpedo tube. He seemed unconcerned by the weather and just concentrated on the job before him. Sparks showered and the metal plate glowed red-hot beneath the cutting torch. Wilf's hand was just as steady as if this was any normal job. If he survived this task, Monty thought, Wilf would have a tale to tell his friends tonight. Monty resolved to give him some beer money.

At last, the fourth metal plate was removed and the welder was able to extinguish his torch. 'That was a first-class job, Wilf.' Monty slapped the welder on the back in a fit of gratitude.

The welder lifted his grimy goggles and smiled back at the two naval officers. 'Nothin' to it in the end, was there? Always happy to help the Navy.' He began packing up his gear and Monty reached into his wallet. Picking out a ten-shilling note, he handed it to the welder.

'Here,' Monty gestured. 'You've earned a few beers with your mates. We're very grateful.' However, Wilf wouldn't take the money.

'Keep your money, gents. I did it for my wife's brother. He's in corvettes and I call this my contribution to keeping him a bit safer. Cheerio.'

With the departure of the welder, it was now the turn of the naval officers to get to work. Before the torpedoes could be withdrawn, they needed to be made safe and that meant removing the pistols. These protruded from the noses of the warheads and they themselves resembled miniature torpedoes. They included a propeller which, as it rotated through the water with the thrust of the torpedo, wound down the detonators into a position where they could be struck by the strikers and, thus, arm the torpedo. When the strikers were pressed back by a blow in excess of 80 pounds, they fired the detonators that fired the primers to explode the TNT in the warhead. Johnson showed Monty how to remove the pistols. First, he inserted some wooden pegs immediately behind four whiskers protruding from the front of the pistol. These were spring-loaded and when bent back on impact with the side of a ship, they exploded the torpedo, something Johnson didn't want to simulate. Then it was as simple as unscrewing two holding nuts in the nose of the torpedo and withdrawing the cylinders from the cavity in the warheads. However, as with the detonators and primers in mines, Monty knew that these pistols could be lethal, too.

Gingerly, Johnson and Monty placed the pistols on the staging and then went to the stern of the submarine. The stern tube of the submarine had not been damaged so it was a simple job for Johnson to remove the pistol in the stern torpedo. Now they had five pistols to render safe.

Neither of the two officers had any idea of how German torpedo pistols were constructed, so they decided to saw through one with a hacksaw to inspect the interior. This was clearly risky as the heat of the cutting might set off either a detonator or primer, but they pressed on regardless. It came as a shock to discover that the design of the pistols was completely different to those of the RN. The detonators were set into the primers and this meant that any error, such as a screwdriver slipping, would cause a much larger explosion than just a detonator exploding on its own. It was the riskiest part of the whole day's operation, but gritting their teeth, they persevered and trusted to God. The task took them all afternoon, by which time they were both soaked to the skin and very tired, but they succeeded. Now it would be safe for all the scientific specialists to examine the submarine and its equipment. Monty looked forward to a good bath and a hot meal that evening, but most of all, he looked forward to ringing Lucy.

Chapter 6
December 1941

Stephen was disappointed to find himself back in hospital and this time, through his own fault. He had been giving a demonstration on how to deal with unexploded incendiary bombs. The technique he had been demonstrating had been to encase the unexploded bomb with sandbags, although ordinary sand worked equally well. Usually, the incendiary bomb would then go off after three minutes and splutter away harmlessly amongst the sand. However, it hadn't worked on this occasion. Feeling embarrassed by the crowd of sailors looking on expectantly, Stephen had waited five minutes and then approached the bomb to see what was happening. It had immediately exploded. Stephen was taken to the hospital in Stromness with a couple of splinters in one side of his body. He had already been laid up for five days, but the army surgeon who had removed the splinters had advised Stephen that he might be discharged after two or three more days in bed. Stephen was finding it all very frustrating.

Until the unfortunate accident, Stephen had been enjoying his new appointment in the Orkney islands. He had a much more relaxed lifestyle than he had experienced in his first year as an RMSO or, indeed, teaching Physics to teenage girls for that matter, he reflected ruefully. There had been no German mines or bombs to defuze, but he had been kept busy with British mines washed ashore after strong winter gales. The work had taken him all around the Orkneys and he had developed an excellent relationship with the trawlermen manning the minesweepers. There had been no need to adopt the C-in-C's advice to take up a hobby. He had been too busy at sea with one or other of the minesweepers and, four months after crossing the Pentland Firth for the first time, he now had a cast iron stomach in a gale. The fishermen had taught him, too, how to use a rod and line to catch fish. Stephen was now the proud owner of some impressive-looking fishing gear and spent many a quiet Sunday fishing from a pier or beach. He had found it the perfect way to relax.

Stephen picked up the latest letter from Carol. It bore a London postmark of only two days earlier. He was amazed how quickly and frequently mail arrived in this far-off outpost of Great Britain, but it was a huge morale-booster. Stephen had already read Carol's letter three times, but it made him feel closer to her each time he read it. In this latest letter, she informed him that she had written to her parents in the United States (where her industrialist father was working for the Ministry of Supply) to tell them all about Stephen. Surely that was significant, Stephen thought. I mean, if she's telling her parents about me, she must feel our relationship is serious. Yet again, he wondered if he and Carol were destined to be married. The more he thought about it, the more attracted the idea became except... there was a war on and he was engaged in one of the most hazardous activities known to Man. No, were he to marry, he would have to wait until after the war was won, but when might that be?

Stephen reflected on the state of the war. It wasn't going well. The Soviets seemed to have held up the German advance into their country, but the rest of Europe was completely under the German jackboots. It was no better at sea. The *U*-boats were still strangling British maritime trade in the Atlantic and the Royal Navy was under severe pressure in the Mediterranean. Worse, Britain was now under threat from the Japanese in the Far East. Yesterday's newspapers were full of reports relating to the shock of the sinking of the *Repulse* and *Prince of Wales*. However, the commander of one of the minesweeping flotillas had expressed some optimism when he had visited Stephen earlier in the day. He believed that the recent Japanese attack on Pearl Harbour would bring the US into the war. Stephen was willing to grab any strand of optimism with both hands.

More positively, though, Stephen had high hopes of seeing Carol in the new year. Prior to the accident, the admiral had agreed that Stephen needed to gather more information on how to handle oneself if taken prisoner and that meant a trip to London. Then, the admiral had learned that Stephen's investiture with the George Cross would take place at Buckingham Palace in late January. It had been postponed from the previous summer following the accident that had hospitalised Stephen then. The admiral had kindly suggested Stephen could extend his trip to London not just to combine the investiture and visit to the Admiralty, but, since Stephen wouldn't be taking any leave over the festive season, to tack on a few days' leave to the visit. He hadn't informed Carol of his accident and hospitalisation, but couldn't wait to tell her about his forthcoming sojourn south.

*****

Monty had forgotten that Lucy would be teaching on a Monday. As he had to travel back down to London that day, he had only been able to arrange to meet her during her lunchbreak. In the interests of accommodating a man serving his country, the headmistress had kindly excused Lucy from playground duty and Monty's driver had driven them to the local public house. On alighting the car, Lucy had become aware of the state of Monty's uniform.

'My! Look what the cat's dragged in. Is this the new fashion for the aristocracy?' Monty thought Lucy's welcome was hardly warm. He suddenly felt very self-conscious of his dishevelled appearance. His trousers were creased in all the wrong places and filthy, and his shoes had gone white from the wet snow.

'I'm sorry, Lucy. I was on a job in filthy weather, didn't think to wear overalls and I haven't a change of clothes,' he replied more tersely than he would have liked. They entered the pub and whilst Lucy found them a table in a quiet corner of the snug, he ordered himself a beer and her a soft drink.

'I feel very grand having a chauffeur to bring me here, your Lordship. The children were fascinated by your car.' Lucy smiled mischievously as she sipped her lemonade.

'Oh, stop it, Lucy. It's my brother that's the viscount and you know that very well already.' Monty was a little irritated by Lucy's mocking tone and wondered why he had made the effort to pay the call.

'Ah, but you can't deny that you are still an Honourable.'

'I don't, but everyone still calls me 'Monty'. Look, we haven't time for this. I have to drop you back at the school in thirty minutes.'

Lucy leant across and pecked Monty on the cheek. 'Dear, Monty. You rise too easily to the bait.' She smiled impishly. In doing so, Monty was reminded how Lucy's features were very elfin. She had short, dark hair and blue eyes. Monty, too, had blue eyes, but fair hair and he thought her eyes particularly striking against dark hair. Her smile softened his defensive attitude towards her.

'So, what has brought my noble lord to this part of the world?' she continued.

'I had a job in Barrow yesterday.'

'I hope it was less dangerous than that affair at Garston gasworks last year.'

'It had its moments, but I think so. Anyhow, I survived to be able to see you briefly.'

'I've always meant to ask, Monty. Are you a mine disposal officer like my brother? I looked up that oak leaf on your breast and I now know you've been mentioned-in-despatches, so you must be very brave, too.'

'Not at all,' Monty laughed. 'My job is only to investigate the technical issues of German mines. I'm just a bureaucrat. People like Stephen are the brave lions who make them safe and deservedly have the medals.'

'Come, come now, Monty. You're too modest. Stephen has told me it's more than that. But I'll not press you.' Lucy sipped her drink and nodded to a couple of old men sitting in another corner of the snug. Monty was pleased that Lucy was behaving more pleasantly.

'Have you heard from Stephen recently, Lucy? I haven't since he went up to Orkney. That must have been three or four months ago.'

'He sends us letters from time to time. He seems to be enjoying the solitude up there, but I detect a hint of boredom. I think he misses the action of the Blitz. He says he's taken up sea fishing and grown a beard. I suppose it keeps him warm up there.'

'How very nautical,' Monty replied, finishing his half pint. He was clean-shaven.

'Mind you, most of his news is about the gorgeous Carol. Have you met her, Monty?'

'Once or twice, briefly. She's very beautiful. She and Johnny…' Monty was about to speak of a US naval officer who was good friends with both Carol and Stephen, but he recalled that Johnny had been killed in the accident that had put Stephen in hospital in the summer. Lucy reached across and took his hand in hers gently.

'I heard about it all, Monty. Stephen was very upset by Johnny's death. I think you and Johnny were his only true friends.' She and

Monty were silent for a short while, each locked in their own thoughts.

'Anyway, returning to his ministering angel, Carol, I think Stephen's in love. She's the subject of his every letter. But did you know she's Jewish?'

'I didn't, but what of it?'

'I don't know really. We've all been brought up as a family of Quakers, but I confess religion does nothing for me. I'm just worried that those of the Jewish faith might not see it that way. You know… a bit like Catholics.'

'It doesn't seem to have hindered Carol's affection for Stephen, though. Or do you think Stephen's feelings for her are unrequited?'

Lucy thought about this a moment whilst she finished her lemonade. 'He indicates that his feelings are reciprocated, so it probably doesn't matter. Let's hope so. I love my brother very much.' Lucy checked her watch. 'I think it's time to take me back to work, don't you?'

Monty rose and helped Lucy into her coat. Before they left the pub, Lucy turned to Monty. 'Thank you for making the effort to see me, Monty. It was lovely to see you, but I'll say goodbye to you properly here rather than at the school. I have a reputation to uphold.' To Monty's surprise, she gripped Monty in a firm embrace and kissed him on the lips warmly. As he dropped her at the school gates, she merely gripped his hand tightly as she said goodbye before alighting the car. Monty's heart glowed with affection.

*****

Monty was just packing up his desk to travel down to his family home in Wiltshire for a few days' Christmas leave when he received news that the Dutch had discovered intact a German torpedo of the type removed from *U-570*. It had run ashore on a beach of Dutch Guiana. The Dutch Navy requested advice on how to render it safe. Although Captain Maitland-Dougall was a widower and had offered to man the office over the Christmas period, Monty delayed his departure to respond to the request as he saw it as his responsibility to respond. He spent a couple of hours drafting a signal giving precise instructions on how he and Johnson had defuzed the torpedoes of *U-570*. Once the signal had gone, he too was gone.

Chapter 7
January 1942

Stephen was standing on a stony beach about two hundred yards
from the Old Man of Hoy when the telegram arrived. It was his first
view of the great red sandstone stack since his arrival on Orkney the
previous summer. Two mines had parted their moorings and drifted
into the bay. Whilst one had foundered on the beach, the other
refused to come ashore and was bobbing about several yards
offshore, trapped in the circular current. Miraculously the grounded
mine had not detonated by contact with the rocks and, ordinarily,
Stephen's instinct would have been to blow up the mine from a safe
distance, but that would have upset the locals. Stephen had come to
have some affection for the Orcadians. They were friendly and
relaxed. Nothing seemed to phase them and they showed no
outward sign of resentment at the thousands of intruding uniformed
personnel on their peaceful islands. It seemed little enough on his
part to render the beached mine safe and thereby avoid the risk of
damaging the landmark of which the locals were so proud.

The man who had reported the mines had told Stephen that at 450
feet high the stack was one of the tallest in Britain and it was
estimated to be over a hundred years old. Apparently, it had
originally had two legs and this had helped give it the appearance of
an old man standing offshore, but erosion by the waves had washed
away one of the legs and Stephen could only make out any human
resemblance because he was looking for one.

For Stephen, the worst and riskiest part of the operation to make
the first mine safe was the approach to the beach. A boat had taken
him and his team around the island of Hoy to Rackwick Bay. They
had then had to trek across the headland to the Old Man in sea boots
and oil skins before clambering down the near vertical cliffs with the
aid of ropes to reach the beach. By the time Stephen finally
approached the mine, he was dog-tired. The wind was coming from
the north-west and blowing at about twenty-five knots, raising large
waves and several white crests. Now accustomed to rough weather
at sea, Stephen's stomach had fared better than on the last trip past

the Old Man. However, it was now winter and not just freezing cold, but the hard snow pellets and near-freezing spray from the waves were torture to the skin. Gloves reduced Stephen's dexterity to near nothing and, thus, he had been forced to work with his hands fully exposed to the elements. The skin of his hands was now raw with the cold and salt spray, but one of his party had provided him a hot mug of tea to warm not just his hands, but his insides.

Defuzing the first mine had been straightforward, at least for somebody of Stephen's experience working cheek by jowl with three-quarters of a ton of high explosive waiting to go off with less than a second's notice, but the second mine was proving to be more problematic. He had two choices. The first was to return to Rackwick Bay and to persuade the skipper of the trawler that had brought them from Lyness to approach the mine and attempt to lash a hawser to it so that it could be towed to safety. However, unsurprisingly, the skipper was not prepared to do this. It wasn't through lack of courage. The skipper had done something similar many times, but on this occasion, he feared the high sea state would cause the mine to drift into the side of his boat. Leaving the mine where it was wasn't an option for fear it would eventually either hit the beach and detonate or free itself of the current and drift out to sea into the path of the ferry to and from Scrabster. Stephen's only other option was to use the telephone of the local hotel to ring the Officer of the Day at HMS *Porsepine* with a request for a party of sailors to return with .303 rifles in order to sink the mine by gunfire. Having done this, he despatched the trawler skipper to return to Lyness to collect the firing party. It meant, of course, another hike over the headland, descent down the cliff face and climb back up. Stephen's legs already ached with cold and exhaustion and he discussed with his petty officer whether it would be possible to shoot at the mine from out at sea. The petty officer, however, reminded Stephen of how difficult that would be given the sea state. Stephen was forced to agree, but at least he and his team were able to take shelter and a hot meal in the hotel whilst they waited for the trawler to return.

The trawler returned just over two hours later and landed six sailors with a couple of spare rifles for the RMS team. Stephen prepared his team to lead the armed party back over to the Old Man of Hoy, but the skipper stopped him and handed him an urgent message. It was from the flag officer's secretary. As Stephen read it, his eyes welled up with his tears and his already tired legs buckled. The secretary's note enclosed a telegram from Stephen's mother, Jane, to inform Stephen that his father had passed away the day before of a heart attack.

*****

Monty had returned from his week in Wiltshire hoping for a quieter life. It had been a while since he had seen his family and he had thoroughly enjoyed the peace and quiet of the Wiltshire estate, but it had not been without its worries. His older brother and heir to the earldom, Julian, had been running the estate since their father had fallen ill and had managed to combine the responsibility with his duties as the brigade major for the local 129th Infantry Brigade. However, just before Christmas, he had learned that he was being promoted and sent to a staff appointment in Cairo. Monty had taken his share in helping rearrange the estate management and learning some of the detail so that he could cover for his brother's absence. Unfortunately, 1942 hadn't started too well.

Firstly, he received the news that something had gone wrong with the Dutch Navy's attempts to defuze their German torpedo. The pistol had blown up and seven members of the Dutch Navy had been killed. Monty's hands shook when he read the signal. The news brought home to him just what a lucky escape he and Johnson had had in Barrow.

Next, Captain Maitland-Dougall had been in an odd mood. Normally affable and supportive, for the past couple of days he had been on edge and distant. Now he had reprimanded Monty, an event Monty couldn't ever recall happening before. Maitland-Dougall had just returned from a meeting with the Naval Staff.

'Ah, Montcalm. I'm glad you're here. There's something I want to say to you. I've just had an interview without coffee with the Third Sea Lord. And it was all down to you, Montcalm,' the captain said icily.

Monty was astonished at Maitland-Dougall's tone. Since his boss was still standing, he thought it right to rise from his chair and face the music.

'I have just been accused of putting the country to huge expense for no reason. It's those blasted Foxers you persuaded me to order.

54

There are thousands of them in store and all down to your wild guessing. Next time you interrogate a German prisoner, Montcalm, be less trusting.'

It took a minute for Monty to clock that his director was referring to the intelligence he had received at Cockfosters about the Germans experimenting with acoustically-guided torpedoes. Monty said nothing to defend himself, despite the fact Maitland-Dougall had fully supported his hunch at the time. Maitland-Dougall continued.

'The whole thing's been a bloody fiasco and we look fools in the eyes of the Naval Staff. It's not to happen again, Montcalm. Understand?' This time, Maitland-Dougall did pause to give Monty the chance to respond.

'I'm very sorry, sir. I accept it's all my fault, but I'm sure the *Feldwebel* was genuine with his version of events. Perhaps, I over-interpreted the facts as he saw them.' Monty was well aware that in fact it had been Maitland-Dougall who concluded that the mysterious torpedoes were acoustic homing torpedoes and had had his suspicions ratified by Captain Carslake. Maitland-Dougall seemed to recall this as his attitude mollified a little.

'Ah well, Monty. No need to worry. There's plenty of this war left for you to redeem yourself.' The captain then sat down to read his signals and the subject wasn't raised again. However, Monty was mystified by his superior's sudden change of attitude. He enjoyed working for him and this type of behaviour was most unlike him. He wondered whether it might be time for him to seek a fresh appointment.

*****

The death of his father, John Cunningham, had complicated Stephen's plans to spend a few days in London after his investiture at Buckingham Palace. Instead, the funeral had been arranged hurriedly to allow Stephen to attend before travelling down to London. Moreover, whereas he had arranged for his mother and Carol to be his guests at the Palace, his mother no longer felt able to attend. She pleaded that in the absence of his father, she would now have to keep the garage running and, in any case, couldn't face the rail journey to London and back. It was agreed that Lucy would take

55

her place. However, having used up his leave in Lancashire, Stephen was only left three days in London.

Despite the curtailed visit to London, Stephen had enjoyed the investiture and, of course, not just seeing Carol again, but introducing her to his sister at last. As he lay in his room on the night of the investiture, his feelings were a mixture of pride and love. Always a modest man, Stephen had, nevertheless, been proud to meet the King again. He liked the King. Like him, he had to overcome a stammer and yet he didn't let it stop him doing his duty. The King had informed him that this was the first time he had awarded the George Cross to somebody who already held the George Medal. That made Stephen feel very proud.

Carol was as lovely as ever and their relationship seemed as deep as ever. As he lay on his bed, Stephen felt a hole in his heart having had to say goodbye to her earlier in the evening. She had managed only to take one day off from her nursing duties to attend the investiture and he would not see her again before his return to Orkney the following day. He yearned for her to be there on the platform of King's Cross, but she had her duty, too. Even Lucy wouldn't be there as she was catching an earlier train back to Lancashire. He could at least be at the station to say farewell to her before reporting to Captain Currey. He wondered why Currey had summoned him to the Admiralty at such short notice.

The next day, he was back in the offices of *RMS Admiralty*, the Admiralty's only operational command. He couldn't remember when he had last been there. It seemed to have changed little although none of the old hands were there anymore. He would have particularly liked to have seen 'Dusty' Miller again, but he was now serving somewhere in North Africa. He had even tried to visit his best friend Monty Montcalm, but he was down in Plymouth. London suddenly seemed a lonely place to Stephen, but at least he didn't have long to wait to see Captain Currey.

He had last seen Currey in the naval hospital in Stonehouse, Plymouth after his accident. Currey had brought Carol down to see him and conspired with her and the medical staff to arrange for his convalescence on discharge from the hospital to take place under Carol's supervision in the Borders. Stephen thought him a wonderful, warm-hearted man who was loyal to his staff. In Stephen's opinion, many senior officers expected loyalty from their staff, but it only worked in one direction. Currey greeted Stephen warmly and gestured for him to take a seat opposite. Stephen detected little change in Currey's appearance since he had first met him. He was still fair-haired, dynamic in his movements and had eyes that seemed highly alert.

'Congratulations, Cunningham, on the GC. I'm glad we finally managed to get you in front of the King this time.' Currey smiled and reached into his pocket for his cigarettes. 'Do you mind?' Currey paused to light his cigarette. 'Are you still seeing anything of the lovely Miss Templeton?'

Stephen blushed before replying. 'Indeed, sir. She accompanied me to the investiture y-yesterday.'

Currey raised his eyebrows as he lit his pipe. 'Sounds like the stammer has improved, what? Good for Miss Templeton.' Currey tried and failed to blow a smoke ring. 'I suppose you're wondering why I called you in before your return to Scapa. How's that working out by the way?'

Stephen felt on edge that Currey had just changed the subject. 'It's f-fine, sir. I like it up there. The people are v-very f-friendly and the scenery m-magnificent. It's just a long way away.'

'I suppose it is, Cunningham. I remember thinking that in the last show. A brute of a journey, too.' Currey reached for a docket on his desk and leafed through a couple of pages. 'And how goes the lecturing?'

'Ah,' Stephen hesitated. 'I confess it is a bit b-boring, sir. The lectures on dealing with UXBs aren't so b-bad, sir. I understand that, but how to behave as a p-prisoner of war, sir…'

'But I gather you've had a bit more briefing whilst down here?'

'Y-yes, sir. It will help, but I've no experience to d-draw on.'

'I see,' Currey said non-committally. 'But I note from this report, that's not all you've been doing, Cunningham.' The captain left the sentence to hang in the air for a moment. 'I have a report here from Admiral Binney, Cunningham, telling me how pleased he and the senior officer minesweeping are with your work. *"Dedicated"*, *"Ice-cool under pressure"*, *"Selfless"*, *"One of the bravest men I have ever met and yet modest with it"*. Fine words, Cunningham, but not pleasing.' Currey shut the docket and tossed it back onto his desk. Stephen was astonished by the anger in Currey's tone.

57

'I'm s-sorry, s-sir. I d-don't understand.' Stephen felt himself welling up at the disapprobation of the man he admired so much.

Currey's tone became more charged. 'I'll tell you why it's not pleasing, Cunningham. I sent you up to Scapa Flow for a rest. You'd been through a lot and I wanted you to have a break from RMS duties. The last thing I expected was for you to volunteer to take over BDO duties.'

'B-but, sir.' Stephen coloured once more, but this time in distress. 'The admiral asked m-me and I w-was p-pleased to help. I j-just wanted to b-be useful, sir.' Stephen was almost in tears at the injustice as he saw it and this seemed to soften Currey's heart.

'I know, Cunningham,' Currey replied more tenderly. 'And I suppose I shouldn't have been surprised by the news. You are what you are, but there's something you need to get into that skull of yours. RMS officers of your skill and experience are worth their weight in gold. I can't have you taking risks on relatively mundane tasks such as defuzing moored mines. I can give that to newly-trained officers. Whilst our lives in RMS HQ have been considerably quieter recently, this war is going to last a long time yet and Jerry's getting ever sneakier in his design of new mines. You of all people must recognise that.'

Stephen let his superior's words sink in before replying ruefully. 'I'm s-sorry, sir. I d-didn't think of it that way… B-but in f-fairness, sir. I need to keep match fit.'

'I understand, Cunningham. Nobody can change your nature and the last thing I want to do is curb a zealous officer's enthusiasm, but you must understand… We have to preserve in pickle the likes of you, Syme, Mould etcetera until this country really needs you. With the entry of the Americans into the war and Hitler being held up by the Russians, it won't be long before we go on the offensive… and for that to happen, it's all hands to the pumps. I have a new appointment for you. Blast!' Whilst Currey had been speaking, ash from his cigarette had dropped onto some paperwork on his desk. He brushed it away.

Stephen's heart leapt at the news of a new appointment. He hoped it would be back in London. Or even at *Vernon*. That would be an easy train ride back up to London to see Carol. Frankly, even a return to Plymouth would be closer than Scapa Flow.

Currey puffed out huge clouds of tobacco smoke and then picked up his signal pad. 'This time, Cunningham, I really am wrapping you in aspic. I'm sending you to Simon's Town to train the South African Naval Forces in bomb and mine disposal. No doubt you'll come across a few drifting moored mines from time to time, but I expect even you to have a quiet time.'

The news was a bombshell to Stephen. It was most unexpected and he couldn't believe it. South Africa! It was even further away than the Orkneys. He couldn't think how to respond, but made an attempt.

'Is that f-final, sir. I d-don't mind staying in Scapa, sir.'

'It is, Cunningham. I've already informed *Vernon* to provide you a relief from the next RMS course. I know what's worrying you, though.' Currey smiled warmly at Stephen in between puffs of smoke. 'You're thinking of that precious girl of yours, aren't you?'

'Y-yes, sir. I suppose I was. I'm in love with her.'

'Good show, Cunningham. I don't blame you. She's a smasher, but if I know her well enough from our meeting last year, she's the type of girl who'll keep. Let's face it, Stephen. In your present profession, you're hardly a terribly eligible bachelor. Best to postpone thoughts of settling down until after we've won this bloody war, what?'

'I suppose so, sir,' Stephen replied in a crestfallen manner. He had no choice but to agree the captain's advice, but that didn't make him feel less that the bottom of his world had just dropped out.

Chapter 8

Night after night for over a week the Germans had been *blitzing* Plymouth. The locals felt that Hitler was determined to wipe Plymouth off the map and had come up with a new term for the German bombing. They called it *Coventrating* after what had happened to the city of Coventry. The naval base at Devonport had been the principal target, but the city of Plymouth and the town of Stonehouse had been devastated, too. Everywhere Monty looked he could see street after street of houses, shops and businesses reduced to rubble. Civilian casualties had been very high, too. The enemy had dropped a considerable number of parachute mines and Monty had been sent down from London with a small party to help where he could. In particular, he had the responsibility of advising the Captain of Minesweepers how to keep the channels to and from the dockyard clear of mines. Consequently, he was based in the minesweeping HQ in Millbay Docks.

Devonport, with its proximity to the dockyard, had been particularly badly hit. The Royal Sailors' Rest, known affectionately by Jack as Aggie Weston's in honour of Dame Agnes Weston whose charity had founded a series of sailors' rests, had been completely obliterated along with the residential streets of Granby Street and Duncan Street. Monty's heart melted as whilst working out and about on the streets defuzing unexploded bombs, he witnessed the evening exodus of the civilian population heading out of town to sleep on Dartmoor.

Today, Monty was working on rendering safe a magnetic mine. This one had landed outside the front door of the admiral's residence at Mount Wise. The Commander-in-Chief, Plymouth, and until lately the Western Approaches, was a legend in the Royal Navy. As a young lieutenant commander in 1915, Admiral Dunbar-Nasmith VC had taken his submarine through the narrow, shallow and perilous Dardanelles Strait. Despite it being heavily defended by Turkish forts, anti-submarine nets, minefields and torpedoes, Nasmith had not only twice taken his submarine into the Sea of

Marmara, but safely back to the Mediterranean, too, despite the Turks being forewarned of his exit. He and similarly courageous submarine commanding officers had run amuck in the land-locked sea to sink Turkish shipping, damage by gunfire the coast-hugging railway trains and to sabotage railway track and viaducts. They had brought Turkish shipping and railways to a complete standstill and, had the Allies only known when they withdrew from the beaches of Gallipoli, the Turks were within seven days of running out of ammunition. Nasmith had been awarded the Victoria Cross for his exploits.

Monty's prime responsibility was intelligence on German mines and torpedoes, but this didn't stop him getting his hands dirty. He was an experienced officer in rendering safe the deadly magnetic mines the Germans dropped on several British cities with the intent of spreading widespread terror, destruction and disruption. As they were dropped by parachute, they didn't often penetrate the ground. Consequently, when they exploded, they caused much more destruction above ground. Moreover, whilst their fuzes were set to detonate after seventeen seconds, they often failed to explode immediately. Unexploded bombs, UXBs, or mines had an extremely effective disruptive effect on the local population and war effort. Until they were made safe, factories had to cease working, trains had to stop running, streets had to be cleared and even anti-aircraft guns in the vicinity couldn't be fired for safety reasons. It was the Royal Navy's responsibility to render safe these parachute mines on land or in the sea. In the countryside the RMS teams had the option of reducing risk to themselves by exploding the mines, but should the mine have landed in a strategic location, such as next to an armaments factory or on a railway junction, the incident was declared as 'Category A'. For such incidents, the mines had to be defuzed even if it was at the expense of the lives of the RMS teams involved.

Monty's mine was a Category 'A' mine, too, given its proximity to the HQ of C-in-C Plymouth. A huge team of naval, air force and anti-aircraft gunners worked in tunnels beneath the HQ and most of the personnel had had to be evacuated until the mine could be defuzed. Like the mines he had previously rendered safe, this was a Type 'C' magnetic mine, one of the first type the Germans had dropped. It seemed to have no unusual features and Monty felt confident it was within his capabilities to tackle or else he would have called one of the already busy professional RMS officers.

Monty's first task was to prepare his escape route, but one of the RMS teams from *Vernon* had already thought of it for him. They had dug a large bunker in the admiral's front lawn a hundred yards from the mine. They would take shelter further away and had prepared another bunker, but theirs was lined with sandbags. If the mine's clock started ticking, Monty felt he would manage the 100-yard dash in the seventeen seconds it took before the mine would explode. Then again, if the clock had already started and stopped temporarily through damage on landing, who knew how much time he would have and his life would be in the lap of the gods.

A seaman handed Monty a bag of non-magnetic tools, a bucket of water and a bicycle pump before withdrawing to safety. Monty approached the dark-grey cylindrical object, about six feet of which was standing above the ground, the rest buried in the driveway leading up to Admiralty House. He noted with amusement that somebody had already removed the parachute and its cords. The green silk was in great demand with the female sex and even the parachute cords were valuable dressing gown cords. Fortunately for Monty, the fuze and detonator were accessible, about eighteen inches above the ground. There would be no need to dig around the mine or to turn it. Again, Monty smelt that distinctive smell peculiar to the mine. He thought it wasn't a smell he would forget for the rest of his life – however, short that might be!

He opened his bag and carefully laid out his tools in the order he would require them, meticulously like a surgeon before an operation. It was a technique Stephen had taught him on the grounds that in the dark he would know exactly where to lay his hands on the right tool. Then he took the bicycle pump and connected it to the gag, a bulbous, old-fashioned motor horn clipped to a straight length of brass tubing. The tube contained a simple tap and its end was threaded to allow the connection to the pump. After opening the tap, Monty operated the pump until the rubber bulb of the motor-horn was fully inflated and hard. Next, he immersed the bulb into the bucket of water and watched for bubbles. This simple device had been invented by Captain Currey and had saved the lives of dozens of RMS officers. Satisfied that there were no bubbles, Monty was confident that the rubber bulb would not leak. Relieved, he shut the tap and removed the gag from the bucket. Now it was time to work on the mine itself. Despite the cold January morning, Monty could feel beads of sweat beneath his dark cap. He signalled to the observers of the RMS party in the safety of their dugout that he was about to commence operations on the mine.

As part of his intelligence duties Monty had started as an observing officer. It had been his job to record every action of the RMS officer dealing with the mine. RMSOs learned by their dead or injured colleagues' mistakes. The Germans were wise to the actions of the *Vernon* scientists and RMS teams' heroism to learn the secrets of new mines and their variants and, accordingly, every so often they developed new booby traps.

Kneeling on the gravel beside the ton of explosive, Monty held his breath and, ever so gently, fitted the gag's adaptor over the top of the mine's fuze. Careful not to tremble for fear of shaking the clockwork fuze inside into action, he guided the threaded end to its mark and made one gentle rotation. The threads of the adaptor mated with those of the bomb-fuze. Monty breathed at last and then listened for any buzzing to suggest the clockwork timer had started. His world now only comprised the cylinder before him and he blanked out the sound of the seagulls, ships and boats in the harbour and passing traffic. Monty's brain was focused only on the fatal buzzing of clockwork. Mercifully, all was silent within this world. Monty made another turn, waited and listened. His knees were beginning to hurt from the gravel chips on which he was kneeling, but he couldn't afford to shift position just yet. He made a final rotation of the gag to render the seal as tight as possible. Gently, he now opened the tap of the gag to apply pressure to the diaphragm in the bomb-fuze. Suddenly, the silence was broken by the sound of a click.

The safety pin of the fuze had clicked. The bicycle pump and motor horn had fooled the mine into thinking it had dropped into water. Now it would not be set to self-destruct on land when the clockwork timer ran down. However, it was important to maintain that air pressure and, hence, why leaking rubber bulbs were fatal. This meant that Monty couldn't disengage the gag and yet it was now in his way for the next task. It didn't matter. The first hurdle was over and Monty was now able to change his position. After the Barrow incident with the German submarine, he now wore overalls over his uniform and the double layer of trousers cushioned his knees from the gravel, but he reached for a towel on which to kneel. As he moved position, he signalled to the observers that the gag was on and working.

Now it was time to wield the heavy brass pin spanner that had been especially designed for this task. It had two large prongs that fitted exactly into two holes in the keep ring of the fuze. The aluminium keep ring kept the fuze in position. Knowing that the clockwork fuze would no longer run, Monty felt more relaxed, but he kept a constant eye on the pressure of the horn's bulb. Despite having tackled several similar mines, his hands still shook. He blew on them to warm them a little. This was too delicate a task for gloves. The keep ring came free after a couple of turns of the heavy spanner. Wishing he had three hands, Monty now had to manoeuvre the ring up the brass tube of the gag with one hand and, with the other, attempt the more delicate and dangerous task of drawing the fuze from its housing in the mine.

And there it was – a silver-coloured cylinder a mere two inches long and two inches wide capable of blowing Monty to Kingdom Come. Protruding from the cylinder was the black gaine. Still encumbered by the gag, Monty unscrewed the gaine from the main fuze and shook the explosive free onto the piece of hessian he had prepared, but he wasn't out of the woods yet. The rest of the fuze still contained the detonator. Monty placed the empty gaine in his pocket and grasped a screwdriver. He unscrewed the smaller screw in the side of the fuze and once it was free, pocketed it. It acted as the anvil between which the tiny detonator would be struck by the spring-loaded striker held by the other screw. The detonator was only the size of a match head, but nonetheless, contained enough explosive to blow an RMSO's face or arm off. Trembling slightly, Monty turned the fuze over and then his face away before gently shaking the tiny detonator into his hand. With ultimate care, he placed the detonator in a box especially designed to keep it safe. Now he could unscrew the gag and relax for a moment. He signalled that all was well to the dugout. However, despite all his work, Monty had only rendered safe the self-destruct mechanism of the mine. The big job still lay ahead of him.

After a few stretches to release his cramped leg muscles, Monty began work on the main armament of the mine. First, he unscrewed the four screws of the four-and-a-half-inch circular plate covering the main detonator. There were reports that the Germans were now using soft metal screws to make it more difficult for RMS officers to remove the plates, but thankfully, Monty's version still had the original hard screws. Behind the plate sat a large bakelite bung holding the main detonator in place. Removing that bung was not a task Monty relished. Sometimes it was a pig to remove and he had, on occasions, had to seek assistance to get the bung to turn. He turned to the huge four-pronged bronze-handled bung spanner designed for the task. He guided the prongs into place and applied his strength to turning the bung. It didn't move, but made a squealing sound. Sweating despite the cold, he applied more leverage and heaved with all his strength. Just as he thought nothing was happening, he felt movement. He tried again and this time the bung very definitely turned. Soon he was able to work without the heavy spanner and able to turn the bung with his fingers. Having removed the bung, Monty could see the detonator. Now came an awkward moment. He could see two wires running from the detonator to the tail where was housed a nine-volt battery and the magnetic unit of the mine. Previously, Monty would have had no hesitation in cutting the wires. Once cut, there would be no danger of the deadly electrical circuit being in place to fire the detonator, but today he hesitated as he remembered something Stephen had warned him of. Stephen had been a Physics master and Monty couldn't quite remember what he had said, but he did recall that Stephen had warned him how simple it would be to booby trap the mine by setting up a separate circuit. By cutting one of the two wires in front of him, the loss of current might operate a solenoid that would initiate another electrical circuit to detonate the mine.

Monty hesitated. He searched inside the mine as far as he could, but he couldn't see beyond the bakelite detonator. There seemed to be no obvious signs of other wiring, but how could he know? In this game, the death of the first RMSO to find a booby trap served as a lesson for his successors to be wary. There was nothing to be done, though. He had to make a decision. If he had made a mistake, at least he would know nothing of it and leave behind no dependants. He snipped first one wire and then the other...

He was still alive and, for the first time, his world expanded to include the sounds around him. Monty wasn't ordinarily fond of seagulls, but today he was glad to hear their mewing. A destroyer in the Hamoaze whooped and it sounded to Monty as if the ship was saluting his success in remaining alive. However, the mine was still dangerous and Monty's task wasn't over yet.

After wiping away the sweat from his head, Monty rammed his cap back on his head and signalled to the dugout team that he was about to remove the main primer. It was housed beneath a second keep ring immediately below the keep ring of the self-destruct fuse. Monty took hold of yet another spanner and turned the keep ring. It turned quite easily, but Monty remembered not to turn it too quickly. The plug above the main primer was on a powerful spring. He recalled how the first time he had defuzed a magnetic mine, he had removed the keep ring too quickly and the plug had popped out like a jack-in-the box on the end of a spring two feet long. He had thought his moment had come and felt sick afterwards. Now he eased off the keep ring and withdrew it slowly to allow the primer plug to escape the mine. Then he put down the spanner and took up a long rod of phosphor bronze at the end of which were two spring-loaded claws. He guided the rod down into the mine's cavity and felt the claws spring to fasten onto the primer. Finally, he was able to withdraw the primer, something the size of a can of baked beans. Like the Royal Navy's mines, it was packed with picric-acid pellets. Seemingly innocuous, it was still enough explosive to bring down a house, more than enough to trigger the explosion of the one ton of TNT or Hexanite still housed deep within the mine. Monty retrieved the primer and removed the cap with a twist. He poured the contents onto his piece of hessian onto which he had piled the explosive from the self-destruct gaine. With great relief, he used his matches to set light to the two sets of explosives. They burnt slowly and harmlessly with thick, nasty-smelling smoke. Monty went for a short walk whilst the explosives burnt themselves out.

The mine was now safe enough to be taken away to have its main explosive charge removed by others, but Monty had one more job to do. He checked his watch. It was approaching lunchtime and the admiral had suggested that once he had dealt with the mine, they should have lunch together. He still had time for the rest of the job.

So far, Monty had removed four of what the RMSOs called the Crown Jewels, namely the bomb-fuze, the gaine, the detonator and the primer. He didn't need to remove the hydrostatic clock, but it was a matter of pride to Monty to show he, too, could do what the RMSOs achieved almost daily. He picked up yet another especially-made non-magnetic spanner, the biggest and heaviest of the lot. The hydrostatic clock was designed to trigger the mine's magnetic unit twenty minutes after the mine entered the water. On land it held no dangers, unless the Germans had started to add booby traps to them, Monty thought dolefully. There was no room for complacency. Now physically tired as well as emotionally spent, he manoeuvred the huge spanner to unscrew the third keep ring. It came off easily enough and Monty paused to examine the perimeter of the clock now visible, just in case there were signs of booby traps. However, he could see nothing beyond the rim of the clock. He felt around it and again, there seemed nothing untoward. He would just have to chance it. For some reason he shut his eyes as he pulled out the clock unit. It was connected to the rest of the mine by six wires and he quickly snipped them and… there it was. A very neatly engineered Swiss-manufactured piece of precision engineering weighing about six pounds. He had done it. However, as Monty placed the clock on the ground next to the other 'jewels' it struck him that, perhaps, the Admiralty might do something to persuade the neutral Swiss to stop selling these units to the Germans.

Monty signalled the all-clear to the RMS team waiting nearby and started to remove his overalls. The team approached and congratulated him warmly. They would now take over responsibility for moving the mine to a place of safety and either burning out the main explosive or even exploding the mine, probably out on Dartmoor. The petty officer in charge returned to Monty his watch, keys and small change. No RMS officer would be stupid enough to approach a magnetic mine with magnetic materials on his person. Conscious of his sweat-drenched shirt, Monty hoped the admiral's retinue staff might find him somewhere to shower before lunch.

Chapter 9

Although Admiral Dunbar-Nasmith seemed to be genial enough, Monty still sat in awe at his table. The admiral had thinning grey hair, swept back without a parting, and very keen eyes. His three rows of medal ribbons included, on the top row furthest inward, the tri-service crimson ribbon of the VC with its bronze cross. Monty was surprised to see that Nasmith didn't wear the original navy ribbon, but then he knew little about medals having received no other decorations than the oak leaf of someone who had been Mentioned-in-Despatches. Indeed, Nasmith later remarked on the absence of medal ribbons on Monty's chest.

'Sorry it's a cold collation Montcalm. Your chaps forced my chefs to evacuate the galley. Help yourself to more salmon, though.'

Coming from an aristocratic family and having been a successful London barrister, Monty was no stranger to fine food, but even he was impressed by the sumptuousness of the spread on the sideboard awaiting his selection. How had the admiral's Chief Cook and his staff presented such a meal at short notice? Monty was impressed, too, by the admiral taking time out to offer such generous hospitality. No fool, Nasmith seemed to read his mind.

'It was the least I could do, Montcalm, to offer you a few refreshments. Without you, my house and half my headquarters might not now be standing. You must have bloody nerves of steel to deal with those monsters. What do they contain? Half a ton… three-quarters of a ton of TNT?'

'A ton, sir,' Monty replied nonplussed. He found it hard to credit that a man with the VC for entering the harbour of Constantinople and conducting four nerve-wracking transits of the Dardanelles Strait should think that he, Monty, had nerves of steel.

'Well, good on you, Montcalm. You wouldn't catch me doing it for all the tea in China. One thing does surprise me, though.'

Monty halted on his way back to the table. 'Really, sir? And what is that?'

'I note the oak leaf, but where are your medal ribbons? I thought you chaps all had chests full of GCs and GMs. Are you incorrectly dressed, Montcalm?'

Monty blushed and took his seat at the table before replying. 'Not at all, sir. I'm an intelligence officer and not a regular mine disposal officer. It's they who take all the risks, sir, and they deserve all the medals going.'

'Bunkum! I've just witnessed you taking apart one of those beasts. And by the look of it, it wasn't your first, I bet.'

'True, sir. I've taken my share of the load when necessary, but I must stress, sir - I only do it occasionally when the proper RMS teams are pushed.'

'Hmm.' Nasmith laid down his knife and fork for a moment. 'I don't see the difference myself. I think I'll have a word with your senior officer. Who is that by the way?'

'Captain Maitland-Dougall, sir, but please don't worry on my behalf.'

'Maitland-Dougall, you say. An unusual name, but one that seems familiar to me.' The admiral turned to his flag lieutenant. 'Flags, you've a younger memory than mine. Why is that name familiar to me?'

The flag lieutenant was a bright young thing and immediately recalled the name. 'Lieutenant Commander A. S. C. Maitland-Dougall, sir. CO of *Vanquish*. She was reported missing, presumed sunk a fortnight or so ago. We're still waiting for reports of survivors.'

'Well done, Flags. Sharp as ever. You'll have my job by the end of the war at this rate. I can only assume there's a connection. Find out will you, Flags?'

'Right away, sir.' The flag lieutenant immediately stood, leaving half his plate uneaten.

Monty went cold. He knew there was a connection, but kept it to himself. He knew that Maitland-Dougall had a son in the Navy, although not where he was serving. The CO of the destroyer had to be the same man. No wonder his director had been behaving oddly recently. He must be beside himself with worry, Monty realised.

*****

69

The following day, Monty was requested by Captain Minesweepers to deal with a parachute mine that had been observed to fall in the Hamoaze off Number One Wharf. Its presence was severely hampering movements up the river and blocking access to and from Number Two Basin. When Monty turned up, he couldn't see the mine as it was submerged, but he was informed that the position of it had been fixed with reasonable accuracy. Monty decided the best plan was to drag for it and was provided with two sailors, a wire rope, a noose and a marker buoy.

The two sailors rowed out to the mine in a dinghy, towing the wire in a loop. It was a technique Monty had seen salmon fishermen using in the Tweed at Berwick-upon-Tweed, although in their case they had been towing a net and their quest was less deadly. One end of the wire was fixed to the jetty and once the sailors had formed a loop with it around the position of the mine, they returned with the free end of the wire and stepped onto the jetty. They dragged the loop slowly towards the jetty and almost immediately, fouled something they assumed must be the mine. Their next step was to form a sort of lasso using a shackle and the marker buoy. It was a simple enough evolution that Monty had witnessed several times. As the free end of the wire was drawn in, the noose would tighten on the mine and the marker buoy would be floating directly above the mine.

Before long, the mine was snagged and its position marked by the buoy. It was now Monty's turn to go out in the dinghy. His plan was to lower an amatol charge about five feet off the mine and fire it. The charge was intended to be powerful enough to wreck the mine's firing mechanism but not enough to fire the mine and, hence, the five-foot gap. Monty prepared his charge and remotely-controlled electrical wiring mechanism, but just as he was entering the boat, he heard a volley of abuse from the jetty above. The source was a lieutenant with a strong Australian accent.

'What the fuck do ye think you're doing, cobber?' the lieutenant asked, showing no respect for Monty's superior rank, but Monty took no offence. He knew the officer concerned, having worked with him in the London Blitz.

'What's your problem, Fanny?' he retorted to Lieutenant Fanshawe Royal Australian Naval Volunteer Reserve.

'I don't want to die yet. That's my fucking problem. And nor do my boys. What the hell are you playing at… messing about with a magnetic mine whilst there are poor sods up here trying to dig up unexploded bombs?'

Monty alighted the boat and climbed the steps up to the jetty above. He shook hands with Fanshawe. 'Where's your bomb, Fanny?'

'About three hundred yards away. In amongst the railway tracks. Close enough for the shock wave of your mine to set it off. Want to have a look at it, Monty?'

'Fair enough, Fanny. There's nothing more I can do it seems, until you diggers have finished your own messing about.' Monty noted inwardly how strange it was that RMSOs always seemed to want to show off their enemies to their peers. He turned to his two sailors and explained the situation before following Fanshawe towards a line of railway trucks on the dockside. The air was still acrid with the smell of the fires from the incendiary bombs of the previous night's raid and Monty had to step around several puddles from the firehoses still snaked all over the jetties. About a hundred yards away he could see a working party comprising five junior rates and a petty officer.

Fanshawe waved in a friendly manner and his petty officer returned the wave… just as the earth shook and Monty saw a plume of flame, smoke and debris rise from the working party's vicinity. Amongst the debris several bodies rose into the air in a cartwheeling motion. One landed at Monty's feet, but it was clear to Monty that the man was already dead. He and Fanshawe sprinted to the crater, but there was nothing they could do. The lives of six men had suddenly been snuffed out. It crossed Monty's mind that if the bomb had exploded just a few seconds later, he and Fanshawe might have been amongst the dead, too, but there was little point dwelling on it. It was all part of the RMSO's rich tapestry of life.

There was nothing more he could do, but he still had his own mine to tackle. Being underwater it would not have been affected by the shock wave of the bomb's explosion. At the sight of the two ashen faces of his sailors he felt cold-hearted. They were clearly shocked and frightened, but Monty had to carry on regardless. He ordered them to row him out to the mine notwithstanding their obvious fear. Quickly, he lowered his charge into the water and paid out his electrical firing cable as the boat was rowed back to the jetty. He, Fanshawe and the two sailors took cover and Monty depressed the plunger of his firing box. Instantaneously, the water of the river rose in a great plume from the charge's explosion, but the mine remained inactive.

Without any evidence Monty couldn't be certain that he had destroyed the mine's firing mechanism, but he felt confident he had succeeded. Accordingly, he informed Captain Minesweepers that the basin could be re-opened for traffic. The captain had heard of the bomb's explosion and was grateful that Monty at least was still alive. He then informed Monty of a second mine in the middle of the ten-acre Number Four Basin very nearby.

'I'm very interested to see how you chaps work, Montcalm,' the captain said. 'Any objection to my watching from afar?'

Monty didn't like the idea, but a four-ringer outranked him and so he agreed. He followed the exact same procedure, but with two different sailors. One mine had proved enough for them. Again, the procedure seemed to go smoothly and Monty laid his charge. 'Fancy a go, sir?' He offered Captain Minesweepers the opportunity to depress the plunger of the firing box.

'Very satisfying,' the captain replied after the charge had exploded. 'Is that it?'

'It is, sir,' Monty replied as he began to recover his gear for the next task. 'The mine's now safe, sir, and you can re-open the basin.'

Barely had Monty uttered his report than he and the captain were flattened by a huge explosion. A gigantic column of water rose from the centre of the basin and the whole working party was covered by mud raining down on their heads for several seconds. Physically battered and his ego bruised, Monty eventually rose to his feet. He, Captain Minesweepers and the two sailors were covered in mud.

'I'm sorry, sir,' Monty eventually muttered. He felt too sick to speak.

'Don't worry, Montcalm. It's not your fault. You couldn't help it, lad.'

'Maybe not, sir,' Monty replied in a crestfallen manner, 'But I wonder whether we should shut Number Two Basin again. I can't understand what went wrong, sir.'

'I agree, Montcalm. But let's go back to the office and discuss it. We need to clean up and I think we deserve a wee dram.'

As Monty and the captain walked to the latter's office, Monty's mind was churning over the problem. He had seen the procedure working several times, but something had changed. The mine couldn't have been an acoustic version or else it would have detonated immediately the wire had snagged it. The wire had been demagnetised and could not have changed the magnetic field surrounding the mine. He had to warn all RMSOs that the procedure was now unsafe and work out why. He could only think that Jerry had become yet more cunning and come up with a new device to kill RMSOs.

Chapter 10
February 1942

A week after Monty's return to London, he received a note inviting him to a meeting with the Naval Assistant to the Director of Naval Intelligence. The note suggested he and Commander Ian Fleming meet in Fleming's club, Boodle's. The invitation intrigued Monty. He knew Fleming as they had been at Eton together, but their paths had only crossed in Monty's final year there and, even though they had met from time to time at the Admiralty, he didn't know him well. Monty recalled that Fleming had excelled at athletics in his time at Eton and had even won the *Victor Ludorum* trophy, but seemed to think that Fleming had left under a cloud as he didn't return for his final summer term. Even then, Fleming had had a reputation for extravagance and being flashy. Coming from an immensely wealthy family, his grandfather having founded the merchant bank, Robert Fleming, Fleming had caused a stir when he had brought a car to the college. He recalled that Fleming had been regarded with disdain by some of the older boys, but he recognised that such feelings may have been actuated by the Eton rivalry between the gentry and *new* money.

Initially, Monty had wondered why they were to meet in Boodle's and not the Admiralty. After all, the offices of DNI, Rear Admiral Godfrey, weren't far from those of DTMI. Then again, knowing Fleming's reputation for style and doing things with *panache*, it was probably Fleming's way of showing off. However, there was only one way to find out and he penned a note back agreeing to meet the following week.

Monty had never visited Boodle's before, but found it easily enough on St. James's Street opposite its younger offshoot, Brooks's. As a former barrister, Monty had tended to favour the society of the Inns of Court over private clubs, although he was, nonetheless, a member of the Garrick. He knew little of Boodle's other than that it had once been the haunt of Beau Brummell. However, it didn't surprise him that it was discreet and on giving his name to the porter, he was swiftly led to a comfortable bar where Fleming was already settled in a leather wingback chair smoking and reading the newspaper. Fleming immediately rose to greet his guest and extended his right hand. Monty noticed that Fleming used a cigarette holder – an affectation, he thought. However, his greeting was warm enough.

'What are you drinking, Monty? May I call you 'Monty'?' Fleming added quickly.

'Of course, sir. Everybody does. I'll have a pink gin, please.'

A waiter had glided over silently and Fleming nodded to him saying, 'My usual, please.'

'Certainly, sir. Shaken and not stirred. I remember, sir.' The waiter glided away just as silently. Monty wondered what Fleming's usual was.

'I'm glad you were able to come, Monty... and call me Ian. You can drop the 'sir'.'

'Thank you for inviting me, s... Ian.' Monty relaxed in his armchair and examined his surroundings. Firstly, he noted that Fleming had chosen a discreet corner of the bar area. The majority of the other chairs seemed to be occupied by senior army officers, but there was a sprinkling of older civilian members, many of whom were dozing comfortably with their newspapers, no doubt after a good lunch.

The drinks arrived quickly and Monty's curiosity was satisfied. Fleming had ordered what looked to be a martini.

'Were we at Eton together, Monty? I know you were there, but I don't recall seeing you.' Fleming sipped his martini and smiled at the waiter. 'Just right. Thank you.' The waiter retired on his oiled wheels to leave the two naval officers in privacy.

'I was a few years behind you. You left soon after I started.'

'Did you enjoy your time there, Monty? Can't say I did.' Fleming didn't wait for an answer. 'I loved the sport and editing the school magazine, but I was never cut out for the classroom. I preferred my time in Europe.'

Monty recalled that Fleming had been a correspondent for Reuters as well as something in the City before the war.

'I gather you had a successful practice as a barrister before the war, Monty. Did you enjoy the Law?'

'I did, thanks, Ian.' Monty didn't elaborate. He was keen to discover the purpose of the *rendezvous*.

'I've been looking up your record, Monty. You came to my attention after that *U-570* business. You did a good job there. And Admiral Dunbar-Nasmith speaks highly of your work in Plymouth last month. I gather you've been put up for a gong.'

'Really? I hadn't heard.' The news was, indeed, a surprise to Monty, but he didn't dwell on it.

'Oh, I'm sorry for my indiscretion, but then again, Captain Maitland-Dougall probably hasn't had the chance to tell you himself. I gather he's still in Scotland sorting out his son's affairs.'

'Indeed. He's naturally distraught at losing his boy. This war is costing too many lives.'

'I agree with you there. That's why I think we need to move things along a bit.' Fleming finished his martini and gestured for another to be brought over. 'Can I offer you a top up, Monty?'

'No thanks, Ian. I have to get back to the office. Captain Maitland-Dougall's due back on Thursday and I have to prepare some papers for him before my own leave this weekend. You were speaking of *"moving the war along a bit"*.'

'Of more anon. But I note you've been at DTMI for nearly two and a half years. Are you looking for a change?'

It wasn't something Monty had considered for some time. Way back in 1939, he had hoped for something more on the frontline, but he had since seen plenty of action, albeit in the presence of the enemy's machines rather than the enemy himself. Monty considered the question carefully before replying and slowly sipped his gin.

'I'm not actively seeking a change, but then again, I could consider it, Ian… if I could be making a direct contribution to the war effort. I work with a fantastic bunch of dedicated and extremely courageous men and I'm proud to be Captain Maitland-Dougall's Number Two. Do you have something in mind, then?'

'I do and I'm looking for people like you. Do you know much about the Commandos?'

'Of course, but I hardly think I'm the type to join them. If nothing else, apart from my lack of military training, I'm nearly twenty-nine.'

'You might be wrong there, Monty. The Commandos have had mixed success up to now, but a new training centre has been set up in Scotland to make them more professional in future. However, I've something a little different in mind. I'm examining the feasibility of forming our own special intelligence Commando unit. The German *Abwehr* have just such a unit. I'm working up a proposal for this Commando unit to accompany forward units when attacking ports or naval installations. Its role would be to pinch documents and cyphers before the enemy can destroy them. We might even include equipment... or even key personnel. The idea is that the unit works directly under the auspices of the NID.'

'Intriguing, Ian,' was all Monty could say to start. There seemed to be nothing *flash* about Fleming these days. He knew he was highly regarded in the naval intelligence circles and widely regarded as Admiral Godfrey's *Mister Fixer*. Now Monty could see why. He recovered his wits to ask, 'But have you in mind that I should join this outfit?'

'I have, Monty. I'm looking at the... let's call it the Intelligence Assault Unit for now. I'm thinking it should comprise two sections. A military unit comprising experienced Royal Marines to do the fighting and a technical unit. The technical unit would comprise specialists appropriate to the target. For example, signals intelligence, radar or in your case, Monty... torpedoes and mines. Your experience as an intelligence officer along with your hands-on experience of dealing with mines and torpedoes makes you the ideal candidate for the job. It would get you away from a desk, too.'

Monty was overwhelmed by the idea. It was certainly imaginative and might well work. Thinking on his own war experience, he could see why Fleming had thought of him. Moreover, the idea of taking a more direct role in the war appealed to him. He had been feeling a little unappreciated of late, although now he knew of Maitland-Dougall's loss, the pill was easier to swallow.

'When might this unit be formed and where would it be based?'

'If I have my way, within two months. There are several details that need to be mapped out first. As to a base, it would need to be close to London in order to be under NID's control and access training by SIS and SOE. As I said, there's still much to map out. I'm just scouting for talent at present. Do you by any chance speak German?'

'I've picked up a bit through attending interrogations of German prisoners... and of course, I've had to read a fair few intelligence

77

documents in German, but I couldn't claim to speak the language. Would that be a problem, Ian?'

'Well, you know what Mark Twain had to say about German, Monty? *"Never knew before what eternity was made for. It is to give some of us a chance to learn German."* Do you think you could work on your German?'

'I could certainly give it a bash, Ian. It would come in handy for my work at DTMI, anyway.'

'Good. Then can I take it that you be interested, Monty?'

Monty drained his glass whilst he thought about the proposal. It sounded exciting and yes, he did fancy a break from his DTMI duties. It wouldn't do any good to become stale or complacent. He made his decision and laid his glass on the table.

'Yes, Ian. I'm most definitely interested.'

*****

Stephen had heard people say that bad luck comes in a run of three. In that case, he thought, I've had my run this year. Firstly, there had been Dad's death and then his new appointment to South Africa. Now he had received another bombshell. He looked once again at the letter before him, written in a bold, round hand. When he had first opened the letter, he had been ecstatic as it was from Carol. She had started by telling him how proud she had been to attend his investiture at Buckingham Palace and how much she had enjoyed meeting Stephen's sister, Lucy. As he had read her warm words, he had longed to hold and squeeze her almost to death, such was his love for her. The she had dropped the bombshell.

Carol had previously told him that she had written to her parents in Washington to tell them all about their relationship. Now, she had finally received a reply and it was bad news. Mrs Templeton had written to say how both parents strongly disapproved of the relationship and wished to see it end immediately. Carol's mother had explained that this would be the wisest course in the long run as there must be no question of Carol marrying a gentile. According to Carol, her mother had even gone on to explain that were she to disobey her parents, then the marriage would be seen as adulterous and any children she and Stephen might have would be considered bastards. The only alternative to this would be for Stephen to renounce his Quaker faith and to convert to Judaism. This was not something Carol felt able to ask of Stephen and, accordingly, she felt she had no choice but to comply with her parents' wishes and to end their relationship.

Stephen's tears flowed onto the letter as he read this through again. It was as if somebody had cut out his heart and split it into several pieces. He had not resolved to ask Carol to marry him, but he was coming around to the idea. He even wondered about renouncing his Quaker faith. It was less important to him than it had been to his father and now that his father had passed it away, it might be possible, but Carol had expressly forbidden him to do so. Their relationship was definitely at an impasse and he could understand why Carol was so unwilling to disobey her parents. It all seemed so silly in his mind. Surely there was only one God even though people chose to worship Him in different ways. What mattered was that he and Carol were very much in love and surely, God would smile on such a relationship. Was not Man destined to be happy and marriage was a necessary precursor to God's will that Man should procreate. Then again, God had ordained that he be sent to South Africa. Could it be a sign that he and Carol were not destined to be together.

Feeling desperately unhappy, Stephen skipped lunch and went for a long walk after informing the duty officer of his intentions. He couldn't face company just now.

Chapter 11
March 1942

Extract from a minute in the archives of the Naval Intelligence Division (NID):

"MOST SECRET

"PROPOSAL FOR NAVAL INTELLIGENCE COMMANDO UNIT

"One of the most outstanding innovations in German Intelligence is the creation by the German NID of special intelligence 'Commandos'. These 'Commandos' accompany the forward troops when a port or naval installation is being attacked and, if the attack is successful, their duty is to capture documents, cyphers etc. before these can be destroyed by the defenders…

"I submit that we would do well to consider organising such a 'Commando' within the NID, the unit to be modelled on the same lines as its German counterpart and placed under the command of the Chief of Combined Operations, perhaps a month before a specific objective is attacked.

"Signed Fleming NID (17)"

*****

All too soon, Stephen's embarkation leave was over and it was time to bid his mother and Lucy an emotional goodbye. Both women were in tears and Jane seemed unwilling to let him go as he tried to get into the taxi. A number of the villagers formed a crowd to wish him farewell, too. Stephen was touched by their effort, but thought the fuss unnecessary. Whilst he had never been overseas abroad, he knew that South Africa wasn't the end of the world and he felt confident he would be home again within two years. It was going to be a far less dangerous appointment than he had faced in Britain, too. Even so, he felt guilty about leaving so soon after his father's death, but perhaps after his break-up with Carol it was for the best. The thought brought about a stabbing sensation in his heart. He couldn't stop loving Carol, despite her wishes.

Lucy released Stephen from his mother's embrace and whispered to him, 'Don't worry about Mum, Stephen. I'll take care of her, but you'd better make sure you write... often!'

Stephen had already sent his trunk on to Liverpool by train and so the driver had only to take his small suitcase from him. He quickly kissed Lucy and Jane and stepped into the rear of the taxi for the journey to the station, fighting hard to keep back the tears he wanted to shed.

Some hours later, he was back in Liverpool, a city so familiar to him. It was here that he had taught Physics and General Science in a girls' school until September 1940 when the *Luftwaffe* had destroyed the school and rendered him unemployed. He had had no regrets in leaving teaching for the hazardous duties of rendering mines safe and bomb disposal. Mines and bombs didn't tease one mercilessly for one's stutter.

He found his way through the docks and the customs shed before boarding a former Canadian Pacific liner, the *RMS Empress of Japan*. Prior to the war, she had plied the Pacific from her home port in Vancouver to Hong Kong via Japan and China. She had been the fastest liner on the Pacific and able to complete the one-way trip in just nine days. Her three promenade decks were already thronged with Stephen's fellow passengers in a mixture of dark-blue, light-blue and khaki uniforms. Many were waving to the crowds on the quayside and Stephen momentarily regretted not letting his mother and Lucy accompany him to Liverpool, but he had wanted to spare them an unnecessary train journey. The ship's rigging was festooned with flags and bunting and, with the crowds on the liner's decks and the quayside, the whole atmosphere was one of a carnival. Stephen showed his identity card and shipping index card to an official on the other side of the customs shed and received in return a berth and meal ticket.

As he mounted the steep gangway, he prayed that his trunk had arrived safely and was safely stowed in his cabin. The advice he had been given at HMS *King Alfred* in 1940, '*never get separated from your kit, sir,'* still haunted him. However, he need not have worried. A ship's steward guided him to his cabin and there was his trunk awaiting him. He discovered, too, that he was sharing a cabin with an army captain of the Royal Army Service Corps, but the officer was elsewhere. He was pleased to note that his cabin was on one of the upper promenade decks and that it was on the outside of the ship, with a scuttle to offer a view. To Stephen's surprise, the steward apologised for this.

'I'm afraid, sir, you're berthed on the starboard side, that is the right-hand side of the ship as she steams.'

'But w-what's wrong with that?' he asked.

'You might find it a little uncomfortable as we steam further south. The sun shines from the south, sir, that is the starboard side. In my former days in the P&O on the India run, we used to recommend *Port Outward and Starboard Home*, sir... er, hence the term *POSH* for those passengers willing to pay the premium fare for such a facility, sir. But don't worry, sir. This is a fast ship and I'll do my utmost to look after you.'

'Oh,' said Stephen a little non-plussed. He didn't really care about such niceties. He was just excited to be going to Africa.

'Now, most important of all, sir. We'll be leaving for Gourock tonight to join the other ships in our convoy and pick up our Royal Navy escorts for the run south. I don't anticipate any trouble from Jerry, but you need to have your lifejacket handy at all times... just in case, like. And here on the back of the door is a diagram showing your muster station for when we go to lifeboat stations. You won't forget it, sir, will you? We'll be practising every day. You'll see, too, sir, details of your allotted saloon. That's where you'll find the bar and take your meals. I'm afraid we can't offer the service we's used to, sir, but we try our best. Should you have no guests on the quayside, sir, you might wish to take tea in the saloon now, sir. It's on for another half-hour. Just one other thing, sir.' The steward gestured to the scuttle. 'You being a navy man, I'm sure you'll understand, sir. The Chief Officer will publish the time of sunset every day and you gentlemen will be expected to apply the cover before then. The Old Man's very keen on darkening ship. Don't want to attract lurking *U*-boats, do we, sir?'

Stephen marvelled at the luxury of his voyage. It felt as if he was travelling first-class. He didn't care a hoot that he wasn't *posh*. But he thought about the steward's final words. He hadn't considered until then that the troop ship might be a valuable target.

*****

The *Empress of Japan* sailed at 6.15 that evening. Stephen went on deck to watch the operation. Two tugs pulled the liner off the quay and another stood by. Gently, they towed the ship through the narrow dock entrance and into the Mersey estuary. In the anchorage Stephen spied another troop ship flying proudly the colours of the Free French. He wondered where she was bound. The sun had already set, but it was still quite light out to the west where the remnants of the sun had lit up the horizon in a blaze of red and orange. As the ship gathered speed, Stephen regretted not wearing his greatcoat. Although the weather was dry, there was a stiff and chilly wind being generated by the ship's forward speed. However, he waited on deck until it was fully dark and returned to his cabin in the hope of meeting his cabinmate prior to dinner.

Sure enough, a short, slightly rotund man in his late thirties, ginger-haired and with a clipped moustache to match, was standing in the cabin wearing only a towel around his waist. He had just returned from the showers. He and Stephen introduced themselves and whilst Captain Arnold Reynolds dressed, they exchanged notes on their backgrounds. Stephen learned that Reynolds was on his way to Bombay. He informed Stephen that the convoy would be calling at Freetown in four weeks' time before its arrival nearly two weeks later in Simon's Town where Stephen would disembark. It would be a voyage of nearly 8,000 miles. This turned out to be unfortunate.

Stephen's cabin mate had some unsavoury habits. He liked to tell dirty jokes and used foul language. Moreover, he openly and frequently broke wind. Fortunately, the weather was benign enough initially to enable Stephen to air the cabin by opening the scuttle during the day, but it had to be shut firmly after sunset. Then there was the trouble of his snoring. Stephen tried cotton wool in his ears, but there was no diminution of the noise. This was Reynolds' greatest sin in Stephen's eyes as he liked his sleep.

The following morning after a disturbed sleep, Stephen woke to find the ship at anchor in the Firth of Clyde. He went on deck for some precious fresh air and to stretch his legs. He was amazed to see so many ships crammed into the busy waterway. Surely, this was a perfect target for the German bombers, he thought. They could hardly miss. He had his first view of one of the new aircraft carriers as well as a submarine and several flying boats criss-crossing the airspace above. He didn't have the knowledge to tell whether they were Catalinas or Sunderlands. Over breakfast he asked one of the ship's officers how long they would remain off Glasgow and learned that the ship would be spending all day replenishing its water stocks, but all being well and subject to the escorts and the remainder of the convoy having arrived, they would sail for Freetown the following day.

As had been hoped, at 11.00 the following day, the *Empress of Japan* slipped the anchorage and sailed down the river for the open sea. Looking at Ailsa Craig passing by, it suddenly struck Stephen that this would probably be his last view of Britain for two years. His excitement quickened when he was informed that he should put his watch back half an hour at midnight. It really felt as if he was bound overseas.

However, the initial excitement of overseas travel paled within a week. Without any work to do, Stephen soon became bored. In between meals, walks around the promenade decks and lifeboat drills, he tried to take an afternoon nap to catch up with his lost sleep, but it wasn't always possible and he started to become extremely irritable.

Jerry wasn't helping either. As the convoy proceeded out into the Atlantic, it was detected by *Luftwaffe* reconnaissance aircraft south of Ireland. The first days of the voyage started with the sighting of a *Focke-Wulf* Condor long-range reconnaissance aircraft circling the skies outside the range of the convoy escorts' anti-aircraft guns. A few hours later, the convoy would come under attack by enemy *Heinkel* 111 bombers based in France. Fortunately, the *Empress of Japan* herself was never attacked, but the troops and passengers were required to clear their cabins and muster on the upper decks during an air attack. Stephen witnessed two less fortunate ships of the convoy being hit by the enemy bombs, but he hadn't heard that either ship had been lost.

Nevertheless, as the convoy made progress south, life onboard improved tolerably. Firstly, as the convoy sailed off the Iberian coast, it was out of range of even the longest-range enemy aircraft. Furthermore, with the rising temperatures, Stephen was able to spend the most insufferable evenings tucked up in a chair on deck to sleep. Although the ship was a fast liner and capable of over twenty knots, she was restricted to the speed of the slowest member of the convoy and this added to the leisurely feel of the voyage. The sea was blue and there was a pleasant zephyr as Stephen toured the upper decks of the ship. To his delight, he discovered in the ship's library a collection of various Trollope works he hadn't previously read. Moreover, one of the ship's officers had spotted his talent for drawing cartoons of the crew, passengers and shipboard life, and invited him to join the ship's newspaper editorial team. Besides his routine of reading his beloved Trollope and drawing for the newspaper, he enjoyed listening to gramophone music in the saloon or walking around the ship.

The sea chuckled as the stem broke through it, leaving a brilliant-white, foaming wake astern. Sometimes, to Stephen's wonderment, the bows disturbed flying fish that skimmed across the waves before falling back into the water. For many days they were joined by a school of porpoises swimming alongside the ship and taking turns to leap across the bows. Stephen began to think it might be pleasant never to reach the coast of Africa.

That was until the *U*-boats struck. Three weeks after sailing, south of the Canary Islands, the convoy was attacked at night by a German wolf pack.

Chapter 12

There was no longer any doubt. The British had adapted their electro-magnetic sweeps in response to the changes Ernst had ordered to the sensitivity of the German magnetic mines. *Leutnant* Klein had used his charts and tabulations to convince Ernst of the fact. Ernst lit another cigarette. He offered one to Klein, but Klein refused it. Ernst had forgotten that as an actuary Klein had calculated the odds of a shorter lifespan through smoking and from the consumption of alcohol and red meat for that matter. Not that the latter was proving a great problem at present. The British economic blockade was proving all too effective and even the gaunt Ernst had had to tighten his belt. It was all reminiscent of the 1914 to 1918 War. Ernst remembered grimly the death from starvation of his family and stubbed out his cigarette bitterly. The war was already eighteen months old and he had expected his mine warfare strategy to bring Britain to its knees within three months.

'Thank you, Franz. You have made your case well and, alas, confirmed my suspicions.' Klein beamed at the praise and cleaned his spectacles vigorously.

'I think it is time to step up our campaign. Our scientists have already developed the means to target the British who recover our mines, but now we must turn our attention...'

'Forgive me, *Herr Oberstleutnant*, what do you mean by "*target*"?'

'I mean that we are having to become more inventive in protecting the secrets of our mines. Booby traps no less, Franz. We're wiring them or cross wiring them direct to the main charge and no longer small explosive charges. The more the British interfere with our mines, the more of their scientists or mine disposal teams will die. This is total war, Franz!' Ernst had noted how Klein had blanched at his methods. The man was weak and had no place in Germany's war machine. He didn't have the stomach for it.

'As I was saying, Franz...' Klein made no sign to interrupt. 'We must now increase our efforts against the British minesweeping forces. The clicker mine is working well, but the British must have worked out that after six sweeps the channels must be clear. Our naval colleagues have come up with something that might just tip the balance in our favour again.'

'Are you at liberty to divulge the details, sir?'

'I see no reason why not. We are comrades in arms, after all. The *Kriegsmarine* have come up with a plan to develop moored mines once more and to launch them from their *E*-boats.'

'But would not the sweeps simply cut the mooring wires and allow the mines to float to the surface once more, sir?'

'We have thought of that, Franz.' Ernst smiled at Klein in the way one indulges a simple child. 'Initially, the mines will sit on the seabed, but will be fitted with a buoyancy chamber and mooring gear to enable them to float nearer the surface. In that way, they can be laid in deeper water, but here lies the beauty of the idea, Franz. We add a programmable delay mechanism. We can keep the mines on the seabed for days or even weeks before they are released. Imagine, Franz. The British sweep the channels and find nothing after a week. Even if they suspect a mine has been laid, they will find nothing and assume it is defective and have no choice but to declare the channel clear. Days or weeks later... boom! These new mines will bring the minesweeping forces to their knees.'

'I congratulate you, *Herr Oberstleutnant*. It is, indeed, an ingenious idea.' Ernst took great pleasure from the clear look of admiration in his assistant.

*****

Stephen was suddenly woken by the sound of a loud explosion. It was a full moon and the convoy was arranged in four columns. The *Empress of Japan* was in the second from the right column and Stephen was dozing in his steamer chair facing to starboard. He heard one of the ship's sailors exclaim, 'What's that, Bosun?'

'A ship's struck a mine,' the Bosun replied.

Stephen's professional interest was piqued and he dashed to the guardrail to see the scene for himself. The horizon was lit up by a column of flame from one of the convoy. The ship was stopped in the water. Seconds later, another great column of flame and smoke erupted even before Stephen heard the sound of an explosion. He knew that with the ship stopped in the water it couldn't have struck a mine and sure enough he heard a cry from one of the lookouts on a deck above, 'Torpedo, torpedo, torpedo!' Seconds later the alarm bells rang to call everyone to Lifeboat Stations.

Stephen didn't see the track of the torpedo, but it missed his ship and instead struck another to port in the third column. Even though he couldn't see the torpedo strike, he heard the explosion and felt the ship rock violently. He quickly made his way to his lifeboat station and thanked Providence that he had remembered to bring his lifejacket on deck with him. As he reached his boat station, he heard an excited cry from the other passengers and many were pointing at something in the distance. Having poor eyesight, Stephen couldn't see the focus of his fellow passengers' interest so he asked the man next to him.

'It's a *U*-boat on the surface, mate, but he's going to cop it in a minute. Look at that.'

Stephen still couldn't see the U-boat, but he did see the creamy bow wave of a destroyer heading in that direction at full speed. It was fast overtaking the liner to starboard and Stephen thought it a thrilling sight. Despite it being almost midnight, the visibility was perfect and the bioluminescence of the ship's wake lingered on the surface. Then, at a range of about a mile, he saw spouts of water ascending from the sea and only then did he spy the surfaced *U*-boat. She had spotted the fast-approaching destroyer and was diving in emergency, but not before she fired one last salvo. The tracks of the two torpedoes were clearly visible even from a mile and were aimed directly at the destroyer's bows.

The passengers on the boat deck were cheering loudly. It was if they were at a racecourse urging on their chosen horse, in this case the destroyer. Would the *U*-boat dive in time, everyone wondered. Would it matter, those in the know were asking. The consensus was that the destroyer would be able to lay down a good pattern of depth charges and that the *U*-boat's captain had left his dive too late. Then the mood suddenly changed. The destroyer had evaded the two torpedoes, but one of them was fast-approaching their own ship. The Master of the liner had clearly recognised the danger, too, as the ship lurched to starboard in a violent turn and the hull rattled with the vibration of increased revolutions from the engine room. All of a sudden, the hunted had just become the hunter. The left-hand torpedo narrowly missed the stern of the liner, but the other hit the ship's starboard side with a thud. Everyone on deck braced themselves for the inevitable, possibly fatal, explosion, but nothing happened.

The passengers' attention immediately switched to the cargo ship in the outer column looming down on them. In her bid to avoid the torpedoes, the *Empress of Japan* had strayed into the path of the outer column. Again, the ship heeled over in a violent turn, this time to port and Stephen was not alone in wondering if the Master had reacted in time. He could see the approaching freighter swinging to starboard to avoid the collision, but the *Empress* was surely turning too slowly to avoid being hit. Some of those around him were fixed on the destroyer's depth charge attack on the *U*-boat, but he only had eyes for the hulk threatening to cleave their stern with its bows. Ever so slowly, the angle between the liner's stern and the bows of the freighter started to open, enough to give Stephen hope, and a minute later the huge cargo ship passed within feet of the *Empress*.

*****

The *Empress of Japan* remained at Lifeboat Stations for a further two hours, but the action had ended soon after the liner had been struck by the torpedo, except for the hunt for the attacking *U*-boats. A spontaneous cheer passed around the upper decks as word reached the passengers and crew alike that their attacker had been destroyed by the escort. Gradually, the crowds on deck dispersed to return to their sleeping quarters or, in the crew's case, their on-watch stations, but those at Stephen's allotted boat station were asked to remain on deck for some reason. Very soon, the Chief Officer approached.

'Excuse me, gentlemen,' he called. 'I'm looking for a Lieutenant Cunningham. Could you identify yourself, please.'

Stephen stepped forward and held up his hand. 'That's m-me. C-can I help?'

'Good evening, Lieutenant,' the Chief Officer replied. 'I'm sorry to keep you from your pit, but the Captain would like a word with you. The rest of you can carry on.'

Mystified by the late-night summons, Stephen followed Chief Officer Maxwell to the bridge. There, he found a group of the ship's officers huddled around the chart table.

'Lieutenant Cunningham, sir,' Maxwell presented Stephen to Captain Douglas, an avuncular-looking, grey-haired man in his early sixties and sporting WW1 medal ribbons on his chest. Douglas immediately switched his attention to Stephen and thrust out his right hand.

'Thank you for giving us your time, Cunningham. I think we have a problem that's right up your street. Come and look at this.' The other officers made way for Stephen to approach the chart table where a diagram of the ship lay over the chart.

'The Senior Naval Officer, Commander Abrams, told us you're an experienced bomb disposal officer. Indeed, I can see you are from the medal ribbons. Now look here, please.' Douglas pointed to a part of the ship's diagram. 'This is Number Three boiler room. During that latest U-boat attack, we were struck by a torpedo, but mercifully, it hasn't detonated. Instead, it's stuck in a bulkhead below the waterline. It's letting in water, but the pumps are coping. Needless to say, the boiler room has been evacuated, but that leaves us down on power. Do you think you could defuze it?'

'I d-don't know, sir,' Stephen replied. 'I know nothing of t-torpedoes... especially German v-versions.'

'That's a pity, old man. According to Abrams' list, we don't have any torpedo specialists embarked and you're our best hope. Were that fish to explode, I'm not confident the watertight bulkheads would contain the explosion and you know what that would mean?'

'There's a risk of the ship s-sinking, sir?'

'Quite right. Look, I know it's asking much of you, but do you think you could have a look at the damned thing?' Stephen could see the obvious strain on Douglas's face and felt for him. The Captain bore a huge responsibility, not just for the ship, but for the nearly 1,500 crew and passengers embarked.

Stephen didn't hesitate in agreeing to help. 'L-let me examine the p-problem, sir... but I'll need some help.'

'Thank you, Cunningham. I was in the RNR during the last show and I knew I could rely on you. Chief Officer Maxwell will escort you down to the boiler room and make sure you have all the help you need. Good luck, old man. We're all counting on you.' Douglas patted Stephen on the back and shook his hand warmly.

Stephen's descent into Number Three boiler room was like entering a stygian darkness. Power to the boiler room had been cut and with it the lights, but one of Maxwell's men had provided them with head torches to aid their way. As he approached the deck plates, Stephen observed the glow of other head torches by the ship's side. He called up for one of the crew to lower his bag of tools on the end of a rope. Even without the yellow glow on the other side of the boiler room to guide him, he could hear the sound of the seawater cascading slowly into the bilges. A short, stocky sailor introduced by Maxwell as the Bosun welcomed Stephen.

'We're right glad to see you, sir. Thanks for volunteerin'. We ain't got a clue what to do about that sod.' He indicated the source of the water inflow. A large, ugly-looking metal cylinder about three feet in length protruded from the steel side of the ship. Sticking proud of the front of the torpedo was a phosphor-bronze device gleaming in the reflection of the torch light. It resembled a miniature torpedo in itself from which two double antennae had been pressed back by the force of the impact of the torpedo into the ship and now looked like a couple of distorted wire coat hangers. Stephen wasn't exactly sure what they were, but he knew them to be dangerous. With huge care, he examined what could be seen of the torpedo and was extremely wary of touching anything. After a few minutes of this careful examination, he thought he understood the principles of the detonation of the torpedo. Clearly, it had misfired on impact for some reason, but it still contained a huge amount of TNT and the device sticking out from the head of the torpedo would contain sufficient explosive to detonate the TNT. In this way, he assumed the firing mechanism of a torpedo wouldn't be that different from that of a mine and he felt confident he could render it safe. He turned to Maxwell to brief him on his conclusions.

'That thing s-sticking out of the f-front will be the torpedo's p-pistol. It ought to have t-triggered the b-beast to explode on impact. It should be simple enough to remove. You s-see the holding nuts there?'

Maxwell leaned forward and examined the torpedo's pistol for himself. 'Yes, I see. But what about those blade-like things?'

'I don't know. They m-might be there to operate some form of spring m-mechanism to fire the strikers in the d-detonator. If so, they will be s-sensitive and extremely d-dangerous.'

'So how do you intend removing the detonators then, Cunningham?'

'I don't. All I need to d-do is remove the p-pistol, take it up t-top and throw it over the side. But I want to deal with those b-blades, first. If they are there to d-detonate the torpedo on impact, they've c-clearly failed. They're pretty m-mangled, b-but I'm not taking any chances. They m-might g-get in my way. Pass me s-some tape, p-please... and do you have any small w-wedges?'

'Bosun?' Maxwell asked. The Bosun handed some tape and a handful of small damage control wedges.

'Would these do, sir?' he asked.

'I think so, thanks. B-but there are t-too many people in here. Even if the t-torpedo doesn't explode, the p-pistol likely c-contains enough explosive to kill everyone around. C-clear everyone out apart from one v-volunteer with a fire bucket f-full of sand.'

'Fair enough.' Maxwell turned back to the Bosun. 'Bosun, detail off one hand to volunteer to help the officer. Then the rest of you clear out.'

'There's no need to detail anyone off, sorr... beggin' yer pardon like. I'll do it.' The volunteer was a huge stoker, stripped to the waist.' The Bosun nodded to Maxwell as if to suggest he accept the offer.

'Right ho, then. Well done. What's your name?'

'Scott, sorr. I'm yer man.'

Maxwell turned back to Stephen. 'There you are. A ready volunteer. So, what are your intentions, Cunningham?'

'I want the hatch above s-sealed. Just in case I have a m-mishap. Is there s-some way to c-communicate with the compartment above?'

'There's a telephone on the bulkhead over there. It's patched straight through to the Engineer of the Watch. I dare say we can rig a field telephone to the hatch above. What do you have in mind?'

'Once I've removed the p-pistol, I'll place it in the f-fire bucket. I'll need S-Scott to hold it for me and then t-to carry it over to the ladder. W-when I give the s-signal, open the hatch and pass d-down a rope. I'll attach it to the b-bucket and you can hoist it up. You'll need to k-keep doing this until we reach the upper d-deck. Then I'll d-dispose of it over the side.'

'And what's the danger in all this?'

'Once the p-pistol is out, the ship will be s-safe. The torpedo's w-warhead can't fire itself and the torpedo can be removed by d-divers

92

on arrival in Simon's Town. You can s-safely pack the t-torpedo to stem the inflow of water. The risk is t-to those handling the fire bucket, so k-keep everyone else c-clear. Understood?'

'Yes, I understand. Thank you, but what you're saying is that should you fail to remove that pistol properly, it'll be curtains for you and Scott here.'

'I s-suppose so, b-but that's the nature of my t-trade. I remember my old instructor t-telling our c-course, "You're d-dead already, so every day you live is a b-bonus.'

'Crikey, Cunningham! I wouldn't have your job for all the riches of Croesus. Good luck.' Maxwell shook Stephen's hand and then wished Scott luck, too. 'Right, Bosun. Let's leave these heroes to be about their business.'

Within minutes, the boiler room seemed a very lonely place. The only light was from the head torches of the two men remaining. Stephen removed some metal snips from his tool bag and cut each of the antenna wires piece by piece until only a few inches remained of them. There was now less risk of them setting off the detonators inside the pistol. This task achieved, it was a relatively straightforward task to unscrew the nuts holding the pistol in place.

'Right, S-Scott. Where's that fire b-bucket?'

'Here, sorr. I'm ready.'

Stephen removed his headtorch to wipe away the sweat on his forehead before continuing. 'Very good. Give m-me as much light as you c-can and be ready to catch the pistol in c-case I drop it.' Outwardly, Stephen was very calm, but it was no act. Long ago, he had recognised that he had to force himself to enter a calm zone in his head, no matter the risk. The last thing he needed was a shaky hand and he was fatalistic about his chances of surviving each rendering safe procedure. Indeed, in this instance, he was genuinely confident about success. Removal of the pistol would be no more difficult than removing the gaine of a mine and in the torpedo's case, it wouldn't be booby trapped. Slowly and gently, he withdrew the pistol from its home inside the torpedo's warhead. Within a minute, he was able to place it on the bed of sand in the outstretched fire bucket.

'It's d-done, Scott. Thanks for your help. I'll take the b-bucket now. Tell them above t-to open the hatch and l-lower a rope.'

Fifteen minutes later, the fire bucket was on the upper deck of the liner and Stephen was able to throw the pistol overboard. A cheer erupted around him and then a chorus of *For He's a Jolly Good Fellow*. Stephen blushed with embarrassment and was then further appalled to be lifted onto the shoulders of several passengers and crew alike and taken to a saloon for a drink. Whether it was through the beer, the nervous excitement of the past couple of hours or not having slept for several hours, he slept surprisingly well that morning, despite his cabin mate's unsavoury noises.

Chapter 13
April 1942

'You can tell the man from me that he's a blithering idiot. Thank you for the call.' Captain Maitland-Dougall slammed down the telephone receiver and his obvious anger distracted Monty from the report he was preparing.

'That was Syme… ringing from Portland,' the captain said to Monty.

'Not Hugh Syme, the Aussie? He's no blithering idiot, surely, sir?' Lieutenant Syme RANVR was fast becoming one of Captain Currey's rising stars in the RMSO fraternity and had been awarded the George Medal for his work in defuzing a series of mines the previous year.

'No, not Syme. I meant the commander of the minesweeping flotilla down at Portland. He didn't have the grace to await Syme's arrival before ordering his men to sink the Tommy by rifle-fire.'

'Oh no!' Monty groaned and held his head in his hands. DTMI suspected that the Germans had deployed a new form of moored mine that was proving capable of avoiding being swept by the minesweepers. A few of the lighter-weight mines had been recovered floating free, but up to now, there had been no trace of the sinker that held the secret of how these mines remained so elusive. The new mine had been designated as the Tommy. Then, in a stroke of luck, a minesweeper off Portland harbour had discovered a Tommy stationery in the water and still attached to its sinker. Syme had been sent down to recover it.

'Oh yes,' replied Maitland-Dougall. 'I've told Syme to stay down there until your arrival. You'd better get down there pronto. If one Tommy's been laid, there are sure to be others. I'll square Syme's delay in returning with Captain Currey. And give the Commander Minesweepers a personal message from me. Tell him I don't care who his grandfather was. I think he's a bloody fool. If he gets shirty about it, tell him to ring me, but he'd be wise not to do so. Off you go, Monty.'

Fifteen minutes later, Monty was being driven at high speed down to Dorset.

*****

Monty's first task on arrival at the naval base in Portland was to have Syme introduce him to the skipper of the minesweeper who had first discovered the Tommy and then sunk it. The poor skipper was crestfallen to have learned his mistake, but he had only been carrying out orders.

'Never mind, skipper,' Monty placated the man. 'I suppose it was pretty good shooting at least. Now can you show me on the chart where you found the mine?'

'Ah,' he replied sheepishly. 'I can't be sure, sir. You see, I didn't plot its position.'

'What! But surely you plot the position of all the mines you find, skipper?'

'Well, that's to say in ordinary circumstances. But in this case, since we sank it, it was 'armless and not worth plottin'.'

Monty turned to Syme. 'We can't search the whole channel. But that mine's still dangerous. The skipper's men may have sunk it, but all they've done is puncture the buoyancy chamber and not destroyed it.'

'Have you no idea where you sank it, skipper?' Syme asked.

'I suppose I could narrow it down for you from the log. How say you both get yourselves a cup of tea from the wardroom and pop back in an hour? I'll have something ready for you by then. Fair enough?'

Monty and Syme had no choice but to agree, but before taking his tea, Monty made a telephone call to HMS *Vernon* to request some specialist assistance. An hour later, they reported back onboard the minesweeper.

'There, gen'lemen. That's the best I can do.' The skipper pointed to a triangle on the chart in the centre of the wide, swept channel.

'But that's an area of at least ten square miles, skipper!' Syme exclaimed. 'How can we expect to comb an area that size?' Syme turned to Monty. 'Is it worth it, Monty? Shouldn't we just wait for another to turn up, much as Captain Maitland-Dougall suggested?'

'Maybe and maybe not, Hughie. We've been chasing Tommies around the coast for three weeks now and not had a better chance than this. We know there's one down there and we're not quite on our own. I'll explain on the way back to the mess.' Monty took the skipper's chart with its triangular search area marked in pencil. 'I'll need to take this with me, skipper. Thanks for all your help, but we'll take over the search now.'

As the two officers walked back to the wardroom, Monty explained his plan. 'I've asked *Vernon* to send me *Esmeralda* with all despatch.'

'*Esmeralda*? Who's she when she's at home?'

'She's a beautiful seventy-ton yacht, Hughie. Before the war, she was privately owned, but since, she's been fitted out with the most modern echo-sounding gear. Her skipper's a chap called Don Callieu. He's rightly very proud of her, so make sure you sound the right noises, there's a good chap.'

Back in the wardroom Monty and Syme pored over the chart. 'Monty, do you realise that we've 280 million square feet of seabed to search?'

'I'll take your word for it, Hughie, but ten square miles sounds easier. We're going to need several marker buoys, lines and some bronze grappling hooks. I'll speak to Commander Minesweeping. He owes us after all.'

'Why bronze grappling hooks, Monty?'

'To trail behind us to pick up anything lying on the seabed. They have to be bronze to avoid setting off the mine.'

'Good point, Monty. I forgot. As you Brits would say, this operation sounds dodgy. But we'll never do it with just one boat, Monty. Could we not ask for another?'

'That's a good idea, Hughie. I don't see why not. Leave it with me.'

Just then Commander Napoleon, the Commander of HMS *Attack*, the Coastal Forces training base in which Monty and Syme were sitting, approached them.

'Why, hello, Monty. How's tricks? Long time no see.'

'Oh, hello, Boney.' Monty stood and introduced the commander to Syme. Napoleon and Monty were old friends from their days competing together in naval sailing regattas.

'So, what are you doing here? I heard you were in London these days.'

'We're looking for a needle in a haystack. We suspect there's a new type of German mine on the bottom somewhere in the swept channel. We need to find it urgently. *Vernon* are despatching a boat fitted with echo-sounding gear to help us scour the seabed, but we've just been discussing the need for a second boat.'

Napoleon mused over the problem for a minute and then suggested a solution. 'I might be able to help you there, Monty, but one favour deserves another. I suppose all Australians can sail, Syme?'

'Indeed, sir,' Syme responded.

'Splendid. In return for some sailing instruction from you, I'll tell you where you can lay your hands on an old drifter fitted with Asdic. Do we have a deal?'

'Asdic! Why that would be of great help, Boney. What's the deal, then?'

'I've a couple of Wrens who I want to learn some seamanship. We've a couple of beautiful little boats here and I can free them up for a couple of hours sailing instruction in the forenoon tomorrow. I doubt you'll be ready to start your search before the afternoon.'

Monty turned to Syme with a questioning look. Syme responded with a puzzled expression, then shrugged his shoulders and nodded. 'Agreed, Boney,' Monty replied. 'But where do we find this drifter with the Asdic?'

'I'll show you. It's alongside a berth in the harbour. It was left behind when the anti-submarine training unit moved up to Scotland, so it doesn't belong to me, but I'll find you a crew if you can skipper it.'

'No problem, Boney. Syme can skipper her.'

'Er, Monty. I can't. I haven't got a ticket.'

'Oh, come now,' Napoleon intervened. 'What the eye doesn't see, the heart doesn't grieve for. There's a war on. Remember the Nelson touch.'

'Go on, Hughie. I'll need to be in the *Esmeralda*. Don't worry. I'll take responsibility.'

*****

It was a sunny, but blustery day in Dorset. White fluffy clouds scudded quickly across the blue sky. Both Monty and Syme wore overalls and seaboots over their uniform, offering some protection not just from the cold wind, but the water in the boats. The two Wrens were similarly attired in overalls, but wore plimsolls. One was shorter and dumpier than the other with blond hair almost the colour of the fine white teeth she frequently showed as she smiled. Monty thought her quite sweet, but still allocated her to Syme's instruction, much to Syme's chagrin as the taller Wren was quite striking in looks. Indeed, her height seemed to be her only fault in Monty's eyes as she was a good inch taller than him. However, she was slim, muscular rather than curvaceous and with long brown hair that she wore in a bun. Monty thought her quite captivating.

Monty began by explaining the names of the different parts of the boat to Georgina Wells, but she seemed somewhat distant during his introductions as if she wasn't happy to be there. Monty persevered and suggested she step into the boat. He offered her his hand after explaining that the boat would rock a bit, but she ignored him and stepped confidently into the stern and sat ready for him to board and cast off the painter. The wind immediately took the small dinghy quickly across the harbour and Monty was thankful he had taken the precaution of taking in two reefs of the mainsail. The boat cleaved through the water and both occupants were quickly covered in spray, but Monty was pleased to see that Georgina seemed to be enjoying the ride.

They quickly approached the exit from the harbour and Monty made ready to go about. He handed Georgina the sheet to the jib and explained what would happen next and what she was expected to do. She smiled shyly back him and Monty felt quite the hero. He wondered whether Georgina might be flattered by his attentions and even find him attractive, but his thoughts were quickly overtaken by the need for action.

'Ready to come about,' he called and seconds later, 'Lee ho.' He pushed the tiller away from him and made to step across the boat. Georgina for her part swiftly let fly the starboard jib sheet and expertly stepped across to the port side, deftly avoiding the boom, and hauled in the port jib sheet. The manoeuvre was expertly done, Monty thought. He smiled some encouragement to his student.

'That was well done, Georgina. I don't think you could have done it better. Would you like to try your hand at the tiller? I'll keep an eye on you, so just relax.'

'Thank you, sir. If you're sure?' she replied and smiled back him sweetly. An arrow pierced Monty's heart.

As soon as they had exchanged positions, Georgina hauled in the mainsheet tauter. The boat immediately picked up more speed and took on a sharp heel to Monty's alarm.

'Don't haul in too tightly, Georgina,' he chided. 'We don't want to capsize on your first outing, do we?' Georgina merely laughed in reply.

'But this is such fun, sir.' She stretched out her long limbs to lean further out of the boat to give more stability and released her hair from the bun. It flew in long tresses in the wind, further melting Monty's heart. 'Perhaps you should tighten the jib sheet, sir?' she called.

Monty was affronted by the suggestion, but then accepted it was called-for. He was astonished at Georgina's confidence. She seemed to be a natural at sailing. He surreptitiously looked at her profile. With the wind blowing her hair, her lithe body taut against the boat and her countenance of sheer joy and excitement, she looked divine. She seemed the sort of girl with whom one could fall in love easily. To his alarm, he realised that his attention had been too drawn to the Wren at the expense of keeping a sharp lookout. Out of the corner of his eye he observed a tug towing a large barge and on a converging course.

'Watch out, Georgina! Let me take over.' He moved across the boat to take the tiller, but Georgina ignored him. Instead, she called out, 'Standby to gybe!' Before Monty could argue, she followed up with, 'Gybe oh,' and to Monty's huge surprise, manoeuvred the dinghy safely across the wind to head away from the tug.

Once he had caught his breath after his confusion, Monty burst out laughing. 'You've been sailing before, haven't you?'

Georgina smiled sheepishly. 'A bit, sir. My father taught me. He was a keen ocean-going yachtsman and I was always his first mate. We twice rounded the Horn in a windjammer before the war. Actually, I hold an Extra Master's Ticket in Sail.'

Monty was stunned. He had never come across anybody with such a qualification before, male or female. His admiration for her strengthened immeasurably. 'You minx,' he replied. 'Why didn't you say?'

'Commander Napoleon never asked, sir. And in any case, sailing's a far more enjoyable way to spend a morning than sitting in a stuffy Ops Room.'

'Very well then, Georgina. You keep the helm and we'll just have some fun.'

Over the next two hours, Monty enjoyed some of the best dinghy sailing he had experienced outside of a race. Georgina was an even finer sailor than Marcia. It slowly dawned on him that he was smitten. As they unrigged the boat and stored it again, Monty resolved that he must see Georgina again.

'Look, Georgina. I'm quite often down this way. How about I give you a call next time and we go out to dinner?'

Georgina pondered the question a minute. 'That sounds wonderful, sir, but I'm not sure my fiancé would like it.'

Monty was almost struck dumb, but eventually spoke. 'You're engaged?'

'Sorry, sir, I am. To one of the RAF pilots in Coastal Command.' She looked at her wedding finger. 'I'm sorry if I misled you, sir. You see, I never wear my engagement ring when sailing in case I lose it.' Monty merely blushed in reply and seeing his discomfort, Georgina went on to say, 'I'm sorry, sir. It just doesn't seem to be your day.'

By late afternoon, both Monty and Syme were searching the seabed off Portland harbour in their separate boats.

Chapter 14
May 1942

For four weeks, from dawn until dusk, seven days a week, Monty, Syme, Callieu and their crews steamed up and down parallel tracks across the ten miles the minesweeper's skipper had marked as the likely area for the Tommy. Neither the grappling hooks, echo-sounders or Asdic detected a thing. Like the others, Monty had given up hope of finding anything and was now convinced the skipper had erred in his calculations. He had even suggested calling off the search as being a waste of both time and resources. He felt sure his desk was piling up, too, but Captain Maitland-Dougall, after consultation with *Vernon*, had insisted that the search should go on at the expense of anything else. Monty's fear of destruction by the mine had been replaced by exasperation, boredom and hopelessness.

All that changed on the twenty-eighth day of the search when a grappling hook from Syme's drifter snagged something. Then the second line suddenly went taut and Syme ordered the drifter to stop engines. As the drifter continued forward, the grappling hooks appeared on the surface and, snared between them, was the mooring wire of a mine. Syme immediately hailed the *Esmeralda*. Callieu then slowly and carefully manoeuvred the yacht in close to Syme's drifter. Monty's heart was in his mouth as the seamen aboard the *Esmeralda* secured their own lines onto the mooring cable.

For two hours the two boats co-operated in manoeuvring carefully to haul the mine to the surface. Although Monty was expecting a magnetic Tommy mine to be drawn to the surface, there was still the possibility that this was an old-fashioned contact mine, quite capable of blowing both boats and all men onboard to smithereens through clumsy handling. Eventually, the mine's sinker appeared and finally, the mine itself. With supreme care, the seaman winched it up onto the deck of the *Esmeralda* and Syme crossed over to delouse it.

'I suppose the batteries will be flat by now, Hughie,' Monty suggested.

'That's an optimistic view, Monty. After all the bad luck we've had in the past four weeks, I'm not taking the chance.'

There was nowhere to hide from the mine, so Monty saw little harm in helping Syme with the task of making the mine safe. Sure enough, Syme was right. The batteries weren't flat and the mine was very much alive, but to their delight, it was the new type of mine. They had found their Tommy. Now it was up to the *Vernon* scientists to devise a method for the minesweepers to cope with it.

*****

A week later, Monty was in his office reading an unnerving report. Another of the Australian RMSOs had reported finding the bomb fuze of the mine he was delousing covered in pitch. It meant that he couldn't apply the gag to hold the fuze safe whilst he removed it. The Germans clearly held a grudge against the British and Australian RMSOs. The unlucky Australian had had no choice but to handle the bomb fuze whilst it was still live. Through a combination of skill, luck and nerve, he had managed to withdraw the fuze without incident, but just as he was unscrewing the gaine, the fuze's clock had started running. Fortunately for the RMSO, he just had enough time to finish unscrewing the gaine and throw the fuze into an adjacent field before it exploded.

The shrill jangle of the telephone disturbed Monty's reading. It was Commander M at HMS *Vernon*. 'Monty, there's been a cock-up and a row's brewing. I'm sending Syme up to you on the next train. You and he need to get yourselves to the Bristol Channel ASAP.'

'What's the problem, sir?' Monty was all ears. Commander M was usually unflappable.

'Last week, the Bristol Channel was raided and it now seems four mines were dropped from two aircraft unbeknown to the mine-watchers. The first anyone knew of it was when somebody heard an explosion about two miles off the pier at Weston-super-Mare. In my opinion it was clearly from a mine exploding after automatic detonation by the self-destruction fuze, but it seems the local bods didn't have the common sense to put two and two together and deduce that where there's one mine, there are likely to be others.'

'Have you now had confirmation of this, sir?' Monty interrupted.

'Too bloody right, we have. Earlier today, at low water, somebody spotted three dark spots way out in the main channel. I think they're Sammies!'

'Oh, my word!' Monty exclaimed in horror. 'And this is the sixth day since you think they were dropped?'

'Give the man a coconut. You're spot on, Monty.'

Monty immediately grasped the problem and could see why a row was brewing. The Sammy was a conventional magnetic-acoustic mine designed for dropping into water. However, recognising that the British were recovering their mines when accidentally dropped on land, in too shallow water or in water that dried out at low tide, the Germans had come up with a self-destruct mechanism. A diaphragm in the mine would be depressed by the pressure of deep water and the magnetic and acoustic firing mechanisms then armed. However, should the diaphragm not be depressed or the mine brought shallow, such as by RMSOs, then a six-day clock would arm the mines' self-destruction mechanism.

'And when is low tide, sir?' Monty asked. He knew the mines would detonate as soon as the pressure was taken off the diaphragm. Whilst the mines would have been laid in thirty feet of water, the tide in the Channel was such that the mines had already come shallow once.

'23.00. The tide's flooding, so we've about eight hours before the mines come shallow.'

'But that's not enough time, sir. Even when Syme gets here, it'll still take us four hours to reach the coast. What time is Syme's train due in?'

'15.12, all being well. Look, Monty, I know the situation's not ideal, but we still have to do something. Syme's not happy about it either.'

'Very well, sir. I'll meet him off the train and high-tail it to Weston-super-Mare.'

'Good man.' The telephone line went dead.

*****

Monty was concerned about Syme's health. He looked exhausted and tense. Since their exploits searching for the Tommy in Portland, Syme had barely had a day's rest. The day before, he had been

104

delousing two Sammies on the mudflats off Horsea Island and it had clearly taken something out of him emotionally. However, the job had to be done and at least Syme had managed to get some badly-needed rest in the car.

On arrival at Weston-super-Mare, they met with the Naval Officer-in-Charge and were briefed on the situation. The NOIC was an elderly commander who had retired after the last war, but been brought back to service. Commander Simmonds struck Monty as being past it.

'So, what are you going to do?' he asked them in his diffident manner. Monty was surprised by the tone of Syme's reply.

'Me? I'm going to do nothing. You should have called somebody in six days ago.'

'Steady on, Hughie,' Monty whispered to Syme. 'You're addressing a senior officer.' Monty put it down to tiredness and nervous strain, but fortunately, Simmonds seemed to be a little deaf and didn't appear to have heard Syme.

'But… but you can't just do nothing. I mean, what are you here for otherwise?' Simmonds replied.

'There's nothing I can do, sir,' Syme said a little more emolliently. 'Those mines are going to blow up tonight around about low tide. There's nothing to stop them. They're far enough offshore not to do real damage, but they're going to take out every window on the waterfront. If I were you, sir, I'd advise your local residents to open their windows between say, 22.30 and 23.30.'

'But it's freezing outside, man.'

'Sir, it's good advice,' Monty chipped in. 'Better to have one cold night than to freeze for several nights without windows.'

Simmonds glumly accepted the advice and set about it. It was too late for Monty and Syme to return to London, so they accepted the offer of a bed in the house of one of Simmonds' neighbours.

The following morning it came as no surprise to the two visiting naval officers to learn that there was glass everywhere on the seafront. Either the residents had chosen not to believe the advice or had shut their windows too early. Monty felt sorry for them. With the shortage of materials and glaziers, it would take some time for repairs to be effected. However, both he and Syme were surprised to learn that only two of the mines had exploded. It left them in an awkward spot.

'Hughie, notwithstanding your reservations, we're going to have to delouse that mine. It's almost mid-channel and interfering with navigation.'

'Not me, mate. It's too dangerous. Destroy it by gunfire if you like.'

'Come on, Hughie. This isn't like you.'

'Monty, I don't think you understand how these Sammies work. After six days the clock on the mine sets the self-destruction arming circuit by bringing together two platinum contacts. Once that circuit is made, it would be suicide to try to recover or, heaven forfend, try to delouse it.'

'But it must be a dud, Hughie, or else it would have destroyed itself like the others, Hughie.'

'And you're asking me to bet my life on that chance, mate?'

Monty was in a quandary. He had enough respect for Syme to know he was right, but he felt it was his duty at least to try. 'Fair enough, then, Hughie. I'll give it a go. I've defuzed several magnetic mines in my time. You can always dig yourself a foxhole within hailing distance to give me advice should I need it.'

Syme laid his breakfast cutlery down carefully and stared intently at Monty before asking, 'Have you ever deloused a Sammy or even any acoustic mine, Monty? No. I can see you haven't.' Syme went back to eating his fried eggs, leaving Monty stuck for words. Monty pushed away his plate. His stomach felt knotted with worry about an unexploded mine in the main channel. Nothing more was said between them until Syme finished his eggs. Then after a large gulp of tea, he spoke.

'Strewth, Monty! You look more blue than my jacket. You make me feel guilty. All right, I'll do it, but don't say I never warned you.' Syme flung his napkin onto to the table. 'But I'll need your help, so it's your funeral, too, if this all goes pear-shaped.'

Monty brightened considerably. 'Absolutely, Hughie. I'll be there. So how do we go about it?'

Syme thought over the problem for a short while. 'I'm not tackling it from the shore side. It's two miles out and too long a walk. In any case, we'd get stuck in the sands. No, we'll approach it from the sea, so we'll need a motorboat and a dinghy.'

Monty checked his watch. It was just after 08.00. 'I'll fix that with Simmonds. If we set off at 09.30, that should give him time to make the arrangements and we can be in position well before low tide.'

'That sounds fine, Monty. You go see Simmonds then. I'll have another cup of tea. I think I'm going to need it!'

*****

Despite it being May, it was a cold and overcast day as Monty and Syme set out across the Bristol Channel to search for yet another sunken mine. Not knowing which of the mines had not exploded, they couldn't be sure of its exact position, so they drifted up and down in the vicinity waiting for the water to fall sufficiently to expose the mine. Soon after 10.00, Monty thought he could see a ripple on the ebbing tide, suggesting an obstruction to the water's outflow. Syme ordered the skipper of the boat to cut his engine. This was a magnetic-acoustic mine, after all, and it was live.

The boat drifted slowly towards the mine with the ebbing tide and when about one hundred yards from where Monty had seen the ripple, the sighting was confirmed as that of the mine. Part of a dark cylinder was beginning to emerge from the water. There was no sign of its parachute.

'Right, skipper,' Syme said. 'That's far enough. We'll transfer to the dinghy and then you need to get well away from us. Just drift with the tide and don't restart your engine until you're well clear.'

The skipper seemed only too glad to discharge his two passengers and their tools. Only about two hundred yards away, he restarted his engine, churning up the mud to release a foul smell of rotting fish. Both Monty and Syme held their breaths, not on account of the smell, but for fear the engine noise would trigger the mine, but after a few seconds, they breathed again. Syme took the oars and rowed gently towards the mine, letting the tide do most of the work. About thirty yards away, he stopped rowing and removed his trousers. From this distance, Monty could see clearly the dark outline of the mine. It was a large one and he recognised it as a Sammy. He was concerned about the way it lay in the sand. The detonator was uppermost and that meant that the primer and bomb fuze would be submerged in the mud and sand. He, too, began removing his trousers. There was no point in ruining them. He and Syme would be working waist-deep in the sea, but Syme stopped him.

'No, Monty, wait.' He handed Monty the oars and dinghy's painter. 'You stay with the boat, Monty.' As Monty made to protest, he continued, 'No, Monty. It's not that I'm protecting you. We can't let the boat run aground or else we'll be stranded, too. You stay within hailing distance with the dinghy and keep her afloat. And there's something else, Monty. That mine's been submerged in up to thirty feet of water, so the self-destruct mechanism isn't my only problem.'

'What do you mean, Hughie? Oh, my word! I see what you mean. The hydrostatic clock's armed it already.'

'Precisely, Monty. That means the detonator to the main charge is more of a worry than the self-destruct mechanism, although I'll need to gag it first anyway for safety's sake. Given that the fuze is buried in the sand, I'm glad I don't need to apply the horn to gag it.' Syme reached into a pocket of his reefer jacket and withdrew the small box containing the screwdriver and pins now used to gag mines. The crafty Germans had become wise to the motor horn and bicycle pump procedure to fool mines dropped on dry land that they were in water and had added a vent to the fuze so that air pressure from a bicycle pump merely bled into the fuze pocket, but the Admiralty scientists had kept up with the game by inventing yet another countermeasure.

'I'll tackle the detonator first and then move onto the fuze and the primer. Depending on the lie of the mine, though, I might need a hand to turn the mine or to bale the water as I dig down for them, so I do need you on hand, Monty.'

Monty saw the sense in Syme's words and agreed. Syme slid over the gunwale of the dinghy and entered the water. 'Jesus! It's cold,' he gasped. He sank to his knees in the mud, taking the water to his waist. 'Ugh! This is horrible,' he exclaimed.

'Will you be all right, Hughie? It's filthy stuff,' Monty asked solicitously.

'We've both worked in worse, Monty. Kindly pass me my tools.'

'True enough, Hughie.' Monty passed Syme his tools. 'Good luck, old chap.' The two men shook hands and Syme trudged off towards the mine, each step accompanied by both a squelching and sucking sound, and a sickening stink of sour mud and decomposing fish. Monty tied the dinghy's painter to one of the oars and stuck the oar in the mud below to tether the boat. He realised he would have to move the boat as the tide receded, but he wanted to be as close to the action as possible for now. Gagging the fuze wasn't going to be straightforward, after all. Hughie would have to lie on his side, dig down into the mud and sand and then remove a tiny screw from the fuze before finally pressing home the gagging pin into the screw hole. It was something RMSOs practised in perfect conditions, but these conditions were far from perfect.

The two men had earlier agreed that there could be no question of shouting. The noise would be enough to trigger the mine. Instead, Syme would indicate progress in achieving pre-arranged steps by signal. It meant that Monty didn't know how well or otherwise the Australian was faring. He saw Syme walking around the mine with great difficulty as the mud sucked his legs down. With nowhere else to put it, Syme laid his tool bag in the water and disappeared behind the mine. Monty had no idea how deeply buried the fuze would be and was tempted to join Syme and help him dig into the mud for it. However, despite the difficulties, Syme reappeared after a couple of minutes and signalled completion of the first stage. He had successfully gagged the mine's self-destruct fuze.

Monty placed a hand in the water and withdrew it quickly. It was freezing cold. He thought of Syme immersed to his thighs in not just the cold water, but the freezing mud beneath. Moreover, should anything go wrong, he had no escape. The mud would hold him fast. Mind you, Monty reflected, he wasn't going to get far enough away in the dinghy either.

Syme held up a screwdriver. It meant he was about to unscrew the plate covering the detonator. Monty knew it would require a steady hand to unthread the screws of the plate, but Hughie's fingers must be either numb, trembling with the cold or both. Monty shivered involuntarily at the thought of it. He tried to think of reasons why the mine had not destroyed itself. Had the batteries run flat? It was unlikely, he thought. They were charged to 180 volts and in six days would not have discharged that much. Could the clock be running slow, say a day late. Again, this was unlikely. They were probably still Swiss-made and Monty hadn't heard of any running faultily. No, more likely the jolt of landing in the water had caused something to misalign, but then the slightest vibration from clumsy handling by numbed hands might reverse the misalignment. He shook his head. There was no point in thinking this way. He couldn't do anything about it. Everything depended on Syme's skill and experience. The thought reminded him of his friend Stephen and he wondered what he would be doing now. Certainly not stuck in an open dinghy in the freezing Bristol Channel fifty yards from a live mine. No, he thought, Stephen would be enjoying the life of the Gods on a luxury ocean liner on his way to the warmth of South Africa.

Chapter 15

As April turned to May, so too, did the passengers and crew of the *Empress of Japan* change into tropical uniform. Stephen appreciated the white cotton in place of his blue serge, but it came at a cost. For a start, he couldn't launder it himself as it had to be starched and that meant sending it down to the ship's laundry where its Chinese crew worked around the clock to wash and press the uniform items, often crushing the buttons in the process. Laundry costs hadn't previously been a concern to him. Then the starched uniforms would come stiff as a board and until the day wore on and they softened, it sometimes felt like wearing a suit of armour. Stephen wasn't complaining, though. He was tanned, well-fed, relaxed and healthy. He had even managed to quit smoking. With the *U*-boat attack far behind them, it was hard to imagine he was at war. He chided himself for the thought. Three ships from the convoy had not been so fortunate.

Stephen's first sight of Africa was that of a hill in the distance towards lunchtime. The convoy was approaching Freetown, the capital of Sierra Leone and in preparation, the convoy's Commodore ordered all four columns to form one column for entering harbour. Stephen felt sorry for the commanding officers of the escorts dashing amongst the convoy trying to shepherd the merchantmen into the new formation. The air was becoming ever humid and Stephen could see mist rolling down from the hills ahead.

After lunch, Stephen returned on deck and now he had a good view of the African coast as the ship entered the river leading to Freeport. He found it disappointing. He had imagined jungle coming down to the water's edge and the natives paddling about in canoes. For some reason it instead reminded him of a seaside town in North Wales, with the hills in the distance, great open beaches and a busy harbour. Moreover, it was raining and the sky was turning blacker and blacker. Despite the now heavy rain, the heat was almost unbearable and sweat poured down the back of his shirt. The river and port were teeming with shipping, including warships. Stephen was advised that the two great battleships swinging at their buoys were the *Rodney* and the *Nelson*. The liner anchored some distance off the town and Stephen was too far off to see any sign of life. It had been promulgated that the ship was programmed to stay in port for two nights and shore leave would be granted, but Stephen decided it wouldn't be worth going ashore. The town and the climate were uninspiring. His first steps on the continent would have to wait until Cape Town. Instead, he wrote to his mother and sister. Then, as an afterthought, he penned a few lines to Monty. Although their friendship had cooled over Monty's relationship with both his sister, Lucy, and this Oxford chum of his, Stephen was prepared to be forgiving. After all, in their trade life was too short and friendships were valuable. If only he had thought this way earlier. Was religion more important than love? He wished he'd responded to Carol's last letter. No doubt a girl like her would have found somebody else by now.

*****

Monty watched Syme remove the cover to the detonator of the mine and then turn to signal that he was about to start work on stage three, the removal of the black bakelite bung that covered the detonator to the main charge. Monty and Syme had already discussed how this was probably the most dangerous stage coming up. Something had gone wrong with the mine's main firing circuit between the detonator beneath the bung and the self-destruction switch. Accordingly, Syme waved his hands to usher Monty further away to a safer distance of 400 yards. This was an acoustic as well as a magnetic mine and turning the bung to access the detonator chamber could be a notoriously noisy task. Moreover, the mine had been in the water almost a week and the bung would have expanded to an even tighter fit.

Despite the risk, Monty gestured his refusal to withdraw to safety and for Syme to carry on. It was a risk and a long shot, but Monty thought that were the mine to explode, he might get away with it from this distance given that it was partially buried in the mud and still had some water around it to absorb the shock. He wanted to be close by in case Syme needed a hand. It would be hard work manoeuvring the huge bung spanner to unscrew the bung and might need the strength of two men. Monty wasn't a religious man, but all the same, he uttered a silent prayer for Syme. He was coming to like the Australian.

With his heart in his mouth, Monty watched Syme lift the huge bung spanner and crouch over the mine as he began work on removing the bung. Every few seconds, Syme froze motionless, perhaps listening for the fatal sound that might precede his instant death or waiting for the acoustic unit to reset itself. It took an age and Monty realised he had stopped breathing, but at last, he saw Syme hold the spanner aloft in one hand and lift the bung in the other. Stage two was completed safely. He wasn't done yet, but once Syme cut the detonator wires, the rest of the delousing process should be relatively straightforward. Syme pocketed the bung and then delved inside the cavity of the mine to cut the wires of the firing circuit, but he seemed to be taking a long time about it. Monty worried that something was wrong.

After an eon, Syme signalled to Monty that he was, indeed, in difficulty and needed help. Like a shot, Monty sprang over the side of the dinghy, not even bothering to remove his trousers, and waded towards Syme.

Monty was grateful that he had previously thought to remove his seaboots. The mud sucked him thigh-deep every step and had he been wearing his boots, he might have become stuck. Monty had never been an athlete or sportsman, but somehow, he reached Syme by force of adrenalin.

'What's up, Hughie?' he whispered in fear of the mine's microphone.

'Bloody Jerry's out to kill me, that's what. Short wires!' Monty saw the look of absolute exhaustion on Syme's face. The combination of the search for the Tommy, the defuzing of the magnetic mines in the previous few days and now this. The man had gone his length. Syme went on to explain.

'I can't pull the circuit wires out to cut them. Bloody Jerry's rumbled us and there's no slack to form a loop. Are your hands dry, Monty?'

Monty understood the problem, but was surprised by the question. There were two wires that needed to be cut to render the mine safe, but they had to be done in the right order, or else… Short wires meant that Hughie couldn't see which one to cut first. Monty examined his hands carefully. He had to answer Syme truthfully. Both their lives depended on it.

'Yes, Hughie. They're dry. Why is it significant?'

'Monty, I'm giving you the choice. Wade back to the dinghy and get the hell out of here or help me and face almost certain death. But there is another option.'

'Go on, Hughie.'

'We both abandon the bastard and destroy it by gunfire. I've had my fill of it. Who cares if a few more ruddy windows are blasted out?'

Monty thought about the option, but he could see in Syme's face that he wasn't seriously considering that plan. It looked like Jerry had upped his game and the reason this mine hadn't self-destructed might be that it was a new variant that had been dropped with the others to coax the minesweepers into a fatal trap. If they destroyed the mine, they would never know.

'What's the other option, Hughie. Why do you need dry hands?'

Syme visibly relaxed knowing that Monty had resolved to stick with him. 'I need you to cut the wires, Monty. I'm soaked and if I were to cut the wrong wire first, I'd act as an earth and trigger the self-destruction switch. If you do it, we've maybe a fifty-fifty chance. But you'll have to do it blind.' He paused to let his words sink in. 'You still want to chance it, mate?'

Monty didn't reply immediately. He reflected on his life to date. It hadn't been wasted. He had had a successful career as a barrister before the war and were he to survive the war, he would have every chance of picking it up again. But he knew that if he walked away from this mine, he would spend the rest of his life, however long that might be, regretting it and forever wondering if it was down to caution or cowardice. This was his moment to prove himself… to himself. Moreover, it was his duty. The men at *Vernon* needed this mine intact and he had to take any chance of giving it to them. In any case, he was the spare and not the heir to the earldom. He reached his decision.

'Very well, Hughie. For Eton, Oxford and England. I'll do it.'

'Good on you, mate. For Melbourne, Australia and… oh, I can't be bothered with all that upper crust claptrap. Let's just get the bastard done.' The two men stared at each other with huge respect for the other and smiled. 'Forgive me if I don't shake your hand, Monty, but it's been a privilege to know you.'

'Likewise, Hughie. Right, where are the pliers?'

Syme handed over a pair of wet pliers, so Monty carefully dried them on the chest of his jacket and wiped his hands on his chest for good measure. He took a deep breath, bent over and inserted the pliers into the cavity of the mine, groping for a wire. He had no choice in its selection as his fist hid the wires from view. He found a wire and gripped it lightly with the jaws of the pliers.

'Right, Hughie. I've got one. Say your prayers. Here goes.' Monty squeezed the pliers and immediately180 volts kicked through his body with a spitting of sparks. The electric shock threw him backwards and he lost control of the pliers. The last thing he heard on this earth was the sound of the pliers clanging against the steel hull of the mine as his back landed on the mud and in a shallow puddle. He lay there spread-eagled and his legs twitched for a few seconds.

But he wasn't dead, after all! He became conscious of his surroundings again and realised that he was still alive. He saw Syme staring at him ashen-faced, too shocked to speak. Slowly, it dawned on Monty that both he and Syme should be dead. He noticed Syme holding the pliers for grim death. He had clearly had the presence of mind under the most extraordinary of circumstances to catch the pliers as they rebounded off the mine to prevent them entering the shallow water. Monty wondered if Syme was a cricketer. Then he had another more chilling thought. The clanging noise of the pliers should have triggered the acoustic mechanism, but it hadn't! What was wrong with the blasted mine? Gingerly, he rose back to his feet, taking care to avoid immersing his hands in the surrounding puddle.

'Strewth, Monty! Are you all right?' Syme eventually whispered.

'I think so, Hughie. Just a bit shocked.'

'Ha, bloody ha. You nearly gave me a heart attack.'

'Sorry about that, chum,' Monty replied sourly. 'I think I've just had one.' He took the pliers off Syme, wiped them again and returned to the mine's cavity without a further word. He reasoned that by chance he had tried to cut through the live wire of the firing circuit. Had he tried the other wire, he would have created and earth and set off the self-destruction switch. If he could find the same wire and cut it through this time, they might just have a chance. He groped about blindly in the cavity and thought he had found his wire. He could feel teeth marks on it from his first attempt with the pliers. Carefully, he took hold of the wire between the jaws of the pliers and gritted his teeth before applying pressure to make the cut. Bang!

Again, Monty was flung backwards into the mud and he felt as if his right hand and arm had been blown off, but there they were, clinging onto the pliers for dear life. He just lay in the mud, literally stunned. He was in pain and he didn't think he could go through it all again, but he knew he must and as Macbeth's soliloquy went, *'If 'twere done when 'tis done, then 'twere well it were done quickly.'* Rather creakily, Monty rose to his feet once again.

For the third time he approached his man-made enemy. Without a glance at Syme, he inserted the pliers back into the cavity, found the wire and held it firmly in the pliers. He gritted his teeth and summoned all the strength of his body to be released through his right hand and squeezed the pliers. Yet again, he felt the electric shock passing through his body, but this time he stood firm and made the cut. He withdrew his hand and dropped the pliers. His hand was completely numb. He turned to Syme questioningly and flopped down onto the sand, a nervous wreck.

'Is that it, Hughie? Have I done it?' His voice croaked. Syme responded by putting a hand on his shoulder.

'Well done, old son, but we're not quite done yet. We need to tape the ends of those wires to insulate them and your hand's in no fit state to do it. Leave it to me, mate.' Without brooking any argument, Syme reached into his tool bag for some insulating tape. Monty was relieved to hand over the task. Of course, the insulation tape was wet and Syme had difficulty getting it to stick around the bare ends of the cut wire, but eventually, the mine was ready for the next stage. They still had to remove the primer to the main charge of the mine, the gagged self-destruct mechanism and the hydrostatic clock. However, the primer was buried in the sand. Syme went round the back of the mine to survey the situation.

'Strewth, Monty!' he exclaimed. The tide's gone out quickly and the dinghy's almost aground. 'You'd better tow it out to deeper water and wait for me.'

Monty looked around him dreamily and saw the veracity in Syme's words. Wearily, he stood up. 'But will you not need a hand to turn the mine, Hughie?'

'No, I think not. In any case, you're hardly in a fit state to help, if you don't mind me saying, mate. With the tide out, it's dried out around the base of the mine and it should be a cruisy job digging down to the primer. Leave it with me and go and rescue the boat.'

Again, Monty saw sense in Syme's words and he made to drag himself off to the dinghy, but a thought stopped him. He turned back to Syme.

'What about the spring, Hughie?' Within the cavity of the primer was a spring connected to the primer charge. The spring was prone to *twang* as it was released and it was thought by the boffins that this noise alone would be enough to activate the acoustic unit and explode the mine. There were two schools of thought amongst the RMSO fraternity on how to deal with the spring. Some thought that it would be best to withdraw it in one fast motion and hope for the best. However, Monty knew that Hughie favoured withdrawing the spring slowly, keeping it under constant pressure and only releasing the tension one click at a time.

'You have a point, Monty, but thanks to you, the detonator to the main charge has been made safe, so I reckon I'll take my chances with Stewie Mould's method. Don't tell him, mind.'

Surprised, Monty trudged back over the sand to the dinghy. At least the going was easier this time. When he reached the boat, however, he didn't climb into it, but moved it to waist-deep water and waited for Syme. He just couldn't manage to clamber over the gunwales with one fit hand and he felt exhausted. However, it didn't take long for Syme to remove the fuze and primer. Hughie had been able to dig down deep enough to yank out the primer and spring in one swift movement. The mine was now safe, but the job wasn't yet complete.

Through a combination of the cold of the water and his recent shock, Monty started to shiver and his teeth to chatter. He willed Syme to hurry up with the task of withdrawing the hydrostatic clock. It wasn't as if Hughie needed to do it, he grumbled to himself impatiently. The *Vernon* team could do that job, but ingrained professionalism determined RMSOs to finish the job. Although the clock was harmless, the RMSOs didn't think it beyond Jerry to hide some booby trap behind it. Better the death of one RMSO than a team of *Vernon* specialists in the mining shed. In August 1940, the Germans had done something similar with deadly effect.

Finally, Syme staked the mine carefully to avoid it being carried away on the next tide and collected his tools and the parts of the mine together. The *Vernon* team could now recover the mine safely in due course and remove its ton of explosive. He ambled back to the dinghy with the air of a man who knew he'd done a good job, but as soon as he saw Monty, he showed concern.

'Come on, Monty. Let's get you back. I'll row.'

*****

Some days later, back in London, Monty read *Vernon*'s report on the Sammy recovered from the Bristol Channel. His bandaged right hand shook as he read it. He and Syme should have been dead! The experts had examined the hydrostatic clock and discovered some corrosion in the points that should have set off the charge. Monty and Syme had literally come within millimetres of death!

Chapter 16

Stephen and his fellow passengers could smell the southern half of Africa for several days before they saw it. The days were now pleasant and balmy with a long, languorous swell as the ship crossed the Bay of Guinea, directly heading for the African coast. Soon, the land appeared to port in the distance, blue-grey and mysterious. Stephen began to anticipate his first steps on the African shore. Once the ship closed the landmass and turned due south, birds were sighted, but none that Stephen recognised. The surface of the blue sea was often disturbed by patches of brown and green from vegetation and flotsam being ejected from the continent by its mighty rivers. After five weeks at sea, like so many others, Stephen gladly anticipated the arrival of the *Empress of Japan* in Cape Town. According to the Chief Officer, the liner was due to be renamed there as the *Empress of Scotland* now that Britain was at war with Japan.

A few days later, it came as a great disappointment to Stephen to learn that the ship's programme had changed. No longer was it to put into Cape Town, but it would first be rounding the Cape of Good Hope for Durban. From there, instead of going on to Bombay, the ship would form part of a westward-bound convoy and then call in on Cape Town on the return. However, Stephen learned that part of the convoy was still being detached for Cape Town and he decided to approach the SNO about it. He found Commander Abrams getting dressed for dinner. Unlike Stephen and many other RNVR officers, Abrams possessed mess kit.

'Excuse me, s-sir, have you heard about the change in p-programme?'

'I have, Cunningham. We're going on to Durban and dropping off the cargo and troops bound for Bombay to pick up another ship. What of it?'

'But I'm m-meant to t-take up my new appointment in S-Simon's Town, sir.'

'Ah, I see. Nothing else for it, though, Cunningham. You'll just have to arrive one or two weeks later. Not your fault. These things happen and I'm sure the war will wait for you,' he added unhelpfully.

'But, sir. I've b-been at sea f-for five weeks already. D-don't you think I should be w-working?'

'Maybe you're right, Cunningham, but what do you expect me to do about it. Taking passage in a convoy's not like calling a taxicab. In any case, after Durban, the ship's turning back and calling into Cape Town on its way west.'

'Could I not t-transfer to one of the ships g-going direct to Cape Town, s-sir?' Stephen was almost pleading now. Abrams whistled loudly in reply.

'Really, Cunningham! You are the limit. Naturally, we're all grateful for your work in defuzing that torpedo, but you're not that special. Even were the Master to agree to your preferential treatment, the Commodore wouldn't. It would mean stopping not just this ship, but an inbound ship to launch a boat for you. All the time that puts two ships at risk of attack from loitering *U*-boats. It's not on, Cunningham. Now, if you will excuse me, I have to change.'

'I see, s-sir,' Stephen replied dejectedly. 'I hadn't thought of it that w-way. B-but would it b-be quicker for me to take the train from Durban, sir?'

'Gosh, you are keen. I rather doubt it, Cunningham. Moreover, it's a hellish uncomfortable journey. Take my advice. Sit it out and enjoy another week of leisure, albeit enforced. Thank you, Cunningham.'

Recognising that he had been dismissed, Stephen left the SNO's cabin.

*****

'Sir. Wake up, sir.' Stephen felt somebody shaking him roughly by the shoulder. He slowly roused. 'Sir. Are you Lieutenant Cunningham?' Stephen was sleeping on a steamer chair to escape the oppressive heat in his cabin. Although he was wearing pyjamas, he wore his reefer jacket over them. He looked up at the person shaking him, but without his spectacles, he could only see a blurry outline of a head.

'Y-yes, I am,' he replied groggily. He felt inside his jacket for his spectacles case and on donning his spectacles, observed a seaman rousing him from his slumbers.

'What's up? Wh-what's the time?' he asked.

'Just gone five bells of the Middle watch, sir. I've a message for ye from Commander Abrams. He says if yer still keen on getting' off the ship, now's yer chance. But you'll have to be quick.'

'Have you found him, Bell?' A young third officer joined the conversation.'

'I have, sir. This is 'im.'

'Right, Cunningham, we've a boat being prepared to take a casualty across to one the destroyers. She's going to take the poor man into Cape Town. Commander Abrams said you were keen to get to Simon's Town ASAP. Now's your chance, old man.'

Stephen immediately came alert. Of course he wanted to go. 'How long h-have I got?'

'Ten minutes. Grab yourself what kit you can. Bell here will help you, but you need to be at Number Sixteen Lifeboat Station by 03.00. Bell will show you the way there, too, but if you're late, the boat goes without you. Understand?'

'Thank you, sir,' Stephen replied excitedly.

'Don't call me, sir. I'm a mere Third Officer. Good luck.' The Third Officer pushed Stephen in the direction of his cabin and then headed back to his duties.

Twenty minutes later, Stephen reached the boat being lowered to take the casualty over to a waiting destroyer. He was a few minutes late as he had struggled to collect his kit together, but Reynolds, who had necessarily been disturbed by the commotion, had promised to pack up Stephen's belongings and have them ready for onward shipment to Cape Town. Lightly packed, but with his bag of precious tools, too, Stephen stepped into the boat. His fellow passenger was a stoker who had been badly burned by a steam leak in one of the boiler rooms. In the moonlight Stephen could see he was bandaged up like a mummy and he heard his low moans each time the seamen lowered the stretcher with a jolt. It was but a trice before the falls were released, the motor engaged and the boat was crossing the short distance between the liner and waiting destroyer. Rather than the grand arrival he had expected, it seemed that Stephen would be slinking into South Africa in the dead of night. He wondered if he would ever be reunited with his baggage.

*****

A few days later, Stephen became aware of how fortunate he had been to land at Cape Town and not to continue his voyage to Durban in the *Empress of Japan*. Now based in the South African naval base of Simon's Town in False Bay, south of Cape Town, he was summoned soon after his arrival by the base engineering officer. He was tasked to give his opinion on the cause of damage to a destroyer repair ship, HMS *Hecla*. She had been part of the convoy in which Stephen had taken passage, but on crossing the Agulhas Bank off the southern tip of Africa, had suffered a tremendous explosion in which twenty-one of her ship's company had died, 116 had been injured and three were missing, presumed dead. Commander Jervis wanted Stephen's opinion on whether the *Hecla* had been torpedoed or struck a mine.

Accompanied by the ship's navigating officer, Lieutenant Commander Alexander, Stephen gazed at the hull in absolute awe. The ship had made her way to Simon's Town under her own steam and been quickly docked at the expense of a cruiser that had previously occupied the dock. Judging by the damage, Stephen thought it a miracle that the repair ship had not sunk. It looked as if the explosion had occurred right underneath her great workshop and stores. Debris from dozens of torpedoes and mines littered what was left of the decks below. Mercifully, they had not exploded, too, but almost the entire keel, about forty feet wide and 150 feet long, had been blown upwards in a huge cupola shape. Every deck right up to the upper deck was a twisted and mangled mess.

'G-golly, sir,' Stephen exclaimed. 'It's a miracle you m-managed to bring her in.'

'Looking at her now, I'm amazed, myself. It was a tricky business judging the right speed you see.'

'I don't f-follow, sir,' Stephen replied.

'I mean that I knew that had we put too much speed on, the keel might have buckled. What I hadn't realised until now, was that had we not maintained sufficient pressure from the screws turning, the poor old thing's back might have broken.'

'I don't know about that, sir, b-but I can be certain that you struck a m-mine.'

'You're thinking of the shape of the keel inwards? Big enough to fit the dome of ruddy Saint Paul's in it, I shouldn't wonder.'

'Exactly. You say you struck in d-deep water?'

'About a hundred fathoms. That's why we thought it must have been a torpedo attack... but I can see now that we were wrong.'

'It would have been a m-moored mine. P-probably floating twenty or thirty f-feet below the surface.'

'And we've no sweepers down here, have we? I'd better pass on the news to the Naval Control bods. They'll have to assume there's a whole ruddy minefield in that area. Thanks for your help.'

Alexander trudged off, his gum boots making a slurping sound in the mud with each step. Stephen remained looking at the ship's hull above, deep in thought. It was a reminder of how potent a little explosive could be underwater.

*****

It was already light as Monty was driven back to London from the Norfolk coast. Monty had hoped to catch up with some sleep in the back of the Humber after an eventful night, but the intensity of the June sunshine even at 05.00, rendered it too hot to sleep. Instead, Monty opened the car window and breathed in the scented country air. It was enough to revive him from his slumbers. Self-consciously, he examined his hands and wrists for the umpteenth time. A few days after the defuzing of the Sammy in the Bristol Channel, the skin of his right lower arm and hand had peeled off like a glove. The doctor had put it down to the effects of the electric shocks and assured him that the skin would regrow. This it had done, but on this latest examination, Monty could see that the colour of his right hand was much paler than that of his left. However, there was nothing he could do about it. He was just grateful he hadn't lost his arm or... worse.

He shuddered and turned his mind to the mystery surrounding the mine that had been dropped four days earlier. A German minelaying aircraft formation had been plotted approaching the Norfolk coast, but one of the aircraft had broken away and headed several miles inland before dropping its payload. It seemed clear to the RAF that this was no navigation error, but a deliberate act. The mine had failed to explode and the local Land Incidents officer, Lieutenant Eric Crane RNVR, had had no hesitation in calling the Admiralty to express his suspicions, meaning Monty had been despatched *at the rush* to Norfolk. On arrival, he had been able to confirm Crane's identification of the mine as one of the German's relatively new Sammy mines, an acoustic-magnetic mine. The odd thing was that the safety pins had been deliberately left in the mine before being dropped from the aircraft so that there was no means of the mine arming and detonating itself. Monty already knew from his experiences in the Bristol Channel the month before that the mine had been fitted with two fuzes, the second being a self-destruction fuze that would destroy the mine automatically if the hydrostatic clock didn't register the pressure of a certain depth of water. Both he and Crane had, therefore, been highly suspicious that this might be another *gift* from the Germans, packed with booby traps to kill an unfortunate RMSO or *Vernon* scientist. But this hadn't been the case. Neither Monty, Crane nor the scientists sent up from *Vernon* had discovered anything out of the ordinary.

Monty knew from experience that it would be unwise to return directly to his flat for a wash and shave before reporting back to the office. Sure enough, despite it being only a little after 07.30, Monty found Maitland-Dougall already hard at work at his desk. The captain seemed excited to see him back.

'So, Monty. What did you discover?'

Monty outlined the work done in Norfolk and the absence of any booby traps.

'Indeed,' Maitland-Dougall replied intrigued. 'So, this seems to have been a premeditated act to drop into our laps one of Germany's latest secret weapons.' He paused to reflect further. 'But that had to involve not just the pilot, but the navigator and an armourer at the *Luftwaffe* base... Possibly even the members of the rest of the squadron. That's some conspiracy!'

'I've had the same thoughts, sir, but whatever the motives of the individual members of the *Luftwaffe*, sir, we've certainly fetched up a prize.'

The captain didn't reply for a short while, but seemed lost in his thoughts. He then turned to his desk and picked up a file. 'Interestingly, your ears must have been burning in Norfolk. I've had two forms of communication concerning you.' He waited expectantly, but Monty didn't make any enquiry.

'It would appear that I have both good and bad news to impart, but before I appraise you of the contents of the memos I have received, let me assure you, Monty, that I regard you as a first-rate officer. You're intelligent, incisive and courageous. I have rarely come to distrust your judgement without regretting it afterwards. I'm going to be sorry to lose you and I intend recommending you for promotion.' Maitland-Dougall smiled warmly at Monty.

'Lose me, sir? Am I being reappointed? Or are you, sir?' The news was a complete surprise to Monty.

'It seems you are, Monty, and that's bad news for me. Your name has been mentioned in some very high places. Does the term *Intelligence Assault Unit* mean anything to you? I can see from your face that it does. Admiral Godfrey informs me that with immediate effect you're to report for training as a commando. I further understand that you volunteered for the new role.' The captain looked at Monty expectantly.

Monty immediately blushed. 'Er, that's right, sir. I'm sorry... I should have told you. Commander Fleming approached me and it sounded an interesting proposition.'

'I'm sure it will be, Monty, but what pains me is why you should want a new appointment. As I've said, you're doing excellent work and making a real difference.' Maitland-Dougall wore a peeved expression and sighed before continuing. 'I can only think it might have something to do with the roasting I gave you over the acoustic torpedoes. It was most unfair of me and I could cut out my tongue...'

'No, please, sir!' Monty interrupted in embarrassment. 'I know about the loss of your son, sir. You were under enormous strain.'

'Oh, so you had heard, but my outburst was still unforgivable... especially as it was I that came to the conclusion that the trials were of acoustic torpedoes and not you. I beg your pardon, Monty. Most sincerely. However, there's nothing to be done now. The wheels have spun too far. Admiral Godfrey has already had the approval of Mountbatten, MI5, SIS and the other service intelligence chiefs. Like it or not, Monty, it's a life in khaki for you now.'

'I see, sir. Does DNI elaborate on where I'm to report for my training, sir?'

'No, he doesn't. I suggest you wander along the corridor to see Fleming about it. He seems to be the driving force behind the whole initiative. Read the memo if you like.' Maitland-Dougall passed over the piece of paper. 'However, you'll note that you will not be lost to me completely. It says that after training, you'll work directly to DNI on an operation-by-operation basis. In between operations you'll return here.'

Monty quickly read the memo. He was astonished by the news as he had had no further conversations with Fleming since the lunch in Boodles.

'Thank you, sir. I'm relieved that I'm not leaving DTMI completely, sir. I have found the work most satisfying. Would you mind if I went to see Commander Fleming now, sir.'

'No, I think you should, but hang on a minute. I said that I had two memos about you. The second concerns a piece of excellent news all round. Would you like to hear it?' Monty noted that Maitland-Dougall had suddenly appeared quite animated. 'Remember that shindig of yours with Syme in the Bristol Channel?'

Monty winced. 'I certainly do, sir. Only now is my right hand and arm returning to normal.'

'Well, I'm pleased to tell you that your efforts and courage didn't go unnoticed. You're to be awarded the George Medal, Monty. Well done, old chap.' Maitland-Dougall slapped Monty on the back and shook his hand vigorously.

Monty was stunned by the news. Suddenly, to have all his efforts and courage of the past two and a half years recognised! It was a huge honour, but then a thought struck him.

'But what about Hughie Syme, sir? He was the recognised RMSO.'

Maitland-Dougall looked away and replied, 'Indeed, Monty. He's to get the George Cross. By rights, you should have had the same medal and I pushed hard for it. After all, you both faced equal risks, but their Lordships felt that since Syme was in charge of the operation, you should have the lesser award. I'm sorry, Monty.' The embarrassed captain turned back to Monty.

'Not at all, sir. I think that's just the way it should be. I was Hughie's observing officer and assistant, after all.' Monty genuinely felt this way.

'It's good of you to take it that way and, if you don't mind me saying, typical of your character.' Monty noticed his superior beginning to well up. 'Anyway, many congratulations, my boy. I think you'd better cut along and see Fleming. Then you can tell me how long I have to find a replacement for you.' Maitland-Dougall turned back to his desk and wiped his eyes with the back of his hand.

Chapter 17
June 1942

On his first night at Achnacarry Castle, Monty decided to forego dinner, despite his hunger after twenty-four hours of arduous train travel from London to the Lochaber region of the Highlands of Scotland. He was too tired to eat and just longed for his bed. That afternoon, he and a number of Dutch Army personnel had alighted the train at Spean Bridge and been met on the platform by their instructors. Monty had had no particular expectations of what to expect, but what had awaited him had been a complete shock for him and the Dutchmen.

  He had not been surprised to discover that as a lieutenant commander he was the senior trainee amongst the four officers and thirty other ranks, but he had not appreciated that the officers would train side by side with their men, without deference to their rank, apart from a token greeting of 'sir' from time to time. They were met on the platform by their commanding officer for the next six weeks, Captain Haze, a tough-looking Yorkshireman and his troop sergeant, Sergeant Nichols, a grim-faced Scot with a dreadful scar down the right side of his face. Having deposited their kitbags in a Bedford lorry, the men had wandered about the station admiring the view of Ben Nevis. Even Monty hadn't ever seen it before, but then had come the bombshell. To their astonishment, there was no transport laid on to the training camp. Instead, they were to march the seven miles from the station to Achnacarry Castle and any man who didn't complete the march within 60 minutes would automatically fail the course and be *RTUd*, that is Returned to Unit. Fortunately for him, Monty hadn't yet been issued any military kit or a rifle, so he didn't have to carry any kit, but his soldier colleagues had to carry their Field Service webbing and rifle, a total weight of thirty-six pounds.

  Despite not carrying a heavy load, it had been the most physically demanding task Monty had ever undertaken and, fortunately, one of the Dutch officers and a dark-skinned private had chivvied him along the route and almost carried him the last mile of the way. They had, also, supplied him the contents of their canteens. It was a blisteringly hot day in mid-June and Monty's heavy serge naval battledress had been sodden on arrival at the camp. To add to the suffering of the whole troop of men on the forced march, the Scottish midges had enjoyed a wonderful feast at their expense, driving them all mad. Two of the Dutch soldiers had not been able to manage the pace and, having failed to meet the cut for the march, been returned immediately to the station for onward travel. Now there were thirty-two. Monty had not had time to wear in his boots properly and his feet were now blistered and sore. His legs were on fire, too, and he had barely been able to stay awake for the welcome briefing from Lieutenant Colonel Vaughan, the Commando Basic Training Centre's commanding officer.

Monty had thought Vaughan an odd sort of man to be commanding the camp. He was aged about fifty with a pencil-thin moustache. A veteran of the last war, he had served in the trenches in the ranks and after the war, become a drill sergeant and then the Regimental Sergeant Major of the Buffs (the East Kent regiment). Soon after the onset of the latest war, he had been promoted to officer and quickly risen to his now exalted rank. However, he made no attempt to hide his unmistakeable London accent. Sergeant Nichols had warned all the new recruits that Vaughan was tough and totally uncompromising about standards, so they had better learn to measure up quickly. However, this was now all beyond Monty as he fell into a deep sleep.

*****

After a blissful sleep, Monty had the time to appreciate his surroundings. The grounds in which the Commando Basic Training Centre (CBTC) was set and its castle were the seat of the Cameron Clan, Chief of whom was Sir Donald Cameron of Lochiel. Achnacarry Castle sat on the banks of the River Arkaig and amongst beautiful, but daunting mountains, including Scotland's highest, just eighteen miles away. The lawn outside the castle had been replaced by an asphalt drill square around which were a myriad of wooden huts and corrugated-iron Nissen huts. Monty and the Dutch Army shared one of the Nissen huts and the only advantage the four officers enjoyed was that their sleeping accommodation was separated from the main dormitory by a thin partition. However, they all shared the same canteen facilities. At breakfast Monty estimated that there were about 200 trainees present, most of them British, but he was surprised to see a fair cross-section of Americans, Frenchmen and other Dutchmen, too. He learned that the dark-skinned private who had helped him the day before was one of four trainees from Java in the Dutch East Indies. He was surprised to see that their fellow Dutchmen seemed to shun the four Javanese and they sat on their own for breakfast. He wondered how that fitted in with the *esprit de corps* so necessary for commando operations.

Soon after breakfast, Monty and his new colleagues were issued with a plethora of new kit. Mercifully, Monty was able to put aside his sweat-stained blue battledress in favour of a khaki version, a knitted commando cap and a woolly jumper. Those men who completed successfully the six-week commando training would be issued with a green beret to demonstrate their new status. However, this coveted accolade seemed impossible to achieve after the briefing on their forthcoming training regime. The men of the new intake were introduced to their instructors, without exception a bunch of tough and fit men, some of whom had been on the recent raid on St Nazaire. Monty and his fellows would receive instruction in small boat handling, climbing and abseiling, orienteering, survival, map reading and vehicle operation. In addition, they would be trained in demolitions, the use of a variety of weapons, including the Commando knife, and close-quarters combat. However, the two instructors Monty feared most were the sergeant and his assistant who would bully them through an intensive regime of physical fitness. Whilst some of this would all be water off a duck's back to the soldiers, it was extremely daunting for Monty and for the hundredth time this month, he wondered why a naval officer needed such training. Indeed, he had raised the matter with Fleming when he had been told he was to attend the course. After all, the course would be tough enough for soldiers and marines, but Fleming had said it was just an experiment for now and, in any case, would help Monty bond with the other commandos on operations.

*****

Ernst couldn't believe his eyes. As he read the telegram again his eyes dimmed and he really struggled to make out the words. '*Killed in Action*'. Little Maxi was dead! How could that be? He was the younger brother. The telegram offered no information on the circumstances of Max's death. Ernst had images of Max being burned alive as his Stuka crashed to the ground. Where would that have been? Was he still in the Balkans? He suddenly had another thought. Would anybody have informed Else? Probably not, he thought, as she wasn't Max's next-of-kin. It wasn't the sort of news to put in a letter to her. Of course, he would have to go to Berlin to give her the news in person. But what could he tell her? He knew nothing more than the stark contents of this telegram. He had to know more and that was another reason to go to Berlin.

*****

Ernst was relieved to discover the appearance of Berlin had changed very little since his last visit. Of course, the British bombers had mounted several raids on the city, but they had been largely ineffective. England was just too far for heavy bombers to mount any serious raids and then only in the summer with the longer nights and clearer nights. It did have the effect of disturbing the Berliners' sleep, though, as they had the inconvenience of having to take to their shelters. The previous year, the Russians had tried, but again without success. Berlin's weather seemed to strike the enemy bombers as effectively as the *Luftwaffe* air defences. However, the British Navy's economic blockade was having a more serious impact on everyday life in Berlin. The rations for bread, meat and fat had been cut once more. Even potatoes seemed hard to come by. Ernst had heard his brother officers complain that it was down to the need to feed all these foreign workers. Accordingly, it was a comfort that the grain harvest had been reported as a good one, although Ernst was starting to wonder if this might just be morale-boosting propaganda.

Of greater concern to Ernst right now was not food rationing, but how to penetrate the labyrinthine bureaucracy of the *Luftwaffe* headquarters. Little Maxi's dive-bomber wing had formed part of Air Fleet Two, *Luftflotte 2*, whose headquarters had been in Brunswick when Max had been fighting in the Balkans. However,

Ernst now learned that the headquarters had moved to Italy in the previous winter and, accordingly, none of the staff were available to meet him. However, he had then had a piece of luck. By chance he had come across an officer who had served on General Schott's staff when Schott had been Ernst's superior officer. Schott had since been promoted and moved to a new appointment in Jever, in Lower Saxony. However, the staff officer had agreed to make a few enquiries and the following day had introduced him to *Oberst* Hagen, a full colonel in the *Luftwaffe*.

Ernst struggled to hide his shock at meeting Hagen. The man had lost his left eye and half his face, including his left ear, had been burnt away. As his mouth had been burnt, too, it curled downwards and gave the impression when Hagen spoke that he was snarling. However, Ernst quickly recovered and saluted Hagen smartly.

'Sit down, Scholtz. It is an honour to meet the brother of Max.' Hagen sat down and immediately withdrew a gold cigarette case from his jacket. He offered a cigarette to Ernst, but Ernst declined. After lighting the cigarette, Hagen threw the match away nonchalantly over his shoulder and took a deep drag on the cigarette. Like Max, Hagen wore the throat decoration of the Knight's Cross.

'Reinhard tells me you are anxious to learn the details of your younger brother's death.'

'Yes, sir. All I know is what was in the telegram and that was nothing.'

'Alas, such messages are perfunctory these days. What do you wish to know?' Hagen started to cough. 'Ach, I should give these things up. My lungs are still damaged by smoke inhalation.' He pointed to the side of his face. 'As you can see, I have suffered on the *Führer*'s behalf, but at least I survived... unlike poor Max.'

'Colonel, could you tell me how my brother died?'

'Ah, yes. You should be proud of him. He was a real hero and I envied him. His wing was one of the best ship-killers I have known. You should have seen them over Crete. I can't recall how many of the Royal Navy ships his wing sent to the bottom. Max always led from the front and inspired his aircrews to emulate his many successes.

'I suppose you could say that we were rivals in a way. Both our wings were sent to North Africa in support of Field Marshal Rommel. Life was good to start. We switched from anti-shipping operations to direct support of the *Afrika Corps*.' Hagen broke off for another coughing fit.

'I swear this is Russian tobacco. They couldn't kill me on the Eastern Front, but maybe these will get me.' To Ernst's surprise, Hagen then withdrew another cigarette and lit it with the stub of the first cigarette.

'So where was I, Scholtz?'

'You were supporting the North African campaign, sir.'

'Ach, yes. We enjoyed life to start. We supported the *Panzers* and helped roll up the British Eighth Army. After we took Tobruk, I heard that we rounded up over 30,000 prisoners and tons of equipment. We were unstoppable and it was only a matter of time before we pressed on to the Suez Canal.'

'So, what went wrong, sir?' Ernst felt it a presumptuous question.

'Our miserable Allies let us down. The fucking Italians couldn't keep us supplied and we were starved of fuel and ammunition. The British had no such issues and were able to build up their Air Force. They even had some good pilots from South Africa. Slowly, we started to lose air superiority. As our own fighters dwindled or ran out of fuel, so did the support for our precious *Junkers* 87s. We were suddenly vulnerable to the Allied fighters. That's how I came to look like this.' Hagen gestured towards his burnt face.

'I was jumped by two Hurricanes and had to bale out over the sea… but not before my aircraft caught fire.' Hagen studied his cigarette thoughtfully and in silence.

'Is that what happened to Max, sir?' Ernst interrupted Hagen's reverie.

'I suppose so. I was in a field hospital in Italy when it happened, but I heard later that he died after leading an attack on an Allied convoy. Max personally destroyed a tanker and went on to attack a British cruiser. His aircraft was damaged by the cruiser's anti-aircraft fire. According to witnesses, Max refused to bale out, despite the damage, as his gunner was badly wounded. He seemed confident he could make it back to base, but about ten minutes later, Max and his escort of two *Stukas* and half a dozen fighters were jumped by a formation of about twenty Allied aircraft. Six of our aircraft were shot down, including that of Max.'

'Did he suffer, sir? Did his aircraft catch fire?'

'I don't know, Scholtz.' Hagen ground his second cigarette out in the ashtray. 'I know that's not what you wanted to hear. All I know is that the *Luftwaffe* has lost a superb leader and a great hero. I fear we will lose our foothold in Africa, but that's another story. I hope I've helped you.' Hagen stood to signal that the interview was over. Ernst stood, too.

'Thank you, sir. You have been very helpful.'

As Hagen left the room, Ernst wondered just how useful the meeting was. He still didn't know exactly how little Maxi had died, but at least he knew the circumstances. It was typical of Max to put his own safety at jeopardy to save his gunner. Ernst could only hope that the end was quick and take comfort from the fact that Max had died a hero.

Chapter 18

Ernst had had to invent an excuse to remain in Berlin. He misled his staff that he had to remain for further meetings, but even that extension was finite. It had, thus, come as a huge relief when he had finally tracked down Else's new lodgings. She had not been at her previous address and nobody had known, or perhaps keen to know, details of her new abode. It had shocked Ernst to hear Else described by her former landlady as a filthy Jew. She was only one eighth Jewish and a pretty little thing. Moreover, she had been Little Maxi's choice of wife. Ernst had really worked hard to restrain himself from hitting the old crone when she had followed up her insult by spitting. After several days and some greasing of palms, he had finally tracked down Else to a tenement in Bernauer Strasse in the Wedding district of Berlin.

The local name for the district offended Ernst's fascist leanings. It was known as 'Red Wedding' on account of the large concentration of Communists living in the district. Prior to the war and the *Führer* cleansing the area of many of the more militant inhabitants, the area had been the scene of many violent clashes between the Communist *Roterkämpferbund* and both the Berlin Police and the Nazi Party. Today it remained a poor working-class district renowned for its prostitution and high crime rate. How could Else have fallen to this, Ernst wondered as he gazed up at the dilapidated five-floor tenement building overflowing with noisy and dirty children. Sitting on the steps were several men smoking. Their pinched faces and blank stares reminded Ernst of his own poverty after the last war. He had witnessed starvation from too close a quarter and the anger at the loss of his family once again burned within him. He enquired of them the whereabouts of Else, but was only met with suspicious and sullen shrugs. His smart uniform seemed so out of place here. Standing on the steps of the tenement, Ernst looked to his left to see a worker sweeping the street. Like many of the residents around here he wore on his breast a yellow star depicting him as a Jew. He shook with anger. Had Else been reduced to this, too?

After several blank responses, one of the layabouts on the steps directed Ernst down the narrow alley leading to the building's back yard and told him to ask for Anna. Ernst wondered if it was a trap. Would he find a couple of thugs waiting to pounce on him and slit his throat for his wallet. He unbuttoned his holster as a precaution and grasped the pistol gratefully. The alley was dark, but soon opened out into a poorly-lit yard piled high with rubbish and in which yet more urchins were playing. He held out a few *pfennig* coins and asked two of them if they knew Anna. The girl pointed to a first-floor balcony behind him, grabbed the money and ran off with the boy. On the balcony, Ernst saw a woman old before her time alternately engaged in pegging out her washing and rocking the perambulator taking up most of the balcony's space. He called up to the woman.

'Excuse me, madam. I'm looking for *Fräulein* Else Beckmann. Can you direct me to her apartment?'

The woman laughed in reply. 'Her apartment, you say? Where do you think you are? Back in Charlottenburg? Noone has an apartment round here, *Liebling*. Else shares a room with me and my five kids.'

Ernst hadn't thought he could be any further surprised. Else and this harridan with her five brats sharing one bedroom! It was insufferable.

'And she isn't here now either, before you ask. She's at work. How else do you think we eat?'

'Thank you, my dear lady, for making that clear,' he replied politely. 'And where is *Fräulein* Beckmann working?'

'At the Jewish hospital.' Seeing Ernst's blank look, she added helpfully, 'On the corner of *Exerzierstrasse* and *Schulstrasse*... No, you're a stranger to this district, aren't you? Back out the building, turn left and then after two hundred metres, turn left into *Brunnenstrasse*. Carry on for another three kilometres or so and that'll take you straight to the hospital. Else is supposed to come off shift at seven o'clock, but she usually stays later. Ask her if she can pick up some flour on her way home, if you see her.' The woman returned to hanging up her rags on the line.

Ernst walked briskly up *Brunnenstrasse*, hoping the exercise would ease his depression. He felt awful to see Else reduced to such straitened circumstances. Would the Fatherland have treated her so badly had she and Little Maxi had the time to marry?

Thirty minutes later, he arrived at the entrance to the hospital. His shock on seeing Else's new lodgings was as nothing to that he suffered now. A line of people, all wearing the yellow star of Saint David, stood outside the hospital waiting to be admitted. A constant flow of ambulances entered and left the hospital. It seemed chaotic. On entering the hospital itself, Ernst was further surprised to spot the staff all wearing the star of Saint David on their white uniforms, too. Ernst had joined the Nazi Party as a means of advancing his career and although supportive of the *Führer*'s policies to make Germany strong again, he had not really given politics much thought. Until today, he had given little thought to the effect of the Race Laws on the Jewish population. Like most people he knew, he had supported the view after the last war that many Jews had been profiteers and he had been unsympathetic to their cause when the Nazis had begun to confiscate their businesses or restrict their business practices. But having seen many Jews serve with valour during the war, he had never subscribed to the view that as a race they were *Untermenschen* or sub-human. He certainly had not supported the acts of violence and destruction of property perpetrated by members of the Nazi Party against the Jews on *Kristallnacht* in November 1938. But nor had he spoken out against it, he chided himself now. Like countless others he had simply been too afraid to swim against the tide to speak out. Moreover, his own livelihood and that of Max had seemed more important than that of a minority he deemed as an alien culture. Today, Ernst began to question that way of thinking.

He jostled his way in to the reception desk and, thanks to his uniform, was quickly allowed to reach the front of the queue. He asked after Else. The receptionist showed no surprise or alarm that a high-ranking uniformed officer wanted to see a member of staff during working hours. He wrote down the name of a department on a slip of paper and handed it to Ernst without a word. Ernst noted that it was the *Schwesterheim* or nurses' residence. What would Else be doing there, he wondered. He made to ask the receptionist for directions, but the man pre-empted him by pointing to a corridor leading off to Ernst's right. Ernst bridled with anger at the man's insolence, but recognised that the receptionist would be under pressure from the huge, snaking queue. Further down the corridor a harassed female nurse gave him instructions on how to make his way to the nurses' residence at the back of the hospital. Within a few minutes, he finally found Else at a typewriter in an office also manned by three elderly men in white coats. They bore the yellow star on their white coats, but Ernst was relieved to see that Else didn't.

Else started with surprise at seeing Ernst, but then her visage changed to alarm at his presence. She jumped to her feet.

'Colonel Scholtz! What are you doing here? How did you find me?' A look of horror passed over her face as she realised that Ernst must have traced her to the squat on *Bernauer Strasse*. The three men in the white coats, also, stood in deference to Ernst's rank and eyed him suspiciously.

'May I take a few minutes' break, doctors?' Else asked.

'No, Else,' one of them replied after a bolt of fear struck him. 'You must not address us as doctors. We are now *Patient Handlers*.'

'Of course. Forgive me. I forgot.' Without waiting for permission, Else grabbed her handbag and ushered Ernst out of the office into the corridor.

'What is it?' she asked impatiently. 'Has something happened to Max?'

Ernst hid his feelings and lied effortlessly. 'No, of course not. I happened to be in Berlin and thought I would drop by to ask how you were and if you had news of him.' Ernst felt he couldn't spring the truth on her just yet. 'Is there somewhere we could talk?' He looked around him and noted that this part of the hospital seemed quieter.

'Of course, colonel. There is a sitting room just over here.' She led the way to a small room off the main corridor with a notice denoting it as for the use of the staff only. 'I'm sorry, but I cannot stay long. As you noticed, I am at work.'

'I understand, Else. Forgive my intrusion, but I couldn't leave Berlin without calling.' He took a seat diagonally opposite Else. 'I did call at your last address, but was surprised to find you had moved... and to Wedding! Does Max know your new address?'

Else looked down in embarrassment. 'I have only told him to write to me here, but I haven't heard from him for three months.' She looked up quickly. 'Was there any mail for me at my old address? Is that why you are here?' she asked hopefully. 'Have you news from him?'

'I'm sorry, but there was no mail for you in your previous apartment and you last heard from Little Maxi more recently than I. I have to say that you weren't spoken of well and I'm not sure any of your previous neighbours would have given me any mail in any case. What's happened? Why did you move... and to such an address?'

'Ah. You tracked down my new address, then. Anna must have told you how to find me here. Then I cannot hide my shame from you.'

'Shame? What shame? I'm just surprised to see you in such surroundings. Do tell me what happened, dear Else.' Ernst leaned forward and held Else's hand tenderly. 'Can I help in any way?'

Else removed her hand slowly. 'That is kind of you, colonel. Max told me how good a brother you were to him.' Else looked away and bit her lower lip. She seemed to be trying to make some form of decision so Ernst remained silent, too. After releasing a loud sigh, Else turned back to look at Ernst.

'There is no point in me lying to you, colonel. You have seen my present circumstances. I was forced out of my home by my neighbours and the local police.' She coloured as she continued. 'They said that Jews were not welcome in the neighbourhood. An official even warned me that were I to draw attention to myself by complaining, my name would be added to the list of Jews to be deported.'

'Deported? Deported where?' Ernst was flabbergasted by the thought.

'To the East, of course. Had you not heard? Large numbers of Jews are being sent to labour camps.' Else looked at Ernst with a look of contempt that he should not know such things. 'And don't think it an ugly rumour, my dear colonel,' she added bitterly. 'My work here gives me personal knowledge of the truth.'

Ernst wrung his hands in angst and replied quietly, 'I'm sorry, Else. There is so much I don't know. Why are you here? Why were there so many people queuing to enter the hospital? They didn't all look sick. And do call me Ernst.'

Else half smiled and looked less angry. 'I'm sorry, Ernst, I shouldn't be taking my anger out on you. The fact is, I don't regard myself as a Jew. I was brought up a Catholic, but recently I have been forced to think more of my partly Jewish heritage. Once I was evicted from my previous home, I came here because the rents are cheaper and only then did I really see what I had chosen to ignore previously. We're treating the Jews worse than animals. We all already knew it, but we're all too afraid to speak out. I needed work, the hospital offered me just enough to live on and I was keen to help where I could.'

'I understand,' Ernst replied softly. 'I suppose we have all quietly colluded with the policy of antisemitism, but I honestly hadn't really seen the consequences until today. They must hate us.'

'Not at all, Ernst. Like us, they just want to find a way through life... just to survive. We're all just humans.' Else looked away and tears welled up in her eyes. Ernst wanted to comfort her, but it didn't seem appropriate. Instead, he changed his line of questioning.

'So, what do you do here, Else?'

'Me? I'm just a secretary in the Transport Complaints Office. The title conceals our true purpose. There are six doctors, six... Oh, I forgot. I'm not allowed to call them doctors now. It has been decreed that not only may Jewish doctors no longer treat non-Jews, but they are to be addressed as *Patient Handlers*. No wonder so many left the country or went into hiding whilst they could.'

'I didn't know that. But you digress.'

'I have. I'm sorry, Ernst. Altogether, six *Patient Handlers*, six nurses and six secretaries including myself, form a committee to review the cases of Jews appealing deportation on medical grounds. No doubt you saw the queue of patients wanting to register for such an appeal. Naturally, we have tried to grant as many exemptions as we can, but it's become more difficult. Our work is supervised by the Office of State Security and now we have Aryan doctors supervising our cases. In any case, we can only delay the inevitable. We can only offer a delay of a maximum of three months. Even pregnant mothers cannot escape deportation, unless about to give birth, and then they are deported with their babies after six weeks. We work two shifts from eight in the morning until eleven in the evening and it's just depressing. The patients often stand for hours before they can be assessed and then, if they are genuine cases, we are under pressure to treat them in the hospital as quickly as possible. Despite the lack of staff, our surgeons are completing twice as many operations as last year.'

By now, tears were rolling down Else's cheeks and Ernst offered her a clean handkerchief to mop her eyes.

'Thank you, Ernst. This is very unbecoming of me, but you haven't heard the worst.' Else sniffed and worked hard to bring her emotions under control, but she hung on to Ernst's handkerchief. 'One of the duties of the hospital staff is to man first-aid stations at the railway stations for the deportees. Some are then required to join the trains to care for the passengers, but the strange thing, Ernst, is that not one of the staff has ever returned to the hospital… and there are dark rumours…' Tears began rolling again and Else was on the verge of sobbing. 'I can hardly bear to think of it… It's being said that these work camps are no such thing. That the Jews are being sent to camps to be murdered. Could that be possible, Ernst?' Else gripped Ernst's arm tightly. 'You're a member of the military. Could that be possible?'

Despite his shock at Else's words, Ernst remained calm and patted gently the hand gripping his arm. 'No, Else. Not possible. It would be against the Military Code. Wild rumours always abound in wartime. Put it out of your mind, Else.' He paused before continuing, but he couldn't postpone the dreaded task any longer.

'I'm afraid, dear Else, that you must prepare for a shock. I'm sorry I lied, but I *have* come about Max.' He took hold of her hand tightly. In return, Else looked horrified at what he might say and yet her eyes pleaded him to lie if it was bad news.

'I regret that Max is dead, Else. Shot down. I've been to the Air Force Headquarters and there's no doubt, but witnesses reported his death as instantaneous. There was no fire. Typically, he died saving another airman.' Else pulled her hand away violently as she took in the news and then beat her fists on her lap quickly and hard.

'It can't be. He was so fond of life and so young. Please tell me it's a mistake and he was only wounded and is a prisoner of war.' She looked Ernst straight in the eyes with her own eyes full of tears. Ernst couldn't bring himself to speak and just responded with a wretched look. Else looked down.

'So, it's true then. I've lost everything.' Her words cut Ernst deep.

'I'm truly sorry to bring you this news, Else. I loved my brother, too.' Ernst suddenly made a decision without thinking through the ramifications. 'And to that end, I'm going to stand by you as if you had already married. Let me find you some better accommodation. By all means stay working here, but let me help.' He almost pleaded the last words.

Else stood up and touched Ernst gently on the shoulder. 'It's a kind offer and, perhaps, I might seek your help, but for now, Ernst, I need time to myself to take in the news… and I really must return to work. Would you think it rude if I let you find your own way back?' She thrust out her hand to shake that of Ernst. Dejectedly, Ernst took it.

'But thank you for coming, Ernst. It can't have been easy for you and I appreciated it being you. Please write to me when you return to the coast.' With great dignity in Ernst's view, she shook his hand firmly, stiffened her back and exited the room.

Chapter 19
August 1942

The short, blond, khaki-clad officer alighted from the train at Bay Horse, near Lancaster. It was a common sight in wartime and would not ordinarily have generated any notice or quizzical looks, but on both upper shoulders he wore a flash inscribed 'RN Commando', instead of pips on his epaulettes he wore wavy stripes showing the rank of a lieutenant commander and, most striking of all, this officer wore a green beret with the Royal Navy crown pinned on it. Monty might well have worn his naval uniform, but he could not resist showing off his newly-acquired green beret. Having successfully completed the course, despite his expectations and previous limited military training, he had been granted a week's leave before he had to report to the Naval Intelligence Division at the Admiralty. He had decided to make a brief stopover in Lancashire to see Lucy Cunningham and her mother before going on to Wiltshire to see his family. He had to admit to himself that he had felt some pride in the awe with which some of his fellow servicemen had regarded him on the train from Scotland. Although barely a year had passed since their formation, the Commandos were already being regarded as elite troops and to be fair, on his chest he now wore alongside the bronze oakleaf for being mentioned-in-despatches, a silver oakleaf denoting the award of the King's Commendation for Bravery for his work in Admiral Dunbar-Naismith's garden, and the very rare crimson and blue striped ribbon of the George Medal.

However, despite his new heroic status, unlike when he had been working for DTMI fewer than three months earlier, he no longer had access to a car and driver. He had no choice but to walk with his kit the two-and-a-bit miles from the station to the village of Dolphinholme. Before the death of Lucy's father, he might have been able to arrange a lift since John Cunningham had operated the local garage and taxi service. However, what was two to three miles to a newly-trained commando?

Monty had rung ahead to book a room in the local public house and an hour later he was ordering dinner over a pint of a local ale. It was too late to call on the Cunninghams, but he used the pub's telephone to inform Mrs Cunningham that he was staying nearby and, if convenient, would call the following morning. He was disappointed to learn that Lucy was out on one of her charitable calls and unable to come to the telephone, but he was relieved to learn from Jane Cunningham that Lucy would be free after chapel the following morning. Monty looked forward to seeing her surprise at his new uniform.

The following morning, Monty knocked on the front door of the Cunningham's house adjacent to the garage. He noted without surprise that the garage was under new management and hoped that the business had been sold. To his delight, it was Lucy herself who answered the door.

'Can I help you?' she asked, looking at him suspiciously. To Monty's chagrin it was clear that she didn't recognise him.

'Good morning, Lucy. It's Monty.' He removed his precious beret to reveal his fair hair and more of his face. Lucy almost jumped with surprise.

'But it can't be,' she replied. 'What happened to your crumpled uniform?' Monty blushed at the memory of his last visit following his visit to Barrow. 'Don't just stand there, you fool. Come in.' She stood aside to let Monty enter the hall and called through to Jane, 'Mother, we've a soldier come to call.'

'Really, lass?' Jane replied. 'But we're not expecting anyone. Show whoever it is into the parlour. I'll be through in a minute.'

Lucy followed Monty through to the parlour and scrutinised Monty quizzically. 'Well, well, well, your Lordship. You have changed since your last visit… and I don't just mean the uniform. You've lost weight and look fitter. Sit down and tell me all.'

Monty was disappointed at the mockery of her greeting. When they had last parted, there had been some trace of affection in Lucy towards him.

'I've been on a course in Scotland. It was purgatory really… being forced to climb mountains and cross rivers crawling along ropes. As I told your mother last night, I'm on a week's leave and just thought I'd call in on my way south. You look well.' Monty was flattered to note that Lucy had clearly taken some care in her appearance before greeting him.

'But why the change of uniform and what's that... 'RN Commando' badge on your shoulders?'

'I can't really say, Lucy... I don't mean for security,' he added quickly. 'I mean I don't rightly know myself yet. I'll find out next week when I return to London. No doubt I'll then be back in a blue suit.' Just then, Jane entered the room and nearly dropped the tea tray with the shock of seeing Monty.

'Oh, it's Mister Montcalm! I had no idea it was you.' She laid down the tray and embraced Monty warmly. 'Lucy's such a tease. What's this soldier uniform, then?' Jane stepped back to observe Monty more closely. 'Oh, my Lord!' she exclaimed and covered her mouth with her hand. 'I recognise that medal ribbon from Stephen's uniform. It's the George Medal. My, Monty, whatever have you been up to. You're a hero!' She kissed Monty on the cheek. 'Look, Lucy! The George Medal.'

This time Lucy seemed impressed and dropped her mocking tone. 'Goodness, Monty. I should have noticed. Come on, tell us what you've been up to. I'll pour the tea.'

Monty was pleased that Lucy was back on familiar terms with him. 'There's not much to tell, really. I helped a chum defuze a new type of mine in the Bristol Channel and somebody put us both up for a gong. Nothing like Stephen's heroism, of course. This tea really is refreshing, Mrs Cunningham.'

'I'm sorry I couldn't offer you slice a cake, lad, but we can't get the sugar,' Jane replied. 'But why are you dressed as a soldier?'

'It's just temporary, Mrs Cunningham. I had to do a course in Scotland and khaki was more practical for traipsing up Ben Nevis and back. I'll no doubt be back in naval uniform soon.'

'Don't give us that, Monty,' Lucy retorted. 'We're both aware what the Commandos are doing. You've been trained to go on their raids, haven't you?'

'Honestly, Lucy. As I said a few moments ago, I don't know what I'll be doing and nor why. Anyway, enough of me. How's Stephen?'

'You know he's been posted to South Africa? We had a long letter from him saying he had arrived safely and was getting settled into his new job. When was that, Lucy?'

'About ten days ago, Mother. He posted it in June. He didn't say much, though, Monty. You know how taciturn he can be, Monty.

Most of it was a description of the flying fish on the voyage and the weather in Simon's Town. He seemed cheerful, though.'

'Lucky devil,' Monty replied. 'All that sunshine and not much to do, I bet. He'll be living the life of Riley.' Monty replaced his tea cup on its saucer and placed both on the table. 'Now, Lucy, it's a lovely day and I've never been round Dolphinholme. Would you mind showing me around?'

Lucy quickly finished her own tea and promptly stood. 'I'd love to. You wouldn't mind would you, Mother?'

'Not at all, lass. It'll give me time to prepare lunch. Mister Montcalm, you will stay for lunch, won't you. It's just a chicken salad.'

'I'd be delighted, Mrs Cunningham, but please call me Monty. After all, I feel almost at home here.'

'I'm right pleased to hear you say that, Monty. Now enjoy your walk and don't come back for at least an hour. I want my kitchen in peace.' Jane looked at Lucy meaningfully, but Monty didn't understand the silent message.

Within thirty minutes, Monty was realising that it had been a bad idea to wear his khaki battledress. Lucy led him along the River Wyre and down to the mill. The mill was working flat out, noisily churning out worsted cloth and Monty wondered if the cloth was being woven to manufacture uniforms. It was here that Monty met several workers, mainly women with a few disabled and old men, who treated him as a hero for being a commando. He felt a fraud. He had only completed the Commando course, a feat in itself, but had certainly seen no action and it was embarrassing to admit this. Lucy found it most amusing.

'You realise that my reputation has been enhanced considerably in the village now, Monty? Walking out with a commando. My stock is so high.' She giggled - coquettishly in Monty's opinion.

'Is that what we're doing, Lucy? Walking out together, I mean.'

Lucy responded by first smiling and then taking his arm. 'I think so. We have known each other a while now.'

The remark pleased Monty and gave him some food for thought as they returned back along the river bank, walking arm in arm, but in silence. Eventually, Monty made up his mind.

'Lucy, I have a favour to ask.'

'Try me, Monty.'

Monty fingered his GM medal ribbon. 'The thing is, Lucy, I've been gazetted for this George Medal, but with all the rush to send me up to Scotland, I've yet to be invested. No doubt, I'll find out when it's to be on my return to London, but I wondered if you might accompany me to the Palace for it… I'm hoping it will be before the start of the new term.' He looked at Lucy anxiously. Lucy smiled pleasantly back, but took a little time to respond.

'I've probably a little more experience of these things than you, Monty, as it happens. Mother and I attended Stephen's last ceremony. Are you aware that only two guests may attend? What about your parents?'

'Oh! I hadn't thought of that. I can't very well ask my mother without my father. Drat!' The smile faded from Monty's face as he considered the problem. He arrived at a solution.

'Look, if the timing's right, would you still travel down to London to meet me? I could ask a friend to put you up and you could meet my parents.'

'That sounds rather daunting, Monty. And doesn't being introduced so formally to one's parents suggest too much about our friendship?'

'Oh!' Monty repeated. 'I hadn't thought about how it might be construed… but I don't frankly care, Lucy.' Monty let go of Lucy's arm and took her hand instead. 'Lucy, you must realise that I love you.' He looked pleadingly into her eyes, praying that his advances wouldn't be rebuffed.

'I know that. You're a dear thing, Monty,' she replied and kissed him briefly on the lips. 'Let's just see what happens, shall we?'

Monty felt deflated and the pair finished their walk in silence.

Chapter 20

'Glad to see you looking so fit and well, Monty.' Fleming ushered Monty into Room 39 of the Admiralty, a less luxurious setting than Boodles. 'And congratulations on the new gong. You won't have room for many more soon. How was the course?'

'To be honest, Ian, I hated it, but I'm glad I did it.'

'Really? I'd have thought a few weeks in the glens during summer would be fun,' said Fleming lighting a cigarette. 'Smoke?' He offered his pack of cigarettes to Monty, but the latter declined them. 'What was so awful about it, then?'

'I think the biggest challenge for me was the physical side of it… and not just the marching. Tossing logs, I ask you. Colonel Vaughan certainly takes no prisoners. I thought I'd die. Of our course only two thirds made it through. I hate the sight of Ben Nevis now. It would have helped had I had longer prior warning of the course so I could prepare for it.'

Fleming removed a gold encased notepad from his inside jacket and extracted a gold pencil from it. 'I'll make a note of that, thanks, Monty. You were only the first of several dark-blue chaps I want to put through that training.' Fleming smiled apologetically.

'And why would a naval officer want to learn to scale cliffs or mount small boat raids at night?'

'I think that will become clear when you go on your first op, old thing. If you're going in with the Royals, you'll need to keep up.' The hairs on Monty's nape tingled at the mention of going on an operation, but he didn't interrupt Fleming's flow. 'Indeed, I might try to attend the same training myself… If I can tear myself away from my desk. Any other feedback I should have?'

'You'd be mad to do the course without good reason, Ian. Did you know that they use live ammunition on the final exercises? One of our Dutch troop was wounded by a bullet and I heard a Frenchman had been killed.'

'No, I didn't know that. Colonel Vaughan clearly means business and sets high standards. How else might we prepare naval personnel for the course?'

'Since you asked, Ian, I think some more military training. We had to become adept at stripping down and using all sorts of weaponry and I hadn't handled a rifle since my days at *King Arthur*. Two of the Dutch officers on my course had to give me extra tuition or else I would never have handled the course. And demolitions is something else. I know one end of a detonator from another and have handled this new plastic explosive before, but I bet most sailors haven't.'

Fleming made another note and then closed his notepad and replaced the pencil to suggest there would be no more feedback. He leaned forward earnestly. 'Thank you, Monty. I'll bear it in mind and, perhaps, discuss it with one of the Royal Marines staff. But for now, I expect you want to know what's in store for you.'

'It has been on my mind. Yes.'

Fleming rose and selected a file from a drawer in the office desk. 'There have been a few positive developments since we last met, Monty. Firstly, the concept of the Intelligence Assault Unit, IAU, has been approved. It's to become a permanent body under the command of the new Chief of Combined Ops, Lord Mountbatten. To update you, the new force will now comprise three elements. A military section comprising Royal Marines only – as before, they'll do all the necessary to get the rest of the unit into the target – kick the doors down to let you in, as it were. Then there will be a naval section comprising officers trained by the NID in intelligence duties. Finally, there's the technical section or troop. It will comprise solely RNVR officers with specialist knowledge of documents, submarines, wireless, radar, mines and torpedoes. As you know, that's why I sounded you out earlier in the year. However, given your record as an intelligence officer, I think you might fit equally well in both the naval and the technical troops. That's why I wanted you to do the full Commando course.'

The penny dropped with Monty on hearing the latter few words.

'I've had approval to recruit 45 permanent members of the IAU for the naval and military troops, but the composition of the technical troop will be according to the nature of the planned pinch.' This time, Monty had to interrupt.

'And do you have any such pinches in mind?'

'Ah! I was coming to that. Don't worry, all will be revealed. You might be putting your training to good use quite shortly. Should you

149

survive, you can then tell me just which bits of your course weren't useful.'

Monty didn't like the doubt expressed about his chances of survival, but ignored the comment. 'So, what are your plans for me now, Ian?' he replied instead.

'I want you to remove yourself and your dunnage down to Amersham. There's an old derelict farm near there that's the HQ of the IAU.'

'It sounds idyllic,' Monty retorted sarcastically.

'Cold Comfort Farm it may be,' Fleming replied, 'But it's ideal for our purposes. Good countryside with plenty of hedges and fields for our night exercises and room to store safely all our kit, including the weapons and explosives. I'll have a driver take you there. Mountbatten's keen to follow up the raid on St Nazaire with another very soon and you'll begin your training immediately.'

'More training?' Monty queried.

'I'm afraid so, old chap. If you can't take a joke, you shouldn't have joined.'

*****

Before dawn on the 19th of August, Monty was crossing the Channel and heading for Dieppe harbour as part of *Operation Jubilee*. 10,000 British and Canadian troops and 60 squadrons of Royal Air Force and US Eagle squadrons were intent on giving the Germans a bloody nose. The IAU, embarked in the gunboat HMS *Locust* were part of the Royal Marines 'A' Commando participating in the raid. *Locust* had been built for operations in the Yangtze River, but had seen action at Dunkirk. Ordinarily, her flat bottom, ideal for her original role on inshore operations, would have made life extremely uncomfortable for the men crossing the Channel that morning in her, but it was a still and even warm night. Most importantly, it was moonless.

The raiding force was spread out to hit six different beaches along twelve miles of enemy-occupied coast, four of the beaches in the town itself. The men landing on these beaches comprised infantry, largely Canadian, and were supported by tanks. Their objective was to take and hold Dieppe for a short while to test the feasibility of making an opposed landing when opening up the Second Front.

Meanwhile, the outer wings, comprising Royal Marines commandos and some US Army Rangers, were tasked with destroying two large coastal batteries threatening Allied shipping in the Channel. The *Locust*'s objective was to disembark her 200 Royal Marines commandos in Dieppe's harbour. The majority of the marines would then cut out all the barges and trawlers they came across for *Locust* to tow out to sea, but the IAU had a completely different objective. Their target was a hotel along the quayside of the harbour. This was the headquarters of the local *Kriegsmarine* and Fleming wanted the IAU to seize the German Navy's cypher machines, code books and whatever secret documents his men could discover.

Monty stood on the bridge of *Locust*, doing his best to keep out of the way of the bridge crew led by Commander Ryder VC. Like the other members of the IAU, Monty wore a steel helmet and carried a backpack, but he wasn't encumbered with a Lee-Enfield rifle or Bren gun. He merely carried a Webley pistol on his hip for self-protection. More experienced hands would deal with the enemy. Until this morning, Monty had thought the live pyrotechnics used by the training staff at Achnacarry frightening. He had spent many mornings racing across Loch Lochy in small boats in practice raids on the shore, but not even Colonel Vaughan had been able to lay on the spectacle before him now. Waves of RAF Hurricanes were shooting up the shore defences with cannon fire. Others were engaged in dogfights above with silver *Focke-Wulfs*, joined by dotted lines of red tracer. More worryingly to the men onboard the gunboat, they had engaged the attention of the German gunners ashore. Both from escarpments to the left of the harbour and from the clifftop to their right, shells were being aimed in their direction. Ryder ordered speed for fifteen knots. Soon afterwards, just as Monty saw ahead the mole protecting the narrow entrance to the harbour, one of the shells struck home with a gigantic explosion. Instinctively, Monty hit the deck and cowered in a ball, his arms over his head. It wasn't that he was paralysed with fear, he was just numb with the shock of the explosion.

The first sense to return was his smell. Monty couldn't hear anything, but his nose detected the whiff of burnt explosive. Then his hearing returned and he heard groans of pain from the bridge roof. Slowly, he stretched out and checked himself for wounds. He was fine and he staggered to his feet. In his peripheral vision he spotted the entrance to the harbour moving to his left as the Captain tried to steer his command away from the concentrated fire. For the sake of something to do and to occupy his mind, Monty headed for the noise of the wounded. To his shock, a huge section of the upperworks on the starboard side had disappeared. The pained moans were coming both from the deck below and the bridge roof. With the ladder from the bridge roof to the deck below reduced to nothing more than a tangle of molten metal, Monty jumped down to assist the throng of wounded below. Already a sick berth attendant was on hand.

'Anything I can do to help?' Monty asked.

'Aye, sir. There is. That red-haired lad over there.' The SBA pointed to a slumped figure against a pock-marked bulkhead. 'He's done for, sir. Would you go through his pockets and remove any personal stuff to be sent back home? Orders are for all the dead to be thrown overboard. I'll get someone else to give you a hand with that later, sir.'

Monty did as directed, but thought it the worst thing in his life. To pick the pockets of a corpse, even for the best of reasons! The marine lay there, his blue eyes staring at the fading stars above, his facial expression almost one of surprise. But for the mass of blood and body tissue where his chest had once been, it might have made for a peaceful scene. As Monty went about the frightful task, he heard every gun of the *Locust* open fire with a deafening din on the cliff top above.

A few minutes later, another red-haired man, but this time a young lieutenant, helped Monty heave the red-haired corpse over the side. It was young Lieutenant Huntington-Whiteley, a fellow Etonian and grandson of Stanley Baldwin.

'Monty, there's been a change of plan.'

'You do surprise me, Peter!'

Whitely ignored the sarcasm. 'Instead of disembarking in the harbour, we're to board a tank landing craft and land at Red Beach. It's only a mile from the harbour. Other than that, the plan holds. You okay?'

'I'm fine, thanks, Peter. Lead the way.'

Soon afterwards, now in full daylight, Monty scrambled down the rope nets into the bottom of the waiting Landing Craft Mechanised (LCM). As the senior officer and following the custom of the

Service even in the thick of action, he was the last to embark and immediately the LCM's skipper, a scruffily-clad young sub lieutenant, ordered his small crew to cast off. Whilst most of the marines took shelter behind the bullet-proof ramp forming the bows of the landing craft, Monty made his way to the wheelhouse in order to gain a better view of the events unfolding around him. To his surprise, the LCM joined several other landing craft to form a flotilla just a mile off the town's main beach. Protecting the flotilla were Free French minesweepers giving fire support with heavy machine guns and a few strange vessels that seemed no more than mere platforms for 20-millimeter Oerlikons and 40-millimeter 'pom-pom' guns.

Monty's view of the beach was soon obscured by a thick and choking bank of smoke laid to protect the flotilla from the German guns. Mercifully, the LCM passed through it unscathed and appeared 200 yards off the sloping beach ahead, itself a graveyard of men in khaki, tanks and other landing craft. The marines surged forward, ready to wade ashore as soon as the LCM beached and the ramp was lowered. Monty hung back in the wheelhouse. His responsibility was to follow in the wake cut by the marines. As a result, he witnessed the first landing craft hitting the beach and immediately coming under a welter of shell and heavy machine gun fire. Nonetheless, the ramp was lowered and the men stormed the beach, led by a major. Minutes later, Monty saw the major sheltering in the cover of a burnt-out tank and signalling back to his CO that the enemy force was too strong. Reports that the beach had been taken by the Canadian infantry were clearly flawed and Monty saw in another landing craft the Commando's colonel wearing white gloves to gesture to the remaining landing craft to fall back.

The sub lieutenant commanding the IAU's craft immediately spun the wheel to open the distance from the storm of gunfire on beach. Monty lost sight of the CO's landing craft, but looked back as his own LCM steadied on course. About five other landing craft had obeyed the order to withdraw, but to Monty's horror, the command craft received a direct hit from a shell. Some of the survivors had been lighting smoke pots in the hope of putting the enemy gunners off their aim, but already fuel was spreading on the surface of the sea around the stricken landing craft. Inevitably, the fuel ignited and the landing craft was lost in a sea of flames. However, just as Monty was intoning a silent prayer for his own deliverance, the LCM came to a shuddering stop. 'We've run aground on something underwater,' he heard the skipper shout to his crew. Unnervingly, the LCM tilted to port savagely, throwing everyone off their feet. The young sub lieutenant rushed over to the side to survey the cause of the problem, but immediately clutched his stomach as it was stitched with a line of bullets. Monty immediately took command and threw the engine levers into reverse in an effort to free the LCM from the obstruction, but whilst the two Ford V8 engines growled ferociously, the LCM didn't move. They were stuck fast and worse, the guns ashore were finding their range.

Monty shouted to Huntington-Whiteley. 'Get your men off, Peter. It's every man for himself now.'

Huntington-Whiteley waved in acknowledgement and turned to his sergeant. 'Sergeant-major, everyone off-kit and swim for it, but see if you can get that ramp lowered first.'

'Aye aye, sir,' the sergeant-major replied and passed on the orders to the other marines before grabbing a Bren gun and returning fire up at the cliffs. Meanwhile, a group of marines started to kick the ramp door down. Others were tearing off their packs and webbing before inflating their Mae West life jackets. Their preparations were rudely interrupted by a German shell. Whilst it didn't cause any additional loss of life, it did shatter one of the diesel tanks to release fuel into the sea. Monty had visions of the colonel's craft going up in flames and shouted urgently at the sergeant-major. 'Everyone over the side NOW! And I mean NOW.' He pointed at the spreading pond of fuel leaching into the sea on the port side and to a man, everyone realised the implications. They needed no further orders.

Monty slit the laces of his boots with his Commando knife, removed his boots and battledress blouse and then began pushing the laggards over the side. Only when the sergeant-major and Huntington-Whiteley were ready to abandon the LCM did he slip over the side with them. Most of the men were heading for the beach, just thirty yards off, but Monty could see it was laced with machine gun fire and, in company with Huntington-Whiteley, opted instead to swim parallel to the beach.

Despite it being a warm August day, the water was cold and the two men quickly tired. It was a further hour before they were eventually rescued by one of the strange floating gun platforms.

This they discovered was the new Landing Craft (Flak) or LCF. However, Monty's troubles weren't over when the LCF deposited him onboard the destroyer, HMS *Calpe*. The *Calpe* was not only acting as a hospital ship for the raid, but as the headquarters ship for the general commanding the 2nd Canadian Infantry Division and as such, was a prize target for the *Luftwaffe*. In the absence of prolonged air cover, it wasn't long before an attack got through and the ship was bombed, killing or wounding a quarter of her ship's company and many of the survivors rescued from the beaches. The adrenalin coursing through his veins earlier had long dissipated. As Monty listened to the sounds of the air attack and screams from the wounded, he kept repeating to himself, 'Oh God, don't let me die.'

Chapter 21
September 1942

Although it had not been his choice to serve in South Africa, Stephen had to admit that he was enjoying life there, although he would have relished more to do. The resident population of both Simon's Town and nearby Cape Town could not have been more friendly. Some of the Boers still tended to be anti-British, but as they tended to live inland, Stephen rarely encountered them. However, to his horror, initially at least, his duties included running the officers' tennis club. He had never played tennis in his life and feared the social aspects of his new duties. However, he had taken some lessons and now found himself a popular partner for the mixed doubles. A number of tea planters in Ceylon had sent their wives to South Africa, fearing an attack on Ceylon by the Japanese. The ladies were always looking for single men with whom to partner at tennis or the many dances organised locally. However, Stephen drew the line at dancing and he had learned to avoid partnering some of the planters' wives on the tennis courts. A significant number seemed predatory.

Other than his commitments to the tennis club, one of Stephen's main duties was training members of the newly-formed South African Naval Forces (SANF) in bomb and mine disposal. Despite the work not being arduous or time-consuming, he had been granted an assistant, Sub Lieutenant Jan Kronje, formerly of the South African volunteer reserves. The previous day, a German moored mine had washed ashore and Stephen had shown Kronje how to render it safe. Now they were in Cape Town docks in front of four very enthusiastic officers of the SANF. Kronje introduced them.

'Sir, this is Lieutenant Boucher... Sub Lieutenant de Kok... Sub Lieutenant Steyn and finally, Professor McCain from Cape Town University.'

Stephen noted that McCain was dressed, too, as a sub lieutenant in the SANF, despite his exalted academic title. He shook hands with them all before beginning his lecture.

'Good m-morning, gentlemen. As it happens, by chance we have here a genuine example of a German m-moored mine. It came ashore yesterday on the b-beach.'

Stephen noted a certain unease amongst his audience, most of whom had stepped back a pace. He laughed.

'D-don't worry. Jan and I made it s-safe yesterday.'

'It still contains nearly a ton of TNT, though' Kronje added mischievously. 'Isn't that right, sir?'

'Y-yes. That's true,' Stephen replied quietly, 'But I assure you it's s-still quite safe.' He kicked the mine, releasing a loud and hollow ring, before taking a hammer to one of the horns. All bar the professor in the audience immediately hit the deck in prone positions. Sheepishly, they rose after twenty to thirty seconds and dusted themselves off.

'TNT is a k-killer in the right circumstances, gentlemen, but it's quite stupid. The real d-danger is in the firing circuits and these can be quite c-clever.'

Knowing that amongst his audience there might be some mining engineers, Stephen enquired if any of them had experience of firing circuits. The professor raised his hand.

'I head the Department of Electrical Engineering at the university, *bro*.'

'Then I'm delighted to m-meet you, P-professor.' Stephen leaped forward to shake McCain's hand once more. 'You probably know m-more on this subject than me.'

'*Yebo*, some might think that, but judging from those medal ribbons, we'd all be *dumkops* to ignore your words of wisdom.'

For the next thirty minutes Stephen explained the different methods the Germans and British used to fire their mines. He had brought along with the mine the large screwed plug he and Jan had used to force the mine's spindle back into its disarmed position and showed them the detonator and charge they had removed.

'Now, according to Jan, you w-wanted some excitement this morning, so we're g-going to show you how to b-burn out the explosive.' A further murmur of disquiet went round the South African officers, but Stephen ignored it and nodded to his assistant. 'Jan…'

Kronje removed the plate screwed at the base of the mine and laid out some oily rags and a pair of wooden tongs, such as might be used for washing clothes. 'Professor, you might wish to help with this. I suggest the rest of you stand upwind.' Kronje handed the professor some matches to set alight the rags, before using the tongs to place the burning wad inside the mine's cavity. Stephen continued his lecture.

'Gentlemen, the safest w-way to dispose of a mine or unexploded b-bomb is to blow it up in a safe p-place. If that's not p-possible, make it safe by removing the d-detonator and charge.' The TNT was now burning well with a dark cloud of sulphurous smoke, causing some coughing.

'An alternative to b-burning the explosive is to s-steam it out, but the b-best way of all, is just to b-blow up the whole thing. Who doesn't like a g-good b-bang?'

*****

'Sir, but you must come.'

'N-no, Jan. I w-wouldn't enjoy it.'

'But that's nonsense, sir. According to Sonja, Julia's a real *punda*. I mean really good looking.' Stephen continued to look unconvinced.

'In any case, Sonja can't leave her guest behind and she's really looking forward to the event,' Kronje pleaded.

Stephen was moved by the plea. He didn't want to attend HMS *Afrikander*'s wardroom Ladies' Night, and he certainly didn't want a blind date, but nor did he wish to spoil his young assistant's evening.

'Go on, sir. Be a *bielie*,' Kronje replied persuasively. Stephen took another look at the concern in the young officer's face and his heart melted.

'Very well, then. B-but I'm doing it for your little *b-bokkie* and not you.'

'What do you, *pommies*, say? You're a real Gent? Is that right, sir?'

Stephen laughed. 'G-get out of my sight before I change my m-mind.'

*****

158

Julia Webber-Tarr was, indeed, a real *punda*. She was tall, slim and very athletic-looking. Her dark hair was cut shoulder-length with a fringe that was just too long to show off her dark eyes to best advantage. However, the attention of most of the men present wasn't drawn to her eyes and face, however beautiful they were. Their eyes were drawn like magnets either to the enormous diamond pendant presented by her low-cut evening gown or the two large, curved breasts in whose valley the pendant nestled. On seeing her, Stephen could barely speak with the surprise. She was possibly the most beautiful woman he had ever met.

Stephen had been nominated as the wardroom's vice-president and as such, was seated at the bottom of one of the tables with Julia to his right and Sonja to his left, Kronje sitting on the other side of Sonja. Julia appeared at total ease in the company of the *Afrikander*'s officers and their ladies. Despite her position at the bottom of the table, she was gaining much attention. Sonja, on the other hand, seemed a mousy young woman who made little effort to make conversation with him, clinging instead to Kronje. Accordingly, whilst relieved that he didn't need to make much conversation, Stephen felt a little lonely in his place.

An officer to Kronje's left made a remark about the size of the diamond in Julia's pendant.

'It's not mine,' she admitted. 'It belonged to my late-mother and Pa normally keeps it in the bank, but I insisted on bringing it along tonight. Such a beautiful jewel is wasted in a bank vault, don't you think?'

Unlike many of the South Africans Stephen had met, Julia sounded very English. He decided he ought to make some effort to make conversation with her.

'F-forgive me for m-mentioning this,' Stephen cursed the fact that his stutter had worsened through nerves. 'You d-don't sound v-very Afrikaans. D-did you g-go to school abroad?' he finally uttered.

'How clever of you to notice... Was it Stephen? After my mother died, Pa packed me off to a school in England. It was on the south coast, near Brighton.'

'N-not Roedean?' Stephen asked.

'It was. Do you know of it?' Julia turned to him and it seemed to Stephen, took an interest in him for the first time in the evening. Her eyes fixed on his medals.

'I d-do. I did my naval training d-down the road at Lancing. B-by then the g-girls had moved to Cumbria, though.'

'Really? And why was that... er, Stephen?' It was the first time that she had used Stephen's name.

'As ever the w-war. The Navy t-took it over for t-torpedo training.'

'I didn't know that.' Julia sipped her wine and there was a return to the lull in conversation, but she broke it. 'I hated it there, but it could have been worse. I might have been sent to the sister school in Jo'burg. Now that would have been rather too close to home.' She laughed. She indicated Stephen's medals. 'Have you seen much action, then?'

Stephen almost blushed at the attention. 'N-no. None at all. This is my f-first t-time outside Britain.

Julia frowned in puzzlement. 'But you seem to have more medals than most of the others around here.'

Kronje had clearly been listening in to the conversation and cut in. 'Don't let his modesty fool you, Julia, my dear. You're addressing a real legend.'

'I'm confused, Jan. You've no medals. Half the officers here have no medals. For what precisely are they handed out?'

'No need to be confused, *Engel*. Tell her, sir.'

This time Stephen did blush in embarrassment, but his confusion was spared by a Royal Navy lieutenant to Julia's right, himself sporting the Distinguished Service Cross.

'Allow me to explain, Miss. From his left to right the officer is wearing the silver leaf of the King's Commendation for Bravery, the George Medal and finally, the George Cross. At a guess, I'd say you're a mine disposal officer.'

Stephen was still too flustered to reply, but Kronje responded instead and rather proudly. 'He is, sir, and I'm his assistant.'

The officer raised his glass of wine to Stephen. 'I salute you, sir. I doubt I will ever meet a braver man. I'm Arthur Sandys-Clarke of the *Shropshire*. May I know your name?'

'C-Cunningham. S-Stephen Cunningham.'

'Cunningham, hey? Not related to ABC, are you?'

'No.' Stephen shook his head and returned to his knife and fork, but felt Julia's hand over his right hand. She grasped it gently.

'You're not a talkative *oakie*, are you? Don't worry. I'll talk for us both, shall I?' Stephen just looked at Julia with relief.

'Very well. I'm Julia Webber-Tarr. I live near Kimberley. My father owns a diamond mine there... and a few other business interests, besides. My Ma died when I was nine. I have a sister three years younger. She's married to a lecturer at the university in Cape Town, so I come down quite regularly to see her. She and Sonja are good friends, so that's how we met. Now other than my age and vital statistics, which I can tell you are far too much a gentleman to be interested in, I can't think of anything else to say about myself, so it's over to you. Tell me something about yourself.'

Gradually and patiently, Julia teased something of Stephen's life story out of him, but nothing would persuade him to tell her about his work and how he earned his medals. He did tell her about his investitures, though.

'So, you've actually met the King?'

'Yes. Twice actually.'

'*Eish*! Did he speak to you?'

'Yes, but I can't remember everything he s-said. I was too nervous. B-but he did say I was the only man to whom he had given the George C-Cross and the George Medal.'

Julia patted his hand. 'There. You must be very proud... and your stammer's improved. Who knows? You might yet start to enjoy yourself. Tell me, have you seen much of South Africa yet?'

'No. I've not been here long enough yet... But I am going up to G-Ganspan with Jan soon. I don't kn-know where it is, though.'

'Really? What a coincidence! That's only about 60 miles from my home. What are you doing there? It's a bit of a one-horse-*dorp*.'

'I'm not sure I should b-be telling you.'

Kronje must have been listening in to the conversation as he interrupted. 'It's no secret, sir. Everyone knows about the naval armaments' depot there. It's handy for both coasts and too far inland for the Germans and Japanese to bomb. I bet you already knew that, Julia.'

'Actually, I didn't, Jan. But I did hear that there's an internment camp nearby for the Germans from SWA.'

'SWA? Where's that?' Stephen asked.

161

'South West Africa,' Julia replied. 'It used to be a German colony and until the war, it still housed several thousand German speakers. Anyway, that's beside the point. You must tell me when you're visiting. You could come and stay for a while.'

The idea appealed to Stephen, but he politely declined. 'I'm afraid we w-won't be there long. We just have to inspect the m-munitions and destroy anything d-defective or out of date.'

'But isn't that dangerous?' Julia clasped her pendant to her breast and Stephen found himself looking at her chest with wonder. Worse, Julia seemed to have noticed and didn't seem to mind. Stephen looked away, blushing.

'N-not really. I hear there's a large s-salt p-pan nearby. We can s-stand a thousand yards clear if n-necessary.'

As the evening wore on, Stephen was surprised by how relaxed he began to feel in Julia's company. Most surprisingly, he made only a token protest before agreeing to join her on the dance floor, something he hadn't done since his days at university. Despite his natural modesty, he couldn't help basking with pride at the envious looks of his fellow officers, although their partners seemed more interested in the diamond at her breast. He had been careful not to drink too much of the local wines, but he, nevertheless, felt intoxicated by the sweet smell of Julia's skin, the touch of her hair against his cheek and the feel of her slender body against his. He felt himself becoming aroused and, guiltily, he had to adjust his position lest Julia should discover his secret desires.

Chapter 22
October 1942

With little else to do in Simon's Town, Stephen had become an avid reader of intelligence reports related to the use of underwater mines. One particular report had stirred his imagination. In December the year before, Italian divers had used a new form of 'human torpedo' to enter Alexandria harbour and attach charges to Royal Navy warships at their moorings. They had succeeded in sinking two battleships and damaging a destroyer and a tanker. The charges had been either suspended from the bilge keels of their targets or placed on the seabed directly underneath the ships. In all, just six highly trained and courageous men had crippled the Royal Navy's Mediterranean fleet, leaving it with no battleships. Warmed to the subject, Stephen had gone on to read that earlier in the year, the German *Abwehr* or military intelligence service, inspired by their Italian allies, had started forming its own small units of divers specialising in sabotage missions, known as *Marine Einsatz Kommandos* (MEKs). According to one snippet of a different report, the German breathing apparatus supplier, Dräger, had just patented and tested in the Aegean a new form of rebreather device with the air being contained in a back-mounted bag. Stephen was aware that rebreathers had been developed during WW1 for escape apparatus for both German and British submarines. However, this latest version had the advantage that divers could use it without fear of their oxygen bubbles escaping to the surface. They would be ideal for further sabotage attacks such as that performed by the Italians. The news led Stephen to ponder how he and his fellow RMSOs might render safe the explosive devices left behind by the enemy divers. More pertinently, what could be done were the Germans to attack the naval base at Simon's Town?

A week later, Stephen penned a memorandum to the Chief of Staff to the C-in-C South Atlantic Station. He had thought long and hard about his submission. He had concluded that the only way for RMSOs to render safe enemy-laid underwater charges would be for them to be dealt with *in situ*, that is by RMSOs trained to dive. This was not a radical idea. The Royal Navy had long been carrying out such training and the year before, Stephen's best friend other than Monty, the American Johnny Johnson, had been killed whilst diving on an acoustic mine. However, there were no such trained officers on the South Africa station and Stephen had just requested permission to learn to dive. Memories of his initial training as an RMSO had caused him some misgivings. His course had been given an introduction to diving at HMS *Excellent*. Stephen still recalled not just the claustrophobia he had suffered underwater, but the cruel and vindictive instructor, one CPO Diver 'Bunny' Warren, a coarse brute of a man who had deliberately crippled temporarily one of Stephen's fellow students, a Lieutenant Charles Lawson. However, Stephen was prepared to put his fears and discomfort aside for the good of the Service.

*****

Ernst now had a guilty secret and one that if revealed, would lead to his arrest by the *Gestapo*, torture and eventual execution for treason and yet, his recent visit to north-west Poland had started so well.

Firstly, he had passed through Berlin and had the chance to meet Else again. Some weeks earlier, she had finally accepted his offer to rehouse her in better accommodation, but had insisted on remaining in the Wedding district. She had feared that were she move back to one of the more salubrious districts of Berlin, she would once more face discrimination and eviction on the grounds of her partial Jewish ancestry. Moreover, she had wanted to continue her work at the Jewish hospital, although how long that might last, she couldn't be sure. Else had informed him that soon after his visit in the summer, the *Reich* Security department had decided that all elderly Jews were to be deported to the Theresienstadt ghetto in Czechoslovakia. The policy left little reason for her committee to continue since now only the younger and fitter Jews remained in Berlin. Moreover, since Jews were now banned from using public transport and ambulances weren't available to them, the hospital's workload had decreased markedly.

In installing Else in her new apartment, Ernst had thought it much as how he imagined it would be to set up home for a mistress. The thought had even induced him to consider the possibilities of making

Else his mistress. She was after all, very attractive and, he hoped, grateful for his help. He had even gained some sexual gratification in imagining how Else might perform in bed. Dreaming of how she might look naked and the pleasure she might offer him in return for his generosity, he had enjoyed an extremely arousing session with one of his favourite prostitutes. However, the following day, the idea had appalled him. Else had been his brother's fiancée and his offer of help had been purely out of altruism. He blushed with the shame that he could have thought to take advantage of her vulnerability.

From Berlin, Ernst had taken a long and uncomfortable rail journey to one of the AEG factories manufacturing the magnetic fuze units for the Navy and Air Force mines. This particular factory was located in Poland and he was considering using it to produce components for his latest idea, the pressure mine. Such a mine would not be triggered by magnetic or acoustic influences, although the Air Force wanted it to be combined with an acoustic unit and the Navy a magnetic unit. As a ship or submarine passed through the sea its hull would displace the water through which it was passing and the new mine would detect the change in pressure. Ernst's trials to date had not shown any proven method to sweep such mines and he had high hopes for them. However, more work still had to be done before he could seek High Command approval to put the mine into production.

It was during Ernst's factory tour that his life had not only been turned upside down, but endangered forever. Since the summer, Ernst had learned that many German factories relied on Jewish slave labour and this factory was no different. As he had passed down the assembly line for the latest magnetic units, something had drawn his attention to one of the workers. Like the rest, he wore shabby striped clothing on which was sewn the Jewish yellow star, but the man's demeanour separated him from his fellow unfortunates. He, too, looked emaciated by starvation and older than his years, but there was a light in his eyes missing in the other slave workers. Whilst they worked in a dull fashion with lifeless eyes, and cowered slightly as he and the factory's supervisors passed, by contrast, this man's eyes sparkled and he had an air of unusual confidence about him. When the rest of the tour party were examining a nearby bench, Ernst approached that of the unusual Jew. The man

165

immediately lost his confident air and surreptitiously tried to cover the unit on which he was working. Indeed, his look quickly turned to fear as Ernst stood over his shoulder and removed the rag covering the unit. On doing so, the blood drained from Ernst's face. Etched in one side of the magnetic unit's compartment was a Star of David and the words in English, *'We are with you!'* The Jew began to tremble and looked up at Ernst pleadingly and fearfully. Still shocked by his discovery, Ernst examined the magnetic unit. It didn't take more than a couple of seconds for his expert eye to note that none of the wiring of the firing unit had been connected. It was a clear case of sabotage.

As he now lay on his bed recalling the incident, Ernst still didn't understand why he had merely handed the metal cover to the Jewish labourer for him to fix and cover his treachery. Why had he not reported this act of deliberate sabotage to the factory foremen? Instead, he had merely exchanged a look of understanding with the Jew before the latter had quickly screwed on the cover plate. What if the magnetic unit was later discovered to have been sabotaged and somebody remembered Ernst examining it? What if the Jew was caught sabotaging other units and, under torture, revealed Ernst's silent complicity in his work? Despite the low Lübeck temperature outside, Ernst sweated throughout his sleepless night.

*****

To be back in naval uniform was a great relief to Monty after his trials and tribulations in the raid on Dieppe. When he had volunteered to join Fleming's IAU, he had felt unappreciated and the prospect of action had offered a thrilling and welcome break from his office routine. Since then, his work had been recognised with the George Medal and he now realised that although unexciting on the surface, his intelligence work was vital to the war effort. Moreover, he still broke out in a cold sweat sometimes when he thought of the blood and carnage he had seen close-hand on the botched Dieppe operation. Fleming had been pleased, despite the operation's failure, and warned Monty to expect another mission before the end of the year. In the meantime, Monty was enjoying the tedium of life in London and was working on a special project.

Monty had long been intrigued by how the Germans swept the British mines. If he could work out how that was done, then other elements of the Admiralty might be able to disrupt the enemy's mine clearance efforts. Before embarking for Dieppe, one of Fleming's colleagues in DNI had tipped him the wink that a loose-tongued German seaman had talked in a waterfront bar of his ship being fitted in the bows with '*a whacking great lump of iron, a kind of huge magnet*'. It seemed obvious that the Germans' equivalent of the towed 'Double-Ell' magnetic sweep was a ship especially fitted out to destroy magnetic mines in the waters ahead of its path, but Monty's participation in the raid on Dieppe had prevented him following up the lead. However, a recent cache of documents captured in Dieppe now focused Monty's attention back on the problem.

The documents mentioned a ship the Germans called a *Sperrbrecher* or barrier-breaker, and that these ships were used to destroy the British magnetic mines by emitting lines of magnetic force ahead of their path. When the magnetic field created reached a mine, the mine's magnetic firing unit would be triggered and the mine would explode harmlessly. A seed of an idea started to germinate in Monty's brain and he quizzed one of his scientific colleagues about it.

'Why certainly,' his colleague had responded. 'If you could discover the parameters of the magnetic field generated by the *Sperrbrecher*, then my associates could design a mine that wouldn't explode ahead of the ship, but right under the keel of the bally thing.'

Monty put in a request to his intelligence colleagues to ask the French and Belgian agents to gather any further information possible on the characteristics and operations of the *Sperrbrechers*.

*****

Monty was surprised by how quickly the Allies' secret agents on mainland Europe came back with the precious information he had requested. When Captain Maitland-Dougall returned to the office, Monty briefed him on the findings.

'I think the Germans are having to put far more effort into mine clearance than we had appreciated, sir. I've just discovered that their

Sperrbrechers are quite hefty ships. They might otherwise be more gainfully employed as freighters or even armed raiders.'

Maitland-Dougall sat down and turned to Monty. 'And how is that so, Monty?'

'According to these intel reports, the *Sperrbrechers* are around 10,000 to 14,000 tons in displacement and over 400 feet in length.'

'Phew,' the captain whistled. 'I take your point. Go on.'

'There's not much else to add, sir. Apparently, the magnet and electrified coil in the bows weigh 400 to 600 tons. Naturally, the hulls have been reinforced to protect the ships from the close-proximity explosions and in case that doesn't work, the holds have been filled with empty casks and drums to add an extra reserve of buoyancy.'

Maitland-Dougall took out the reading spectacles he had recently taken to wearing and gestured to Monty to hand over the report.

'And another thing of interest, sir,' Monty added as he handed over the report, 'The ships are well-armed with anti-aircraft weapons and when not clearing mines, they're being used as escorts for convoys or *U*-boats. They're in use all the way down from the Baltic to the Bay of Biscay.'

Maitland-Dougall scanned the document quickly and thought hard about its content. 'That's all very well, Monty, but we still have no details of the vessels' magnetic signatures. And I'm not sure we have any hope of gaining it… short of finding ourselves a technician willing to turn traitor, I suppose.'

'I fear you may be right, sir. The intelligence officer with whom I discussed the report didn't offer reassurance on that point either, sir. It's all very well for our agents to overhear snippets of a conversation between tipsy seamen, but the technical information we're after is hardly the subject of bar room talk.'

'Hmm. I suppose a bribe might work, but it would mean our agents taking even more risks. Are you still set on this idea of yours to sink a *Sperrbrecher*?'

'Given what we know now, sir… Yes, if at all possible. I hadn't appreciated before the value of these ships to the enemy.'

'Well, we'll have to see what turns up. For now, however, that's not your concern, Monty. I've just returned from a meeting with the Combined Ops staff and they're laying on a special operation next month. Fleming and his gang have put in a bid for your participation, so it's back to khaki for you for a few weeks, Monty.'

Chapter 23
November 1942

In early November, Monty was, indeed, back in khaki, this time onboard HMS *Malcolm*, the last of the *Scott*-class destroyers built at the end of the Great War. Despite her venerable age, she had seen plenty of action and had helped with the evacuation of the BEF at Dunkirk in 1940. Surprisingly, she now flew the American Stars and Stripes at her masthead in place of the usual White Ensign. In company with another Royal Navy destroyer, HMS *Broke*, she carried the IAU and 600 US Rangers from the American 34th Infantry Division. The two ships were providing support to the Eastern Task Force of *Operation Torch*. The US and British military planners had decided to invade North Africa. Not only was it hoped that the invasion would enable the Allies to expel the *Afrika Korps* from Tunisia and Libya, but it would serve as a rehearsal for the ultimate aim of a landing on Continental Europe. It would be the first time that the US Army would have a chance to engage the enemy. Under the command of General Eisenhower 107,000 largely American troops embarked in 500 transports and 350 warships converged on the northern coast of Africa. The huge armada was then divided into three task forces supporting landings to the west in Morocco, in the centre at Oran in Algeria and to the east at the capital of Algeria, Algiers itself.

As a mere lieutenant commander Monty wasn't privy to the plans for the whole operation, but he was aware that the brass hats believed the Vichy French Armistice Army would not oppose the landings in Algeria. However, given that the US government had recognised that of Marshal Pétain and the British had instead backed General de Gaulle's French National Committee as a government-in-exile instead, it was less likely that the Vichy forces would open fire on American ships and forces. Moreover, after the Royal Navy had sunk the French fleet at Oran in 1940 to prevent it coming under the control of the Germans, the Vichy French Navy was known to be extremely hostile towards the British and for this combination of reasons, the two Royal Navy warships flew the Stars and Stripes and the troops landing at Algiers would be carrying US flags prominently.

It was a moonless and chilly night as the two destroyers zig-zagged across the Bay of Algiers in the early hours of Sunday 8th November. As they lounged on the upperdecks of the destroyer, Monty could hear his fellow commandos regaling the fresh-faced American troops with tales of fierce firefights either during the raid on Dieppe or, for some, in Norway and even Madagascar. In the early days of their passage from Britain, the Royal Marines had often shown off their skills at shooting and unarmed combat and Monty had heard some of the 'dough boys' refer to their British colleagues as a rugged lot. However, although lacking combat experience, Monty didn't think the US troops would be a pushover either. As members of the *élite* Rangers, they had all undertaken similar training as the Commandos. This batch had been amongst the first to arrive in Britain and had all undergone training in amphibious operations in Belfast docks. At the suggestion of Lieutenant Colonel Swenson, a former prison warder in the US and now commanding the Rangers unit, Monty now wore a Colt .45 on his hip in place of his usual sidearm. Swenson had even offered Monty an M1 carbine, but Monty had refused on the grounds that he didn't expect to be doing any fighting. That was a task for the marines. In their short time together since Gibraltar, Monty had learned to appreciate Swenson's quick sense of humour, but not his choice and language at times. One of his officers had confided to Monty that Swenson was tough, dynamic and aggressive. Monty didn't doubt the assessment, but he thought Swenson might be a racist.

The task for Swenson and his men was to land in the port of Algiers and to capture the facilities before they could be destroyed by the defending forces. This part of the operation was given the name of *Operation Terminal*. Swenson had been briefed that a secret deal had been concocted between the Americans and Vichy French so that whilst the Allied invasion wouldn't be supported, the French would probably not fire against them. Accordingly, all the men had been ordered not to open fire unless fired upon first. The Royal Marines were said to be a 'Special Engineering Unit' supporting the capture of the port facilities, but in actual fact the real task of the IAU was to storm the French Admiralty HQ, blow the safes and steal as many secret documents as possible. As a fairly fluent French speaker, Monty was present to prioritise the expected haul. A Marine lieutenant was in charge of the combat operations.

Despite the darkness of the sky, Monty could see the bow wave of the *Malcolm* gleaming brilliantly against the dark sea as the ship built up speed for the approach to the harbour of Algiers. The bows had been specially reinforced to allow the ship to ram the harbour boom. The ship shuddered with the acceleration and Monty could taste as well as feel the acrid soot being expelled by the funnels.

'It sure looks a beautiful place,' Swenson remarked. Monty hadn't heard him approach.

'Indeed, sir. I once sailed here when I was a student. I recall the rows of white-washed buildings high up on the hills. It looked quite beautiful then... There was something fascinating about the meeting of the Arab architecture and culture... You know, the mosques and *kasbah,* and the French replication of their Parisian Avenue *Haussmann* with their promenades and wide boulevards... all meeting in one spot. Now, I can't but think how envious I am of a place where there is no need for a blackout. Look at the street lights along the coast and in the town itself.'

'I guess I'd have to agree. We Americans don't seem to appreciate that back home. It came as quite a shock in Northern Ireland. It all seems so peaceful here. Perhaps we were unnecessarily worried about those French gun emplacements.'

Barely had Swenson spoken when suddenly, somebody was cutting the power to these very same streetlights and the sky was rent by the bright cones of searchlights. 'Jeez!' Swenson exclaimed. 'You'd think the French were expecting an attack.'

'Just what I was thinking, sir. I wonder how reliable this American-French secret deal is. You don't think we could have been betrayed, do you, sir?' Monty felt the grip of his Colt .45 for reassurance.

'Who the Hell can say, Monty? I'd better assemble my men.' Swenson dashed down the ladder to the upperdeck below. Monty reflected on the part of the brief for the mission where it had been stated that the Americans had dropped leaflets on the North African cities proclaiming messages of friendship for the French people and how it was only the German and Italian occupying forces that were the enemy. His ruminations were rudely interrupted.

The destroyer was suddenly bathed in light from searchlights ashore and within a minute, the guns of the *Batterie des Arcades* above the city disturbed the air with their ominous rumble and orange-red gun flashes. It only took two salvos to score a direct hit amidships on HMS *Malcolm*. Monty felt the heat of the shells passing through the air and then heard the rattle of shrapnel across the superstructure, but mercifully, the forward funnel had provided some cover to his rear on an anti-aircraft platform and he was unscathed. However, on the deck below he could see others had been less fortunate. The US Rangers were so tightly packed together, just a few pieces of shrapnel had caused carnage. With the ship's position pinpointed by the glare of the searchlights and being at near point-blank range, the battery's guns couldn't miss and another salvo rocked the destroyer, this time causing a fire. Steam and sparks erupted from the after funnel and Monty could feel and hear the ship's speed reduce rapidly. *Malcolm's* Captain took evasive action and the ship heeled sharply to starboard in a tight turn, causing Monty to lose his balance and fall to the deck. He elected to remain there as he heard shells screaming overhead and the screams of the wounded. It all seemed like a repeat of the raid on Dieppe.

To Monty's alarm he felt something warm and wet under his chest and he panicked that he must have caught a piece of shrapnel in his side, but he couldn't feel any pain. He carefully felt around the damp patch of his battledress tunic, but the moisture wasn't sticky. Another burst of a shell illuminated the scene and to his relief, Monty recognised the moisture as emanating from a ruptured hot water pipe. He then noted that the ship was listing to starboard and at much reduced speed. Tentatively, he rose to a crouch and looked at the wreckage below. Men were busy with firehoses tending to the midships fire, but they seemed to be winning the battle. In the light of the flames and shell bursts now directed at HMS *Broke* Monty almost vomited at the sight of a US Ranger yelling for a medic whilst forlornly using his bare hands to try to stem the flow of blood gushing from the stumps of his severed legs. Elsewhere, he spotted several ammunition boxes scattered on the upperdeck, some of which were on fire. Bravely, two of the marines were cutting the lashings securing the boxes and dumping the boxes over the side before the mortar rounds could explode.

Another huge crash sounded nearby accompanied by cheering. Looking up, Monty saw that the aptly-named *Broke* had broken through the boom protecting the harbour. Someone immediately laid a course for the *Malcolm* to follow her through the gap in the boom. Thankfully for the GIs onboard, the other ship was drawing the enemy's fire as HMS *Malcolm* seemed to be limping along at about a mere four knots. In between the artillery fire Monty could hear the sounds of church bells even though it was only 05.30.

Glancing forward, Monty noticed Swenson marshalling his men to the port side of the ship, but the commandos had remained on the starboard side under the protection of the forward funnel. Monty slid down the ladders to seek the lieutenant in command of the troop. To starboard he spotted the *Broke* smash alongside the mole opposite them and begin to disgorge her embarked troops ashore. By contrast, the *Malcolm* gently bumped alongside her mole, but the US Rangers were no slower in disembarking. The Royal Marines lieutenant gave the order for the commandos to get ashore. Now wishing he had accepted Swenson's offer of the carbine, Monty followed the men over the flimsy gangway ashore wedged between the two experienced marines designated as his close protection team.

The first thing Monty noticed as he and his unit ran along the *Quai de Fécamp*, was the smell of alcohol in the air. Short of fuel for their vehicles, the French and Algerians were using alcohol as a substitute and the exhaust vapours hung heavily over the streets. More importantly, however, he noted that it was obvious the French weren't offering merely token resistance. Swenson's troops were coming under heavy machine gun fire at the southern end of the port as they set about capturing the port facilities. As soon as they could find suitable cover from the Vichy gunfire, Monty called a council of war with the Royal Marines lieutenant and his colour sergeant.

'Alf, we've been misinformed. Clearly this op's not the cake walk we were promised. How do you rate our chances of reaching the French Admiralty building?'

It was the colour sergeant who replied. 'It'd be bloody murder, sir. There's two heavy machine guns set up already and… if my ears don't deceive me, sir… that's the sound of the French bringing up a tank.'

'And I hate to trump your bad news, Colours, but look out to sea,' the lieutenant added.

Monty turned to look in the direction the officer was indicating and to his dismay, he saw both destroyers withdrawing. It was a sensible decision, Monty reflected. The French gunners had zeroed in on both ships and were giving them a dreadful pasting. However, the implication was obvious. Until reinforcements could be brought up from the rest of the task force, Swenson's Rangers and the IAU were on their own. He weighed the odds and came to a decision.

'That settles it, gentlemen. It would be futile to try to storm the French HQ now. Instead, we'll turn to Plan B, the Italian Armistice Commission.' Both Royal Marines nodded in agreement. The Commission had always been their secondary target.

Following the fall of France and the signing of the Vichy Government's Armistice, the Germans had left the Vichy regime in charge of North Africa, but insisted on setting up a commission to ensure the Vichy Government complied with the terms of the Armistice. Whilst the main office of the Commission was based in Wiesbaden, members of the Commission regularly visited Algiers and shared offices with those of the Italian Armistice Commission, set up similarly following the Armistice with the purpose of overseeing Italian interests in North Africa and the south of France. DNI suspected that the German Commission was a front for the *Abwehr*. The combined offices were situated about six miles from the harbour in a villa overlooking the city.

'Right then, sir. Plan B it is. Let's get going,' the colour sergeant replied.

Leaving behind the sounds of gunfire, the two-dozen members of the IAU loaded their packs and set off to the west of the city at a brisk pace. By now the sun was up and it was already getting hot and, as the city stirred, dusty. Monty was singularly surprised to see how little attention the Algerians paid the hot and sweaty, heavily-armed force of invaders as they trotted along the streets. Perhaps they thought the troops were French, he wondered. He noted that the Royal Marines had exchanged their steel helmets for their treasured green berets and he decided to do likewise. After all, he, too, had worked hard to earn the right to wear it.

In a little over two hours the troop approached an expensive-looking white villa with fine views over the sea and surrounded by a high wall and two large iron fretwork gates. The latter was no barrier to the sergeant and his six men as they climbed it and overpowered the sentry. They reported back to their colour sergeant that the villa was occupied by a mere seven Italians, none of whom had wanted any trouble and had surrendered without even a token of resistance. Relieved, Monty and his escort entered the villa.

Monty was met with the pleasant smell of pasta and tomatoes. The arrival of the IAU had disturbed the Italians at their breakfast and the smell reminded Monty's stomach that he hadn't eaten for hours. After the adrenalin-fuelled opposed landing in the port a few hours earlier and then a strenuous trot six miles uphill carrying a full pack, Monty's stomach felt entitled to make its presence felt. However, there was work to be done before he could think of food. Whilst some of the marines kept a watchful eye on their prisoners, the remainder fanned out to search the building.

Disappointingly, their finds didn't amount to much. Apart from a fully functioning radio set and the Italians' weapons, there were just a few documents of low classification, but Monty did have a stroke of luck. In the pocket of an old greatcoat left behind by an Italian officer, he found a copy of an Italian codebook. It was hardly just reward for the risks the unit had taken to get here, though, Monty rued. However, just as he was resigning himself to joining the marines and Italian prisoners in a breakfast of pasta, one of the marines asked to speak with him.

''Scuse me, sir. You know 'ow you said to look art for any typewriters, Chalky an' I jes broke down a locked storeroom cupboard and found a funny lookin' typewriter hidden in there. It might be of in'rest.'

Monty flew down the corridor to join the marine, Chalky, beside a smashed cupboard door. Gently, he retrieved the machine in question and it certainly wasn't a typewriter in the ordinary sense. It had keys at the front of the machine, but above the keys was a lamp board and three sets of rotors to the rear. It was obvious to Monty that this was a coding device foolishly left behind by the latest and clearly lazy or at best negligent *Abwehr* visitors. Monty tingled with excitement. This was why he was on this operation. It had never been expected that anything of interest related to torpedoes or mines might be 'pinched' in Algiers, but Monty was one of only two

176

officers trained to operate with the IAU to have been briefed in signal intelligence or SIGINT.

As Monty understood it, the Germans had developed a machine they called Enigma for easily transposing signals into a code that the receiver with the same type of machine could read off in plain language just as easily. He had been shown a photograph of what to look out for, but this machine was different. Apparently, the transmitting and receiving operators had to know how to set up the rotors in a specific way each day so that what was received wasn't gobbledygook. Accordingly, Monty had been briefed to look out for scraps of paper containing random numerals hidden around the desks of cypher clerks. He hadn't been cleared to know how the intelligence bods were cracking the enemy's cyphers for fear he might be captured on a raid and spill the beans under interrogation. Even Fleming claimed not to know for the same reason, but it was obvious that the capture of the coding machines would help enormously. Monty felt sure that the capture of this machine made the IAU's raid completely worthwhile, but how was he to despatch the precious pinch home?

*****

The IAU spent the night in the Italian Armistice Commission building drinking French beer and eating Italian food. The chef was very obliging and the marines thought it wasn't a bad way to spend the war. The Italians seemed very pleasant fellows and thought more about returning home than prosecuting the war. The events of the following morning were strange, though. It started when six armed *gendarmes* of the French Police turned up at the gate and politely requested to speak to the officer in charge. Suspiciously and covered by several marines, Monty went out to meet the inspector in charge.

'*Monsieur*, my men have come to offer you protection,' he said in heavily accented, but good English. 'A surrender is being negotiated.'

The news came as a surprise to Monty, but he had no intention of offering his men's surrender without a fight. The codebreaking machine was too valuable a pinch to abandon.

'I'm sorry, Inspector, but we were not party to any surrender and have no intention of giving ourselves up without a fight.' The Royal Marines lieutenant gave a brief command and at least a dozen marines suddenly appeared with grim looks of defiance.

'No, no, no, *monsieur*!' the Frenchman exclaimed. 'It is er… *compliqué*. Mostly, the town is prepared to surrender to the Americans, but elements of the traitorous forces of Pétain have surrounded the American infantry and refuse to surrender.' The policeman spat to one side and then smiled. 'However, reinforcements are on their way and I have no doubt that by tomorrow, the Americans will control the city.'

'Really?' Monty replied in astonishment. 'So why would we need your protection, Inspector?'

'Ah!' the inspector shrugged. 'That is, also, *compliqué*. *Admiral* Darlan is in command of all military forces here, but he says he only has the authority to surrender the city and not the rest of Algeria. Your situation here is, therefore… unclear. You are on the outskirts of the city and some might argue outside the city limits. Do you understand?'

'Not really, *monsieur*. Please explain.'

'The building here has diplomatic status and my men are here to afford it, its staff and… ah, *visiteurs*, diplomatic protection… at least until the situation is clearer. *D'accord?*'

Monty thought the situation bizarre, but he wasn't in a position to argue. 'In that case, *Inspecteur*, my men will retain their weapons… at least until the situation is, as you say, clearer. I suggest you and your men remain outside.'

The policeman looked crestfallen at Monty's response. 'Ah, that is a pity. I had hoped my sergeant and I might join you inside to toast your army's success.' He smiled earnestly at Monty and Monty readily understood that the inspector and his men had no love for the Vichy regime.

Smiling, he took the inspector by the arm and ushered him indoors. 'That sounds a very sensible idea, inspector. I believe Italian wine is quite tolerable and I have seen a few bottles about. Please ask your sergeant to join us. Tell me, how did you know we were here?'

'Oh, that was easy. You would be surprised by how many reports I received about foreign troops entering the Commission building. Algiers is a very… close city and nothing escapes our notice.'

*****

A few days later, the IAU and the US Rangers were reunited on the quayside waiting to embark for home in the sloop HMS *Black Swan*. As well as the precious coding machine, the unit had snatched nearly two tons of documents from the Vichy Admiralty HQ, several of them German and Italian. Admiral Darlan had finally agreed to surrender North Africa in return for being made the Allies' High Commissioner for North and West Africa. It had been a confusing few days and Monty was pleased to see Swenson alive and well. Sadly, that was more than could be said for HMS *Broke*. She had sunk out at sea after evacuating the harbour.

'I'm relieved to see so many of your men survived, colonel. You seemed to be in a pickle when we last saw you.'

'We were certainly in a real jam, Monty, and unable to fight our way out of it once the French brought up tanks. We were forced to surrender.'

'I had no idea, sir. So, what happened?'

'We surrendered to some colonial troops, from Senegal, I think. No sooner had we surrendered when the thieving black bastards stole our watches, jewellery and wallets. Fortunately, after I complained to a proper French officer, he stood the bastards against a wall and threatened to shoot them unless they handed everything back within two minutes. My boys were real upset, I tell you. Otherwise, we didn't fare too badly. We managed to distract the French long enough to prevent them destroying the port facilities, at least.'

'What about casualties? And were you treated well, sir?'

'Not to start. Quite apart from the Africans stealing our valuables, some fucker of a French commander stuck a pistol in my stomach, threatened to shoot me unless I gave details of the rest of the task force's landings and then to imprison my men in a dungeon. Had he not been restrained, one of my sergeants would have killed him with his bare hands. However, a French Navy captain stepped in and ordered the French to treat us with respect. We were then bundled into a van and taken to the French officers' mess and treated to a very fine dinner.'

'It sounds quite bewildering, sir.'

'It sure was, but in actual fact, some of those Frenchies weren't bad chaps. I don't speak French, but some of my officers told me that many of the officers even supported the landings. They thought that it might be the best way to achieve a free France, but then there were others who resented any outside interference, be it British, American, German or Italian.'

'So how long were you kept prisoner, sir?'

'Only a day. It was kind of odd, me being a prisoner. You know I used to be an assistant warder at the Minnesota State Penitentiary?'

'I had heard, sir. Did you lose many men, sir?'

'Yep. A few, sadly. Fifteen dead and thirty-three wounded. How did your guys get on?'

'We didn't do too badly, sir,' Monty replied vaguely. The discussion was interrupted by the siren of the sloop. 'I think your ship's ready to sail, sir. I'd better let you join your men onboard.'

'Are you not joining us, Commander?'

'I fear not, sir. Change of plan. You know how it is, sir. I'm getting a lift to Blida for onward transport by air to Gibraltar before returning home. Perhaps we'll meet again, sir?'

'I do hope so, Monty. Take care of yourself.'

Chapter 24
December 1942

'You did very well, Monty. Thank you.' Fleming lit a cigarette before continuing. 'The pinch of that Enigma machine has really pleased the cryptographers down at Bletchley Park. Apparently, it's enabled the chaps to read six weeks of German back traffic. Moreover, it's confirmed the value of the IAU. I have a strong feeling that soon we will no longer be experimental, but established.' Fleming took a long draw on his cigarette with satisfaction and studied the ceiling.

The mention of Bletchley Park intrigued Monty. He hadn't heard it spoken of before. 'Bletchley Park, Ian?'

'Yes, there's a unit there trying to read German signal traffic. It's all very hush-hush. Full of crossword solvers and mathematicians, I gather. Don't ask me more as all I know is that the capture of code books and Enigma machines makes the lives of the cryptanalysts much easier, that's all.'

Monty suddenly thought of Marcy. She was a gifted mathematician and working at Bletchley Park. Working on statistics my foot, he thought. He thought of her with renewed respect. However, there was a subject he was keen to raise with Fleming.

'Ian, I was wondering if I'm really suitable for this IAU work.'

'Suitable? By Jove! Of course, you are. You've just proved that. What more do you want? Another gong?'

Monty coloured with anger as he responded. 'No. Of course not. And I'm happy to be employed wherever I can be of best service. My point is that I'm a specialist in torpedoes and mines. I'm no soldier. Might I not be better employed with the IAU when there's a more specific target? In that way, I could spend more time on my duties at DTMI.'

Fleming took another drag on his cigarette before lighting another. 'You have a point, Monty. I'll give it some thought. As it happens, I do have somebody else in mind to replace you.' Fleming stubbed out his first cigarette and turned to his paperwork.

Feeling slightly snubbed, Monty returned to his office where he found Captain Maitland-Dougall awaiting his return with enthusiasm.

'Good trip, Monty? I hear the *Torch* landings were a complete success.'

'It was a bit mixed, sir. Nobody expected such resistance from the French.'

'I can't understand the surprise. Never trust a Froggie, Monty. They're a back-stabbing lot who will side with anybody not on our side. Anyway, now you're back, I have some interesting news for you.'

'That's good, sir,' Monty replied as he hung up his cap.

'Look at these photos. Tell me what you see. The RAF sent them through for you soon after you left for the Maghreb.'

Monty noted the photo showed three ships, one large and two small. The caption explained that it had been taken from 15,000 feet over the German naval base at Lorient. With the use of a magnifying glass, Monty could see that the two smaller vessels were minesweepers towing magnetic mine sweeps. That suggested that the bigger vessel was a *Sperrbrecher* and sure enough, Monty spotted a semi-circular patch of disturbed water merging with the wake of the ship. He looked up at Maitland-Dougall for his analysis.

'The RAF photographic interpreters identified the larger ship as *Sperrbrecher A.I.* They assumed that the minesweepers had exploded a mine. What are your thoughts, Monty?'

'I don't see how that's possible, sir. The minesweepers aren't on the right course to do that.'

'Precisely. That's why I asked the RAF at Medmenham to reevaluate their interpretation. They came back with this.'

Monty took the piece of paper from the captain. It gave more information on the exact position of the minesweeping force and details of the *Sperrbrecher*'s recent activities. More interestingly, the RAF had deduced from the course of the vessels, the depth of water and the wave patterns following the explosion that the mine had a charge of 740 pounds of explosive. A series of other photographs taken at the time over a period of seven-and-a-half seconds had enabled the photographic interpreters to calculate the speed of the ripple after the explosion and the speed of the *Sperrbrecher* of six to seven knots. From that they had calculated that the mine had been exploded between 450 and 525 feet ahead of the *Sperrbrecher*. Impressed, Monty handed the report back to his superior.

'Well done the PI boys at Medmenham. This is an excellent report, but…'

'It's not definite enough for our scientists?'

'Indeed, sir. According to this report, the ship hadn't stayed on a steady course and I don't think the calculations will be accurate enough for the scientists to work out precisely the magnetic signature of the *Sperrbrecher*, sir.'

'I have to agree, Monty, which is why I've eagerly awaited your return. So, get your backside down to *Vernon* and arrange some trials to compare overhead photographs of a series of controlled explosions with this recce photo to check the data.'

'Overhead photos, sir? Are the RAF laying on a photo-recon Spitfire for us?'

'No, Monty. Better than that. They're going to offer us an autogyro. They've proved useful in calibrating coastal radar stations, so will be just the trick for our purposes.'

Monty was again impressed with his Air Force colleagues.

*****

It struck Stephen that Simon's Town wasn't a bad place to learn to dive. Unlike the water off Portsmouth harbour, the South African water could be warm and clear. One even had the choice of two oceans nearby. Moreover, Stephen felt himself fortunate to have been taught by a couple of Chatham dockyard divers. Their only student, his training was one-on-one and the divers were civilians, meaning that they weren't hidebound by discipline and regulations. They had taught Stephen that diving could be fun. Another piece of luck was that his course had taken place in December, one of the best months to learn to dive in South Africa. The water in False Bay had been warm and the current minimal. He had been amazed to see such a diversity of marine life amongst the kelp forests. He had come across several very playful and entertaining seals. His dives had not just been restricted to the waters of False Bay either. He had experienced the cooler Atlantic waters off Cape Town, but he had declined the opportunity to dive off Gansbaai on the southern coast.

His instructors had suggested it would be a great place to view sharks! Stephen shuddered at the idea of being taught to dive by the likes of CPO Warren in HMS *Excellent*. He had almost put Stephen off diving for life.

'You seem deep in thought, sir.' Kronje spoke. 'Are you thinking about the Christmas Ball?'

'Er, n-no.' Stephen came out of his trance. 'I was thinking more of how b-best to use my diving skills. I hope I don't have to render s-safe any underwater mines, b-before I've had more experience.'

'Ah. Could you not help the dockyard divers with some underwater repair work?'

'I've already offered, b-but they suggested I needed m-more training and experience underwater.'

'A bit chicken and egg that, sir. *Ja*-nee, I don't know, hey. Just how are you to get the experience to be able to gain more experience of diving?'

'I'll think of something. So why were you asking about the b-ball? You are still c-coming?'

'Too right, sir. Sonja's really looking forward to it. Indeed, sir,' Kronje looked around and then spoke quietly and conspiratorially, 'I intend using the occasion to ask her to go to the next level.'

'N-next level? What do you mean, Jan?'

'You know, sir. Ask her to marry me. I thought it would be romantic. You hear me, sir. It being Christmas.'

'Oh, I see. Congratulations, Jan.'

'No, sir. Congratulations are a bit premature, sir. Wait until she's accepted me, my little *liefie*.'

'I see,' Stephen answered noncommittally. He was a little bored of hearing about his assistant's love life.

'You know, Julia's really looking forward to it, sir. Are you sure that you don't want to accept my aunt's offer of a bed for the night?'

'Quite sure, thank you, Jan.'

'Seems like spilling money, sir, but I suppose you can afford it.'

'Jan, have you checked the d-demolitions for t-tomorrow's lecture?'

'Not yet, sir. Plenty of time later in the afternoon.'

'I think now w-would be a good time. Just in case there are any p-problems.'

'Oh, *lekker*. I'll attend to it right away, sir.'

Kronje left Stephen in peace and now his thoughts did turn to the forthcoming ball. Since the Ladies' Night he had been in fairly regular communication with Julia and he was looking forward to enjoying another evening of her company. Notwithstanding the generous offer of Kronje's aunt to accommodate Julia with Jan's intended, Sonja, Stephen had booked her into a hotel on Saint George's Street, just ten minutes' walk from the naval base. Of course, Jan was right, he conceded to himself. It was taking a fair slice out of his monthly salary, but he knew Julia to be accustomed to finer things than sharing a room with Sonja, good friends or not.

*****

Once more, Julia appeared stunning, not just to Stephen, but to everyone else in HMS *Afrikander*'s wardroom. Her mid-brown hair was tied back, but several long strands hung loose over the magnificent diamond necklace she wore. Instead of the huge diamond pendant she had worn at the Ladies' Night, on this occasion she wore a necklace with a double row of brilliantly-dazzling diamonds and a single, small pendant of diamonds surrounding a single emerald to match the colour of her silk dress and gloves. Again, her dress was low-cut to show off her curvaceous chest, but this time it was square cut and less obviously drawing attention to her cleavage. Stephen was captivated. He was the envy of his brother officers as he led her to the small table they were sharing with a couple of other junior officers and their ladies, including Kronje and Sonja. He pinched himself. How could he have attracted such a beautiful escort?

As they sat opposite each other, Stephen checked himself from admiring the diamond necklace and changed his gaze to Julia's face. She smiled back at him to show off her fine white teeth and he noticed that her eyes were a soft brown. For some reason, he had thought them green when they had last met, but then he recalled with a pang of conscience that it was Carol who had green eyes.

'So, Stephen,' she opened the conversation. 'No more medals, I see. What can you have been doing?'

'Er, n-no. Things are quiet around here.'

'You are looking good on it. You've taken on a tan since I last saw you.' Stephen blushed slightly.

'I've b-been learning to d-dive. In between dives, there w-was much time to s-sit in the sunshine. It really is a lovely c-country you have here.'

'I'm glad you think so, but you should have come to see me in Kimberley when you were at Ganspan. I would love to show you more of the country.'

'Ah. I'm s-sorry, but there just w-wasn't the t-time.' Stephen wriggled uncomfortably on his chair. 'You are looking very b-beautiful tonight, Julia.'

'Why thank you for the compliment, sir, but are you suggesting I look different tonight? Was I less good-looking the last time we met?' Julia frowned in mock disappointment and it took a moment for Stephen to catch her meaning.

'N-no. I m-meant... You...'. His words tailed off in embarrassment, but Julia rescued him.

'It is I who should be sorry, Stephen.' She took hold of his hand. 'I was teasing, don't you see? A woman enjoys being complimented.'

For a few moments Stephen was able to relax as the stewards served their table with white wine. Julia asked to see the label.

'At least it's local, I suppose.' She nodded to the steward to continue pouring the wine.

'Is it not a g-good w-wine then?' Stephen asked nervously.

'Don't worry. It's fine. It's a Chenin Blanc from Paarl. I just prefer our own Stellenbosch Chardonnay, that's all. It's absolutely fine.' Julia again took Stephen's hand and squeezed it reassuringly. The naval steward looked bemused and moved on to the next table.

'You said 'S-Stellenbosch', Julia. I thought that was n-nowhere near Kimberley.'

'You're right, Stephen, but my family own an estate over there. It's better known for its red wines, but I happen to think the Chardonnay a very good example. Do you like wine?'

'I'm not sure.' He raised his glass to smell the bouquet. 'In England, I've only ever drunk b-beer or whisky. I only had my f-first glass of wine on the way here.'

Julia's face lit up. 'Then you must visit us in Stellenbosch. It's only a few hours by train from here and I could teach you a little about our wine. Come on. When's your next leave?'

'Er, I d-don't know. It d-depends on young Jan, here.'

Kronje paused his conversation on hearing his name mentioned and tuned into Julia and Stephen's conversation.

'But you must be due some leave over the festive period. Surely?' Julia turned across to Kronje. 'That's right, isn't it, Jan. What are the leave arrangements?'

'The Boss kindly offered to cover for me over the Christmas period, but I'll be back on the fourth. You could take some leave then, sir, couldn't you? After all, you've been here the thick end of nine months and are due some.'

Stephen looked down at his lap. He felt part of a pincer movement. It was true that he was due leave, but he'd never before thought about it. However, it wasn't just the chance to explore more of South Africa that attracted him, but to spend more time with Julia… How might that work out?

'I suppose so,' he finally responded. I'll look into it after the weekend.'

'Thank you, Stephen.' Stephen felt a foot rubbing slowly up his calf and Julia looked him lovingly in the face. His heart melted.

*****

It was a lovely, balmy evening, so Stephen offered to escort Julia back to her hotel on foot. Moreover, he needed the fresh air. Unused to wine, his head needed clearing. It had been an enchanting evening, only marred by the number of times other officers had cut in on the dance floor. He felt a tinge of jealousy. He wanted her to himself and was now glad he had agreed to visit her in Stellenbosch. Surely, then there would be no competition for her attention. Julia had a shawl to protect her bare shoulders from the sea breeze, but nevertheless, cuddled up to him as they walked. His loins stirred at the memory of the footwork under the table for much of the evening. It seemed clear to him that Julia reciprocated his feelings towards her and he dearly wanted to kiss her, but Saint George's Street was too public an arena. His heart, thus, lifted when she invited him to come up to her room to say farewell. He felt sheepish as they passed the staring night porter of the hotel.

At the entrance to Julia's hotel room he held back cautiously.

'Thank you, Julia, f-for a wonderful night. M-might I see you again b-before you go?'

'Oh!' Julia turned back to him in surprise. 'You're leaving so soon? I thought you might at least have kissed me goodbye.'

'B-but, of course. I w-want to.'

'Do you, Stephen? Do you really want to kiss me goodbye?' Julia looked at him coyishly and a barrier within him broke. He embraced her and kissed her full on the lips. To his surprise and relief, she didn't resist, but returned his passion and even teased his teeth with the tip of her tongue. After what had seemed an eternity of hedonism, but in fact only twenty seconds, Julia broke off the embrace. 'Come on, Stephen,' she whispered. 'We can't carry on like this in the corridor. I have my reputation to consider.' She opened the hotel room door and led him inside.

This time it was Julia who took the lead in kissing Stephen. She nuzzled his ear and whispered, 'I've never had a man in uniform make love to me before.' She led him gently to the bed, sat on it and pulled him quickly on top of her.

Stephen had crossed the Rubicon. After kissing Julia passionately all over her face and ears before moving down to her neck and throat. She moaned with pleasure and writhed beneath him, giving him the confidence to move lower to her breasts at which Julia pushed him back. Embarrassed and ashamed, he pulled away.

'I'm s-so s-sorry,' he mumbled.

'Don't be such an ass, Stephen. Unzip me.' She turned her back to him and with no more hesitation, Stephen quickly lowered the zip before turning her back to face him again and peel off her gloves. Gently and tenderly, he released each of her breasts in turn and gazed on them with wonder. He had never seen such large breasts before and noted that each of the areolae had puckered to produce long, dark nipples. To his fascination, as he stroked her nipples, they grew even longer. Instinctively, he bent down to kiss and then lick them gently. They grew yet bigger and more erect as Julia moaned appreciatively in response and this gave him the confidence to continue. Urgently and impatiently, he removed her gown before slowly peeling down her drawers. His heart pounded as her full nakedness was revealed to show the bare patches of secret, pale flesh against her darkly-tanned body. He was transfixed. Having taught General Science at his girls' school as well as physics, he was well aware of the female anatomy, but this was beyond his imagination.

'For God's Sake, Stephen,' Julia protested. 'Don't just stand there gawping. Take your clothes off.'

Two hours later, Stephen made his way slowly back to his cabin in the naval base. The sentry on the main gate gave him a sly, sideways look as he offered his salute, but Stephen didn't care. His time with Julia had been divine and he couldn't wait to book his leave to stay with her in the new year.

Chapter 25
January 1943

Early in 1943, Monty learned that Fleming had agreed to replace him
on IAU missions that weren't expecting to pinch mine or torpedo
related information or equipment. Moreover, Fleming's high hopes
that the IAU would become established on a permanent basis had
come to fruition. The unit was now called 30 Commando, although
for now it would still operate under the cover name of a 'Special
Engineering Unit' in the field. Monty went down to Southampton to
bid the men farewell as they embarked in the liner *Durban Castle* for
South Africa. The men now seemed to walk six inches taller since
their return from Algiers and it was clear to Monty that the new
recruits held the members of the Maghreb raid in some awe. The
unit had been expanded by several new volunteers for hazardous
service and was now commanded by another lawyer and RNVR
officer, Lieutenant Dunstan Curtis. Curtis held the DSC for
distinguishing himself in command of a Motor Gun Boat during the
failed Dieppe raid.

On his return to his DTMI office, he found Maitland-Dougall in an
agitated mood.

'Monty, if my suspicions are correct, I owe you an apology. Read
this.'

Maitland-Dougall handed Monty a short report from the
Operations Division. It concerned a fast convoy of six tankers that
had left Trinidad with one Royal Navy escort vessel. As the convoy
had passed through the South Atlantic, they had come under attack
from *U*-boats. Of significance was that they had all been torpedoed
from the stern.

'Do you suspect…?' Monty left the words hanging.

'Bloody right I do, Monty. Your *Feldwebel* didn't let you down.
It's just taken Jerry longer to deploy their acoustic homing torpedoes
than I had expected. You'd better look into whatever intel we have
on the new weapons. In the meantime, I've suggested an immediate
signal to issue your Foxers to all ships.'

*****

'Rabbi, I've come to seek your advice on a very personal and complex problem.'

'I will do my best to give you honest counsel, Carol. What is the nature of this problem?'

Carol Templeton paused before responding and breathed a heavy sigh.

'I've met a man who I would dearly love to marry and I know he feels just the same way about me, Rabbi. Weel, at least he did the last time I saw him,' Carol added mournfully.

'That sounds wonderful news to me, my child, so where does the problem lie? Is this man unsuitable in some way? What do your parents say?'

'My parents haven't met him. As you know, they are both in Washington, but I have written to them about him. The problem is…' Carol hesitated and wrung her hands. 'You see, Rabbi, he isn't of the Jewish faith.' She looked imploringly at the elderly Rabbi.

'Ah! I can see that would make a great difference to your father. He is a strict adherent of *halakha* and the *Talmud*. What was his reaction?'

'It was my mother who wrote. She wrote that my news had upset them greatly and my father was particularly distressed. Indeed, he expressly forbade any considerations of marriage. He went so far to say that were I to defy him and marry this man, any bairns with whom we might subsequently be blessed, would be classed as illegitimate by our faith. That couldn't be true could it, Rabbi?'

'Mmm. That depends, but I see your problem, Carol. Tell me a little of this man. Have you known him long?'

'Several months, Rabbi. He's a very *braw* man… a real *laoch*. One of the Navy's mine disposal officers. I first met him when he saved my house and those of my neighbours by defuzing a bomb near the reservoir.'

'I remember the occasion, Carol, but I never heard to whom some members of our congregation should be grateful. Forgive me, I interrupted.'

'I offered him the use of my bathroom… I wasn't there at the times he used it, Rabbi,' Carol quickly added to avoid any

191

misunderstanding. 'It was all very correct. However, the effort of days of tunnelling made him ill and I returned home one evening to find him collapsed and in a serious condition. With the hospital's help, I nursed him back to guid health and our relationship developed from there.'

'And what of this man's religious convictions? Does he have any?'

'He's a Quaker, Rabbi.'

'Really? But I thought they were pacifists and wouldn't sign up to the military.'

'Aye, he *is* a pacifist right enough, but saving the lives of civilians by defuzin' mines and bombs didn't offend his religious sensibilities.'

'I see. The trouble is my understanding of the Quakers is that their faith is deep-rooted. I cannot, therefore, imagine him to be the sort to be persuaded to take up our faith.'

'No Rabbi. I don't think his faith is very deep-rooted, though. He told me that it was his late-father who held the strongest beliefs. He served in an ambulance brigade on the Western Front during the Great War.'

'A brave man, then… and one who certainly practised what he preached. But forgive me for asking this, dear child. It's an impertinent question, but I need to pose it. Do you really love this man? Could it be mere hero worship?'

Tears welled in Carol's eyes as she responded. 'I love him more than anythin', Rabbi. True, he is my *laoch*… hero, but he's kind, gentle and he makes me laugh. I really miss him.'

'And where is he now, Carol?'

'He's been posted to South Africa. I haven't seen him for o'er a year… not since I wrote to tell him we couldnae marry.' Carol sniffed and had to reach for her handkerchief.

'What? So, you've already told him you can't marry and haven't seen him for a year? Why on earth are you seeking my advice now? Surely, the affair is over?'

'Because I'm hoping not, Rabbi. As a nurse, I've met several men over the past few months… even been romantically inclined with one or two, but it's taught me to realise that none could ever match up to my dear Stephen. If anything, the past year's absence has taught me that I really do love him and want to spend my life with him. I was hoping you could offer me some guidance on the Jewish law on this matter, Rabbi.'

'I think I understand, Carol, but I'm not sure my advice will help. To sum up your options, it would seem that on the face of it, you have three. Firstly, you could renounce your faith or risk the opprobrium of your parents by marrying this man anyway. Naturally, as your Rabbi, I would be unhappy for you to take that course of action. Alternatively, you could ask this man, Stephen, I think you said, to convert to Judaism. If he doesn't feel as strongly about his Quakerism as his father, he might be persuaded to do so. Or thirdly, you might move on, Carol. Who's to say that this love of yours hasn't found another soulmate, particularly after your letter?'

'Rabbi, were it a simple matter, I would give up my religion for this man. I cannae see that God expects my love only for him. Surely, he would encourage my love to be shared. And why would it matter how my husband worshipped God? After all, surely the important matter is that we both worship the same god? However, I could never betray my parents in such a manner... Perhaps you're right. Stephen might have found someone else, but I would kick mysel' if I didnae find out how he feels and give him another option. Tell me, Rabbi, does Jewish law specifically forbid marriage with non-Jews?'

'Ah, my child, that really is a difficult question. There is no hard and fast answer, I'm afraid. It depends on one's interpretation of Jewish law, a subject that has been controversial for centuries. The Orthodox view is that the *Talmud* asserts marriage between a Jew and a non-Jew is prohibited and, thus, not valid under Jewish law. As such, any issue would be seen as illegitimate. This seems to be the interpretation your father is making.'

'Is that your interpretation, Rabbi?' Carol asked quietly.

'My dear, you put me on the spot, but I will do my best to answer. Under British law marriages between Jews and non-Jews are recognised by the State. Accordingly, were you to go against the wishes of your parents by marrying this man... and the question is a little academic given the passage of time since you wrote to end your relationship... But were you to marry and have children, then there is no question of them being regarded as illegitimate. I hope that clears up that point.'

'Thank you, Rabbi. I am relieved to hear it, but it's not the main issue, is it? How do we reconcile our different faiths under *Jewish law*?'

'It is a thorny issue, indeed, my child and I don't think I can give you a clear-cut answer. As I said before, it is down to interpretation and different Rabbis see Jewish law differently. To put it bluntly, and I don't subscribe to this view, some Jewish leaders see interfaith marriage as an act of rebellion against Judaism, punishable by excommunication. The more liberal subscribe to the view that should our children end up by marrying non-Jews, then we should not turn our backs on them. I am one of those who think that it is better to continue to give such couples our love and support in the hope that even if the non-Jewish partner in the marriage doesn't come to convert to our faith, the children will be brought up as Jews.'

Carol took the old Rabbi's hand and squeezed it fondly with tears in her eyes. 'You're a good man, Rabbi.'

'Oh, away with you, girl. It's just age. As one grows older, one becomes more sentimental, I suppose.' The Rabbi brought himself up short. 'I've just had an idea, Carol.'

Carol beamed with joy. 'Really? Please let me hear it.'

'I warn you, Carol, that it might not be enough to satisfy your parents, and in particular your more conservative father, but have you heard of *Noahides*?'

'Vaguely, Rabbi, but I can't remember the definition.'

'If your Stephen is of strong religious convictions, then it might apply. In certain circumstances our faith allows a Jew to marry a non-Jew who truly believes in God and is willing to live by the Nohaic Covenant. Essentially, it means living by Seven Commandments, not dissimilar to the Ten Commandments of Moses and there is no reason why a Quaker wouldn't. Your loved one would then be regarded as *ger toshav*, that is a *God-fearer* under Jewish law.'

'But that would be marvellous, Rabbi. I think you've solved the problem. How clever of you.'

'Hold hard, Carol and don't get ahead of yourself. Remember these things aren't set in stone. It's down to interpretation. Your father might not agree with this interpretation and it would require some accommodation by your intended.'

'But it's worth a shot, Rabbi. Look, I've taken in the principle, but not the details of what you've jes said. Please, Rabbi. Would you be willin' to set it all out in a letter to my father?'

The Rabbi was silent for a moment. 'Of course, child, but not yet.' He held up a hand at Carol's obvious look of dismay. 'You must write a letter of your own first. You must write to Stephen to advise him of this conversation and then to establish his present feelings towards you. I'm sorry to lay it on thick, Carol, but when a man is rejected in his proposal of marriage, you can't expect him to remain a monk for the rest of his life... er, that is if the Quakers have monks.'

'Of course, I'll do that, Rabbi. Oh, you're such a wise and dear wee man.' Carol kissed the Rabbi warmly on his cheek. 'Thank you, thank you.'

The Rabbi's heart melted to see the joy radiating from Carol's pretty face.

Chapter 26
March 1943

The trap was set and every day, Monty and Maitland-Dougal scanned the intelligence reports for any indication that their plan had worked. Two months earlier, Monty had worked with the *Vernon* scientists to conduct controlled explosions of mines and have the shock waves photographed from the air. On one hair-raising evening he had embarked in a minelayer to supervise the laying of two German mines that had been previously rendered safe. The operation had been conducted at night to avoid detection by the *Luftwaffe*, but it had been a stormy night anyway. That had meant a heavy swell had been running and Monty had had his heart in his mouth as the two heavy mines were swung outboard and laid off Portsmouth, one in five fathoms of water and the other in ten. As the minelayer had rolled in the swell with the heavy mines on the derrick, Monty had feared either might have swung inboard and dropped with a heavy crash onto the deck. Fortunately, the crew of the minelayer had seen and done it all. The laying had gone off without a hitch. The positions of the mines had been marked with buoys and cable laid back to the shore to allow them to be detonated remotely in daylight the following day.

The RAF had despatched one of their autogyros as promised and once it was directly overhead each of the mines, they had been detonated. The resulting photographs had been good enough to allow comparison with the earlier photographs of the *Sperrbrecher* detonation. This had enabled the scientists to calculate accurately the strength of the ship's magnetic field. Then had come the waiting game. The RAF had deployed the newly and specially-designed anti-*Sperrbrecher* mines amongst a pattern of regular magnetic mines in the patrol area of the *Sperrbrecher* and reconnaissance aircraft had been overflying the area for the past two weeks.

Maitland-Dougall flicked through his pile of fresh signals whilst Monty read the latest reports about the new German acoustic torpedoes.

'Anything new, Monty?' the captain asked as Monty laid down a docket with a sigh.

'Not really, sir, but I've been examining a theory about the sinking of the *Repulse* and the *Prince of Wales*.'

'But that was over a year ago, man! And moreover, the Germans weren't involved. I hope you're not off on a wild goose chase, Monty.'

'Just hear me out, sir. As we both know, although the *Repulse* was of the Great War vintage, she had been modernised and the update had included the fitting of anti-torpedo blisters... blisters twelve feet thick, sir.'

'I think I know which way your mind is running, Monty.' Maitland-Dougall abandoned the signal pad and gave Monty his full attention.

'According to the post-mortem on the attacks, *Repulse* managed to avoid nineteen of the torpedoes dropped against her and only five of the others struck her. The *Prince of Wales*'s steering gear was put out of action by only the second torpedo to hit her. That hit her in the stern, damaging her propellers and taking out the steering gear. Obviously, she then became a sitting duck for the Japanese and it only took three more torpedoes to send her to the bottom. Now think about it, sir. How did the Japanese get so lucky with just a few torpedoes? Either they have exceptional pilots...'

'Or exceptional torpedoes.' Maitland-Dougall slapped his thigh with enthusiasm. 'Monty, I don't think anybody has considered this before. Well done. So, what next?'

'I was thinking that the Americans must have recovered some Japanese torpedoes over the last year. I've a contact with the US Navy here in London, sir. Might I approach him to put the word out for any information on recovered fish, sir?'

'Good idea, Monty, and then... What is it, PO?' The discussion had been interrupted by a red-faced telegraphist bearing a piece of paper aloft.

'I thought this might interest you, sir, so I brought it up immediately. You said to keep a special eye out for information on German minesweepers, sir.'

Maitland-Dougall snatched the signal from the petty officer's hand and scanned it quickly. 'Eureka! Monty, I swear you're a wizard.

RAF Photo Reconnaissance report the sinking of *Sperrbrecher A.I.*
Well done again, Monty. Thank you, PO.'

As the telegraphist withdrew, Monty considered the impact of the
news. No doubt the *Sperrbrecher* had suffered casualties. Monty
suddenly felt sick at the thought that he had probably been party to
the killing of unarmed German sailors. Like the Royal Navy's
minesweeping forces, those sailors were just doing their job. Just as
suddenly, he needed a breath of air and he left Maitland-Dougall
staring after him open-mouthed.

*****

A week into his holiday in Stellenbosch, Stephen could now tell the
difference between a Sauvignon Blanc and a Chardonnay, but at
times he still had trouble distinguishing between a Cabernet
Sauvignon and a Merlot. However, telling the difference between a
Pinot Noir from a Pinotage was quite straightforward. Despite his
newly acquired knowledge of wine, he still couldn't see the point of
it. What was wrong with good, old-fashioned English beer to
quench one's thirst? He was careful to hide his opinion from Julia,
however. She and the French cellar master, Marcel, had waxed
lyrically about flavours such as cigar boxes, leather, plum and cassis,
none of which Stephen's nose or palate had been able to detect. It
had seemed tosh to him, but he had just smiled appreciatively. Now
the two were engaged in a protracted discussion on the optimum
proportion of Merlot and Cabernet Sauvignon to produce a French-
style wine. Stephen felt excluded and contemplated his experiences
of the past week.

It had been obvious to Stephen that Julia's family were wealthy
from the extravagance of her jewellery, but that had been nothing to
the wealth exhibited by the family's wine estate. At its heart was the
manor house in which he was temporarily residing. A Rolls Royce
and chauffeur had met him at the station and as the car had swept
into the magnificent gates, Stephen had gasped aloud at the size of
the house at the end of the oak and palm lined long driveway. It had
a magnificent white façade in the Dutch colonial style and was
reputed to house forty bedrooms. Stephen contrasted it to his family
home attached to the garage and comprising just three bedrooms.
According to the *Afrikaans* chauffeur, the whole estate extended to

over 400 acres. Stephen couldn't picture that in his head, but he knew by comparison that a neighbouring farm in Dolphinholme comprised a mere thirty acres. How could one family live in such excessive grandeur when there were so many deserving poor about?

To Stephen's further embarrassment, the family dressed for dinner every evening and ate very grandly. In anticipation that he might need to dress up, he had taken the precaution of packing his best uniform and a few wing collars, but whilst no comment had been passed, the morning after his arrival had heralded the arrival of two Indian tailors. They had measured every inch of his lean frame and within 48 hours produced for him a dinner jacket with a pair of patent leather shoes, two lightweight suits, several shirts, two pairs of handmade brogues and even a riding outfit complete with knee-length leather boots. Stephen had felt so ashamed. He had been made to feel a pauper in need of charity. Julia had laughed it off as a token of her father's gratitude towards a man who had served his country with distinction, but the shame continued to burn within him every evening as he donned the splendid dinner jacket.

He was beginning to feel drowsy. It wasn't just the daily lessons in horse riding that were tiring him out. It was Julia's seemingly insatiable sexual appetite. Her father had returned to Kimberly three days earlier and since then she had been his near inseparable bedtime companion. He wasn't complaining, though. Despite his lack of experience, he had instinctively and quickly learned the ropes and prided himself in giving Julia pleasure. She had said to him one evening that he was the first man who hadn't treated her body as a rugby ball. His attentions had been reciprocated, too. He heard his name mentioned and refocused his attention on the conversation between Julia and Marcel. Marcel offered him a glass of red wine, one third full.

'Miss Julia thinks this wine might please you, *Monsieur*.'

Instead of sipping the wine immediately, Stephen treated it as he had been taught to do so. He first examined the rim around the top of the wine. It was a chestnut-brown. Next, he swilled the glass and examined the veils as they drained down the side of the glass. They were distinct, but not enough to suggest the wine was too sugary. Then he examined the colour. The colour had faded from its original deep red and was now quite tawny. He concluded that this was a fairly old wine. He had remembered that the tasting of wine requires three senses and only the last was taste.

He swilled the wine around more in the glass and then sniffed it. The bouquet was extremely pleasing. He was learning that he enjoyed the fruitier wines and even his untutored nose could pick out the smells of plums and cherries. He could smell vanilla, too, and wondered if the other flavour might be chocolate. He couldn't be sure. He sniffed again. This time he picked out a definite aroma of blackberries and the chocolate aroma smelled more of caramel. Finally, he tasted the wine whilst both Julia and Marcel looked on intensely. He immediately tasted the fruits he had detected with his nose and now he could definitely taste a little chocolate. He swilled the wine in his mouth and sucked air through his teeth. The wine felt smooth and velvety. There was no doubt in his mind that he was tasting an elderly Merlot. He swallowed the wine to looks of disapproval from his audience, but he didn't care. Coming from a poor family, his mother had insisted that he and Lucy cleared their plates and Stephen didn't see why drinking wine should be any different. Moreover, he found it unsavoury to spit wine into a spittoon and thought it unbecoming of Julia. Even to his inexpert palate this was a good wine and he savoured another mouthful.

'Well?' Julia asked. 'What do you think it is and what do you think of it?' Marcel looked on with a worried expression.

'I'm fairly sure it's a M-Merlot and probably one that is at least t-ten years old, my dear.'

The two onlookers looked at each other, nodded and smiled with satisfaction. 'I told you he'd like it, Marcel. I'm glad you liked it, darling. It's a twenty-eight and I'm sending you back to Simon's Town with a case of it.'

'B-but I c-can't accept it,' Stephen stammered. 'It's too generous.'

'Nonsense, Stephen. It will serve as a souvenir of your visit until you can next come. Now don't be a glutton by finishing the glass. You'll be too tipsy for our picnic. I thought we'd ride out to the Drakenstein mountains. It'll be lovely and cool over there.'

Stephen groaned inwardly. His thighs and buttocks had had no chance to recover from his riding lessons and Julia had been particularly voracious that morning. Julia had clearly picked up signs of his reluctance as she added,' Oh, come on Stephen. Don't be a baby. It's only about twelve miles on horseback.'

*****

Only twelve miles on horseback he thought. Every muscle in Stephen's lower body ached and he was quite certain he wouldn't be able to perform in bed tonight. In any case, he just didn't have the energy. To Julia's disdain, he had given up trying to trot his mount. He just didn't have the strength in his thighs anymore and he was happy to slouch in the saddle whilst the horse walked the trail towards the mountains in the east. Besides, it must be 80 degrees, he guessed, and that was just too hot for physical exercise. Nonetheless, he trudged on behind Julia. He sensed that his torture might end soon as the mountains loomed high before him and to the south. The valley through which they were riding was extremely pretty and the trees lining it offered some shelter from the early afternoon sun. Everywhere was a mass of pink flowers.

They crossed a river, leaving the vineyards behind and the landscape turned to scrubland dwarfed by the sheer cliffs and rugged peaks of the Drakenstein mountains. Soon afterwards, Stephen spied ahead a camp of some sort, surrounded by three or four vehicles. As they neared it, he recognised one of the estate trucks. Julia turned round to him and shouted, 'Come on, Stephen. Trot on. We're nearly there.' She urged her mount into a canter and left him in a cloud of dust. With one last vestige of effort, Stephen dug his heels into the flanks of his horse to will it to trot after Julia. Unable to sit in the stirrups properly, his bottom took a painful knock, but it was only a hundred yards to their *picnic* site.

This was like no picnic Stephen had ever before encountered. A large awning had been erected to the side of which was a form of grill over an open fire from which tantalising smells were emanating. A trestle table covered with a linen table cloth and weighed down with china and cutlery stood nearby. To his amazement, underneath the awning were a couple of rattan armchairs replete with cushions and side tables. Stephen was accustomed to picnics of a few sandwiches, boiled eggs, fruit and pop. This was a full-blown banquet. How the wealthy live, he pondered for the thousandth time this week.

He dismounted stiffly and was grateful to hand over his horse to one of the estate grooms. There must have been about a dozen servants on hand to prepare this *picnic*, all of them black. He recognised three or four of them from the house, but not the others. He flopped down in one of the armchairs and was immediately glad of the soft cushion.

'Really, Julia. Wh-when you said we were going for a p-picnic, I imagined a hamper or something s-similar. This is magnificent.' He gazed in wonder at the activities going on around him.

'Oh, it's nothing special, dear. I thought I would treat you to a typical *braai*, that's all.'

'A *b-braai*? Is that the same as a barbecue?'

'I suppose it is. But they're part of our heritage and important social events here. There's a bit of a ritual over the building the fire, but I won't bore you on the subject. However, they tend to be a bit heavy on the meat, so I've asked the *braaimaster* to include some local fish and shellfish. Do you like fish, Stephen?'

'I like fish and chips, but I s-suspect that's not what you have in mind.'

'Fish and chips. That conjures up memories of school, eating them on the seafront wrapped in newspaper. It was lovely, but no. That's not what we'll be doing today. Now, listen. I'm not going to tell you what you're eating until you've tasted it. I want to surprise you with a few of our local meats and fish. If you don't like it, you don't have to eat it.'

'Oh. You're not g-going to s-serve me snake and c-crocodile, are you?'

'Do you know, I hadn't thought of that, but no, my darling. It'll be nothing quite so exotic. Another time, perhaps. God, I'm glad of the shade.' Julia loosened the top buttons of her blouse to reveal more of her cleavage and tired as he felt, Stephen, nonetheless, felt the stirrings of lust within him. 'It's a pity the river's so far away, we might have gone for a swim.'

'But I didn't pack a bathing costume anyway.'

'Who needs a bathing suit, dear?' Julia replied mischievously and very deliberately opening her blouse further to give him a glimpse of treasures to come.

The meal when it was served was delicious. Stephen wasn't as keen on the spiced sausage, but the rest was wonderful. The fish had been a steak of yellowfin tuna and alongside the lamb chops he had enjoyed an ostrich steak. The texture and flavour of the meat was like nothing he had ever tasted before. However, the *pièce de resistance* had been the grilled rock lobster, basted in garlic butter and lemon juice. Stephen had refused the cooled white wine as he was already drowsy enough, but he had enjoyed the chilled lemonade. He wondered how the staff had managed to transport the ice here, but couldn't be bothered to ask. Needing a walk to allow his lunch to shake itself down, he and Julia walked a couple of hundred yards away from the camp and sat down in the shade of a rock on picnic blanket. Before long, they were both lying down cuddled together.

'Are we still on your father's estate, Julia?'

'No. That last lot of vineyards belong to a neighbour.'

'After B-Britain, the country is so vast. And the c-climate so lovely. It's a far c-cry from Orkney.'

'But I thought you came from the north of England.'

'I do. It, too, is a b-beautiful place, but much s-smaller. I was based in Orkney before my transfer here.'

'Do you like it here then, Stephen?'

Stephen rose on his elbow surprised by the question. 'Of course, I like it here. It's like p-paradise. One wouldn't know there was a w-war on.'

Julia wriggled closer to him. 'I'm glad you think that way, darling. You know this will all be mine when Daddy dies? He's splitting his assets equally between my sister, Sylvia, and me, but I'm to inherit the estate.'

Stephen sat up. 'Wh-why are you t-telling me this, Julia?'

'Well,' Julia shrugged. 'Just in case you thought you might want to settle here after the war is over.'

His mind reeling, Stephen stammered, 'D-do you mean s-settle here permanently?' Julia reached up and pulled him down on her.

'Why not? I'm not unattractive, am I? And it's time I was married. I'm fed up with the old cats saying how dreadful it must be for one's younger sister to be married before me. In any case, Stephen. I think I love you.'

Stephen lay back at Julia's side. He was shocked by Julia's forthright words. Truth be known, he hadn't thought of marriage since Carol's rejection. He found Julia infatuating and, if he was honest, he was enjoying the sexual relations, but marriage? He stared at the cloudless blue sky and absorbed the warmth of the sun like a reptile. South Africa was such an idyllic land and were he to marry Julia, he would never want for anything. He could even arrange for Mum and Lucy to come out to join him. And the war wouldn't last forever. After all, the Allies had landed in North Africa and were rumoured to be driving back Rommel's *Afrika Korps*. All the same, it was a bit of a shock. He became aware that Julia was expecting some form of response.

'To b-be honest, Julia, I hadn't thought that far ahead. Of course, I'm very fond of you, but whilst this d-dreadful war rages, I can't think too far ahead. I'm in a high-risk trade, after all.'

It was clear from her eyes that his reply had disappointed Julia. 'Will you at least think about it, my dear?'

'Of c-course, Julia. It's a w-wonderful idea, b-but we've only known each other for a few weeks or months. G-give me a little time.'

'You're not ruling out the idea, then?'

'N-no. Of course, n-not.' He leant over and kissed her passionately to spare further conversation on the subject.

He must have drifted off to sleep as an hour later, Julia shook him gently. 'Come on, we need to head back.'

Stephen sat up and as he did so, his body rebelled. He just couldn't imagine riding back. With Julia's support, he stood up stiffly.

'You poor old thing. I can see you're in no state to get back in the saddle. We'll have to drive back.'

'But what about the horses?'

'Oh, don't worry about that. The *kaffers* will walk them home.'

It was the first time Stephen had heard Julia use the term and it shocked him. 'But is it not a long way to walk back, Julia?'

'Don't worry yourself about trifles, Stephen. It's what Daddy pays them for.'

Stephen bristled inwardly at the comment.

Chapter 27
March 1943

Stephen was in his own world underwater. It was peaceful and the water of Durban harbour was not only clear, but warm. The harbour divers had asked for help in removing a rock on the seabed obstructing the anchorage for visiting destroyers. Whilst they were competent to operate the pneumatic drills for boring holes in the rock, they needed an expert in underwater demolitions to set the explosive charges. Stephen had been only too happy to offer his services.

He rather liked Durban. It had a more relaxed air than that of Simon's Town and was quite old-fashioned. Unlike Simon's Town, though, a blackout had been enforced at night since the previous year. He had heard it said that during one of the battleship HMS *Warspite*'s visits in 1942, the then Vice-Admiral, Sir James Somerville, had complained bitterly that the lights from the shoreline were silhouetting his fleet and rendering the ships sitting targets for a possible *U*-boat attack. Eager to please, the Durban Corporation had then gone so far as to suspend the running of the trolleybuses running along the shore for fear that arcing from the trolley poles and wires might be seen out to sea. The trolleybuses had been replaced by diesel-fuelled buses. Then, following the sighting of a Japanese reconnaissance aircraft overflying the harbour a few months earlier, the blackout had been observed more strictly, even when the Eastern Fleet wasn't in port.

Durban was an important stopover for the Allied convoys *en route* to the Middle and Far East and so the harbour entrance was protected by gun batteries and anti-submarine nets. For fear of Japanese aerial bombing, the Bluff, overlooking the harbour, bristled with anti-aircraft batteries and the RAF and Americans operated flying boats to mount anti-submarine patrols far off the coast. From time to time, the drab-grey colours of the troop convoys and visiting warships would be enlivened by the regular visits of hospital ships bringing the wounded for attention at the nearby military hospitals. These ships were painted white with a green band running the length of the hulls and a large red cross painted amidships. In addition to the wounded, the hospital ships brought large numbers of troops suffering from tuberculosis contracted in the Western Desert and these patients were transported by rail to Johannesburg.

Stephen was using Explosive 808 to break down the underwater rock. It resembled green plasticine and was in use by the Special Operations Executive in occupied France for sabotage purposes. Ever since a consignment ready for dropping by parachute into France, and labelled *Explosif Plastique*, had been given to the US scientists, it had become known as *plastic explosive* or *PE*. Being malleable, it was ideal for Stephen's use as he could shape it to apply its explosive force in exactly the direction he required. However, he was careful not to use more than five pounds of it at a time. He couldn't risk damaging the nearby posts, or dolphins, to which the destroyers would tie up in the absence of a full-length jetty.

One of the reasons Stephen enjoyed this task was that by working alone and separated from the surface it gave him the chance for uninterrupted thought. He had been giving much thought to his relationship with Julia and the prospect of settling down with her after the war. At first, the idea had had its appeal, but he now had second thoughts. Perhaps it was the egalitarianism of his Quaker upbringing, but there seemed something very wrong about a section of society that could live in extreme wealth amongst such prolific poverty. Moreover, the untethered racist behaviour and language towards the native South Africans offended his religious scruples. It was a long time since he had attended a meeting house, but he still believed in God and that all people under God were equal in his eyes. He now realised that during his leave in Stellenbosch he had been blind to the snobbery of Julia and her family, but he had been enchanted by her and, he was ashamed to admit to himself, he had been proud of his sexual conquest. But the novelty of sex had both physically and morally tired him. He was fond of Julia, but it wasn't love. He thought of his feelings towards Carol. He had worshipped her and would have been content only to spend the rest of his life in her company. Whilst she, too, was undoubtedly beautiful, he had resisted any sexual longings for her. He regarded her as standing on a pedestal and he had had too much respect for her to consider anything more intimate than a kiss or hug. With Julia it had been different and losing his virginity to her had just happened. He hadn't planned it. He couldn't explain his feelings, even to himself. However, thinking of Julia, what was he to do about her? She had expectations that he would marry her. What if it was already too late? Might she be bearing his child? She had always been scrupulous about inserting her cap prior to sex, but it wasn't foolproof. After all, she had admitted to him one night that she had once had an abortion. He had been very upset by her admission. Not only did he find the idea of a termination abominable morally, but it suggested a certain casualness on her part towards life. It was, perhaps, the principal reason why he had started to dislike Julia the more intimate their relationship had become. How long was it now since his leave? Five weeks. She might only now be missing her period. It would be inconceivable for her to abort his child and he would have to do the right thing by her. What a mess! But what was he to do about it? He knew he needed to end their relationship, but how was he to do so without hurting her? He wasn't sure he had the moral courage. But then if she was already with child... He shuddered, despite the warmth of the water and realised he must concentrate on his work.

Working deftly from experience, he connected three explosive charges with benign-looking detonator cord resembling a white clothes line. Benign it might have looked, but in the right hands the cord could have deadly effects. He inserted a detonator with its waterproof cap into the centre charge. It was a relatively simple job then to connect this detonator to an electrical cable running to the surface. Once an electric current was initiated by a dynamo exploder box, it would detonate all three charges simultaneously and shatter the rock into several pieces. Having completed the work to his satisfaction, he signalled to the support crew above that he was ready to return to the surface.

*****

Monty was enjoying a quiet drink with an RMSO in the New Yorker bar one evening. Situated on Park Lane it was a little off the beaten track from Whitehall, but it fitted in with the irregular hours of the RMSO fraternity as the bar opened at 15.00 when the London pubs shut. It was a smart venue with prices to match, but money was the least of the worries of men who didn't have high expectations of surviving the next incident. A good-looking redhead caught his attention. She wore her lovely hair long, just beneath the shoulders and after the hair, the feature that caught his interest was her broad smile and lovely, white teeth. He guessed she was only a couple of inches shorter than him at a height of, perhaps, five-feet-four. She seemed familiar to him, but he couldn't place her immediately. His colleague noticed his obvious interest.

'Lord! Look at the tits on her,' he exclaimed. The woman was, indeed, large-chested.

'Don't be coarse, Alf,' Monty replied. 'I'm sure I've met her somewhere.'

'Well, I wouldn't mind an introduction, old man. She's gorgeous. I've seen her in here a few times. According to the barman, she's a nurse at a hospital nearby, but I can't see a nurse's wages paying her way here. Come to think of it, I've never seen her in uniform... Not that I'd mind that.'

As the woman surveyed the room, Monty smiled at her. To his delight, their eyes met and she smiled back at him with a look of recognition. Then it hit Monty. He did know her. She was Stephen's girlfriend, Carol somebody, and they had met once, or possibly, twice in Stephen's company. He gestured for her to join him and Alf and she came across cautiously.

'You're Stephen Cunningham's friend, Monty, aren't you?' she said in her soft Scottish Borders accent.

'Indeed, I am. It's clever of you to remember me... Carol, isn't it? I remember you. Will you join us for a drink? This rascal is Alf Preston. Alf, this is Carol... Er, I'm sorry...'

'Templeton. Carol Templeton. Pleased to meet you, Lieutenant.' Carol offered her hand to Alf.

'Do call me Alf and I'll call you Carol,' Alf replied, first shaking Carol's hand and then pulling up a chair from another table for her. 'What'll you have?'

'An old-fashioned, please. That's very kind of you.'

'You'll be lucky to get any orange in it, but I'll see what I can do.' Alf went off to the bar.

'So, Carol. It's a long time since we met. Are you keeping well?' Monty asked.

208

'Oh, not bad. And yerself? You're looking leaner and fitter than when I last saw you. And where did ye get the tan?'

'I'm fine. Fair to middlin' as Stephen's folk would say. As for the tan, I was in North Africa for a short while. Nothing terribly adventurous, though.'

'Oh aye? I see ye got yerself a medal, though. They don't hand out the George Medal with tubes o' Smarties. Talkin' o' Stephen, have ye heard from him recently?'

'Not for a few months now. You know he's not the best correspondent and, to be honest, I've been a bit busy myself recently. You know he's in South Africa now?'

'Aye, he wrote to me after he arrived, but nothing since then.'

'I see. I gather it's all off with you two anyway. Is that right?'

Carol fiddled in her handbag for a few moments before replying. 'Aye. That's right enough. My parents objected, ye ken?'

'What? I hadn't heard that. But they've not met Stephen. I presume you told them what a splendid chap he is?'

'Aye, of course, but they had their reasons. Oh thanks.' Alf had brought her drink across.

'We were just discussing a mutual acquaintance, Alf – Stephen Cunningham.'

'Cunningham? A legend in his own lifetime. I'm sorry to say I've never met him, but I've certainly heard of him. He's one of the coolest chaps in our outfit. Nerves of steel.'

'I'm afraid I can't stop long. I'm meeting a friend here, ye see, and then we're going to the theatre, but since I've bumped into you, Monty, I jes wanted to ask you. How long does it take for mail to reach South Africa?'

'Lord! Who can say these days? I suppose about four weeks, but then convoys get diverted or delayed and… I regret to say ships can be sunk with their mail onboard. Why do you ask?' Carol seemed relieved by Monty's answer.

'Oh, right. I thought it went by air. Nothin' to worry about then.'

Monty took one of Carol's hands gently. 'Are you worried after Stephen, then?' Carol removed her hand slowly.

'Och, no! It's just that I wrote to him last month and haven't received a reply yet. I thought, mebbe, he'd chosen not to write back.'

'Give it time, Carol. I'll tell you what. I'll write to him myself and say that we'd bumped into each other. I'll tell you if I hear back, but I'll need your address. Oh! I think your friend's just arrived. There's a young woman over there trying to attract your attention.'

Carol looked over her shoulder. 'Aye, that's Kathy. I'd better go. But wait a moment.' She withdrew a pen and notebook, wrote down something in it and tore out the page for Monty.

'Thanks, Monty. It's kind of you. And thank you, too, Alf, for the drink. It was nice to meet you.' Carol wandered over to her friend and after exchanging greetings, the two women left the bar.

'My, Monty! What a stunner. Tell you what. I'll give you a quid for a copy of that address.'

*****

'Have you made any progress on the acoustic torpedoes yet, Monty?' Maitland-Dougall asked. 'I've just been put on the spot by the Joint Intelligence Committee.'

'Nothing of significance as yet, sir. I've heard nothing from the Americans about any special Japanese torpedoes and the Germans seem to have suspended deployment of the Gnats.'

'Gnats, Monty?'

'Sorry, sir. The new acoustic torpedo's been given the codeword 'German Naval Acoustic Torpedo'. The Foxers seem to be doing the trick, though, sir.'

'All very well for the ships that have them, but what about the ships overseas who've not yet had the chance to be issued with your noisemakers, Monty?'

'True, sir. Moreover, some of the escort commanders have complained that the Foxers are jamming their Asdic sets. We really need to establish the exact frequency on which the Gnats are working to find a way of making the Foxers more efficient. But I'm short of ideas at present, sir.'

'Well, keep working on it, Monty. Something will come up eventually. Meanwhile, I have significant news for you.'

Monty was all ears.

'With the campaign in North Africa winding up, the Combined Chiefs of Staff have agreed a strategy for an invasion of Axis territory in the Med. I'm not privy to the detail, but it could be Greece, Crete, Sardinia or even Italy. Naturally, I don't know any timings either. I gathered from the Combined Ops intelligence officer that your oppos in 30 Commando have made a good impression and Mountbatten wants them involved from the outset. DNI is particularly keen to gather useful intelligence on the German *U*-boats and Italian human torpedoes, so I've been asked to assign a torpedo expert permanently to the invasion forces. That means I'm losing you for the duration, Monty.'

'Me, sir? But I don't know anything about submarines and the Italian chariots.'

'You know about torpedoes, though. And as far as I perceive, these Italian chariots are just manned torpedoes. In any case, you might find out something about these… Gnats.'

'So, when do I return to 30 Commando, sir?'

'I told you, Monty. I don't know any timings, but I suspect none of us will get much notice of the assault, so you'd better be on short notice to move. I suggest you take some leave to sort out your affairs. You might be away for months this time.'

Chapter 28
April 1943

'The Commodore will see you now, Lieutenant Cunningham.' A WRNS second officer ushered Stephen into the office of the Chief of Staff to the Commander-in-Chief South Atlantic.

The commodore was seated at his desk and gestured for Stephen to take a seat opposite. He finished signing a signal and handed it to his secretary. As she withdrew, he leaned back in his chair and felt in his jacket for his pipe.

'So, Cunningham. You requested a personal interview. What's up, old chap?'

Stephen had rehearsed what he wanted to say, but now he struggled to say the words. The commodore filled his pipe with tobacco and looked over it expectantly.

'I've come t-to request a n-new appointment, s-sir.'

'Already?' The commodore raised his eyebrows as he lit the pipe. 'But you've only been here half a dog watch. What is it, a year?'

'Y-yes, s-sir.'

'You seem to have fitted in, all right... and I've had good reports about your work in training the South Africans. I hear you've even been helping out the dockies in Durban. What's the problem? Aren't you happy here?'

'I just f-feel I could b-be more use elsewhere, sir. It's a b-bit quiet here.'

The commodore glanced at Stephen's medal ribbons. 'I suppose for someone with your record, life probably is a bit tame, lad. The George Cross, George Medal and King's Commendation for Bravery... Why, you must be the most decorated man in the Service.'

Stephen blushed with embarrassment and said nothing in reply.

'So where did you have in mind for a new appointment? That is, were it in my gift to recommend it... and I'm not sure I want to. We can't run the war with every Tom, Dick and Harry deciding where they want to serve.'

Stephen started at the commodore's attitude. He had thought it would be easier than this. 'Obviously, sir, I'd b-be happy to return to RMSO d-duties back in Britain, sir, b-but I thought about North Africa, sir.'

'North Africa, hey. Full of flies, man. And far too hot, too. In any case, from what I read, Montgomery's almost kicked out Rommel from there. The *Afrika Korps* and Italians are falling back on Tunisia and there are reports that their troops are already being evacuated by sea. I don't think you'll find much excitement there… if that's what you're really looking for. But I'm not sure that's so. Come on, Cunningham. Spit it out. What's the real reason for this request?' The commodore took several deep puffs on his pipe and seemed happy to wait until he had a full confession from Stephen.

The interview wasn't going the way Stephen had planned and he felt uncomfortable with dissembling, even though it wasn't untrue that he thought his skills and experience might be put to better use in another theatre. He felt he had no other option than to come clean and to rely on the commodore's human understanding. The chief of staff had a reputation for fair play and looking after the people under his command.

'It's true, sir, that I f-find my duties unimportant here. B-but there is another reason for m-my request.' Stephen wrung his hands in anguish, but the commodore merely smoked his pipe patiently and allowed Stephen to continue.

'I've met a g-girl, sir, and I d-don't know how to b-break off the relationship.' Stephen cringed inwardly. This was the most embarrassing conversation of his life.

'You've not put her in the family way, have you, Cunningham?'

'Oh no! N-nothing like that, sir!' Sufficient time had passed since his leave in Stellenbosch for Stephen to be relaxed on that point, but Julia's letters had made it quite clear that she regarded a proposal of marriage as a mere formality to come.

'It's just that the g-girl in question expects something more p-permanent, sir.' His face had flushed considerably.

'I see. And you don't want to hurt the gal's feelings, hey? You're not the first young man to become entranced by a local girl overseas, Cunningham. Who is the unfortunate young lady. Do I know her?'

'I don't think you d-do, sir. She's called Julia Webber-Tarr, sir.'

'Christ, Cunningham! Of course, I know her. Her father's an extremely wealthy industrialist. He owns vast swathes of the Kimberley diamond mines. My God, Cunningham, you struck the jackpot there! The gal's damned pretty, too. Are you sure you want to break off with her?'

'Yes, sir,' Stephen replied very quietly. 'I really do.'

'Umm.' The commodore puffed away on his pipe for a minute. 'Very well, Cunningham. I've dealt with worse problems. I'm not sure we want to upset Webber-Tarr's daughter, so I'll see what I can do… but I'm making no promises mind.'

'Thank you, s-sir'. Stephen rose to take his leave a much-relieved man, but he felt ashamed to have taken such a cowardly way out. That said, there was no guarantee he was off the hook yet, anyway.

*****

Captain Maitland-Dougall's warning had come true. Monty had his orders to proceed to Malta in order to join up with 30 Commando somewhere in the Mediterranean, but he didn't yet know where. Perhaps, he might meet up with his elder brother in Cairo, he thought optimistically, but then again, the General Staff were never close to the frontline and 30 Commando would most certainly be. He had been to see his parents in Wiltshire and noted with concern his father's declining health. Mother was terribly worried about him and it didn't make life easier having two sons overseas at war. However, the estate manager seemed to know his business and that was one less worry to the family.

He was booked on a ship taking passage from Liverpool and it seemed too good an opportunity not to call to see Lucy *en route* to the port, but he had had to postpone his visit until the weekend immediately prior to sailing as she didn't break up from teaching for another week and she was busy in the evenings in her final preparations for the end of term. Feeling disappointed that Lucy couldn't even spare him one evening, he had decided to remain in London until it was time to head north. Then he had had the idea that he might pass one of the final few days of his leave looking up Marcy, but even that hadn't been straightforward. It seemed that she now worked shifts and not only had that caused him difficulty in contacting her on her landlady's telephone in Wolverton, but

214

Marcy's availability had been restricted. However, with perseverance, he had managed a luncheon engagement in a smart Oxford restaurant.

Marcy had been pleased to see him and again, he had noticed how attractive she could appear without her spectacles, but he had forgotten how much taller she was than he.

'Monty, it's lovely to see you again. It's been too long.' She kissed him fondly on the cheek and accepted his offer of a seat. 'You're looking very tanned and healthy. Have you been somewhere nice?'

'I was in North Africa a little before Christmas and I'm leaving for overseas again over the weekend.'

'Oh! That's rather sudden. I suppose I shouldn't ask where you're going?'

'I'm afraid not, Marcy, but it'll be warmer. That's all I can say.' A waiter interrupted them with the menus.

'The soup today is spinach and watercress, sir, madam. Our main course special is fried pollock with a parsley sauce and crispy bacon. Can I bring sir or madam a glass of something?'

Marcy replied, 'Just water for me, please,' and Monty echoed her choice.

They each examined the menu. Marcy was the first to make her choice. 'I have to say that I'm sick to death of Woolton pie and I don't fancy sausages and mash. I think I'll go for the fish. It sounds nice. And bacon, too!'

'That sounds an excellent choice. I'll join you. Would you like a glass of wine with the fish? I'm sure the restaurant keeps some back for its better customers, Marcy.'

'No thanks, Monty. I have to go back on shift later.'

'Shifts, hey?' Monty lowered his voice and drew closer to Marcy across the table. 'Statistics my foot, Marcy. I think I have an inkling of what you do Marcy… And I'm awfully impressed.'

'I've told you, Monty. I work with statistics and if you think any differently, then you should know better than to discuss it.'

'Point taken, Marcy. Mum's the word.' Fortunately, Monty didn't have to dwell on his rebuff as the waiter came to take their order.

'How's life treating you at Bletchley Park, Marcy?' he asked after the waiter withdrew.

'Splendidly,' Marcy replied excitedly. 'It's a simply super place to work. There are all sorts of different sorts there and oodles of social functions. We even have our own recreational club. And the work is really interesting, too, of course.'

'How fascinating. What sort of activities do you get up to?'

'Oh, all sorts of things. There's a bridge club... a gramophone recital every week that I try to attend when it fits in with my shifts. I play tennis in the summer and, this will surprise you... Last autumn I started learning Scottish Country dancing. It's simply thrilling.'

'Are there enough women to make up partners, then?'

'Ah! There lies the rub, Monty. It's the other way around. The women outnumber the men by three to one. We fair wear out the few men who attend, I tell you.'

'You make me feel jealous, Marcy.'

'You jealous? If I know you, you're in love with a different girl every month.' Marcy blushed slightly and looked away. The soup arrived before Monty could reply.

Monty found the conversation a little difficult as neither of them was able to discuss their work for security reasons. It was so long since they had been at university together that they now had few friends in common to discuss, too. However, Monty was happy enough to listen to Marcy's descriptions of her lodgings, social life and people with whom she worked. Other than the grimness of her accommodation near the Wolverton railway sidings, she made life at Bletchley Park sound like that at a holiday camp. The coffee arrived and Marcy suddenly noticed Monty's medal ribbon.

'I say, Monty. Do forgive me for prattling on about myself. What's the medal?'

'Oh, it's nothing to do with courage in the face of the enemy, Marcy. I just helped a chum out defuzing a couple of mines, that's all. He received the George Cross and I received the George Medal as his assistant.'

'Golly! Still, you must have been awfully brave and it must have been dangerous.'

'It was a bit, but my main memory is of horrible, cold and slimy mud.'

'I fancy you're being your usual terribly modest self, Monty.' Marcy reached across and stroked Monty's cheek affectionately. 'I bet the girls are all impressed.'

'Not really,' Monty sipped his coffee. 'There was somebody I had hoped to impress, but it didn't really work.'

'You're not in love again, are you, Monty?' Monty noted that Marcy seemed earnest in the question this time. Her tone had changed from the usual mocking one.

'Actually, I am, Marcy. I met the sister of one of my colleagues in Lancashire. She's a school teacher.' To Monty's surprise, Marcy seemed disappointed by the news.

'And does this paragon of virtue reciprocate your ardour, Monty?'

'I'm not sure… Leastways, I think she's fond of me, but she's never said more. But I have to tell you, Marcy, this time I really am head over heels in love. Indeed, I want to marry her.' It was the first time Monty had thought of marriage to Lucy and he surprised himself by voicing the thought. He detected a certain frostiness in Marcy as he said it.

'I see. I suppose it had to happen sometime, I suppose,' she replied sorrowfully and fiddled in her handbag.

'I had hoped to see her this week, but she's still teaching and I'm off overseas this weekend. I might then have put matters on a sounder footing.'

'But as she wasn't available, you thought you'd look me up instead. To fill in the time as it were.' Marcy's tone had definitely hardened, Monty thought.

'Of course, not… dear Marcy.' Monty reached across the table to take one of Marcy's hands, but she withdrew it abruptly. 'I mean, we've been good friends ever since our varsity days. Why wouldn't I want to see you?'

'Indeed, Monty. Just good friends. Good old Marcy. She'll be up for a free lunch if my girlfriend's not available.' Marcy's voice started to choke and she pulled a handkerchief from her handbag to dab her eyes slightly. She stood suddenly. 'Oh, Monty! You're so… tactless and I'm not going to take it anymore.'

Too startled to stand himself, Monty remained seated. 'But what do you mean? What have I said?'

'Oh, Monty! You really are the limit. I'm afraid I have to catch my train now. I told you I was back on shift later.' She turned abruptly and headed for the exit doors. Monty chased after her and caught her arm.

'I'm sorry, Marcy. I really don't know what I've said to upset you, but please forgive me. I didn't mean to…' Marcy shook herself free.

'Oh, go to Hell, Monty.' Her eyes welling with tears, Marcy burst through the restaurant doors onto the street. Monty just stood there watching her retreating figure before he became conscious that the other diners were staring at him. Turning a deepening pink, he called for the bill and his cap and left as expeditiously as he could.

*****

With little else to do until the rail journey north for the weekend, Monty decided to amuse himself in the cinema. The film was an American Western called *The Ox-bow Incident* and he found it very exciting, but to his dismay, part way through the film a message flashed across the screen. As a variation of the common, *Air raid in progress. Please head for a shelter*, it read instead, *Lt Cdr Thomas Montcalm is to report to the Admiralty at once*. There were gasps of admiration from the audience in his row and that behind as he stood and left the cinema to answer the call. It was no surprise that the duty officer was aware of his whereabouts since he always had to leave a list of his movements with the duty officers, but it was still a surprise since he was now on pre-embarkation leave. He telephoned the Admiralty immediately and was informed that a staff car was on its way to take him to an aerodrome for passage by air to his new appointment. This was a total surprise to Monty. He had expected a long sea voyage, after all. He asked the duty officer to inform Lucy or her mother that he would not be meeting them over the weekend, after all. It was very disappointing. He had looked forward to seeing Lucy and had even thought about buying a ring to take with him, but he felt a sense of excitement, too. What could be so important that he was being given the VIP treatment?

The car duly arrived and Monty had no difficulty in persuading the driver to drop by his digs in order to change into khaki and collect his gear. Subsequently, he caught a naval aircraft to an airfield near Bristol of all places. The Fleet Air Arm crew weren't able to tell him why. It was all very mysterious, especially as he didn't arrive in Bristol until after midnight to a completely blacked out aerodrome. However, there the mystery unravelled. Monty was directed to a hut on the edge of the airfield where he discovered that he was joining a small number of VIPs flying from Whitchurch to Lisbon. Monty was surprised to be classed as a VIP. The other passengers seemed to be a couple of army staff officers, a general and several civil servants. However, as one by one they were required to confirm aloud their names and next-of-kin, Monty recognised the name of one of his fellow travellers being that of a government minister and realised that a woman was included in their party. Some of the passengers seemed quite nervous. Monty assumed that like him they were concerned for their safety and a lieutenant colonel seated next to him confirmed this.

'A commando, hey? Don't often see you chaps about. Ever flown this route before?'

'No, sir. This is my first time. Actually, do you know where we're going?'

'What? You don't even know where you're bound? It's Lisbon. I'm then going on to Gibraltar. I dare say you will be, too. After all, if you're a spy, you wouldn't be in uniform, what?'

'A spy, sir?'

'My, you are a first-timer. This route's laid on for spies and escaped POWs.' The colonel gestured with his head to the woman sitting quietly on the end of the bench opposite. 'Every now and then, a few mortals like us are allowed to take the flight if we're pressed for time – along with members of the government, of course. I've had to do it occasionally. Mind you, since the end of last year, it's become more fraught with danger. Bloody Jerry!'

'What do you mean, sir?' Monty was aware that air travel carried its risks.'

'You may have noticed that we're operating from a civilian airport.'

'I hadn't, actually, sir. I've just stepped off a Navy 'plane and it was too dark to see anything.'

'We're taking a civilian DC3… KLM under charter to BOAC. Until November last year the Germans left such aircraft alone out of respect for Portugal's neutrality, but that's since all changed. Did you hear of Leslie Howard's death?'

'You mean the actor, sir? *Gone with the Wind* and all that.'

'That's him. His 'plane was shot down on his return from Lisbon. There are rumours amongst the *cognoscenti*, you know…' The colonel tapped the side of his nose confidentially. 'Jerry may have thought him a spy and deliberately shot him down. Their spies in Lisbon keep an eye on passengers travelling this route, you know, so watch out.'

The news chilled Monty, but he had no further time to consider it as he and his fellow passengers were called to board their flight.

Chapter 29
May 1943

When news of Stephen's reappointment came through, events moved quickly. He had barely had time to make his farewells to his colleagues in HMS *Afrikander* before he had found himself on a train to Durban. There he had embarked in a troopship bound for Port Tewfik at the northern end of the Red Sea. He had quickly learned that life in South Africa and onboard the troopship had been one of luxury compared to that of North Africa. Immediately on disembarkation, he and several army troops had been taken by lorry on a three-hour bumpy and dust-ridden journey to a make-shift transit camp. The best accommodation that the transit camp had been able to provide for him and three other officers of similar rank was a tent and this had had no furniture. Instead, he and his mess mates had been issued with blankets and told to bed down on the desert floor. The night of his arrival had been torture. Firstly, he had been surprised by the cold of the desert night and then, on awakening, he had found his bedding infested with dozens of black beetles. However, the one advantage the camp had offered was its proximity to the Pyramids and Stephen had had high hopes of being able to visit them in his free time. He had presumed he had been reappointed to help clear mines from the Suez Canal

His discomfort was unexpectedly terminated, though, with fresh disappointing news. After breakfast, he had been given fresh instructions to travel by rail to Alexandria. Fourteen hours later, including a three-hour stop in Cairo, he had found himself in Alexandria. So much for his hopes of visiting the Pyramids, he had thought. However, even then his travails were not yet over.

It was with a shock that Stephen had reported to HMS *Nile*, the shore base at Ras El Tin providing logistical and administrative support to the Royal Navy in the Eastern Mediterranean, only to discover that there was no appointment for him there, after all. It seemed that with the collapse of Rommel's forces in North Africa, personnel movements had become fluid and disjointed. It was with some embarrassment that Captain Rolleston, the Flag Captain to the Rear Admiral Alexandria, welcomed Stephen on his joining call. Rolleston had served during the Great War and retired as a commander before being recalled to service and given the acting rank of Captain.

'Damned silly mix-up, I'm afraid, Cunningham. I say, you're not related to the CinC, are you?'

'N-no, sir,' Stephen replied automatically. It was a common enough question.

'Eh? Ah well. It seems you've come a long way for nothing, but these things happen in war. A shame as you've a distinguished record. I'll contact the Admiralty and see what they want done with you.'

'Is there n-nothing I can do here, s-sir?' Stephen was starting to wonder if he might have been better staying in Simon's Town.

'What did you have in mind?'

'As you know, sir, I've plenty of experience in mine and bomb d-disposal, b-but I've recently learned to dive, too, sir.'

'Really? You are a brave chap. We could have done with you in '41. Might not have lost two battleships to the Eyties. The trouble is, Cunningham, the work's largely been done. The harbour's clear of mines and the Royal Engineers deal with anything left over from the *Luftwaffe* raids long back. I don't know whose idea it was to send you here, but frankly, Cunningham, your skills are a bit specialist for our needs. You'd be more use back home.'

Naturally, Stephen felt disappointed, but uplifted by the news he might be able to return to England. He wanted to check on his mother and he missed the camaraderie of having other RMSOs around him.

'I'll tell you what, Cunningham. Take a breather for a week or two. Take in the sights. I can recommend the palace. Do you fish or ride?' Stephen nodded without explanation. 'Splendid. Plenty of opportunity for both. We'll contact London and try to get you shipped out of here as quickly as we can. Can't say fairer than that.'

*****

Three weeks later, Stephen was experiencing his first taste of Malta. It was a shock. Despite his experience of the *Luftwaffe*'s bombing raids on Britain's major cities, he was, nonetheless, appalled by the devastation of the densely populated island. Lieutenant 'Tiny' Rowland briefed him on some of the history of the siege. Rowland, known as 'Tiny' thanks to his huge height of six-foot-six inches, was another RMSO and Stephen had been sent to relieve him.

'This m-must be the most heavily bombed place on Earth, Tiny.'

'Sadly, I think that's true, Stephen. I still can't believe they sent you to take over from me. It must be two years since we last met.'

'Longer, I think, Tiny. It was in Birmingham, C-Christmas 1940.'

'So, it was. You've a good memory, Stephen. What an awful shout that was… But nothing compared to this.' Rowland gestured to the remnants of the walls of the bar in which they were sitting. The *Luftwaffe* had refashioned it as an open-air bar.

'B-but how did the civilian p-population endure it? Living in this rubble.'

'Stoically, I'd say, but that wasn't the worst. Imagine a quarter of a million people trying to cram into the few shelters available. Added to the malnutrition caused by the food shortages, they quickly became cess pits of disease. Dysentery, tuberculosis and typhoid were rife, but thankfully, the convoys have been getting through for some time and Jerry's not paid us a visit in ages. I heard someone say that we had 3,000 air raids in '41 and '42.'

Stephen fiddled with the cross stud on his GC ribbon and muttered, 'Some p-people really earned their medal.'

'I say, Stephen. Your stutter's improved miles. It's barely noticeable now.'

'You should hear me with s-senior officers, Tiny. I'm all jelly.'

'It's going to take a huge effort to rebuild the island, but I'll be sad to leave it now.'

'Really? S-surely, you've suffered enough? I mean, two years of this.' Stephen gestured to the detritus around them.

'Maybe, but I met a local girl and we were married a year ago. I feel settled here and it seems a pity to leave just as all the hard work's done.'

'Congratulations. But there must still b-be plenty to do.'

'I wouldn't be too sure of that, Stephen. Of course, there's plenty of unexploded ordnance around, but the island's crawling with Royal Engineers and RAF ammunition technicians. I can't see Jerry mounting too many mine laying raids now we've gone on the offensive. Had you heard that we're likely to be going into Crete or the Greek mainland next?'

'It would make more sense to go for Italy or even S-Sicily.'

'Where did sense come into it, old chap. War is hardly a rational thing, is it?'

'Have you heard d-details of your new appointment? Is it b-back home? Can you take your wife?'

'Hold on, Stephen. Yes, I've had my new appointment and I'm not going anywhere near England. I'm joining a so-called *Naval Demolition Unit*.'

'G-good gracious. What's one of those?'

'I gather I'll be going to Crete, Greece, Italy or wherever as part of the next invasion. There are a few *NDU*s being created and our task will be to destroy sandbars and underwater obstacles.'

'Golly! That sounds exciting.'

'Maybe, but don't say that to Maria, my wife. She's anxious enough about me leaving her as it is.'

'What a pity. I'd quite fancy the challenge. I don't suppose we could swap c-could we?'

'I think that glass of *Kinnie* has gone to your head, Stephen… And it doesn't even have any alcohol in it. 'Twere it possible, I'd bite your hand off. I feel quite at home here and then there's Maria to consider. Thanks, though, old pal.' Stephen thought Rowland quite moved by his offer.

'Well, why not? I'd happily volunteer to take your place in one of these NDUs. You're well in with the admiral. Why not ask him?'

'I suppose I could sound him out, but I bet you a pound to a pinch of salt that nothing can be done. Come on, I'll buy you another *Kinnie*.'

*****

Operation Husky, the Allied invasion of south-east Sicily on 10 July 1943, was an even bigger event than *Operation Torch*, comprising as it did 2,000 ships, 4,000 aircraft and 150,000 men. General Patton took his American Seventh Army ashore in the Gulf of Gelaand. Montgomery's Eight Army landed further east in the Gulf of Goto. 30 Commando went ashore at Cape Passero immediately behind the initial assault wave.

From Lisbon, Monty had travelled down through Spain overland to Gibraltar and onward by sea to Algiers where he had finally caught up with the rest of 30 Commando. The Commando was now under the charge overall of a Lieutenant Commander Riley with Monty in command of the Technical Troop. Unfortunately, Riley and Monty hadn't hit it off initially. Monty had shown Riley his orders to the effect that under certain circumstances the entire Commando would be put under Monty's tasking and Riley had not taken it well. In his turn, Monty didn't like the apparent lack of discipline within the Commando under Riley's leadership. He thought Riley a maverick who didn't make any effort to stamp out thieving, truculence and even fighting amongst the men.

The Allies seemed to have taken the Italians by surprise and Riley wondered if they had been lulled into a sense of false security because the assault had taken place on a bright moonlit night. Even so, it was clear that the First Airlanding Brigade had suffered many casualties. In an audacious move, 2,000 men had been sent by gliders to capture a key bridge in Syracuse. It was obvious that through the inexperience of the American pilots towing the gliders, they had released the gliders too early. On the approach to the coast, the men of 30 Commando had watched the gliders overfly them and seen several drop short into the sea. The following morning, the men had been traumatised to see hundreds of corpses, many of them from the South Staffordshire regiment, washing ashore against the cliffs. A large number were missing the top section of their heads for some reason. A marine had disgusted his colleagues by suggesting that the skulls reminded him of toilet bowls. The comment had not been appreciated. Monty had the satisfaction of learning that there was a limit to bad taste, even amongst the Royal Marines.

Now safely established ashore, 30 Commando separated from XXX Corps to proceed independently to their first target, a German coastal radar installation. They met with little resistance on the way, but the Germans defending the radar station were of sterner stuff. The Royal Marines of the military troop attacked the station and, whilst a firefight ensued, the small number of German sailors were no match for the battle-hardened veterans of the Maghreb. Unfortunately, the time gained in defending the installation had given the Germans the opportunity to blow the self-destruct charges and there was little equipment left worth salvaging and sending back to the boffins in England. However, remembering the raid on Algiers, Monty thought to search the greatcoat of the naval officer in

225

command and now lying dead amongst his men. It wasn't his first experience of rifling the pockets of the dead, he remembered. Monty's German was sufficiently good to recognise that within the officer's greatcoat pocket were not just a handbook for the radar set, but a complete and detailed set of notes taken by the officer on his long radar course.

Operating with speed, there was no time to bury the dead Germans and the Commando pressed on further down the coast to a Radio Direction Finding station manned by the Italians. The Italians offered no resistance and Monty's troop hit the jackpot – a complete set of the *Regia Aeronautica Italiana*'s cyphers and frequencies for their aircraft's homing beacons for the present quarter. The information would be of vital importance to the RAF in Malta. Overall, reflected Monty, it hadn't been a bad night's work. A marine and corporal were left behind to guard the installation for further investigation.

*****

The men of 30 Commando pushed north to Augusta in the wake of the Eighth Army. Monty didn't think it a welcoming spot. The city had been relieved first by men of the Special Raiding Squadron, a unit of the SAS, and then the Black Watch. The port had been bombed by the RAF and shelled by the Navy. Rats scurried about everywhere and the stench of faeces and rotting corpses in the high heat was sickening. However, the commandos had no time to consider such problems. They had to race to search the city for documents and equipment of interest before the soldiers looted or even destroyed them. At the nearby seaplane base Monty was overjoyed to be handed an Enigma machine complete with its plug board. Somebody had tried to destroy the rotors with a hammer, but Monty felt sure that the unit would still be of great interest to the boffins at Bletchley Park. The thought prompted him to look back on his lunch with Marcy in Oxford three months earlier.

He had considered Marcy's outburst extraordinary. All the years he had known her, he had considered her a sweet and even-tempered girl, but something he had said had clearly upset her. He hated leaving on bad terms and had written her a letter of apology, but received no reply. Then again, the absence of a reply wasn't significant. Mail to the Mediterranean theatre was all over the place at the moment with the Allies' rapid movement further and further eastwards. A strange thought had struck him, though. He recalled that Marcy's composure seemed to have become disturbed when he had mentioned his relationship with Lucy and then uttered his previously unspoken thought that he would like to marry her. He and Marcy had been good chums for years, but might she have been jealous? Could it be that she was attracted to him in a way that suggested they could be more than just good friends? It was only then that he recalled their last but one meeting. Marcy had kissed him passionately as they had parted. Why had he not remembered? Imagine, life with Marcy! She was very attractive without her spectacles and awfully bright. She was a good crew for the boat, too. It was food for thought, but what was Riley saying?

'You've just got to see this, Monty. Come on.'

Monty followed Riley somewhat reluctantly. He was feeling jaded but what Riley had to show him was worth the effort. Instead of radar to detect aircraft, the Italians had installed a hall of bizarre-looking giant trumpets for detecting aircraft sound. These were connected up to a control panel showing the speed, altitude and course of the detected aircraft. It was a magnificent piece of engineering, but so antiquated.

'Would you believe it, Monty? It seems that the Germans didn't trust their Italian allies enough to share the secrets of radar. I'm intrigued what else we might discover on the island.'

Chapter 30
July 1942

A few days after the invasion of Sicily, Monty was particularly keen to race across the island to the west coast where lay the *Regia Marina*'s largest base on the island, the arsenal of Trapani. Monty was keen to inspect the Italian Navy's torpedo storage facilities for any sign of Italian or German acoustic torpedo variants. Before leaving London, he had read an intelligence report that the Italians might have developed a radio-controlled torpedo. The pre-war naval attaché had written a report to say that he had witnessed trials of an air-launched torpedo that trailed a wire connected to a radio buoy. The torpedo was guided by an operator in the launching aircraft by sending radio signals to the buoy which were then relayed via the wire to the torpedo. It marked its position to the operator with a trail of fluorescent liquid. According to the attaché's report, he had been much impressed by the manoeuvrability of the torpedo and the surface targets had not been able to evade it. The torpedo had been improved by the addition of a parachute to facilitate its release at altitudes of up to 3,000 feet, but the Italian generals had been less impressed than the British Naval Attaché with the torpedo's performance and had directed the trials to be discontinued. However, Monty had read a more recent intelligence report to suggest that the project had not been abandoned. Moreover, the design had been improved to the extent that trials off Pola had recorded speeds of 65 knots when British and American torpedoes were only capable of about 45 knots. If Monty could discover one of these new weapons, it would be a real coup both for 30 Commando and DTMI. Unfortunately, the Commando ran into the 15th Panzer Division.

The jeep in which Monty, Riley and two Royal Marine NCOs were travelling led the column of a Bedford truck carrying a dozen marines and a couple of motorcycle outriders. Somewhere near Agrigento on the southern coast, out of nowhere it seemed, there was a great flash and the road ahead of them disintegrated from the burst of a tank shell. The jeep was thrown off the road by the blast, but fortunately nobody was killed. Shaken up, Monty scrambled to the side of the road and took cover as best he could.

'Look, sirs. Over there,' one of the NCOs shouted and pointed across the road. With careful scrutiny, Monty could just make out movement of half a dozen tin helmets in the British style. It appeared that some of the army had established a defensive line against the tanks.

'What do you think, Quintin?' Monty asked Riley.

'I'd say we'd be safer over there than here, but first we have to cross the damned road. Come on, let's just go for it.' Without waiting for any reply from Monty, Riley dashed across the road, followed by one of the NCOs. The Germans responded immediately with a burst of machine gun fire. Horrified, Monty watched the bullets rip up the road in a straight line following the two men, but mercifully, they rolled into the bank on the other side of the road. Monty realised that, despite the Germans now being forewarned of their intentions, he and the other NCO needed to follow suit. He decided it was best not to think of it and hurled himself across the road, expecting any second to be ripped apart by a hail of machine gun fire. The Germans did, indeed, respond and Monty felt a stabbing pain in his left hand, but somehow, he and the NCO found themselves safe across the road. However, they were no sooner congratulating themselves than a tank shell burst nearby and covered them in stones, earth and shrapnel. Monty had left his tin helmet behind with the jeep.

'Dig, for fuck's sake,' Riley roared. The NCOs had their entrenching tools with them, but the two officers were reduced to using their bare hands to dig the earth beneath them. Within minutes, they were joined by two members of the 8th Durham Light Infantry.

'Howay man,' one of them greeted the commandos. 'We can see you've ne'er worked down a mine. Gi' us a go, sor.' The two Durham men quickly set to with their own picks and shovels to dig the four men a deep trench. Meanwhile, one of the NCOs noted that Monty had taken a bullet clean through his left hand and applied a dressing to stop the bleeding.

'There ye are bonny lads. Y've a reet canny home fer now.' The infantrymen looked around the newly-dug trench with professional pride.

Riley felt in his jacket pocket for some cigarettes and handed two packets over to the former miners. He gestured to the NCOs to do the same. Monty didn't smoke. 'Thanks, lads. We're very grateful.'

'Oh, that's purely belta of you, sor. We'll be away back to ar'ain hyem now then.'

For the next two hours Monty and his colleagues cowered in their temporary home whilst the Panzers were driven back by a combination of artillery and airpower. Not for the first time, Monty decided that he preferred dealing with the hazards of rendering mines safe to life as a soldier. One's actions were in one's own control and if one failed, well, it would be too late to worry about it.

*****

Their pride dented and with Monty's left arm in a sling, Riley and his men pushed on up the coast. Without the jeep, Monty rode in the back of the Bedford truck and observed the retreating landscape. It was covered in vines and in an effort to distract himself from the pain in his hand, Monty tried hard to remember the local grapes. He remembered Nero d'Avola and Frapatto, but couldn't for the life of him recall a white grape. It was on the tip of his tongue. Manzanilla? No, that was Spanish. Then it came to him. Inzolia, of course. It was used in Marsala wines. Suddenly, the truck screeched to a sharp halt. A minute later, Reilly joined Monty at the back of the truck.

'There are signs up to say we're about to enter a minefield, Monty. I think we'll have to turn back. It's a job for the sappers.' Monty clambered out of the truck to stretch his legs. He gazed at the sea on the horizon. It was a lovely, deep blue, covered with an armada of shipping. In the distance could be heard the boom of artillery fire and aerial bombing. A few years ago, the scene would have been one of beauty and, above all, peace. A marine shouted to call his and Riley's attention to a young boy approaching the convoy on foot through what was denoted as a minefield.

The lad waved at them enthusiastically. He was skinny and very dark skinned, dressed in plimsolls, shorts and a torn vest. The men were used to such sights. The boy would be begging for something, no doubt. Riley gestured for one of the marines who spoke a little Italian to come forward.

'*Attento! Miniera!*' he called, but the boy came on regardless. He came up to the truck with a wide smile that revealed two missing front teeth.

'*Ci sono solo poche miniere. Posso mostrarti la strada,*' the boy replied.

'What's he saying, Finlay?' Riley asked.

'I canna say, sir. His accent's a bit thick.'

'Hark whose talking, Finlay,' a sergeant interjected. Finlay tried again, supplementing his language skills with sign language.

'*Attento! Miniera!* Boom!' The marine mimicked walking on the road on tiptoes.

'*No. Miniera non molti.*'

'He says there aren't many mines, sir.'

'Ask him if he knows where they are, Finlay.'

'*Dove sone le miniera?* Savvy?'

'*Si signori. Posso mostrati.*' The lad tapped his chest and gestured to the roads and vineyards.

'I think he's sayin' he can geed us, sir.'

'I'm not sure we should trust him, Monty. We'll wait for the sappers, shall we?' However, Monty would brook no delay in his quest to find a guided torpedo.

'No, Quintin. I say we carry on. The lad wouldn't have walked along this road if he really thought it mined. Let's give it a go.'

'Very well, Monty. You're in charge… for the moment.' Riley turned to his sergeant.

'Very well, Sergeant. He's our best shot. Have we any chocolate?'

'Yessir.' The sergeant rummaged in his haversack and withdrew a bar of Cadbury's.

'Finlay, tell him that if he can show us the way, this will be his.' However, the lad clearly understood the sentiment and shook his head.'

'*Niente cioccolato. Sigaretta.*' The boy mimed smoking a cigarette.

'Cheeky bugger,' Riley responded. 'He can't be more than fourteen, but very well.' He pulled out a packet from his own haversack and held them up. The boy replied with three fingers.

'Christ almighty! Now he's haggling. Right, who's got some fags on them? This is my last packet.' Reluctantly, two marines each held aloft a packet of Woodbines. Riley snatched them and nodded his agreement to the boy. Turning to the sergeant, he said, 'He can ride on one of the motorcycles and lead the way. If the other motorcycle runs parallel, we'll follow in the truck two hundred yards astern and try to follow their tracks. Let's get going. We've wasted enough time already.'

Standing on the privilege of rank, Monty decided that this time he would sit in the front of the truck with Riley and the driver. The young Italian seemed quite happy to ride pillion on a motorcycle and led them off the road through the vineyards. Monty wondered whether the mines were anti-personnel versions or anti-tank mines. It would make a big difference. If the latter, the weight of the motorcycles and their passengers wouldn't be enough to trigger a mine, but the fifteen-hundredweight truck would be a different matter.

The path through the vines was steep and bumpy, making for an uncomfortable journey, and at the worst of the jolts, Monty momentarily feared that they had struck a mine. However, the diversion was a short one before their guide led them back onto the road. It seemed that if the road was mined at all, it was only for a length of about 600 yards. Waving them farewell, the lad ran off happily clutching his cigarettes. No doubt he would make a small fortune selling them, thought Monty, but good luck to him.

Once back on the road, the going was good and the unit soon found themselves at the naval base in Trapani. The only enemy troops they had encountered had been a coastal defence battalion. Despite outnumbering the commandos in spades, they didn't put up any resistance and immediately surrendered. It seemed that the Italian soldier had no love for his German allies and no interest in fighting. However, given the need for speed, Riley, on his part, had no interest in taking prisoners and had too few troops to provide guards. He merely told the battalion to make a pile of their weapons and to hand themselves over to the Americans who were landing at the Castellammare del Golfo further up the coast.

Monty was pleased to find the arsenal at the naval base intact. Two warehouses contained a vast array of weapons; sea mines in one and torpedoes in the other. However, Monty was disappointed only to find conventional torpedoes and none showing any form of guidance system. He moved into the mine shed in company with Riley.

'My God! I've never seen such a place,' Riley exclaimed. 'There must be hundreds of them… All neatly stacked and pristine. Is this what you came for?'

'It's certainly a good find, Quintin. I'll need to take a few to pieces in order to remove samples of their firing mechanisms for *Vernon*.'

'But aren't they live, for Christ's sake?'

'That depends on your definition. Most of the mines contain about three-quarters to a ton of HE. The bigger ones two tons, but…'

'Each one! But…' Riley did a rough count of the number of mines. 'But that means there's about three to four kilotons of explosive around us… And you want to go fiddling with them!'

'I'll need some help, too, I'm afraid.' Monty held up the arm in his sling. 'It's a two-handed job.'

'Hang on a minute. What did you mean, *"It depends on your definition"*? Are these fuckers live or not?'

'Quintin, you know very well from your experience with demolitions that explosive on its own isn't dangerous – save for nitro-glycerine, that is. It needs a primer and detonator to set off the charge. Whilst I'm sure these mines will have their primers fitted, I doubt the armourers would have inserted the detonators. It would be crazy to do so until they were ready for launching. Furthermore, they won't be armed. Those mines over there with the horns are contact mines. The horns contain glass tubes that, once broken on contact with a hard surface, will set off an electrical circuit to detonate the mines. Those cylindrical mines will be a mixture of magnetic or acoustic mines, possibly a combination of both. They usually require a hydrostatic clock linked to the pressure of seawater to arm them and then they would still need an outside influence such as noise or a change in the magnetic field surrounding them for them to be triggered. I can't see that happening here.'

'Thank Christ for that, Monty. It feels spooky seeing them sitting there, even evil. So, you're saying they're completely safe, after all?'

'I didn't say that, Quintin. I'm not primarily interested in the main charge of the mines, but the firing mechanisms and fuzes. The fuzes themselves might contain up to a pound of RDX or some other explosive content, more than enough to kill a man and… even such a small explosion would ruin our day in this warehouse. As you said, there's quite a bit of HE waiting to go off should I make a mistake.'

Monty saw the blood drain from Riley's face before he could reply. 'Er, just how many of these mines do you intend to take apart?'

'Just one of each of the more modern versions, say half a dozen.'

'And is it likely that any of them will be booby-trapped?'

'That's just the chance I have to take. My main reason for being here is to learn the latest nasty surprises the enemy have in wait for our RMSOs.'

Riley was stunned into silence for nearly a minute. He kept looking around the warehouse in shock. Finally, he spoke.

'This isn't a job for which I can call for a volunteer to assist you. It looks like you and I might be earning our harps and wings together if you blow it… I didn't mean to say that.'

'That's your choice, Quintin. But I have to do this and I can't do it on my own.'

'Erm. How long do you think it'll take?'

'A few hours, I'm afraid. I don't plan on hurrying and… I don't know what difficulties I might come across.'

'Right then. Let's get on with it, then. You've certainly got balls, Monty, I'll say that for you. I'm sorry to say that I misjudged you.'

'Think nothing of it. Could one of your men fetch my tools for me?'

Chapter 31
July 1943

A short, scrawny soldier drove Stephen and his luggage from the port to a former school in the town of Augusta on the south-eastern coast of Sicily, facing the Ionian Sea. In the distance to the north, Stephen could hear the *crumps* of artillery fire. The Eight Army was attempting to drive out the Germans and Italians defending Catania before pushing on to Messina. It was a typically hot July day and Stephen wished he could have swapped his army-issue khaki unform for the crisp, starched-white tropical uniform of his naval contemporaries at sea. However, the khaki was more practical for bomb disposal duties. Since he had focused on scientific and mathematical subjects at school and university, he had had little education in Classics. Over his last couple of months of service in the Mediterranean, this had been something he had increasingly regretted. The war was offering him, free of charge, a Cook's Tour of the ancient civilisations. Even so, he was aware of some of Augusta's history. The world-renowned physicist Orso Corbino had been born in Augusta. Corbino had gone on to serve as an eminent professor at the nearby University of Messina specialising in the influence of external magnetic fields on the motion of electrons in metals.

A large, stubby castle built on the hill above the road caught his attention. 'Do you know the name of that c-castle, c-corporal?' he asked his driver, a soldier of the Durham Light Infantry.

'Ah can't say ah do, sir. Looks bloody old, though, dunnit?'

Several pedestrians on the roadside interrupted with cheers and waves as they passed. A little girl even waved a small Union flag.

'The locals s-seem remarkably friendly,' Stephen remarked in surprise at the welcome.

'Aye, that they do, sir. It don't matter that we and the Americans 've bombed the hell out o' the toon. Ah think they's jes grateful to see the back o' them Fascists, like. It's the same al'over, sir. We've bin given a reet royal welcome.'

Stephen burst into a fit of coughing. The dust from the bombed-out buildings mixed with the sand of the beach was caught up in swirling patterns by the onshore breeze. The American jeep had become the favoured form of transport for British forces, but it was open-topped with no sides. It was another reason not to be wearing tropical whites, Stephen thought once he had his breath back.

'Here ye are, sir. Hame, sweet hame, sir.' The driver braked sharply, kicking up another cloud of dust, outside the playground of a small school from which a Union flag flapped lazily in the light breeze. 'Better than kippin' in tents, leastways, sir. Ah'll jes gi' ye a hand with your bags shall ah, sir?'

'No, thanks, corporal,' Stephen replied, hefting his tools and kitbag from the back of the jeep. 'I'll m-manage. Thanks for the ride.'

'Nay bother, sir.' The driver saluted Stephen and then turned the jeep back towards the harbour in yet another cloud of dust before accelerating away. Stephen returned the salute with gritted teeth to avoid inhaling the dust. He then patted himself down and reflected that only soldiers seemed to show him respect for his rank. Many sailors and especially the senior rates, seemed not to regard RNVR officers as *proper* officers. No matter, he thought. He had been briefed this would be the way at the *King Alfred* training establishment and was used to it by now. It didn't matter to him as much as getting the job done. Whilst he thought it rude and insubordinate, he accepted and understood how sailors with ten or so years of service and experience wouldn't take kindly to accepting the authority of RNVR officers with just two months of training. There again, he had served for almost three years now.

Abandoning such thoughts, he strolled through the school's main entrance and was amazed that the first person he came across was Lieutenant Charles Lawson. Lawson was a tall, slim and dark-bearded fellow RNVR officer. Stephen and Lawson had trained together at *Vernon*. He didn't like Lawson much, though. The last time they had met was in the Midlands. *Was it Birmingham or Coventry?* He couldn't remember. *Was that two years ago? Perhaps longer?* All he could remember was the cold, the devastation and his fear in tackling so many mines in so few days. He had heard since that Lawson had had the misfortune to be working on a mine on the top floor of a warehouse on the Thames when the fuze's clock had started to run. With no nearby cover, he and his assistant had had no choice but to jump into the river, but unfortunately for them, the tide was out. Lawson had broken both legs on the mudflats below and his rating had been killed.

'Cunningham! I can't believe it,' Lawson exclaimed warmly as if he really meant it. He shook Stephen's hand vigorously. 'It's so good to see you. Let me give you a hand.' Lawson picked up Stephen's tool bag and put his other arm around Stephen's shoulders to usher him into a classroom now being used as a mess hall. Stephen was surprised by the warmth of Lawson's welcome.

The mess hall was occupied by a warrant officer and five able seamen in the middle of a game of crib. There was no separate messing and accommodation for the officers, warrant officer and junior rates in the demolitions party. It was something to which Stephen had become accustomed and he preferred the arrangement to the strict segregation between the ranks of the Royal Navy elsewhere. After all, they were a tight team.

'Fix us up two mugs of char will you, Nobby?' Lawson asked of one of the junior rates.

'Aye aye, sir. Just give me two minutes and it'll be right up.' The seaman laid down his cards and Lawson signalled to Stephen to take a seat in an armchair by the window.

'It's not much, but its home for now, Cunningham. The engineers did a good job in patching the place up for us and we're quite comfortable.'

'Who's in charge here, Lawson?'

'We come under a Captain Gregson. He's in charge of minesweeping and port clearance up at HQ. He's not a bad chap. We were at Eton together. Pretty much leaves us to our own devices.'

'So, what are we d-doing here?'

'I say, Cunningham. Your stutter has improved immeasurably… and you've an amazing medal haul. Well done.' Stephen blushed at the compliment and started to doodle in his notebook.

'As for our duties,' Lawson continued, 'There isn't much to do at present. The Eyties seem to have been taken by surprise and didn't bother to mine the harbour here, but Gregson doesn't expect us to be so lucky in Messina. The Yanks are fighting their way up the north coast from Palermo whilst Monty fights the army's way up the east coast. The plan is we meet at Messina before crossing the straits onto the Italian mainland, but Jerry's stiffening the backs of the Italians and conducting a well-organised withdrawal. We're just hanging around until we're required to check out the harbour.'

'How do the men keep b-busy?'

'Mainly by playing crib, but I'm trying to start a bridge school. Do you play bridge by any chance?'

'N-no. I don't play cards.'

'Pity. Never mind. The locals are friendly and there are a few bars and restaurants open. The local wine's very good and plentiful. With any luck, we won't be here long.'

*****

Despite the disappointment at not finding a guided torpedo, Monty had made one significant find amongst the mines. Along with the magnetic and acoustic mines, he had discovered a new type of mine that appeared to be triggered by changes in the water pressure around it. It contained a new type of explosive, too. The Germans were calling it Hexogen, but Monty recognised it as being very similar to the British RDX, Research Department Explosive. However, the next few weeks were proving disappointing to the Commando.

The Germans had clearly recognised that Italy was losing the war, but they weren't going to allow the Italians to be routed. Field Marshal Kesselring was staging a very well organised, staged withdrawal towards Messina where his men were crossing the Strait of Messina onto the Calabrian mainland. All 30 Commando could do was to follow in the wake of Patton's Seventh Army as they made steady progress north across the island. Why wasn't the RAF or Royal Navy using their superiority in the air and on the sea to destroy the lighters and barges ferrying the thousands of retreating Germans with their ammunition, equipment and vehicles Monty and Riley wondered. Moreover, it was a dispiriting business making their way slowly to Messina. The route was littered with the corpses of dead Germans and Italians. The days were very hot, the air stank of rotting meat and bluebottles buzzed in swarms as they nested in the putrefying flesh. The ground was very rocky so the GIs were finding it hard work to bury their own forces and nobody, it seemed, could be bothered with the dead of the enemy. The locals just averted their gaze and moved on.

'Finlay,' Riley called. 'Ask those peasants why they don't at least bury their own, for Christ's sake.'

A few minutes later, the marine returned. 'They're superstitious, sir.'

'Superstitious of what, Finlay?'

'They talk of *Il malocchio*, sir. I think it means 'evil eye'. As far as I can gather, sir, it's because the men have died with their eyes open. The peasants seem to think that the corpses are staring at them with a malevolent eye, sir. Pure rubbish, of course, sir.'

'You don't need to tell me. Let's get out of here.'

'I did hear something else, sir.'

'Go on. Spit it out.' Riley was impatient to move on.

'Mussolini's been deposed in a military coup, sir. A Marshal Badoglio's replaced him, sir.'

'Now that is interesting, Finlay. But it's not going to help us today. Let's keep moving.'

The men continued their slow journey along the coast and did make one interesting find by luck. They came across a crashed communication truck. It turned out to be a very important discovery as it was a travelling wireless interception station that the Germans were using to gain intelligence from Allied wireless transmissions. The German occupants were all dead, but their pockets produced some useful documents, including cypher crib sheets. How far I've come, Monty reflected. From a career at the Bar to rifling the pockets of dead men!

Unable to enter Messina until it had been liberated by either Patton or Montgomery, Riley decided to hole up in a villa near Milazzo, a mere twenty miles from Messina, and to await developments.

*****

To the naval demolition unit's dismay, it took a further three weeks before the US Third Division was able to enter Messina, by which time, Stephen thought he knew Augusta like the back of his hand and had visited all the historical buildings. The morning after Messina was captured, Captain Gregson sent for Lawson. Lawson returned to the school in high excitement and summoned all members of the naval party for a briefing.

'Good news, chaps. The Americans have taken Messina and most of us are now required to clear the harbour. Captain Gregson wants us to conduct an immediate recce and to report back. Mister Bratley,' Lawson turned to the warrant officer. 'I want you to select five able rates and pack up to leave immediately. A Bedford's on its way as I speak.'

Lawson turned to Stephen. 'Sorry, Cunningham, but this is my show. Gregson only wants one officer on the recce and knows me better. I'm leaving you behind three ratings as a back-up party. Sorry.' Lawson extended his right hand.

Naturally, Stephen was disappointed by the news, but could see Captain Gregson's logic. He took Lawson's hand and shook it warmly.

'I'm jealous, b-but good luck, Lawson. I'll help you gather your gear.'

Fifteen minutes later, Stephen and three disappointed junior rates bade their colleagues farewell and waved after the retreating truck.

Chapter 32

At last, Messina was liberated by the Americans and 30 Commando were able to begin their search of the town for any useful intelligence. However, the job was hampered by the presence of German Teller land mines littering the town. Moreover, Monty only just managed to save in time the life of one particularly enthusiastic marine. The marine had discovered an Italian Navy wireless set intact. Just as he was about to switch it on, the hairs on the back of Monty's neck prickled.

'Stop!' he shouted. 'Don't move!' Treading warily, he borrowed the marine's bayonet and began a systematic search around the radio set. Sure enough, besides the usual power and aerial cables, he found a wire in the back of the set that shouldn't have been there. He traced it beneath the desk on which the radio was sitting and down to the deck. There it disappeared between two floor boards. Ushering the marine to step away, slowly and gently, Monty used the bayonet to prise open one of the floor boards. Sure enough, beneath the floor he found a stash of TNT. He disconnected the wires to the explosive and breathed a sigh of relief.

'Send for Lieutenant Commander Riley,' he instructed a now ashen-faced marine.

A few minutes later, Riley appeared. Monty showed him what he had found and Riley was visibly shocked. 'Sergeant,' he called. 'Warn the men that anything and everything could be booby trapped if it can be lifted, pulled, or any damn thing. I mean pictures, pianos, canteens, weapons and even bog handles. Savvy?'

The sergeant eyed the TNT and replied quietly. 'Yessir. Leave it to me.'

The ground shook as another artillery bombardment from across the strait came in. 'It's about time our troops took out those buggers,' Riley responded. Then the noise of the artillery fire was drowned out by an even bigger explosion. The building rocked around the men.

'Bloody hell! What was that?' Riley exclaimed.

'I think it came from the harbour, sir. Leastways there's a plume of smoke a mile high over there, sir. I think we'd better take a look.'

*****

Two days later, it was Stephen's turn to be summoned to HQ to meet Gregson. Poor Gregson's face was badly swollen with several mosquito bites

'Take a seat, Cunningham. I'll not beat about the bush, but it's bad news.' Stephen immediately worried for his mother and sister. 'Lawson and his party have had an accident.' Stephen's worries cleared guiltily. 'It's bad, I'm afraid. Lawson and his team discovered the harbour at Messina littered with depth charges. From what I gather, attached to the depth charges was some form of device they didn't recognise and as soon as they started to lift it, the whole thing went off. It's most mysterious.' Gregson leaned back in his canvas chair and seemed to deflate in Stephen's eyes.

'W-were there any c-casualties, sir?' Stephen asked, all of sudden concerned for the welfare of Lawson now that he knew the news didn't concern his family.

'I'm afraid so. Lawson, along with Mister Bratley and three others... Killed outright. In fact, there were only two survivors... junior rates and they're both in hospital, one of them very badly injured. It's a disaster! Charles was at Eton with me, but in my younger brother's year. I didn't take to the fellow at first, but... They're both gone now.'

'Oh, my Lord!' Stephen exclaimed. In the past three weeks he had come to like Lawson. He had changed since their days at *Vernon*. Gregson interrupted his thoughts, though.

'The thing is, Cunningham, the job's still got to be done. In just eight days that port has to be open for the arrival of the shipping to support the advance across the straits. I want you to take the remains of your party there immediately. Carry on where Lawson tragically left off. For God's sake, find out exactly what happened, the state of the harbour and then brief me on what you're going to do about it. I don't need to mince words, Cunningham. If we can't get that port open within eight days, there'll be hell to pay. The whole success of the Italian campaign is at stake.'

242

Stephen was stunned by the news, not just the loss of five brave men's lives, but the timescale to clear the harbour. He stood up. 'Leave it with me, sir. I'll do my b-best.'

'I know you will, Cunningham. If there's anything you need, don't hesitate to ask. I'll take it all the way to Admiral Cunningham or General Montgomery should I have to.'

*****

Stephen's first task was to interview the two survivors of the accident in Messina. One of them was expected to be in hospital for a few weeks only, but the other much longer. Fortunately, both were *compos mentis* enough to answer Stephen's many questions. It became clear to him that the depth charges had been booby trapped in some way to prevent them being lifted. The least badly injured survivor even described them as '*Death to Touch*'. Stephen determined he wouldn't make the same mistake as Lawson, not for his own sake, but to ensure the Allied crossing of the Messina Straits wasn't delayed.

His next task was to survey the harbour. Not even the destruction of the *Blitz* had prepared him for what met him in Messina. Allied bombing and artillery had completely obliterated the town. Rubble lay everywhere and barely a building was left standing. The stench of human and animal corpses in the high-summer temperatures was overpowering and many of the US GIs he passed were wearing cloths over their mouths and nostrils. Several Italian labourers were being put to work to clear the dead and destruction. If anything, the harbour area was even worse. Not a single facility remained intact and Stephen wondered how it would be restored for the arrival of the Allied assault force in just eight days' time, but first things first. He had to render the harbour safe. Commandeering a rowing boat, he instructed his two ratings to row him around the harbour.

Stephen peered over the stern of the boat into the harbour water below. It was very clear and the visibility good enough to see down to a depth of about forty feet. The sailors in the hospital had told Stephen that they had been trying to lift three depth charges linked together by steel wires. They thought either the wire or one of the charges had hit the harbour wall to cause the explosion. Stephen suspected there was more to it than that and took his time in examining the depths of the harbour. The water was warm so he even dived carefully into the harbour to take a closer look at the wire links. Indeed, it took him four days before he was able to make his report to Gregson who had driven up to see how he was progressing.

'I've discovered what happened to Lawson's party, sir. B-booby traps.'

'I suspected as much, Cunningham. Tell me more.'

'Firstly, sir, the harbour is riddled with explosives. N-not just the water, b-but the quays, too, sir. There are scores of d-depth charges lying around in the pumphouses and the substations, sir. I s-suspect some of them will be b-booby trapped. I c-could do with some help with them to speed things up, but the water's mine. There are about another forty depth charges in the water, linked to b-booby traps. They are quite strange d-devices and I suspect they include a trembler device. That's what k-killed the previous party, sir.'

'The Jerries are bastards!' Gregson stared at the harbour water with incredulity. 'All right, I'll ask the pongos to give you a hand with the explosives on the quays, but you'll have to train them in what to do. And what are you going to do about the devices in the water? Can you do it, man?'

'I'll try, sir, b-but I'm not going to lift the depth charges whilst they're still c-connected to those booby traps, sir. We've seen that's a fast route to Hell.'

'I agree.' Gregson removed his cap and mopped his fair hair with his handkerchief. His face was now far less swollen. 'So how do you intend tackling those infernal devices?'

'I want a d-diving suit, sir.'

'What? But you're not a qualified diver. I'll send you a couple of my best divers, if that's your plan.'

'I learned to d-dive in South Africa, sir. It'll be fine. By all means send me some help, b-but I need to inspect those b-booby traps myself, so I need a diving suit, s-sir.'

'Very well, Cunningham. It shall be done. You're the star turn round here just now, after all.'

*****

The following day, two naval divers turned up in Messina with a brand new Siebe Gorman diving suit. Stephen had not met Petty

Officer Davies before, but he was dismayed to meet the Warrant Officer (Diver). Their paths had crossed before. Warrant Officer 'Bunny' Warren had been his course's diving instructor at HMS *Excellent* in 1940 and had clearly been promoted since then. Stephen remembered the short, stocky Scotsman as foul-mouthed, disrespectful and, above all, a bully and sadist. Warren seemed surprised to see Stephen again, too, and even more surprised to see Stephen's medal ribbons. He kept any profane thoughts to himself. At HMS *Excellent*, Stephen had been cowed by Warren's bullying approach, but no more.

'Right, Mister Warren. I want one of you to take the new suit and to test it out. Then your next task is to take a hacksaw each and to c-cut through the wire wrapped around those metal cylinders connected to the depth charges, but take care. They're b-booby trapped... with a contact mechanism, I think. I want them separated s-so I can see what they are.'

Stephen saw Warren exchange a look of unease with Davies at the prospect of handling booby traps. Stephen had no doubt they had heard of the fatal accident, but he had no qualms concerning their sensibilities. This was the sort of job for which Royal Navy divers had been trained and clearance of the harbour had to be completed at all costs. Whilst the divers began changing into their diving suits, he instructed the two junior rates to rig a winch in order to commence lifting the depth charges once they were safe.

'It needs to be extremely stable, s-so rig it with four legs in place of the usual three. And I want plenty of hooks reeved through the pulley so that we can lift the charges evenly.'

The men set about their tasks under Stephen's supervision, but it became clear to him that the job was going to take too long. He needed more hands. His activities were interrupted by the approach of a Royal Engineers captain and his sergeant. Both wore the insignia on their sleeves of bomb disposal experts.

'Good morning,' the captain greeted Stephen. 'Captain Harvey Farquhar and Sergeant Allan. We gather the Navy needs our help.'

'Yes, we certainly d-do. Lieutenant Stephen C-Cunningham. I'd be grateful if you and your men c-could clear the quays of various explosives, b-but watch out for booby traps. I'll show you what I've found in just a minute.' The two divers were now ready to enter the water, so Stephen ordered the junior rates to act as their attendants whilst he showed Farquhar and his sergeant around the harbour.

Stephen detected a drawl in Farquhar's accent. 'Are you C-Canadian, Farquhar?'

'Gee. How clever of you. I sure am. My folks emigrated from Scotland when I was just a bairn. We live in Truro, Nova Scotia. You know it?'

'N-no. I'm afraid not. I've never been to Canada.'

'You should go… once this damn war's over. Jeez… Look at 'em go.' Farquhar was interrupted by the noise of a squadron of American P-40 Warhawk aircraft flying low over the port heading north-east to the Italian mainland. 'I'm not sorry to see Jerry getting a bit of his own medicine, I can tell you,' Farquhar continued once the aircraft had passed overhead.

'How long have you b-been here?' Stephen asked.

'Three weeks. We were one of the first units in once the town was taken. It still wasn't easy, though.' Farquhar examined one of the piles of depth charges in a building along the quay side. He felt underneath for one of the booby traps Stephen had indicated. 'Make a note, Sergeant.' He turned back to Stephen.

'My men can deal with this sort of booby trap, but we've never dealt with depth charges. Your line of country, methinks.'

'True, b-but it's not difficult. I c-can show you how or my men can do it.' Stephen heard the sound of artillery fire in the distance and then the rumble as the shells hit the already shell-struck town.

'Was there much fighting, then?' Stephen had never been in combat and was interested in how it felt.

'Not on the ground. Jerry and the Italians had retreated across the Strait by the time we arrived. But look for yourself.' Farquhar pointed to the Italian mainland on the other side of the Strait. 'That's Calabria… the toe of Italy and it's only three miles off. Until our air forces take them out, we're still directly under the guns of the Italian coastal batteries. You and your men may need to take cover from time to time… or else have some helmets to hand. At least we're now spared the regular visits from the *Luftwaffe*. It wasn't pleasant.'

After an hour showing Farquhar around the harbour, Stephen returned to his men working on separating the depth charges from their booby traps. To his surprise, he found both divers on the quay smoking.

'What are you d-doing?' he addressed Warren. 'Why are you not in the water?'

Warren eyed Stephen malevolently, but remained polite in his reply. 'We're tekkin' ah break. Need to tek a rest break at reg'lar intervals on this type of job. Did I not teach ye that?'

Stephen felt anger rising in his breast, but remained calm and civil. 'B-but you've not been d-down an hour.'

'Aye. Forty minutes. But them's the regulations. Difficult and risky work this an' we daren't risk gettin' oo'cr tired.'

Stephen had no answer to this, but it might have found it more credible from another warrant officer. 'So, what progress did you make?'

'Not much. The trouble is every time ye try to cut the wire it brings those blasted packages closer to the depth charges. We canna risk them knockin' agen each other, can we?' Warren gave Stephen a look of defiance. He clearly didn't expect to be contradicted.

Stephen took a deep breath to contain his anger. 'How many wires did you c-cut then?'

'None as yet. It's difficult work sawin' under water, ye know.'

Now Stephen really was having to work hard to control his anger. Warren had not once called him 'sir'. That was something he could accept, but his attitude was entirely belligerent. Worse, the job wasn't going to get done at this rate. He made a quick decision.

'How's the new s-suit?'

'Jes fine. Nae problems.'

'Very well,' Stephen retorted. 'From now on, I'll d-do the diving. You can act as my attendants.'

'What?' Warren snorted. 'But yer not qualified.'

'Oh yes, I am. I was taught by Chatham d-dockyard divers in Simon's Town.' Stephen was pleased to see the look of surprise on Warren's face, but then Warren just shrugged and flicked his cigarette into the water.

'Well, it's yer funeral.'

Stephen quickly changed into the new diving suit. 'Yer not doin' it right,' Warren remonstrated, but Stephen knew his method was quicker and ignored Warren. Very soon, he was in the water tackling the first wire. Only now did his anger subside. It was the worst example of disrespect he had encountered in his career, to date… and from a warrant officer, too! But it wouldn't do to be emotional in the same water as forty depth charges primed to explode should he make a mistake.

It took thirty minutes to cut the first wire. Stephen had to admit that Warren had been right that the job was difficult and, moreover, that he had to watch out that the jerking of the wire as he cut it didn't bring the booby trap into contact with one of the depth charges. Once one of the booby traps was free, he surfaced to examine it, but didn't yet dare risk having it lifted out of the water. He saw that the booby trap comprised two cylinders linked by an electrical cable. He suspected that the upper and smaller cylinder was the contact fuze, so he left that alone for the moment. Keeping the two cylinders well apart, he removed the outer cover of the lower cylinder to expose three wires. With this eventuality in mind, he had some wire snippers attached to his suit belt. He cut the first wire, moved his cutters further along the second wire and cut that, too. Finally, and again staggering his cut, he cut the third wire. The charge was safe and he was now able to repeat the procedure to render the first cylinder safe. He and his team could now use the winch to lift the depth charges to which the cylinders were linked. Stephen took each hook and dived again to attach them to the network of cables linking the depth charges. At last, they were ready to lift the first three depth charges to the surface, but they still had to be disconnected. Ninety minutes later, each charge was separated and ready for lifting. Stephen left this to the four ratings and exited the water. He was hot and tired and badly needed water.

The men were forced to stop work by a German artillery barrage raining down on the port, but the shells did no damage in their immediate locality. On emerging from the shelter of an already crumbling building, he was surprised to find Gregson standing on the quay, immaculately dressed in crisp tropical whites. Stephen had asked Farquhar to have his men cordon off the area in which they were working, but Gregson had clearly breached the cordon. One couldn't fault his courage.

'Bloody well done, Cunningham. Here. Take this.' Gregson passed over a canteen of water that Stephen quickly emptied. 'How are you feeling?'

'Fine, sir.' In fact, Stephen felt exhausted.

'But why are you doing the diving. After all, that's why I sent Warren and Davies to you.'

'I thought it would be easier, s-sir. I c-could have passed instructions by telephone to the d-divers below, but it's difficult to b-be precise from the surface. The d-divers won't have come across this type of device before, sir.'

'Nor have you for that matter, Cunningham.' Gregson seemed unconvinced, but didn't pursue the subject. 'But the job's taking too long and you can't stay down there forever. What can be done to help you?'

'Do you have more water, sir?' Stephen was so tired, he could barely think, but another canteen of water cleared his head. 'I need some volunteers to help lift the charges and their b-booby traps to the surface. I can train them to make safe the booby traps once I've s-separated them and I c-can make the depth charges safe.'

'You'll have the men, Cunningham, but one more thing. I've been here for the last hour and I think you should be using a small explosive charge to separate those death traps rather than a hacksaw.'

Stephen was surprised that Gregson had been on the quay so long as he hadn't seen him. He chided himself, too, for not thinking of the use of explosive to separate the booby traps and depth charges. Something like an ounce of plastic explosive should do the job nicely.

'Aye aye, sir. It should d-do the trick.'

Chapter 33
September 1943

It took a few dives before Stephen and his men were into a smooth routine for rendering safe the booby traps in the water and raising the depth charges. Gregson's suggestion of using explosives to sever the wires had proved highly successful. Stephen dived each time to apply the small explosive charges to separate the booby traps from the depth charges. To save time he called for volunteers to help with neutralising the booby traps. To his amazement, there was no shortage of volunteers for the hazardous task. However, whilst this included Davies, Warren seemed reluctant to take charge of the activity.

'I reckon someone needs to take charge of those fookin pongos. We dinna want them mekkin a fookin dog's breakfast of defuzing those depth charges, do we?'

It dawned on Stephen that like most bullies, Warren was a coward, but it suited him to have the warrant officer out of his way. Indeed, as it turned out, Warren proved to be stalwart in taking charge of the lifting of the charges from the water. On Stephen's second day of diving, he was in the water for a full twenty hours and made excellent progress, despite the visibility in the water having been reduced almost to nil with all the activity in the harbour. He wasn't just busy in separating the booby traps from the depth charges, but examining, often by touch alone, several other objects in the harbour, most of them harmless, but it was still necessary to *discredit* them and report them safe. Despite the marathon session in the water, Stephen felt too elated to be tired. Gregson was on the quayside to welcome him out of the water.

'My God, Cunningham. You must be superhuman. Mister Warren tells me that was your twentieth dive in the last 48 hours. How do you do it?'

Stephen glowed with pride, but retained his customary modesty. 'Thank you, s-sir, but it's all d-down to the extra help. No d-doubt I'll feel tired when the job's d-done, though.'

'I don't doubt it either, Cunningham. It's a splendid achievement. Mister Warren tells me the wharf's already clear. How much longer to clear the water?'

Stephen reflected a short while before replying. 'Another t-twenty-four hours, I should think, sir. We've d-dismantled or d-discredited over a hundred and fifty objects so far.'

'That's simply splendid. I'd say you deserve a half day off to recuperate, then.' Stephen allowed his feelings to show as Gregson added, 'That's an order by the way, Cunningham. Tired men make mistakes.'

'Very well, sir. Now there's s-something I'd like you to s-see, sir.' Stephen took Gregson to see the line of dismantled booby traps recovered from the water. As might have been expected, inspection of the cylinders revealed the usual detonator, primer and large main charge. However, there was an unusual addition.

'I would value your opinion of this, sir.' Stephen held up a clockwork mechanism for Gregson to examine.

'It looks like a clock to me,' Gregson replied as he turned the device over and over. 'But I admit it looks a bit unusual... and why was it included?'

'Exactly, sir. With your permission, sir, once this job's over, I'd like to run them over to Milazzo.'

'Why Milazzo? What's there, Cunningham?'

'There's a unit of RAF ammunition technicians working there, sir. They can d-dismantle the mechanism for me, sir.'

'Fair enough, Cunningham. Permission granted, but frankly, I don't care what you do once you declare this harbour safe. Your namesake, ABC, has promised Monty we can have 800 trucks a day crossing onto the mainland within 48 hours.'

*****

The next day, as he had always intended, Stephen ignored Gregson's order and worked the full day. As he climbed out of the harbour water that evening after his twenty-eighth and final dive, he was astonished to be met by Warren with a smart salute.

'Jes thought you'd like to know, sorr, the quays and buildin's are safe. I've told Sarn't Harper and his engineers they can secure. I reckons we're almost done, sorr.'

251

The use of the word, 'sir', in Warren's inimitable pronunciation wasn't lost on Stephen. He'd noticed that Davies had started saying it the day before. It was worth more than a medal to his ego.

An hour later at 22.00, Stephen lined up his working party in two smart ranks and awaited the arrival of Captain Gregson. With great pride in his men, he saluted Gregson and reported, '207 devices dismantled or discredited, sir. The harbour is c-clear and ready for use, sir.'

At 04.00, the assault force berthed in the port. A few hours later, on 3rd September, four years to the day since the start of the war, the British Landing Ships (Tanks) began ferrying across the Eighth Army's vehicles and the invasion of the Italian mainland commenced.

*****

With the crossing of the Eighth Army into Calabria, 30 Commando mustered in Messina to await their turn to cross the strait as part of *Operation Baytown*. However, Monty had persuaded Riley to adopt a different plan. This was to leave the Eighth Army's XIII Corps and instead join up with the US Rangers destined to mount their own amphibious assault on mainland Italy. Monty was aware that the Italian armaments manufacturer Silurificio had a torpedo factory at Baia, just 50 miles west of Salerno on the other side of Naples. 30 Commando operated under the direct tasking of the Chief of Combined Operations, CCO, Commodore Lord Louis Mountbatten, but even so, Riley thought it prudent to gain 'sign off' from the Senior Naval Officer present for the change in plan. Accordingly, Monty and Riley sought out Captain Gregson in his headquarters.

'My God! It's young Montcalm, isn't it?' Gregson greeted the two naval commando officers. It took Monty a moment to recall how he knew Gregson and then it came to him. He had fagged for one of Gregson's roommates at Eton. Gregson Minor had been in his year.

'My word! What a surprise to see you here after all this time, sir.' Monty saluted Gregson crisply.

'So, you're one of these famous commandos now, Monty.' Gregson looked at Riley expectantly.

'This is my CO, Quintin Riley, sir. The captain and I were at Eton together, Quintin.'

252

'Pleased to meet you, sir.'

'So, how's Gregson Minor, I mean Jeremy, sir. Did he follow you into the Navy?' Monty asked affably.

Gregson frowned in return. 'He did. He rose to command an *L*-class destroyer, but she was sunk off Bône by an *E*-boat in the spring. Sadly, he wasn't picked up.' Monty wished the floor would open up and swallow him.

'Oh! I am very sorry to hear that, sir. He was a good chap. I liked him awfully.'

'Thank you, Montcalm. But that's war. At least we're on the offensive now.'

Riley was sympathetic enough to change the subject. 'The town seems to be a bit of a wreck, sir. And I see half the mole's gone. That can't have been down to our bombs or shells, surely?'

'No, it wasn't. Jerry's a bastard at times. He booby trapped the harbour to stop our ships using it. Some unfortunate chaps from a demolition party copped it in the first attempt to clear the water. As it happens, Montcalm, you might remember one of them. A Lieutenant Charles Lawson. He was Eton with us, too.'

'Is he dead, sir?'

'I'm afraid so. Five of them took the blast and only two survived.'

Monty was shocked. He had never liked Lawson since their days at Eton. Lawson had always teased him about his short stature, even when they had met at *Vernon* and he had been a rank senior to Lawson. Nevertheless, he hadn't wish him dead.

'I remember him, sir. Indeed, our paths crossed when I was doing some training at *Vernon*. He was on the RMSO course.'

'I have every admiration for those fellows. You wouldn't catch me doing their job. It takes courage I just wouldn't be able to muster. I'm putting his successor up for the VC and he bloody well deserves to get it. You wouldn't have thought it to look at. He's modest, mild mannered and diffident, but he's tough as old boots. You know he was in the water almost twenty-four hours continuously at one point to make those booby traps safe. You wouldn't think he had it in him. Scrawny sort of chap with spectacles… and a stammer of all things…'

'A stammer, sir? What was his name?' Monty thought it had to be Stephen. How many naval officers were there with a stammer.

'Cunningham. No relation to ABC, he claims.'

253

'I don't believe it. Stephen Cunningham. Sir, is he still here? I haven't seen him in ages.'

'Really? Well, it's a damned small world. First Lawson and then bumping into you. And you knowing Cunningham.'

'But is he still here, sir,' Monty persisted.

'I doubt it. I told him that I would arrange for him to go back to Blighty after what he'd achieved here, but damn me, he refused. Keen as mustard, despite being in need of a good rest. He insisted in crossing with the first wave of the men crossing the strait earlier. You've only just missed him, but you'll no doubt catch up with him soon. You're with XIII Corps, after all.'

Riley finally had a chance to speak. 'Actually, sir. That's why we're here. We need to get to Salerno rather quicker than XIII Corps. I can't tell you why, sir,' Riley cut off Gregson's question. 'We've cleared it with General Clark's staff, sir, but we wondered if you might smooth the way with General Dempsey's staff. We don't want to be accused of being AWOL, do we?'

Gregson considered the request carefully before replying. 'I suppose not. Yes, you can leave that with me. I'll speak to somebody to cover your backs. I presume London is content?'

'Ah! Actually, we haven't had the chance to tell them yet, sir. We don't have direct comms with them. That's something else you could help us with. They do grant us some discretion and independence in these matters, but it would help, sir.'

'Very well. You can leave it with me, Riley.' Gregson turned to Monty.

'It was good to see you again, Montcalm. It's a shame you missed your friend, Cunningham. I'm sure he would be disappointed to learn it, too. It's not the only thing he's missed either. Some mail finally caught up with him today. One letter's been half way across the world… South Africa, Alexandria, Malta and now here.'

Monty's sixth sense was alerted. 'I'm sorry, sir. This might seem a strange request, but could I see that letter?'

'That is, indeed, a strange request, but I know better than to ask you chaps your business. Give me a second.' Gregson rummaged through the piles of documents on his desk and pulled out a couple of envelopes. 'Found it. Here you are. Looks like a woman's hand.'

Monty examined the address on the envelope. It was, indeed, a woman's writing and he recognised the handwriting from a slip of paper providing the writer's address. Poor Stephen! Monty hoped the letter would catch up with him eventually.

AUTHOR'S NOTE

As with all my books, I have tried to remain faithful to historical fact. The events described in this story are largely true, but inevitably, I have had to play around with timelines, invent characters and use my imagination in places to make this a novel and not a textbook.

Although they bear no resemblance to the characters, many of Stephen Cunningham's experiences are based on those of Lieutenant Commander John Bridge GC GM* RNVR or Lieutenant Hugh Syme GC GM* RANVR, and those of Monty on events described by Captain F Ashe Lincoln, QC RNVR in his autobiographies. All three men were unquestionably extremely brave. Bridge was, indeed, instrumental in clearing the port of Messina in time to allow the Allies to cross the Messina Strait. Lincoln did serve with DTMI and then 30 Commando in the Mediterranean. His two autobiographies, *Secret Naval Investigator* and *Odyssey of a Jewish Sailor*, provided much material for my descriptions of Monty's activities.

It was Commander Ian Fleming RNVR who envisaged the formation of an Intelligence Assault Unit. It was later renamed as 30 Commando and the unit was reformed in 2010 as the Royal Marines Information Exploitation Group. As in WW2, its role includes intelligence gathering. I drew heavily on Nicholas Rankin's excellent book, *Ian Fleming's Commandos* for an account of the history of 30 Commando and *The Man with the Golden Typewriter*, edited by Fergus Fleming for my descriptions of Fleming.

The final book of the trilogy, *He Who Would Valiant Be*, is progressing. My tale will continue to follow the exploits of Stephen and Monty and, again, will be based on true history.

ACKNOWLEDGEMENTS

I really could not have written this novel without the help of several people. As with the earlier book in this trilogy, it started with Sue Williams, the daughter of Lieutenant Commander John Bridge, GC, GM and Bar, for giving me access to her father's memoirs. Again, I am very grateful to Commander Rob Hoole, Secretary of the Royal Navy's Mine Clearance Diving Officers' Association for helping me with various technical aspects of the book. Tony Boyle, too, was more than generous with his time, not just in correcting my mistakes on rendering safe procedures for magnetic and acoustic mines, but actually showing me how it was done (the book cover is a shot of his re-enactment). Similarly, I received valuable input from Steve Venus, an expert in German explosives and fuzes. Thank you again to Kath Robson who not only proof-read the original manuscript, but offered several suggestions on how it might be improved. John Drummond helped with the design of the book cover.

I have been fortunate, too, to draw considerably from the historical accounts of many other authors. These include not just John Bridge's memoirs, but books by Ivan Southall, Ashe Lincoln, Noel Cashford and Nicholas Rankin. Finally, I wish to thank my wife, Hilary, for her patience, support and input to the book. I hope you have enjoyed reading this book and will leave a review on Amazon and/or Goodreads. Such reviews are the oxygen of publicity to feed the visibility of authors. Thank you to everyone above.

Finally, should you want to be added to my mailing list for advanced notice of news concerning the final book of the trilogy, *He Who Would Valiant Be*, or any of my other books, please email me at the address below.

Website: www.shaunlewis-theauthor.com,
Facebook: shaunlewistheauthor
Twitter: @shaunlewis1805
Email: shaunlewisauthor@gmail.com

www.ingramcontent.com/pod-product-compliance
Lightning Source LLC
Chambersburg PA
CBHW021234250626
47155CB00008B/3016